'Social media has never been this deadly. A brutally brilliant story!' Satu Rämö

'His best yet!' S.J. Watson

'Biting, acerbic, darkly funny and, most importantly, it shines a spotlight on the ridiculousness of modern living, the importance of social media and how we see ourselves' Chris McDonald

'Will Carver uses his unique voice to skewer the vacuous world of wannabe influencers and reality TV ... a savage, scathing, compelling but deeply funny take-down of a fake, narcissistic world' Trevor Wood

'Thrilling, tense and funny ... Will Carver has his finger on the pulse of our society' Michael J. Malone

'One of the most compelling and original voices in crime fiction' Alex North

PRAISE FOR WILL CARVER

LONGLISTED FOR THEAKSTON OLD PECULIER CRIME NOVEL OF THE YEAR
LONGLISTED FOR THE GOLDSBORO BOOKS GLASS BELL AWARD

'Incredibly dark and very funny' Harriet Tyce

'A gripping novel laced with humour and cutting character insight ... a thrill from start to finish. Expect the unexpected!' Sarah Pinborough

'Weirdly page-turning' *Sunday Times*

'Brilliantly original ... plausible, relevant and timely' Sam Holland

'Clever, compelling, funny and it really makes you think' *Daily Mail*

'Wickedly fun' *Crime Monthly*

'Laying bare our 21st-century weaknesses and dilemmas, Carver has created a highly original state-of-the-nation novel' *Literary Review*

'Arguably the most original crime novel published this year' *Independent*

'At once fantastical and appallingly plausible ... this mesmeric novel paints a thought-provoking if depressing picture of modern life' *Guardian*

'This book is most memorable for its unrepentant darkness...' *Telegraph*

'Will Carver's most exciting, original, hilarious and freaky outing yet' Helen FitzGerald

'It's the author's black humour and thought-provoking observations on human nature and our society that ... take over your brain' *CultureFly*

'The final chapters will have you racing through the pages to find out what happens' Crime Fiction Lover

'Arguably the most original writer in Britain' *Daily Express*

'Vivid and engaging and completely unexpected' Lia Middleton

'Equally enthralling and appalling ... unlike anything I've read in a very long while' James Oswald

'Insightful, sharp-minded, and fascinating' Sarah Moorhead

'Thoughtful, challenging and unafraid to examine the impact huge events can have on the human condition ... his most important novel to date' *The Madrid Review*

'Unflinching, smart and entertaining ... as thought-provoking as it is brilliant' Isabelle Broom

'Multi-layered and masterfully written' *Heat magazine* Book of the Month

ABOUT THE AUTHOR

Will Carver is the international bestselling author of the January David series and the critically acclaimed, mind-blowingly original Detective Pace series, which includes *Good Samaritans (2018), Nothing Important Happened Today* (2019) and *Hinton Hollow Death Trip* (2020), all of which were ebook bestsellers and selected as books of the year in the mainstream international press. *Nothing Important Happened Today* was longlisted for both the Goldsboro Books Glass Bell Award 2020 and the Theakston Old Peculier Crime Novel of the Year Award. *Hinton Hollow Death Trip* was longlisted for the *Guardian*'s Not the Booker Prize, and was followed by the literary thrillers, *The Beresford, Psychopaths Anonymous, The Daves Next Door, Suicide Thursday, Upstairs at the Beresford* and *Kill Them With Kindness*.

Will spent his early years in Germany, but returned to the UK at age eleven, when his sporting career took off. He and his partner run their own fitness and nutrition company, and live in Reading with five children and a tortoise.

Find Will at www.willcarver.co.uk and follow him on X and Instagram @will_carver.

Also by Will Carver and available from Orenda Books:

Good Samaritans
Nothing Important Happened Today
Hinton Hollow Death Trip
The Beresford
Psychopaths Anonymous
The Daves Next Door
Suicide Thursday
Upstairs at the Beresford
Kill Them With Kindness

BAD INFLUENCE

WILL CARVER

ORENDA
BOOKS

Orenda Books
16 Carson Road
West Dulwich
London SE21 8HU
www.orendabooks.co.uk

First published by Orenda Books, 2026

A catalogue record for this book is available from the British Library.

ISBN 978-1-917764-28-5
eISBN 978-1-917764-29-2

Typeset in Garamond by Elaine Sharples
Printed and bound by Clays Ltd, Elcograf S.p.A

MIX
Paper | Supporting responsible forestry
FSC® C018072

For sales and distribution, please contact info@orendabooks.co.uk

For those who believe it is more important to see than it is to be *seen*. And for Marc, who was a rare being who tried to live in just this way.

'Always eyes watching you and the voice enveloping you. Asleep or awake, indoors or out of doors, in the bath or bed – no escape. Nothing was your own except the few cubic centimetres in your head.'

George Orwell – *1984*

'In the future, everybody will be world famous for fifteen minutes.'

Andy Warhol

S C R O L L U P

^ ^ ^ ^ ^ ^ ^ ^ ^ ^

^ ^ ^ ^ ^ ^ ^ ^ ^ ^

@JackedUp

(He jumps from a squat to a lunge and back again, then casually hitches up the bottom of his vest to reveal perfectly toned abs.)

'You can achieve results like this by working out for only twenty minutes each day, without lifting weights and still eat the things you love.'

(He takes a huge bite from a burger.)

'Just double-tap now, hit subscribe and let me show you how to get in the best shape of your life.'

^^^^^^^^^^

^^^^^^^^^^

@NotYourGuru

'In order to be successful in your relationship or your business or with money, you have to raise your standards.'

(Cut to the audience nodding in agreement.)

'There are things that you want in life, am I right? But here's the thing, you don't get what you want. You get what you *have* to have.'

♥ 12.1k

^^^^^^^^^^

^^^^^^^^^^

@StorageBySophia

Sponsored

'Four ways to organise your closet better...'

^^^^^^^^^^

^^^^^^^^^^

@HHRetreats

'White sands. Blue waters. Cocktails. Rooftop infinity pool. Luxury like you have never experienced. The third name that appears when you hit *share* is the person you are supposed to take to this five-star escape to paradise.'

^^^^^^^^^^

^^^^^^^^^^

DIARY ENTRY 001 'UNLISTED' VIEWS: 1
COMMENTS: 0 LIKES: 0

(Direct to camera)

'You see these things online. How to lose weight by drinking cider vinegar or free guides to building garden furniture from old pallets. Tips for better sex, or ways to earn ten grand a month by working from home for one hour a day. The people are beautiful. The clothes are stylish. The interiors are gorgeous. It's all the things you want but don't have, right?

Their family or *her* eyeliner or *his* biceps. I get it. Because I want it, too. I see all these things all the time. The fame. The wealth. The abundance. I want some of that. We all do. And I know that creating content is exhausting. You want it to be engaging or strike a chord or start trending. I've done all of that. I've filmed myself gaming and cooking vegan cakes and giving make-up tutorials. My last video received 900 views. Nine hundred. It's not enough to be noticed. That's not influencing anybody.

I want to be heard. Doesn't everybody want to make an impact, somehow? I can only dream of being influential, of understanding celebrity. Of being famous for something. Anything. To be sent shoes and books and concert tickets for free just because I should be seen wearing the right thing in the right place. I mean, it must be magical.

I thought that, if I kept posting great stuff, eventually something would hit. It would take off. I would be noticed. I'd get to experience how these people exist in the world. I could understand what it is that they do day to day. I'd know what it was like to finally be seen.

Then I realised there's a much easier way to do that.

All I have to do is find one of these influencers, break into their house, and live there without them knowing.

PART ONE:
IN DEVELOPMENT

PAIGE BECKERMAN
@TheFitnessPaige
'Get fit. Get healthy. Get happy.'
12.2k Following **4.8M** Followers

Paige turns it off.

All of it.

She goes into her phone settings and swipes the notification slider to the left on all her apps. Every social-media platform, every game, every shopping app. It's gone.

Do. Not. Disturb.

Nobody will be able to contact her or get hold of her for the next two days.

She's off the grid.

Her browser is still active, for now, as she loads the page for her idyllic spa retreat. Acres of woodland to walk around. To escape the noise. A rooftop pool that looks over the canyons, so she knows that there is civilisation but, in that moment, she will not be a part of it. It's not even within touching distance. And that's why these places work.

Relax.

Regroup.

Reset.

Healthy food all day, lovingly prepared for her by somebody else, who has worked out the correct macronutrient ratios for her current weight and physical-activity levels. They do the intense work so Paige doesn't have to.

They'll cover her in mud and wrap her in seaweed, or they'll massage local honey into her skin as she dozes for an hour before washing everything off in a body-temperature milk bath.

Paige smiles.

It's luxury but not in that sense of being excessive. It's a different kind of decadence.

It's what she needs.

Some time to be Paige, not @TheFitnessPaige.

A couple of days away from creating content. She doesn't want to film herself cooking or working out or giving lifestyle advice. She just wants to be herself. She hardly ever gets to do that. She always has to be present, otherwise she will disappear, somebody else will take over.

Paige has never turned it all off before. It's exhilarating.

She could die tonight and nobody would even question it until Monday. The police would have to perform their due diligence, of course, and a quick check of the press would turn up Ariel Dean because of their online feud, but any detective with half a mind would know that it had to be Tom and Dana, the two people from the police sketch who have been tormenting the Hollywood Hills.

But Paige isn't thinking about that. She's looking at the swim-up matcha bar and smiling.

The camera on the opposite wall zooms in on her face. Paige has no idea that it's on, that they have been watching her for the last few days, that they can hear her now, too.

She's being examined.

Always.

Paige lives with nobody, yet desperately needs some time by herself.

And she hasn't even realised that she's not alone.

That the end is going to be filmed.

TWO WEEKS EARLIER...

AUDITION TAPE: ELLIE BOND, 23.
'I don't really think before I speak. I mean, my brain is definitely working but the filter between what I am thinking and what I am saying doesn't always work. And that sometimes gets me into trouble.'

^^^^^^^^^^

^^^^^^^^^^

AUDITION TAPE: MAX FARLEY, 21.
'Look, you know, I can't really sit still. I get bored easily. I always have to be doing something. So, if there's nothing to do, I'm going to make my own fun.'

^^^^^^^^^^

^^^^^^^^^^

AUDITION TAPE: SHONA JACKSON, 26.
'I live a glamorous lifestyle. I'm a queen. I will not let others around me bring me down to the level of a peasant.'

^^^^^^^^^^

^^^^^^^^^^

AUDITION TAPE: BARNABY HUNT, 22.
'I have a great skill for turning people against one another without them realising that I have done it. Luckily, I'm cute, so nobody ever suspects me and that's a great advantage. I don't know what career that is useful for. I don't do it to everyone, of course, just the popular kids, right?'

^^^^^^^^^^

^^^^^^^^^^

Everyone on the tapes is nine out of ten. They're nine hundred and ninety-nine in a thousand. They're one of a million willing to go down on some sex-starved TV executive for an opportunity to live out loud in front of the nation.

Each of them is one of the hundred percent of wannabes who would sign on the dotted line after being presented with the information that appearing on the show will probably ruin their lives.

That's what the studios tell them.

They have to.

'Here's the thing,' they say, sliding the contract across a desk. 'Chances are, your life will never be the same again. But probably not in the way that you are hoping.'

They never really get to the second part of that sentence. Attention spans have dwindled drastically among the social-media generation.

Swipe up. Ignore. Skip ads.

These people have high ambition but a lower work ethic, and that results in an unrealistic, warped view of the world.

The warnings continue.

And they continue to be ignored.

'The press will undoubtedly hound you. They will dig up things from your life that even you have forgotten about. People from your past will come forward with half-truths and lies, looking for their moment to cash in.'

Most people who take part in a reality show do not become famous enough or rich enough to never have to work again. But they do earn too much to just fade into insignificance. They are never going to be able to return to that office job. A lot of them have to move abroad to escape.

There are pockets of Spain where reality contestants go to die.

^^^^^^^^^^

^^^^^^^^^^

AUDITION TAPE: ALYSSA SILVER, 21.
'Maybe people would say that I'm crazy or weird or quiet, I don't know. I don't like people who just say what they're thinking and believe there should be no consequence. I don't care where somebody comes from or how much money their family has, loyalty is the most important quality.'

^^^^^^^^^^

^^^^^^^^^^

The studios don't prioritise the welfare of their guests or contestants. They want conflict and confidence. Antagonism and arrogance. It's all about the ratings.

And, still, armed with all of this information, with all of the history and statistics, everybody signs that contract.

Everybody.

Alyssa would sign it.

And so would Alessandro.

^^^^^^^^^^

^^^^^^^^^^

LESS
I like fashion. Not in the same way as Alyssa. She likes whatever is trending. She flits from one interest to the next. I like hats. I like design.

I also like to go by the name *Less*, rather than Alessandro. I think it gives me an edge. And it allows 'Alessandro' to disappear. I don't want to be Alessandro anymore. I want to be Less.

Less is cool. I've got a cousin, Alessandro, and he goes by *Sandro*. Sandro is not cool. Sandro is a middle-aged guy sipping wine and playing dominoes in Tuscany, discussing tannins and poetry.

Less is into couture.

Alessandro was into couture but that's just another way of saying that he was chased a lot at school. He was also caught a lot. Tripped over a lot. Pushed. Punched. Kicked. And even spat on.

The kids called him *gay*.

Alessandro was gay.

Less is gay.

I'm gay.

But that's not the point. That's not how they meant it. They were saying that I was weird. That I was different. That I didn't belong. And that's the part that stuck. That's the part that really hurt.

Because I was an outsider.

I guess I still am.

I wake up and it feels like my brain is resting heavily in the front of my skull. My mouth is dry. There's pain in my feet from dancing all night at Studio nightclub.

Sure, I know that I should never have touched that speed, but it always feels so fucking great at the time that you forget how much the high gets outweighed by the assault of the comedown the next day.

It's a dirty drug.

Filthy.

Another thing the kids at school would call me, when I was still Alessandro.

I could have gone to a private school, my parents have the money. Perhaps I would have thrived there, been encouraged to explore my *differences*. Maybe I still would have been an outcast. My parents wanted me to grow up having a 'normal' childhood – like they'd had. To mix with kids from all walks of life. That's what they say, but it's bluster. They care about what they look like to others. And sending a rich kid to a regular school is about as on-trend as you can get.

All it meant was that I got picked on by the poor kids, too. And the black kids, the jocks and the goths. Once, I got slapped by a girl from the tennis squad. She caught me so right that my legs buckled.

It was so embarrassing.

The crowd laughed.

They laughed at the gay weirdo in the hat.

And that kid, whose wealthy parents wanted him to have a regular school experience instead of growing up spoiled and entitled, grew up sad and confused and alone. And, I'm not going to lie, a little bit spoiled and entitled. Because so many of my generation are. No matter their class. There's a lack of drive, of entrepreneurial spirit.

Because we can have everything we want and we can have it almost instantly. But, still, we are somehow bored.

Bored stiff.

Bored to tears.

Bored stupid.

Bored to death.

'Oh, God. Why?' I put the pillow over the back of my head and hug it into my ears as the lawn mower passes beneath my bedroom window. I want to curl up into a ball and die.

It's a Thursday. Most twenty-year-olds are either at college or have started working, but my plan is to stay in bed until noon at the very earliest. I'm my own boss. My time is my own. Sure, I'm still studying, aiming for a degree in fashion design with a focus on haberdashery, but I also earn my own money, making one-of-a-kind pieces and selling them through my social-media accounts.

The Boomers and Gen-Xers look at us like we're lazy tech zombies, but some of us have entrepreneurial drive. There are a million ways to get noticed now, to get rich, even. It's not like I came from nothing. I don't pretend that's the case. Everything was bankrolled by the *Mom and Dad Savings and Loan Company*. They bought the initial materials. They converted one of the spare rooms into a studio. (Alyssa's house doesn't even have a spare room.)

I take all the profits.

And there are profits.

I have a healthy online following. Enough to fund my drug and drinking habits, to get me into my favourite night spots, but not so huge that Rachel Zoe is knocking on my door, asking for a bespoke piece for some celebrity red-carpet event.

I'm privileged and I know it. I can't shy away from that. But I'm also not taking that privilege and doing nothing. I don't want to rely on my father's bank account, I want to make it myself.

^^^^^^^^^

^^^^^^^^^

@NotYourGuru
'Self-esteem doesn't come from having things, it comes from the act of getting those things for yourself. Making it by yourself.'
♥ 10.4k

LESS
I want my friend to make it, too.

Alyssa is different to me because she also craves the *fame*. It's maybe even what she craves the most. There's a million kids our age who have no idea what they want to be or the direction they want to take their lives. Sometimes I can't even force myself to think beyond today. I want to work but I want to enjoy my life. Party. Get drunk. Get laid. Who doesn't? But I also want to get paid. I want to make hats. I want to become a fashion designer over anything. I also understand that it is a great privilege to know that at my age.

I guess I'm drenched in privilege, right? I am well aware that most kids don't have my family wealth. Or a family accountant. Or a family lawyer. They don't have that cushion to fall back on. So why feel sorry for me at all, huh? The money doesn't define me. I'm still just a kid. Trying to find my way in a world that is moving too quickly. I experience the same mental hardships that every youngster has to endure to build their resilience in an unforgiving society.

Alyssa certainly doesn't feel sorry for me. I love that about her. Her family manages to get by, but she has to cook most of her own meals and care for her grandmother, who lives with her, now. She takes two buses to college. Somehow, everybody knows the kids who receive financial aid for their tuition. A scholarship would have been great but she doesn't excel in one area. Yet she became best friends with a guy who lives across the other side of town in a giant house, where the gardener is currently mowing the fucking lawn beneath his window, sending vibrations through the walls and into his hungover brain.

I want to shout at him, but I also don't want to move.

Mine and Alyssa's relationship works. It's a real friendship. Alyssa has a hundred ideas a day and I will pretty much go along with anything, as long as it satisfies my fun quota.

There's a party in the Hills.

A new restaurant is opening.

Protest at an art gallery.

Underground fight club.

I'll say 'yes' to all of that.

So, later tonight, once this crapulent headache has subsided and the desire for more alcohol rears its head once more, when we decide to scope out and crash a celebrity gala and Alyssa suggests that we steal a car, I will simply say 'yes'.

Because it's another adventure.

Free fun with my best friend.

Hell, my father is so rich and powerful that he's the only person I can really get in trouble with. And, sure, speed feels great at the time, and I'll do coke, whatever you throw my way, but nothing beats the natural high of pulling the wool over my father's eyes, of getting away with something that I shouldn't be doing.

^^^^^^^^^

^^^^^^^^^

@TheFitnessPaige 'DON'T BUY IT'
♥ 31k ◻ 898
(Direct to camera. Close-up.)
'Five million views.'

(Sigh.)

'Five million. You've seen her. Drinking her morning smoothie with a teaspoon of semen. Forget the vitamin C or the B12 or the magnesium, zinc and potassium. Heck, the amount of protein in a shot of that stuff is about a quarter of a gram. You'll get more from a bowl of oats with chopped banana. And it'll taste nice. And fill you up for the morning.'

(Cover face with hands.)

'Look, drinking a mouthful of cider vinegar every day does nothing but make you wince. There is no sense in putting butter into your coffee unless you like a greasy, fatty film on the surface of your hot drink. And you do not need to find a male friend to masturbate into a yoghurt pot twice a day so that you can boost your daily sodium intake by 0.4%, okay?'

^^^^^^^^^

^^^^^^^^^

Paige comes across like she cares. Like false information is the thing that annoys her the most. She doesn't want people duped by food fads. She's not selling out to grab followers, she is providing a service. She is helping, using science and knowledge and experience.

Like she used to. In the beginning when it was pure and not about likes or endorsements.

She has had enough. There are millions of people who follow her online for her workout videos and nutrition advice. She's beautiful, of course, but so many of these 'fitfluencers' are. They have to be. They are their own brand. Their bodies should be inspirational, aspirational – though ultimately unachievable without the right genetics and absolute discipline they rarely tell you it requires people to look that way.

Paige is aggravated because this other woman has gone online with a video saying that she has a spoonful of her friend's ejaculate in her smoothie, extolling the health and nutritional benefits. The story has taken hold, and everybody seems to be talking about it.

^ ^ ^ ^ ^ ^ ^ ^ ^ ^

^ ^ ^ ^ ^ ^ ^ ^ ^ ^

For You Trending News Sports Entertainment

#SemenSmoothie
102k posts

Game Seven
91k posts

#10CC
13.5k posts

#Lakers
8,564 posts

Ariel Dean
1,041 posts

^ ^ ^ ^ ^ ^ ^ ^ ^ ^

^ ^ ^ ^ ^ ^ ^ ^ ^ ^

Thousands of men are commenting on Ariel Dean's video, offering their own *product*. Some think they are being cheeky, others think they are funny, a lot of the men say something repulsive that they would be too embarrassed to say to a woman in real life.

All are disgusting. Protected by their avatars and usernames.

Many people have clicked out of curiosity and end up shaking their heads in disbelief in much the same way that @TheFitnessPaige is doing in her own video.

^^^^^^^^^^

^^^^^^^^^^

@TheFitnessPaige 'DON'T BUY IT'
♥ **34k** ☐ **912**
'I have a degree in nutrition from Berkeley. I'm also a qualified personal trainer and strength coach. I'm not just some hot chick in Lycra, licking a teaspoon and saying how I thought it would be more salty.'

^^^^^^^^^^

^^^^^^^^^^

Paige is one of thousands of people online doing this kind of thing but, for some reason, something hit and her profile exploded.

No rationale. No explanation. One video just caught hold of something and she continued to grow from there, riding the wave.

Now it's full-time.

Sure, she is still a qualified nutritionist and mentor but, above all, she is now an influencer; she's a content creator. She has a twelve-grand camera, microphones, editing software, a library of rights-free music and sound effects. Some days she feels more like a music-video producer. She has to think about colour and lighting, and which dish to serve her food on before she takes the shot.

There's no worry about being caught in the same outfit twice on her videos because she hasn't bought a pair of leggings or a workout vest for over a year. Parcels arrive most days with free goods for her to place in her reels and all she has to do is tag the company that has sent them.

And now this charlatan comes along and grabs up precious scrolling time with her bogus, soft-porn angle on nutrition.

Well, @TheFitnessPaige is not taking it. She unleashes a tirade of accusations. She calls the woman fake. Clickbait. An airhead. And she dresses it all up as concern for her followers and for people who do not follow her, who might buy into what this snake-oil saleswoman is trying to trick them with.

'Don't buy it,' she signs off. And it's good advice to anyone that will listen. Almost every second of these videos has been planned. The content is curated. It's very rarely a true window into the world of the person who is posting something.

It's a soundbite.

A sales pitch.

A vanity project.

So, @TheFitnessPaige is right, her followers should not believe the things that they see online. They should not take any of these videos at face value.

^^^^^^^^^

^^^^^^^^^

@TheFitnessPaige 'DON'T BUY IT'

♥ **35k** ▢ **967**

'Do not just accept that this sperm guzzler is advising on best nutrition practices. Don't even assume that it was semen on that spoon. It may not have tasted salty. It could have been a mixture of icing sugar and water.

Don't buy it.

Don't believe any of it.'

^^^^^^^^^^

^^^^^^^^^^

@TheFitnessPaige detaches her camera from the tripod and turns off the light – she lights herself from above because it picks up the contours of her muscles better. She plugs the camera into her computer and watches the video. She made her speech eight times. It was scripted. She read from cue cards. There's an AI program that she can run it through to make it appear as though she was looking into the camera the entire time.

The fifth take was best, she thinks.

Colours are corrected.

She adds music.

Then she posts, including all her usual hashtags and the words *DON'T BUY IT*, in capital letters.

She is the real influencer. An oracle. The truth-sayer. (Though her name isn't even really Paige.)

And she has just started a war.

Maybe that was the point.

^^^^^^^^^^

^^^^^^^^^^

ALYSSA

'Have you seen the video?' I don't even say hello to Less, I'm too excited.

'Alyssa. It's before twelve. I'm still dying. Why are you calling me with cryptic shit like this?' Less doesn't want to open his eyes yet, I know that. He sent me a text last night saying he was at Studio. Again.

'Oh, man up, you big pussy. I need someone to talk to about this.'

Only I can get away with talking to Less like this. Because he knows how much I love him.

I wait for him to sit up and find his laptop.

'Okay, bitch, what am I looking at.'

Less is the only man that I would allow to speak to me in this way. Because I know he loves me just the same.

I can hear him tapping away at his keyboard. 'Did you see that woman who puts jizz in a smoothie? Is that even a thing? I mean, I'm here for you if you want to try that. I haven't released for a few days.' He laughs.

'You're disgusting, you know that?'

'I'm just trying to be a good friend.'

He's not disgusting. This is a joke between friends. There's context. We're on the same page. If a stranger online said that to me, it's different. Outrage is justified.

'Put your dick back in your pants and have a look at Paige's profile.'

'It weirds me out when you talk about them like you know them, like they're your friends.'

'She followed me back, so I won't hear another word about it.'

Our usual back-and-forth continues until Less finds what I made him look for.

'You got it?'

'Yeah, I got it.'

'Watch it.'

He does. I wait. I imagine him gazing at the screen, open-mouthed, just as I did. Then he laughs when she talks about all the vitamins that aren't really in semen.

'She's got a bee in her bonnet,' he says down the phone. 'How long is left of this rant. It's not real, though, surely.'

'She cares, Less. She doesn't want misinformation out there.'

'She wants likes and views.'

'She's an influencer.' I do get agitated when Less talks about my heroes like this. I want him to agree with me but he sees things differently, I guess. Those with white privilege can smell their own, maybe.

'I know that. I'm just saying that a fight with another influencer can drum up business for both of them. They might've come up with this together for all we know.'

He says it's weird that I talk about these people like I know them, but he does the same thing. He thinks he understands them more because he's rich. I know he's already stopped watching the video.

'Oh, my God, Less. That other bitch is not an influencer. She's a try-hard. She wishes she was like Paige. She's a gimmick.'

'Most of the people we watch on this thing are gimmicks. Fuck, we watch people play video games. We watch people reacting to videos that we've already seen and reacted to ourselves.'

He doesn't get it.

'Well, I thought you'd be on my side.'

'What are you even talking about? There's no side. If this spunk-swilling sea witch really only wants to boost her profile, Paige has played right into that. She can now do a video in retaliation and get even more views than before.'

I don't say anything. He's right. It makes sense. Of course it does. It's just that I used to be able to count on Less to laugh at the same inane nonsense that I still laugh at. But he has grown more distrustful of things recently, and I don't know what sparked that change.

Our friendship, as unconventional as it may seem, is real. I don't want us to grow apart.

He's the best thing in my life.

^^^^^^^^^^

^^^^^^^^^^

LESS

I lose interest in the video. It's easy to do. There's always something else to look at. I open my fashion profile. I recently posted a picture of a hat that I designed. Some troll has written, 'Why don't you just die?' as a comment. That's a great way to start the day. I had hoped college would get me away from the bullies but hate always seems to find a way.

I roll my eyes but it hurts my head. It's too much. I scroll to the next video. And the next. It's automatic. Even though I'm doing something else. Even though I'm supposed to be in a conversation.

Then I stop.

There's a video of a young woman at a red-carpet event. She is loitering behind a line of people waiting to see whatever stars are getting out of the limousine. A tall woman – undoubtedly a model – exits the car and pulls her fur coat around her. Seconds later, the other young woman has pushed her way to the front of the crowd and throws a pot of red paint over the fur coat.

'Hey, Lyss.'

'What?' She's still annoyed, I can tell.

'Looks like your favourite fashionista has landed herself in some trouble again.'

^^^^^^^^^^

^^^^^^^^^^

ROSIE VELAZQUEZ
@RosieVelazquez
'Fashionista. Activist. Servant of God.'
741 Following **1.1M** Followers

^^^^^^^^^^

^^^^^^^^^^

#BanFur #AnimalsAreNotClothing #CompassionIsFashion
There are no frills with Rosie. She is all of the things she professes to be.

Being a fashionista makes her popular. Being an activist means she is often angry about something. And being a servant of God allows her to live in constant guilt.

But anyone with that level of influence must also have a grasp of business.

The video of her demonstration at the red carpet was taken by a friend. Nobody else was back there with him, they were all at the barrier, snapping pictures of the rich and the famous on their way to another benefit. A gala where they have donated products or plan on bidding for something in the name of charity, playing the role of the concerned citizen as they jet across the country, wearing outfits that cost more than six months of rent in the city.

Rosie can't handle the hypocrisy of it. How dare they wax lyrical about climate change and the environment when their private plane has guzzled precious fuel so that they can travel in luxury. They pretend they care about refugees from war-torn nations, washing up on the shores of neighbouring countries in a drastic effort to escape their appalling lives and save their families from certain destruction. But they just want the Chanel goodie bag.

And don't talk about saving anything if, the day before the event, you are going to boast about the animals that were skinned to make your coat.

Rosie wishes it wasn't so exhausting to care about things.

She knew about the fur because it's so easy to find out anything about anybody now. The modelling world has taken a pretty strong stand against the fur trade, Rosie appreciates that. It's the right thing to do. But somebody always has to be controversial. They call it art or expression but it's rarely the case.

Publicity.

Anything for that fifteen minutes.

Rosie's friend stood way back from the crowd as Rosie waited with her pot of paint and her heart full of rage. The only video circulating the news networks and online gossip sites is the one sold by the perpetrator of the crime. The money made will be used to bail her out and the rest will go to the charity that the woman in the fur coat was allegedly supporting.

Fashionista. Activist. Servant of God. Businesswoman. Philanthropist.

Rosie Velazquez will be manhandled and made to sweat in a cell for a few hours. But she will get to go home at some point and review her protest and update her followers and not issue an apology of any kind. And she will sit on her couch and watch herself on the news. And she will flick through all of her social-media channels and find that the video has gone viral. And she will hate that people will call it a stunt. And she will have a drink and fall asleep on the sofa.

And she will have no idea that hers is the first house that Alyssa and Less will break into together.

And she will have even less of an idea that they won't leave.

^^^^^^^^^

^^^^^^^^^

ALYSSA

I do everything with Less. Everything but this. I've been going at it alone for maybe two months, now.

It all happened by chance.

My mom is awesome. Beautiful, strong, independent. Dad left when I was small. Typical went-out-for-cigarettes-and-never-came-back kind of guy. She keeps us all going. She's amazing. But it's difficult, and she has to work all the time. It's hard on her. She has no life so that I have a chance of having one.

A couple of weeks back, she was about to leave for an evening shift at the hospital. She gave me a parcel.

'It's for Aaron, next door. Can you take it over to him when you get a chance this evening? He wasn't home earlier so I took it in for him. It's getting a little too often, but let's just be nice, eh? Thanks, darling. Don't wait up.' And she was gone. Another ten hours in the hell of healthcare.

I waved her off and then decided to get the delivery over with.

So, I knocked on Aaron's door and it opened slightly. It looked closed when I approached, but it was clearly left on the latch. I don't know why.

'Hello? Aaron?' I poked my head inside. 'Anyone there? I have a parcel for you.'

Nothing.

I stepped inside. Sure, I could have left the package on the mat and shut the door on my way out. But I didn't. It's these little decisions that can end up having a huge impact on our lives.

I still don't know why I did it but I went into the house and shut the door behind me, still holding my neighbour's mail. Maybe it's a generational thing. We see so much of people online, maybe we think we are allowed to know everything about a person. You don't have to be rich to be entitled.

The place was a typical bachelor pad. All the furniture in the lounge was modular and pointing at a huge TV screen with giant speakers in the corner. We can hear when he is watching the game if we are in the kitchen, which I often am because I have to cook most of my own meals and make sure my grandmother is fed and watered.

There was no evidence of a woman's touch, that I could tell. It wasn't disgusting but it was untidy. Not dirty but also not well maintained. Food wrappers. Pizza boxes. Single socks. I kept walking. I went into the kitchen. And that was worse.

'Aaron?' I tried again.

No answer. I guess I knew that there wouldn't be.

There was no way I was going to look in the bathroom. Instead, I went upstairs. Curiosity got the better of me, I kind of forgot that I was technically trespassing. I headed straight into the bedroom. The bed was, surprisingly, made, and an outfit ironed and laid over the back of a chair. Looked like he was going out somewhere.

I had just opened the drawer in Aaron's bedside table when the front door opened and he came home, talking loudly into his mobile phone.

'I'll be there on time, don't worry ... No, screw the Uber, I'll take my car ... Everyone drives bar to bar here, don't worry.'

He ran upstairs and straight into his room.

I was hiding under the bed.

I didn't know what else to do.

I held my breath.

Aaron kicked off his shoes and I saw his trousers drop to his ankles before he kicked them off, too. Part of me wanted to laugh but I couldn't.

I waited until I heard the bathroom door close. He locked it, even though he thought he was the only one there, and, as soon as the shower started, I rolled out from beneath the bed, ran downstairs and threw the parcel on Aaron's sofa before letting myself out to go home.

I ran.

It was a few metres. But when I got in, I was out of breath and my heart was racing. And I couldn't stop smiling. It was such a rush.

'Are you feeling okay, dear? You look exhausted.' My grandmother was concerned. She's sweet and I know that she hates that she's not as independent as she used to be.

'Oh, Grandma, no need to worry, I'm absolutely fine.'

The truth was, I was better than fine.

I felt amazing.

Exhilarated.

And, though I didn't know it at that point, it seemed that I had a new hobby.

I was a phrogger.

^^^^^^^^^

^^^^^^^^^

AUDITION TAPE: MOLLY MINNS, 20.

'I'm super, super bubbly. But, you know, sometimes I can go the other way. Maybe it's a split personality. Maybe it's just because I'm a Gemini. But I've got a wicked sense of humour and people are just going to love watching me because you never know what you're going to get.'

^^^^^^^^^^

^^^^^^^^^^

They are drinking Sauvignon Blanc in the editing suite at Tammy Lowell's house and watching audition tapes. A lot of the tapes are the same. *Crazy* wannabes with energy and big mouths. Stupid people with stupid opinions. The type of contestant that can go on any show. It doesn't matter what they have auditioned for anymore, it's all the same programme with a different title and set-up.

These two women are responsible for shows like *Stay-at-Home Dads of Suburbia* and *Green Card or Get Out.* Their most recent smash hit reality show is *Love in a Women's Prison*, where even the guards are contestants, but everybody is there for affection and attachment.

And a cash prize.

And their chance to be on television.

These powerhouse females could walk down the street and not be noticed, but millions of people have definitely seen their names at the end of something they have watched on TV.

Lincoln/Lowell Productions. Then the sound of a parrot squawking and saying 'Who's the big winner?' People have seen it. They've heard it. And they have no idea who Lincoln/Lowell are.

Edie Lincoln and Tammy Lowell. Friends from college. Media students who got into television through an internship and pure confidence. They are brash and outspoken – Edie more than Tammy – but they work harder than almost anybody in the business. They have to. They've always had to. And success means that they have to push even further to stay at the top of their game.

There's no real struggle for high art. None of their shows get picked up by HBO. They're not reviewed favourably in the *Times*. They make car-crash television. Shows where they can manipulate a situation. Manufacture a scene and pass it off as *reality*.

It's gone past an experiment. The *Big Brother* type of show – where you throw a group of ordinary people together in front of some cameras and watch what they do – is over. It has to be staged. They have to force predicaments.

The contestants are train wrecks. That's what Lincoln/Lowell are searching for. Right now. In the editing suite. With their bottle of wine. There is always somebody dealing with their sexuality or gender or morbid obesity. If you put a black guy on the show, you'd better get his bigoted counterpart. Maybe someone with obvious mental-health issues. A breakdown is always good viewing, and if they decide to take their life once the show has wrapped, that's great publicity for the next season.

That sounds cynical and horrific. But that is Lincoln/Lowell – Edie more than Tammy.

Spinning gold from the darkness of humanity.

Profiting from misery.

Situation after contrived situation.

But Lincoln/Lowell Productions do not shy away from that. They know who they are and they produce the most, and they are viewed the most. These women love what they do. And they'll keep doing it until it doesn't work anymore or they come up with a better idea. Or they get found out. Or they die.

'Let's see if we can get a shortlist of six out of this pile of bottom feeders and we'll get Satmohan to look into them, stalk them for a bit, see if they'll do what we need them to do,' Edie suggests, but Tammy isn't listening. 'What are you watching that's more important than this?'

Nothing.

'Tammy. What are you doing?'

She is watching @TheFitnessPaige's most recent post.

'Edie. Forget the tapes for now. We need to get Satmohan on this psychopath.'

^^^^^^^^^

^^^^^^^^^

LESS

'Morning, Sunshine.' My mother looks at her watch. All I can do is sigh. 'No classes today, I take it?'

She knows damn well that I've skipped whatever I was supposed to be doing this morning but she has no more control over me than she does over her lunchtime bottle of Zinfandel.

'What are you doing?' I'm finishing getting ready and she is doing that thing she does where she potters around my room, moving things about.

'Open the blinds. It's like a god-damned cave in here.'

'Jesus. It's fine. I'm trying to get ready.' I pull my fluorescent-yellow jacket from the wardrobe. I shouldn't wear it. And that's exactly why I do. That's fashion. Alessandro would have picked something to help him blend in. Less isn't like that. Less won't be beaten down. I won't be beaten down. It's okay for me to stand out. I realise that now.

I look in the mirror.

'So, what are you doing today instead of going to the college we pay for?'

I have to bite my tongue. I really don't want to get into it with her. It would be easy for me to say that it's not *their* money, it's my father's money, but I don't want to hurt my mom – no matter how hard she pushes. She's hurting. I can see that. I'm fairly certain that she has already had a drink, because it's too early for her usual brand of antagonism.

'I'm going to rob a bank.' I can't help myself. I'm trying to deflect. I won't be mean to her just because she is mean to me.

She stares at me. Then at my unmade bed. Then back at me.

'I'm meeting Alyssa for a coffee. It's nothing sinister. I'll head in this afternoon. I'm not really missing anything. Honestly.' I don't mention that I have probably missed out on another morning of torment or intimidation, she doesn't need the added worry of my troubles. I head over to my desk, shake a bottle of aftershave to see how much is left in the bottle and spray it on each side of my neck, then twice on my left wrist before rubbing it against my right.

'She's a sweet girl, Alessandro.'

What the hell is that supposed to mean?

'Less, Mom. Call me Less, please. Everybody does.' Apart from the ones who call me weird.

'I'm not doing that. Alessandro, she is a sweet girl. She's not as lucky as you, she doesn't have what you have.'

'I know that. I don't care about any of that.'

I really don't care. I think the world of Alyssa. She's easily the best person that I have ever met. I went to school with the privileged, the wealthy and the working class, and they all had their fair share of bullies and bigots. I don't judge people on their background, I judge them on their character. Because that's what I expect. I don't want to be judged on my sexuality or my choice of hat or the tightness of my jeans or the fact that my father is rich.

I know my mother used to earn her own money. A few catalogues. A billboard advertising toothpaste. She danced, too. She was beautiful. That's what my father liked, at first. But he stopped her from doing what she loved.

Whatever opinion my father had of the woman who would become his wife, it is not a view that I have ever held. I see her sadness. I understand what it's like to be alone. I guess that's why I let her get away with talking to me like a piece of shit. We're both struggling but she's been at it a lot longer than I have, and she can't see a way out.

Besides, if there's one thing I know, it's how to let people walk all over me.

But my mother is the only one who is allowed to do that.

'I'm not saying that you care where she's from, I'm saying that I don't want you to drag her down. She works hard, Alessandro. She struggles. She's a fighter.'

I am hurt by the accusation but I know that my mother is just talking about herself. She's projecting. Sometimes she does this to get a reaction from me so that we argue, then she tells me what's really bothering her. She can't just talk. There has to be conflict first.

'It's a cup of coffee, Mom. She's my best friend. She's real. Our friendship is real.'

'Don't fuck her up. That's all I'm saying. And make your bed before you go.' She walks out, tutting, shaking her head at the dirty clothes still on my floor. I stick two fingers up at her back in frustration.

My mother turns around and I hide my hands behind me. I can feel my cheeks flush, but she didn't see what I was doing.

'What time will you be home? Are you going to miss another dinner so that you can stay out all night again?'

I sigh. The bullies at high school were less persistent with their torment. 'It's just coffee with a friend. We might go out tonight but I'll be home for dinner with you and Dad.'

'Good. Well, grab me a bottle of my medicine on your way home, will you? I'm almost out.'

She's talking about gin. Mother's ruin.

'Not a problem.'

My mother smiles. Then reminds me, again, to make my bed before I leave the house.

A final jab.

I do as I'm told. I pick my clothes up and put them in the wash basket, finish opening the blinds and I make my bed. Then I pick up my wallet and a pack of gum from my desk, and I feel ungrateful for wanting an escape from my privileged life.

^^^^^^^^^^

^^^^^^^^^^

ALYSSA

I'm not *that* sweet.

This phrogging thing doesn't always come off. Businesses are much easier to get into than residential properties but they are much harder to stay in.

For two weeks after the parcel incident, I found myself checking Aaron's door when I knew he wasn't there, to see if it was open. The first few times, I was overly disappointed. My mood crashed. But, when I finally got in again, I went straight to his bedside cabinet to finish what I had started last time.

There was nothing interesting in there. I didn't want to steal anything. I just wanted to be there. And I still don't really know why. I just know that I felt something. Excitement, maybe. My home life is loving and supportive, but we're crammed into a tiny space and I spend a lot of time taking care of my grandma. It's nice to take a break from reality.

I took forty minutes out of my day to sit on the sofa of the man who lives next door, watch his TV and drink one of his beers. I left the can out. It probably still had condensation on the side when he returned, and I bet he didn't even notice.

Or maybe he did and it messed with his mind a little.

Is that my problem? He left his home open.

I wasn't doing anything wrong.

Not really.

Nobody died.

Aaron should have locked his door. Doesn't he know the disenfranchised youth of America are crying out for something to do, a reason to look away from our phone screens for the duration of our four-minute attention spans?

It was too late. I was hooked.

Randy's Doughnuts is an LA institution. It's been there for over fifty years, serving the great and the good. It's too high profile. But Jo's Cro's is up-and-coming. It claims to have been the birthplace of the Cronut – a cross between a croissant and a donut. It's small. Boutique. Grateful for the custom.

I bought three custard cronuts and a black coffee half an hour before closing. With the final queues of the day dwindling, staff were starting to wipe down tables and mop floors and clean out cabinets. I was already in one of the stalls in the bathroom. I left the door partly open in case a staff member came in, and I stood on the toilet seat so nobody could see my feet.

And I got so close. They had locked the back door and switched off the lights behind the counter. Apparently, the assistant manager, Carlos, liked to piss in the women's toilet at the end of the day. Maybe he was being rebellious. Maybe he had some issues with his mother. But he caught me in that bathroom stall and he knew what I was trying to do, and like me, he didn't know why. There would have been nothing to do in there after closing, anyway.

Maybe it's a working-class thing. Having to make your own entertainment because you can't afford to buy it.

He just thought I was a dumb kid and told me it was probably best that I left.

I was lucky it wasn't some Karen closing up that day.

But even though it didn't work out, there was still the buzz. Like a stand-up comedian practising a new set that bombs, the heart rate still raises, it's still an experience.

Like any addiction.

^^^^^^^^^

^^^^^^^^^

@MillennialMotivation
'The only thing better than a twelve-step plan is a co-dependent relationship.'
♥ 3.1k

^^^^^^^^^

^^^^^^^^^

ALYSSA

I want to do this with Less. He's my best friend. We share everything. It would be more fun together. Everything is. Apparently, it's only really a drinking problem if you are drinking alone. I don't want to keep this from Less any longer.

Even the closest of friends have their secrets, but I don't want any with him.

Less is good. He's the sweetest person. He's not like the other privileged one percent. They do what they want because they think that they can, that they are allowed. Less is different. But I still think I will have to ease him in.

^^^^^^^^^

^^^^^^^^^

#CrueltyFreeLiving #EmbraceLife #CompassionOverCruelty #MindfulLiving

Rosie Velazquez sets the camera on her phone to 0.5x, so that she can get more of the police station in the background of her selfie. (Everyone is using 0.5x, right now.) This feature only works with the camera on the back of the phone so she has to take the picture without looking at the screen. She holds it out in front and up high to get the best angle.

It's perfect.

After six attempts.

Capturing a real, spontaneous, moment has never taken so much planning.

She writes, 'Rocking my mug shot' before throwing in a list of hashtags that bear no relevance to the situation – but will be sure to drop onto the right feeds.

It doesn't even take a minute before her device is lighting up with notifications. Likes and messages. Support and abuse. It's all part of the job, part of the game. She smiles as though each one is a validation.

'Taxi,' Rosie yells, holding out a hand into the road. A car pulls up and she hops in the back before giving the driver her address. He either doesn't recognise her or doesn't care. Half the people that get into his car tell him they are off to an audition or they've got a small part in something. He hears the words 'streaming' and 'podcast' more than he ever has before. So maybe he just isn't fazed by celebrity.

She posts on a different platform that she is now *in the cab*. It's not interesting but it has to be done. If she says nothing, she will never be heard. She knows that she has to keep pumping content otherwise somebody else will take her fifteen minutes.

Where she is.

What she's doing.

Who she is with.

If she is eating a nutritious Buddha bowl, she takes a photo, adds a filter that brightens the colours and tags the restaurant. It doesn't always work but it puts her in with a chance.

There are three men waiting by her front gate. They have cameras. Real cameras. Lenses that look like penis replacements. They're waiting for Rosie. Hoping she looks dishevelled and pale, so that they can capture the moment she is at her worst and sell it to the highest bidder.

Vultures.

But, also, strangely necessary in the ecosystem of fame.

'Just pull over here, that's great. Thank you.'

The driver still doesn't appear bothered that his current passenger is about to get hounded by the paparazzi. He's seen worse. He's dropped at bigger houses with more secure gates. The kinds of places that require a minimum of fifteen foaming-at-the-mouth photographers. He tells her how much it costs, and she hands him a few notes that will cover the journey and a generous tip, that Rosie thinks he deserves.

'Good luck, miss,' the driver says as she opens the car door.

It sounds genuine.

^^^^^^^^^

^^^^^^^^^

@Dress2Impress
'Wore all black to look sexy for my man today. He asked me if I was going to a funeral. Yeah, for my motivation to look good.'
♥ 6.7k

There's no chance to breathe between the cab pulling away and the three camera hounds blurting out her name like they know her.

How was prison, Rosie?

Why did you do it, Rosie?

Rosie. Rosie. Rosie.

'Look, can you just let me get to my fucking gate,' she shouts. And that's the picture they want. Rosie Velazquez, righteous do-gooder, animal activist and stylish influencer, losing her cool. A blue vein across her right temple. Teeth gritted.

Come on, Rosie.

It's all good publicity, Rosie.

Smile for the camera, Rosie.

She gets past them and heads up the path towards her front door. They don't follow. They dare not trespass. It's fine to shove a zoom lens into someone's face on a public street and they know that. In fact, it's the best way to get the reaction the tabloids want.

'Come on, Rosie,' one of them calls after her.

She stops. To give them time to get their cameras in place. Then she turns and holds up both middle fingers. It's childish but she was put on the spot. These idiots don't understand the amount of work that goes into setting up the shots that she posts. She considers herself a curator.

Rosie lets herself in and bolts the door shut behind her. She heads straight to the kitchen and opens the fridge. There's half a bottle of some Napa Valley Chardonnay from a few nights ago. She takes out the bottle and sniffs at it. It's almost certainly on the turn by now but it's all she has.

She takes a wine glass from the kitchen cabinet as well as a huge coffee mug. From another cupboard she takes a tin of artisan cocoa powder. Rosie sets the tin next to the mug and takes a picture, being sure to avoid shadows. And then she posts the image.

^ ^ ^ ^ ^ ^ ^ ^ ^ ^

^ ^ ^ ^ ^ ^ ^ ^ ^ ^

@RosieVelazquez
'Finally home from the big house. Hot chocolate and bed needed. Zzzzz.' #GratefulLiving
♥ 457

^ ^ ^ ^ ^ ^ ^ ^ ^ ^

^ ^ ^ ^ ^ ^ ^ ^ ^ ^

She watches the first five-hundred *likes* roll in.

Pours the wine.

Takes it over to the sofa and sips at it while she cries.

She can't tell her followers how she really feels.

^ ^ ^ ^ ^ ^ ^ ^ ^ ^

^ ^ ^ ^ ^ ^ ^ ^ ^ ^

ALYSSA
'You're late.'

'Yeah. My mother was breaking my balls again.' Less is so funny, he never apologises.

'You're always late.'

'What can I say? I'm an artist. I don't like to be restricted by time.' He smiles and I jokingly shake my head in dismay. 'Have you ordered? Are we eating?'

This is the awkward part about hanging out with someone who doesn't have financial worries. I don't have the money to eat out whenever I like. I had to take two buses just to get over here. I am hungry but I need the money. I have to come back later for the party that we're going to try to crash. I don't have a car.

'I haven't eaten yet,' Less continues, he can see I look a bit uncomfortable, I always do when it comes to money. 'I'm definitely getting something. Order what you want, it's on me. For standing you up for so long.' He pushes a menu over to me and picks up the other for himself, trying to make it look as though it doesn't matter.

Twenty dollars is nothing to Less but it's a big deal to me. He knows that and he never makes me feel bad about it.

^^^^^^^^^^

^^^^^^^^^^

LESS

I was only six minutes late; that's pretty good for me. I love my friend from the poorer side of town and, maybe, to the casual onlooker, it seems as though I am attempting to buy her affections. But I'm not. We both know that I fund a lot of our fun, but Alyssa is too proud to actually ask me to do that. She would rather sit here and starve than suggest I pay for anything. My mom is right, she's a sweet girl.

^^^^^^^^^^

^^^^^^^^^^

ALYSSA

If somebody was looking over at our table right now, they might deduce that I am using Less for his money and connections. I am a young woman who is in no doubt about what she wants, but, for all my morally grey areas, I would never exploit my relationship with Less in that way. It's important to me that we're equal. Struggle is relative.

One of us has money and one of us does not. But we are both mixed-up. We're both kind of directionless. We're both what-the-hell-are-we-going-to-do-with-our-lives kids, it doesn't matter how much cash we have in our wallets. Our friendship is one of the only truly real things that either of us has. It's genuine and it's deep. And, in our eyes, at least, unbreakable.

I order a chicken salad. Less gets the burger with fries and a side of onion rings.

'I hate you,' I tell him.

'What?' He smiles.

'You eat like you're at a kid's birthday party and you somehow look great in skinny jeans. It's not fair.' He's got a wonderfully angular face. All cheekbones and chin. He's either a pretty boy or a handsome woman.

'My drunken mother used to be a model. I must get it from her. Those were the days when she only did coke and was fun to be around.'

'Ah, so you got your dad's personality. Lucky it wasn't the other way around.' I push my tongue into the side of my cheek to show that I'm joking. This is how we talk. It sounds like flirting but it's obviously not.

'Quite. So, what do you want to do after this?'

'Go to Rosie Velazquez's house.'

^^^^^^^^^^

^^^^^^^^^^

LESS

'What are you talking about?'

'I just want to see her. I'm not going to ask to braid her hair or anything.'

'We have no idea where she lives.' I take a huge bite of my burger and grease drips down onto the plate.

There's a flicker in Alyssa's eye. She's hot but she doesn't know it. Tanned skin and doe eyes. If I was straight, I could see the appeal.

She smiles like she knows something. It's mischievous but playful and it has my attention. She lays her cutlery down, takes a swig of her latte and pulls out her phone so that she can show me just how she worked out where one of her favourite influencers lives.

Alyssa starts with a picture of the chicken salad that she is eating. But she hasn't taken it. She swipes right. There's a picture of a young man. Mid-twenties. Hair tied up in a top knot. White gravestone teeth. Tattoos all the way up both arms. He's in the seat that I'm sitting in right now.

Swipe right. A view of the menu.

Swipe again. A selfie of both of them outside the café we are sitting in right now. Both of them. Tattooed guy and Rosie Velazquez. I don't know whether I should be worried or impressed.

'You know that you kind of seem like a stalker right now, Lyss? And my mother thinks *I'm* the bad influence. Ha!' I take a napkin and wipe the corners of my mouth. 'Is that why we're here today? In case she comes in again?'

'Noooo. I'm not mental. I'm just making a point.'

She scrolls and shows me a picture of Rosie on her morning run. It plays the songs she was listening to at that point of her workout. Kings of Leon, allegedly. The caption says that she is '...out for a quick 5k, this morning'. There are houses in the background and a street sign.

Alyssa tells me that it took seconds to find a street with that name near the café.

'You can walk to that sign from here.'

'Lyss, you're scaring me.'

'Give over. It's just math. A five-kilometre run means that the sign is within that distance of her house. In fact, it's probably only half that because nobody just goes for a run in a straight line, right? They do a circuit.'

'She's not a fitfluencer, either. Could be lying about doing 5k.' I know this pisses her off.

'Not everyone online is a liar, Less.' Alyssa hasn't had a privileged life but she is still naive. And I kind of like that about her. I feel like I can help. I can guide her.

I shrug my shoulders and throw more delicious cheese-covered beef into my mouth.

Next, a picture of Rosie in her back garden, recommending a book she has been reading in the sunshine. There are hills behind her.

An image of her and the tattooed guy having cocktails on the front lawn. She has tagged the company that does cocktail pouch deliveries. The sun is setting to her right, so Alyssa now knows where the west is. Another picture is less curated. A selfie taken by a hand attached to a heavily inked forearm. I can see a fence and a Volkswagen camper van across the street.

It's an old van. It probably hasn't moved in a while. Cue Google Earth and Street View on Maps. Alyssa went on her own virtual jog around the streets. She found the fence and the van.

'Just come with me and look,' she says. Like it's totally normal.

I just stare at her. I can sense another Alyssa-fuelled adventure. I don't want to look too excited, though. Not yet.

'Don't put this information out there if you don't want to be found.' She says it like it justifies her stalking.

'You want to try a new club or restaurant, I'm in. But this ... I don't know. Sounds kinda...'

'Fun? Different? In-ter-est-ing?'

'Weird, I was going to say.'

'I thought you hated that word.'

She's right. She knows me, and I feel kind of stupid for saying it. Those bullies ruin everything.

'Look, Less, you get bored and your parents buy you a car or some kind of gadget or a summer wardrobe or whatever. I don't have money. I have to find ways to entertain myself for free.'

That hurts a little. I don't want her to think of me like that. She's real. We are real together. I don't feel guilty about my privilege and I know that Alyssa is not trying to make me feel guilty. She already knows that I'll go along with her plan. Because it's different. Because it could be fun. Because it is Alyssa.

She already knows that I will do exactly what she wants.

Because I always do.

^^^^^^^^^

^^^^^^^^^

ARIEL DEAN
@FoodForThought
'My journey towards health and energy.'
223 Following **47k** Followers

Oscar leaves the yoghurt pot next to the sink in the bathroom.

'Is there any way I can do this at home and then bring ... *it* over? It feels weird doing that in there with you waiting out here.'

'It needs to be fresh, I think.' She doesn't know. 'Maybe you could freeze it or something?'

She has no idea what she's doing. She hooked on to some hokum website and thought she'd try it. She'd been down on a few guys in the past. She didn't *love* the taste but a glass of water and blob of toothpaste was always enough to sort that out. Putting it in a smoothie takes away that process. And, according to the blog post she read, written by a man, there are a heap of health benefits.

Oscar was happy to help with the experiment before he realised he would be masturbating in her bathroom while she waited outside. He doesn't like it anymore.

Tired of orgasms.

What a problem to have.

Ariel Dean has had some health issues. She's always had a waif frame, it's natural and it suits her, but at her lowest she was skinny. Too skinny. There's so much she can't eat. Her body has difficulty absorbing certain nutrients.

Medically speaking, it's a difficult area of study. The gut isn't quite as 'glamorous' as something like cancer, and everything is being eclipsed by mental-health issues right now. There's little funding for food allergies and intolerances even though the gut affects so many areas of the body.

From a young age, Ariel has had to monitor her food, make diaries of what she eats, abstain from certain food groups and then reintroduce them to see if they make her sick. Or lose energy. Or bloat. Or want to give up.

So many times she has wanted to give up.

Veganism took off in almost the same way as social anxiety. Everyone was jumping aboard. And Ariel Dean was nothing if not a trend follower.

But it worked.

She had energy, her skin began to glow and her hair had some shine, some body. She didn't feel great, yet, but she felt good. She couldn't remember the last time that had happened.

She discovered kale and avocados and the fact that you could make cheese out of cashew nuts. Like everything that makes you feel amazing, Ariel became obsessed. She experimented with food, she started exercising; she had never had the energy to do that before. But, most importantly, she began to document her journey online.

And people began to watch. And listen.

And take note.

Word spread. It wasn't just her family anymore, or the people in her town, it was other cities and countries. She was nowhere near the level of followers that it takes to be considered 'influential' but her story touched the hearts of thousands of people.

Then she read a blog, written by some undersexed miscreant. Maybe it was meant as a joke, but Ariel was innocent. Her quest was pure. So she lapped it up. And she regurgitated the drivel from the blog post in her video as she added a spoonful of Oscar's best swimmers to her protein drink after a morning jog in the park.

She just wants to be well, and she will try anything to keep things that way. She has spent her life struggling with her health, so she is always looking for answers. And it has made her gullible.

The post went viral for all the wrong reasons. It upset Ariel.

But now some fitness bitch is calling her out. She doesn't know what Ariel has been through to get to this point, but, apparently, that isn't even a consideration.

Ariel is stronger now.

And she's not going to take it anymore.

^ ^ ^ ^ ^ ^ ^ ^ ^ ^

^ ^ ^ ^ ^ ^ ^ ^ ^ ^

ALYSSA

The camper van looks like it hasn't moved for years. The back left tyre is flat and the curtains could do with a dip in bleach. But it's definitely the one from the picture with the picket fence next to it. The sun is high in the sky right now, but it's heading over to the right.

And, on the other side of the road is a building that is unmistakably the home of Rosie Velazquez. The front garden is the same. The door is the same. But it's also easy to tell because Rosie is standing on her steps and stretching her calf muscles.

I can't believe it.

I'm shaking.

'Shit, that's her.' I'm either starstruck or panicked, but I slap Less across the chest in my apparent giddiness.

'Um ... ow.' It didn't really hurt. He just doesn't know why I did it.

'We can't just stand here, it looks too suspicious.' I would love Rosie to know who I am but, right now, I don't want her to even see me.

Rosie is dressed in black. Black leggings. Black vest. Black shoes. And black cap. She's going for a run and she doesn't want to be noticed. She grabs her right ankle with her right hand and pulls her foot up behind her to stretch off her quads. She's lean. A long-distance runner's body.

'Look at this,' Less says, pointing at a paper sign in the window of the camper van. I follow his lead but keep an eye on Rosie in the reflection. She bends over and touches her toes a few times. Then she places her earphones in her ears and walks down her path to where the photographers must have been waiting when she got home from the police station – I saw that online. She opens the gate, turns right and starts to jog.

Five kilometres is her usual distance.

At a decent pace, it means that she probably won't get back to her house for another twenty-five minutes, minimum.

Rosie Velazquez's home will be unoccupied for almost half an hour.

Oh, my God. My mind races.

^^^^^^^^^^

^^^^^^^^^^

LESS

'You know, that's a good price. It wouldn't take a lot to do this old thing up a bit. We could take a weekend trip somewhere. Behave like hippies.'

I'm getting into character, reading the advertisement in the window of the camper van.

'Oh, would you focus. She's gone and her house is empty.'

'You don't know it's empty.'

'What?'

'You don't *know*. That tattooed guy could be there.'

'No way. She'd have mentioned it. She's always going on about their *friendship*. Look, she's just posted about going for a run. We're probably skulking in the background if you zoom in enough.' Alyssa looks over at the front door. There's no deterring her when she sets her mind to something. I admire that about her. She has the drive to be better, just not the focus on something specific that would make it happen.

'What's your point?' I ask.

'You see what she was wearing? Everything skin-tight. No pockets. No bag. She doesn't even keep her phone in one of those armband things that runners wear.'

'Okaaaaay.' I don't know where she's going with this.

'So where's her key?'

I wait for her to answer her own question.

'Maybe she just leaves it under the mat.'

It might seem ridiculous to somebody else, but I know that my parents do it. If they are going out to an event and don't want to carry a wallet or purse because it is too bulky or doesn't compliment the outfit, they will do the same. It's a stupid-rich-person thing. They think they're invincible.

'I'm sure she does. Come on, let's go,' I urge her. I don't know why I'm so nervous.

But it's already too late. Alyssa is walking across the road.

'I'm not going to use it, I just want to see if it's there. You stay and look at the van.'

I know that she is impulsive. Impetuous, even. I shake my head. There's nothing I can do to stop her.

Then a man with long grey hair steps out from behind the camper van.

'Anything I can help you with, young man?'

'Uh, well ... yes. The ... er ... the van. You're looking to sell, huh?'

Oh, shit. A witness.

'It saddens me but yes. I mean, the stories this thing could tell.' He pats the van like it's a dog.

'Oh, I bet.' I look over my shoulder as subtly as I can and take a step to the right so that the old hippie is focused on me rather than the woman walking up his neighbour's path. 'I can see the tyre needs changing but is there much that needs doing on the inside?'

I'm sweating. Maybe this was not such a good idea.

Alyssa is walking towards the steps like she owns the place.

Confidence is key, it seems.

The old man sighs. He's not paying any attention to the young girl who doesn't live across the street. He's reliving his glory years, a guitar and blanket in the back of the van, hitting the road, meeting some waitress in a diner. He has more than a few stories even though he looks as though he has, like so many, settled for a life wasting away in suburbia.

ΛΛΛΛΛΛΛΛΛ

ΛΛΛΛΛΛΛΛΛ

ALYSSA

I don't even look back. I'm a woman on a mission. What's the worst that could happen if I get caught? It's not a crime to look. It's all anybody is doing.

I reach the doorstep. There's a pair of boots outside the door next to a potted plant of some kind. But that's not what's on my mind. I take the two steps up. A glass pane in the door means that I could easily look inside the home of one of my idols, but I've probably seen enough of the place from Rosie's online content.

This is it.

I reach out for the doormat and take a deep breath.

^^^^^^^^^^

^^^^^^^^^^

LESS

'The engine is good, the cooker is good, the fridge is all good. You see these young folk adding TV screens and huge speakers to these beautiful machines. I don't get it.' The old guy is inside now, so I can see right through the window. Alyssa is on her knees.

'What do you want to use it for?' The van owner just wants to know that it's going to a good home; he doesn't really want to sell it.

'I'm sorry?'

'The van. What are you going to use it for? You want to put an Xbox in it or something?'

'Oh, no. No. Nothing like that. My friend is a travel blogger. A writer, you know? She visits places and writes reviews. She wants to write a book about being on the open road.'

I don't know where that came from but, apparently, I'm a pretty convincing liar. It falls out of my mouth.

The old hippie seems convinced.

^^^^^^^^^^

^^^^^^^^^^

ALYSSA

Under the mat, I can see the key. It has to be to the front door and Rosie Velazquez must have left it there when she bent down to touch her toes. But, about ten inches behind, I can see something else. Another key. Identical. Why would she need to leave two keys under the front mat? It makes no sense.

It's too much to think about now. I have come within touching distance. Just a taste. That's enough.

For today.

I take a deep breath, smile, and make my way back down the path.

^ ^ ^ ^ ^ ^ ^ ^ ^ ^

^ ^ ^ ^ ^ ^ ^ ^ ^ ^

LESS

'So, you're interested?' the old man asks. I can tell that he doesn't really want anybody to buy the thing. He has his memories but he still wants the van that gave him so many of those memories. His wife probably just wants it gone from the front of their home.

'Sure. I'm interested.' I can see that Alyssa is on her way back towards me. I start to back away from the camper. I could buy it and set the thing on fire for fun, if I wanted. But I just want to get the hell out of here.

'Nobody has so much as sniffed at the thing for months. You live around here?'

'No. I'm from across town.'

Alyssa appears next to me. Miles of smiles. She is glowing. Buzzing. She needs to save me from this, though.

She puts her arm through mine. 'Honey, you have to stop looking at cars. We have enough.' She fake laughs. It takes me a second to realise what she's doing.

'I can't help myself, you know that.' I smile and kiss her on the head. It's a bit awkward.

The old man looks puzzled.

'If you're from across town, how did you see the advert in the window of my Volkswagen?'

'I ... I saw it online,' I try. Then I realise who I have been talking to – he's an analogue guy in a digital world, no way he's advertising a car he doesn't want to sell on the internet.

'Online? Where do you see that?' The old man closes the door to his van and locks it. He's suspicious now. He never posted an advert on the internet; he probably doesn't even use the thing.

Alyssa tugs at my arm to get away and says, 'Google Earth.' Then she laughs. 'Everyone's on it.'

^ ^ ^ ^ ^ ^ ^ ^ ^ ^

^ ^ ^ ^ ^ ^ ^ ^ ^ ^

#Climber #WhateverItTakes

Satmohan finds out everything he can about @TheFitnessPaige. He scours the internet at first, pulling up profiles from several platforms and collating the information. He finds interviews, both in text and video form. He knows where she grew up and what school she went to, so now he can look into records and speak with former teachers. They will tell him who her friends were. He can then hunt them down through their – usually open for anyone to peruse – online profiles.

He searches through photos and friends lists. If they follow @TheFitnessPaige, it's a good start, but millions of people do. He wants to see if there are any recent selfies of Paige with friends and what area they were taken.

In a couple of hours, Satmohan knows her real name, her qualifications, her jobs before she became such an influential fitness and nutrition guru.

'Leanne Paige Beckerman. Star school gymnast. Average track and field. Decent grades. Middle-class family. Younger brother joined the navy. Parents still together. She's single. Focussed on her career. Honestly, she seems frightfully ordinary. I might be able to find out more with a little more time. Turn over some rocks. Uncover some enemies...'

Satmohan has the makings of a ruthless future producer. He has worked for Edie Lincoln and Tammy Lowell for over a year. He started as their assistant, running errands and fetching coffee, but he showed a tenacity for the business and he networked with the right people. He has his own contacts. Now he acts as a researcher and sometime production assistant to the powerhouse duo. He's been credited on several shows.

Satmohan is what they call 'a climber'.

'She sounds boring as shit.' Edie is not convinced.

They are on a three-way video conference call. Both producers are at home, Satmohan is in a coffee shop with his earphones plugged in.

'You're wrong, Edie,' Tammy chimes in. 'None of these people are what they say they are. They scream self-esteem problems and daddy issues. This girl is no different. But trust me. There is something there.'

Edie is comfortable. She likes making the shows that they produce now. If these people are ready to be exploited in the name of ratings and entertainment, how is Edie the bad guy? She is a facilitator.

Tammy has the vision, though. The numbers aren't reflecting her thoughts yet but she predicts a move away from shock TV and gimmick contestants. The tides are going to turn. There will be a shift from the sensational. No more housemates with dwarfism or Nazi ideals or crippling anxiety or Tourette's or alcohol dependency or a belief that the world is flat. Regular people are coming back into style.

'In an increasingly emotionally disconnected world, viewers are starting to crave somebody to watch that they can relate to,' Tammy reiterates.

A normal person. But a normal person with an abnormal job that keeps them at a distance, so that Tammy and Edie can still fuck with them as much as they want. These new internet stars don't have the support systems like those with actual talent to protect. They're thrust into fame overnight.

'I want to trust you, Tammy, I really do, but I'm finding it hard to see whatever it is that you are seeing. Satmohan, what do you think?'

'I don't know, I've only just started looking into her.'

'Gut reaction?' Edie pushes him. She is always testing his instincts.

He knows he can't hesitate.

'I think Tammy is right. There's something there. Nobody is that clean.'

Both women give a subtle nod like they are jointly proud of their surrogate Punjabi son. Neither has their own kids. They prioritised their careers.

'Have you found out where she lives?' Tammy asks.

'Not yet but it's only been a couple of hours. I can find it.'

'Good work,' Tammy praises. 'Then print off the contract and take it over there. Get her to sign.'

Edie doesn't even know which show Tammy thinks Paige is ideal for.

Tammy has no idea, either.

But she knows that Paige is going to be perfect.

^^^^^^^^^^

^^^^^^^^^^

ALYSSA

Less and I run off and we don't look back until we get out of breath.

The old man doesn't give chase; he's probably just happy that he doesn't have to sell his van.

'What the hell was that?' I can't tell if Less is mad or excited.

'That, my friend, was fucking fun.'

'Well?'

'Well, what?'

'Did you find what you were looking for?'

'Yup. As expected. You rich idiots think you're untouchable. She'd put a key under the mat because she didn't want to carry it with her while she jogs around the block. The thing is, there was another one under there a bit further back. I reckon she must have put one under there when she went out one night or something and somehow forgot about it, or didn't need it in the end. Who knows?'

'That's a little odd.'

It is odd. I wonder whether Rosie would even notice if it was taken. It looks like it has been forgotten about. Unless, maybe, it is left there for tattooed guy.

I'll check again next time.

Oh, wait. Next time?

I'm already thinking about next time. I'm leading this. I know.

I've got a taste for it. Less has no idea that I've been doing this a while. But I know he will love it. He's always talking about how he has an addictive personality.

^^^^^^^^^^

^^^^^^^^^^

@D4ilyMotiv4tion
'Remember that recovery is never linear. Days can be good or bad and some don't even make sense. But each one counts for something.'
♥ 2.2k

^^^^^^^^^^

^^^^^^^^^^

ALYSSA
'A bit of a rush, I have to admit.' I'm testing him. I want my best friend to be with me.

'For you, I'm sure. I was stuck talking to Old Man Marley about the good old days when chicken really tasted like chicken.'

We both laugh. Good. He's not mad.

'So, are you going to buy the van or what?'

'Oh, you're fucking funny.' He pushes me playfully, we're both still breathing hard.

Our day of misdemeanour is not finished yet, though. The plan has always been to try and crash a party in the Hills. Again, it's all about confidence. Walking in like you belong. We've done this kind of thing before in bars, masquerading as young fashion prodigies. Another time we were editors at Scribner. The time before that, we were part of a writers' room at Warner.

It's fun.

Nobody gets hurt.

Nobody that matters.

We agree a time for later. Less says he's happy to get a car and swing by my neck of the woods then head up to the Hills.

'Look, I need to get back home and pick up a bottle of Tanqueray for the old dear. She's probably shaking in a corner of the house somewhere. You going to be okay getting back from here?'

'Yeah. Yeah. I'm a big girl, Less. I have to get back, too, and cook some dinner for my grandma.' Our lives are so different but, in their own ways, they are both shit. Less has financial security but is forced to procure the substances his mother is addicted to. I have the sweetest grandmother and a hard-working mother but I'm almost a full-time carer. I've been getting myself to school since I was small and cooking my own dinners since I could reach the kitchen counter.

We both feel secure at home and insecure within ourselves. We both struggle in groups. We both want to be liked. We both want to make an impact in some way. But we're both also bored, searching for something.

'And I can trust you not to go and use some influencer's toilet or something?' Less smiles and I pretend to roll my eyes. But the truth is, my intention is to go back towards Rosie's house. Not to use the key or take the spare. I'm timing her run. If it is five kilometres, she shouldn't be longer than thirty-five minutes. If that's the case, I will know exactly how long Less and I will have to look around Rosie Velazquez's house the next time we visit.

^^^^^^^^^

^^^^^^^^^^

LEG DAY #028 VIEWS: 1 COMMENTS: 0 LIKES: 0

'You have to keep your chin up and your chest up, that will keep your back nice and flat. Make sure that your chest stays behind your knees. That's right. Good. And remember ... form over speed.'

^^^^^^^^^^

^^^^^^^^^^

Paige speaks directly to the camera as she drops into a squat so low that she could pick pennies up from the floor with a clench.

She uses her go-to expressions. Always thinking about the brand.

The Fitness Paige app launched six months ago and she promised new material every week for those on a monthly subscription. This means uploading recipes and images of the food she prepares, as well as new workouts and motivation. Today she is recording *LEG DAY #028*.

Paige is four minutes away from the end of a thirty-minute routine that will 'blast your glutes and burn up those quads', when the doorbell rings. It's far enough away for the sound to not interfere with the recording. It wouldn't be difficult to pause and edit. It could be done but she wants the workout to be authentic and recorded in one take.

She continues.

'Drop your knee directly below the hip as you step back into the lunge. We're close to the end, now. Stay with me. You're gonna have to dig deep for this next part.'

The doorbell rings again.

Satmohan is persistent.

Paige ignores it again, but it is flustering her. She has the cameras set up faultlessly, in order to capture different angles. The lighting is immaculate. The sound is on point. Everything is perfect. Because it has to be. Because that is the aspiration. That is what she must portray. It's the Paige Fitness brand.

'If you still feel like you need to stretch some more then go to the cooldown area in the app and take another ten minutes for you and your body. Eat well. Recover. And I'll see you at your next workout.' She smiles and balls her fist to show her strength.

#StrongWomen #Fitness #Lifting #Cardio #FitnessMotivation #Training #Wellness

Fade to black.

Paige drinks water and wipes her face with a towel. She takes a breath because she doesn't want to be mad when she opens the door. Even though she is seething. It's been four or five minutes, whoever was there is probably gone. Another parcel from a sponsor left on the doorstep.

Still, she marches down the hallway like she's ready to tear somebody's head off. The video will turn out fine. She's living up to her end of the bargain for the app. New users are downloading and paying for it every day.

Don't forget to like and subscribe.

As she reaches for the door, the bell rings again and startles her. Adrenaline is released and she yanks the door open aggressively.

'Who are you?' she asks, sternly. Eyes wide.

'Sorry?'

'Have you been here for the last five minutes ringing the doorbell over and over again?'

Satmohan stays quiet.

So does Paige.

'I work for Lincoln/Lowell Productions. We make—'

'The parrot thing. At the end of each show.'

'That's us. Well, we are interested in you.'

The anger and frustration dissipates, instantly. Paige is interested in their interest. Satmohan delivers his pitch. He does as he is told, explaining that it's just an idea so far, a pilot. They will need to set up their own cameras around the place – nothing intrusive – and to figure out a structure, what the real story is. What's the angle. That kind of thing. He throws out some TV jargon to excite and baffle her.

Satmohan has no real power. He has no real idea about what the show will be or if it will ever really happen. It looks like another *At Home With X* travesty. He doesn't care about the details – it could be one of their personal projects that never sees the light of day – he's there for one reason. To slide that contract across Paige's dining table, explain how it could negatively affect her life, that it probably won't end up the way that she thinks. And then get her to sign it.

@TheFitnessPaige will sign it.

Because everybody does.

^ ^ ^ ^ ^ ^ ^ ^ ^

^ ^ ^ ^ ^ ^ ^ ^ ^

#BlessedAndGrateful #ThankYouLord #GodIsGood

Rosie Velazquez doesn't come home for an hour.

It's not that she is slow or unfit or that she decided to run ten kilometres instead, it's that she is just like her profile says: A servant of God. She went to church. She had to talk to her Lord.

To ask Him if what she did was right.

To gain His forgiveness.

To ask His advice.

This has been drummed into her from birth. She grew up in a close Christian community. The type of town that nobody ever leaves. Nobody but her and one other. Blair Conroy. But nobody knows what happened to her.

There are two elderly women on the front pew doing the same. Calling out and waiting for guidance. Rosie thinks they look sweet. Like good people. She keeps her phone in her hand but doesn't look at it the entire time she is there.

She's not stupid. She knows that God is not going to answer – her influence doesn't stretch that far. But, somehow, the God who cannot enter into a two-way conversation is the only person Rosie feels truly connected to.

She drops to her knees, clasps her hands together and prays.

'God. I feel so out of control. I thought I had found myself. I thought I knew what I wanted to do with my life. And now everything is spiralling out of control. I don't know who I am anymore. Everybody is watching. There's always somebody watching. I know that you see me. You see us all. How am I supposed to know if I am on the right path? Is getting into trouble part of making a difference?'

This is how it goes; there's no preparation or protection for this new wave of celebrities.

Rosie doesn't want an answer, she just wants to talk and not have somebody pass judgement. Even the *likes* are getting too much. She wants to vent. To get her thoughts off her chest and not be offered a solution.

With her hands still pressed together, Rosie opens her eyes. The two women at the front are in the same position as they were when she last looked. Still and silent. Church is the perfect escape from the speed at which the world seems to be moving.

Rosie gets back up to the seat. She knows that she shouldn't rest like this between runs, that she should keep moving, at the very least she should stay on her feet. She follows @TheFitnessPaige and remembers her saying something about lactic acid build-up.

And that's what she takes away from church today, that she has to keep moving. Keep fighting the fight. Keep posting content. Keep trying to make a difference. Stand up to injustice.

She stands up and a thought for a 'What would Rosie do?' T-shirt design pops into her head.

She thanks God.

The run home feels faster. Rosie is lighter. Less overwhelmed. At the corner of her road she passes a young woman, maybe the same age as her, sitting on a fence next to the street sign. Rosie only catches a glimpse of Alyssa, hunched over her phone screen, smoking a vape. Rosie can smell blueberries as she jogs on to her house, lifts the doormat and takes the key to let herself back in.

Alyssa knew exactly what was happening. She knew who was running past. She was watching the timer on her phone screen.

Fifty-one minutes.

It's slower than she was expecting. She needs to get home to help her grandma but she couldn't leave before she knew how long Rosie Velazquez takes on her daily run. And now she does.

Fifty-one minutes.

What Alyssa doesn't know is that today was different. Today was a church day. Even though Rosie is openly a 'servant of God', she does not preach and she does not mention where or when she chooses to worship. She keeps that separate. It's *her* thing. Not to be shared.

Rosie's daily run takes around thirty-four minutes when she doesn't stop off for a spiritual release. That's seventeen minutes that Alyssa and Less won't have to keep looking through Rosie's wardrobe and bedside table and refrigerator when they return, in a couple of days, to use the key left beneath the door mat.

Rosie pours herself a glass of water when she gets in. She takes the spray bottle she uses to water her plants and aims it at her face. Then she takes a selfie.

^^^^^^^^^

^^^^^^^^^

@RosieVelazquez
'Back home from my daily run and just set a new personal best for 5k.' #CrushingIt
♥ **2.2k**

^^^^^^^^^

^^^^^^^^^

LESS

As a baseline regimen, I cleanse twice a day, exfoliate twice a week and moisturise in the morning and before bed, ensuring to use an SPF moisturiser in the day to protect against harmful UV rays. I have also used hydrating serums and eye creams. It's all part of my skincare routine. I reckon that has something to do with the reason I always get asked for ID when buying my mother's liquor.

I once asked my mother what her biggest regret in life was. She told me that she wished she had started moisturising her neck at a younger age.

It was not the answer I was expecting, I'll admit.

The store owner scrutinises my fake driver's licence but hands it back along with the gin bottle wrapped in a brown paper bag. It doesn't matter how many times I have been asked to prove my age, it's still so embarrassing. Maybe because I still look underaged or maybe because I know my mother will be swilling the cough medicine bottles in the bathroom cabinet if I don't get back to her soon.

I wasn't lying when I said that the class I missed this morning wasn't important. I'm ahead with my designs but I was still hoping to go into college this afternoon to work on a project and pick up a few things so that I can forge on at home. Honestly, you'd think I would have found my people at college, doing the course that I've chosen. But I'm like flypaper for the emotionally insecure. The small-minded seem to follow wherever I go.

Maybe it's me. Maybe I'm the problem.

I wasn't expecting to be a part of Alyssa's deviance today, and I do worry about my mother's state of mind if she doesn't get her fix. I feel like it's the parents who are supposed to put themselves last, not the kid.

I tip the cab driver and watch as he speeds off down the driveway. I look at my front door and think about Alyssa. She was right about rich folk having a feeling of invincibility. They can just leave a key under the door mat. What she doesn't know is that the super-rich don't even lock their doors.

I turn the doorknob and push the front door open. I do have a key, just in case, but I can't remember the last time I used it. Besides, my mother stopped going out about six months back so there's always someone around.

There are two people inside, at the end of the hallway. That bastard gardener, who was mowing grass at God-knows-what-time this morning, while I was nursing a serious comedown. And the other person is my mother, she is looking the gardener directly in the eyes and one of her hands is on his chest. Looks like I'm just in time. I know that if she can't get her booze, she will fall back on another addiction.

'Mother, I'm back. Put it away.' I try to hide my disdain with a joke but I don't think it comes across that way.

She shoos the gardener outside onto the patio. It doesn't seem like there's anything going on between them. Probably just a little flirtation. It's my mother still believing she is a young catalogue model and the gardener not wanting to lose his job.

I watch as she sways her way over from the kitchen. I'm sure she thinks it's a sashay but it most certainly is not. She's slurring something about the groundskeeper and the man who came by to install the sound system. She's definitely taken something.

'You know, you really have to leave the help alone, Mother.' Again, I say it jokingly, but I also mean it. My father won't stand for that.

'You're a good boy, Alessandro.'

'Can you even hear me? What have you taken?'

'You're a good boy.' Her eyes aren't even open, her weight is shifting from left foot to right.

'Mother, should I be worried?' I think she's probably pickled herself from the inside and will live forever as a result, but, if she is going to go, a handful of pills seems the most likely way. It makes walking around the house in the day something of a gauntlet.

Deep down, I know she wouldn't do it. She hates many aspects of her life but she thinks too much of herself to go out like that.

'Give me my medicine, there's a good boy.' She reaches out her hand.

'What is it, Xanax and antihistamines again?'

'Just give me the medicine, Alessandro. Be good.' She looks as though she could fall asleep at any moment.

'Tell me what you're on before I hand anything over.'

'Give me the god-damned bottle, you dirty little freak.'

A moment of clarity. She snatches at the bottle and I let her take it.

'There she is. The woman who gave me life.' I joke but, this time, it hurts me. Words do damage. I'm a grown man and I still want to cry when people call me those names.

My mother takes the gin from the bag and lets the paper float to the floor. She's not swaying now. She's not floating. She takes a step towards me, her only child, to give the vitriol she is about to spit some added menace.

'All I've done for you. This life. This privilege. This boredom that I endure so that you have all the possibilities. And you throw it away. You're not a good boy, Alessandro. You're a disappointment.'

It's evil. A moment of pure venom. I'm surprised that my mother didn't mention my sexuality to really drive the nail in.

What's my choice now? I could cry. I could show her my heartbreak. I could laugh in her face. I could call her pathetic. A has-been. I could mention her wrinkly neck. I could say that the only thing she has done is spread her legs for a successful businessman once a week and drink herself to oblivion. I could tell her that I wish she would just die, that she should take the rest of the Xanax in one go and float the hell away from this shitty life that she seems to hate so much.

I could turn the disappointment back on her, call her a failure, tell her that she's not a mother.

But I can't do that. I would never hurt her. I know too well what it is like on the receiving end.

I wouldn't want her to feel the way that I do, right now. I wouldn't wish that on anybody. I know how much it can damage.

I don't back away, though. I keep my face close to hers, fighting the frustration that could bring tears to my eyes. And I say, 'I love you, too, Mother.'

All that money and it's a miserable household. Alyssa's family has nothing, but at least they have each other. Who really has the privilege? Sure, I've got a nice house, but hers is a home.

I turn and walk away, up the stairs to my bedroom because, if there is one thing that school taught me, it's that you don't give bullies the satisfaction that they have hurt you.

^^^^^^^^^^

^^^^^^^^^^

@TheFitnessPaige
'Got some exciting news. I can't share too much yet but keep your eyes peeled for an announcement soon. New legs workout dropping on the app later today, too.' #Blessed #FitFam
♥ 27

^^^^^^^^^^

^^^^^^^^^^

@TheFitnessPaige finishes talking with Satmohan. She takes the contract and calls her lawyer. She's going to sign and she wants to do it the right way, but she has to go into the office later to get the paperwork checked.

In the meantime, she takes a picture. Enough to show that it is definitely a contract for something but not enough to say what it is about. She places the papers on a burlap table runner with a couple of fresh oranges and a cup of black coffee. It's rustic but with a pop of colour.

Paige hits send and then goes into the kitchen to make a fresh cup of coffee because the one in the picture went cold as she arranged the objects for her photograph.

Her phone starts to light up. She expected that. Her millions of followers will be just as excited as she is about new opportunities to spread her love and positivity, and it's the kind of post that promotes clicks and responses. She can't remember when everything became about that.

But that is not the post she is being notified about.

She taps one of the pop-ups on her screen and is taken to a video. A beautiful woman with long, wavy, shining red hair and glowing skin is staring hard down the camera lens.

Paige realises who this is and what it might be about. She rolls her eyes but continues to watch, anyway.

^^^^^^^^^^

^^^^^^^^^^

@FoodForThought
'CALL OFF YOUR DOGS'
♥ **40k** ☐ **1,254**

'There are eight billion people in the world. There are around four thousand religions. So we already know that people are not going to agree on everything. In fact, it's safe to say that there is endless diversity and we should embrace that. People can go about things in a different way and reach the same state of being. We should be able to worship what we want, dress the way we want, eat what we want, earn money the way we want.

'For anyone who has been following me – and it's suddenly a lot more than it used to be – you will know the struggles I have had. Thank you for going on this journey with me. But you, Paige, you have not been following me like I have been following you. You don't know my story. Yet, still, you take it upon yourself to criticise me for trying something that I read might give me more energy. You throw out a scathing indictment of my methods and motivations to your legions of fans, then sit back as they do their worst.

'My page was a place for hope and optimism. And now it is filled with your trolls. There's a part of me that wants to retaliate but I have no idea what you are going through in your life, right now, just as you had no idea about me. To post something like that, I would assume that you're not feeling great about yourself. So, for now, I am going to leave it. Call off your dogs, eh? And, while I am remaining calm, I want you to know that I do not forgive you.'

(Step closer to the camera.)

'And I definitely won't forget.'

^ ^ ^ ^ ^ ^ ^ ^ ^ ^

^ ^ ^ ^ ^ ^ ^ ^ ^ ^

She is eloquent. Smart. Calm.

It's only that last section that seems like a threat.

Because it is.

Paige turns off her phone and places it upside down on the kitchen counter. She could be reflecting on what Ariel Dean said, thinking about her own behaviour, considering an apology. Instead, she is annoyed that this nutrition charlatan just ruined her moment to celebrate the contract.

The contract that she was told would almost definitely not affect her life for the better.

The contract that she is so desperate to sign.

She's only mad because she knows that Ariel is right.

^ ^ ^ ^ ^ ^ ^ ^ ^ ^

^ ^ ^ ^ ^ ^ ^ ^ ^ ^

ALYSSA

The house smells amazing. Because I don't live in a mansion like Less, if I make something in the kitchen, the aroma spreads to every other room.

It took me forty-five minutes and two buses to get home, but I was on such a high that I didn't even notice.

'Grandma, did you touch the oven while I was out?' I ask, throwing my keys into a bowl on a console table by the door.

My grandmother says nothing. She is sitting in the living room watching one of her gameshows. I know she heard me but I go in and ask her again. 'Grandma, is everything okay?'

'What is *Flowers for Algernon*?' She's talking to the television.

A woman on screen presses a buzzer and says, 'What is *Flowers for Algernon*?' and wins $800.

'Easy,' says the old woman with a blanket over her legs. 'I'm fine, dear.'

I knew she had heard me.

'Did you touch the oven while I was out?'

'Of course not,' she lies. Then, at the television, 'What is *Hyperion*?'

She's right again.

I head back into the kitchen. I can still hear my grandmother mumbling. 'I know how to make pork pibil.' The problem is, she doesn't know how to make pork pibil the way that I make pork pibil, where it is wrapped in a banana leaf and foil, so it can take a slightly higher heat. 'Well, it'll be another forty minutes because, somehow, the oven is twenty degrees lower than the way I left it.'

I can hear the old lady answer another question correctly. I wish she'd move around more, her legs look swollen. She got old really quickly, it was so sudden. She was active before that, she would read. I still see so much of my mother's pretty face in hers, but her body isn't what it used to be.

She's ignoring me again. My phone vibrates. It's a message from Less saying: *My mother*, followed by an emoji of somebody's head exploding next to another emoji of a water pistol. It doesn't quite work but I get the idea.

I text as I walk, apologising and trying to console him with the fact that his mother will be passed out on the chaise longue soon enough. It's difficult to know what else to say other than *It'll be over soon*. I can't imagine Less's life at home, so lacking in warmth. His house is incredible. But it doesn't feel like a home. A show home, maybe. For a show family.

I sit on the sofa and watch my grandma.

'Who is Philip K. Dick?'

Correct.

I can't help but smile. My grandmother is plucky. Turning the oven down. Sipping her tea and playing her quiz shows. It's so simple. She'd be lost in a house like Less's. At least here, we are close to one another.

'I'm going out after dinner, Grandma. Mom will be home from work by nine, so you won't be on your own for too long.'

'Don't worry about me, dear. You're always worrying about me.' Aside, she says, 'What is *I Am Legend*?'

'I love you. I just want to make sure you're okay.' I can't help but smile. Grandma smiles back. It's the first time she has looked away from the TV.

She asks where I'm going out to this evening, and I explain that there is a party in the Hills. 'Less is picking me up in a couple of hours.'

Grandma says how much she likes Less and that she is happy I have found myself a good boy, and I can't help but laugh.

What is Tinseltown?

I explain, again, that we are just friends and that there's no way he would be into me, anyway. Not like that. And then Grandma is sweet about how beautiful I am and how lucky Less would be to have a girl like me. And I remind her that Less is gay. And the old lady misses the next question on the television as she thinks things through.

I look at my phone screen.

Another message from Less. A crying-with-laughter emoji. I know that my friend is almost certainly not laughing in real life. Even though we are always honest with each other, it's ingrained in us to always apply a filter. I'm focussing on my phone, my grandmother, the television and the food in the oven, I have to scroll to see what I said last that was so funny.

Three social-media notifications.

A missed call from my mother.

I excuse myself and take the phone into the kitchen to call back – Grandma isn't even listening to me. It rings twice before my mother answers. There are no real greetings or niceties; it's all about business. Straight in. She has to work a little later tonight. An hour or so. She doesn't want to leave the old woman for that long. Not at night. Things always seem worse in the darker hours.

'Can you get to this party a bit later?'

This is my life. I never go against what my mother says. She does so much for me, I can never say no. Besides, I can't leave Grandma all alone at night.

'Sure. Not a problem.' It's not a problem because Less and I haven't even been invited. (Less knows whose house it is but they have never been formally introduced.) The whole plan to get in might, actually, work better if we arrive once things are in full swing. I mean, I would never say no to my mother, anyway.

This happens all the time. Mom will take any extra shifts they can give her at the hospital. She doesn't get paid a lot and now she has taken in her own mother. Three grown women in one house. My father is either in jail or dead. He has never tried to get in contact and he has never given any financial help.

What is An Inconvenient Truth*?*

'I'll make it up to you, baby, I promise.'

'You don't have to do that, Mom. Honestly, it's fine. I need to leave the pibil in a little longer anyway – Grandma turned it down again.' We laugh. 'Go. Work. Everything is fine at home. I love you. See you later.'

I hang up the phone and send a text to Less asking him to come over an hour later. I'm sure he won't mind.

He comes straight back, telling me that he won't do that, he'll be over at the time we agreed but he'll bring a bottle of champagne so we can get into character for the party.

I smile and agree to the plan. It's probably best that Less gets out of his house, anyway.

Grandma says, 'What is Newton's third law of motion?'

I frantically tap away at my phone screen, the smell of the pork beckoning me to eat.

'Grandma, what is your date of birth?'

'Don't worry, dear, you haven't missed my birthday.'

'I know when your birthday is, I just want to make sure I get your birth year right.'

'It's the sixteenth day of the sixth month of the twenty-sixth year. Easy to remember. Why do you need to get it right?'

I don't answer straight away because I'm typing – and because she is always doing it to me. I press a blue box labelled with the word 'submit'.

'I wanted to make sure I had everything correct on your application.'

'My application for what?' she asks, only half listening. Then, 'Who is D.W. Griffith?'

'To be on this gameshow. You could pay off the rent for a decade.'

'What? Alyssa. Why did you do that? I don't want to be on TV.'

'Oh, Grandma, don't be silly. Everyone wants to be on TV.'

^ ^ ^ ^ ^ ^ ^ ^ ^ ^

^ ^ ^ ^ ^ ^ ^ ^ ^ ^

#TeamPaige #TeamAriel #Feud

These women never stop. They can't relax for one second otherwise the next batch of ruthless talent will be snapping at the heels of their Louboutins and editing their own surnames over the company logo.

They want a pool of willing wannabes to choose from, just in case an idea takes off, so they are constantly watching audition tapes from these hopefuls and filing the ones that will fit the next big idea.

Or the next small one.

Edie Lincoln wants fifty people in a *Battle Royale* scenario. Of course, there won't be murder, but there has to be a way to set up something like that and film it, create some heroes for the nation to root for and villains to despise.

Edie and Tammy have notebooks filled with possibilities. Some could never work and others would be downright impossible – for mainstream television, at least. But among the Arctic survival ideas, wife-swapping idiocy and *Lord of the Flies* rip-offs, there are some gems. So they continue to watch the moronic audition tapes, looking for that something in somebody that will spark.

There's a video call for Tammy from Satmohan. She looks at Edie.

'Pick it up. We need a break, anyway.'

Edie does as she is told and answers the phone.

'Satmohan. Talk to me.'

'She has the contract.' He is wearing his earphones and talks as he walks along the street. People around him assume he is somebody important, who can't afford to waste time by making a call in his office or on the train.

'She signed it?'

'She will. She definitely will. She wants her lawyer to look over it, but I think she's just posturing. She probably already signed the thing, she did everything but rub her hands together when I spoke with her.'

'Great job, Satmohan. I have Tammy here with me.'

Tammy pokes her face in front of the camera. 'Yeah, great job, Satmohan. As always.' Then she disappears to the side.

'You want me to head over or wait around and make sure she talks to this lawyer?'

Edie looks over at Tammy, who is offscreen now. Tammy holds up her hand and screws her face slightly.

'Stick around for a bit and see if she leaves with the paperwork. If you can make some calls while you wait, get hold of some cameras that we can put in her place, that would be helpful. We'll put a bottle on ice and you can pop it once the ink is dry.'

'Message received. I'll check back in when it's done.' He hangs up.

The idea that Lincoln/Lowell Productions has for @TheFitnessPaige is one of their better creations. Documenting somebody who has come from nothing and worked hard to become financially and spiritually successful is always an interesting and often inspiring concept.

But positivity only gets you half the ratings.

Paige is beloved by millions. Her message is very *real* even if her physique comes at a cost. But hers is no Cinderella, rags-to-riches story. She comes from a middle-class background. White suburbia. And she got lucky.

She's not trying to hurt anybody or take over anyone. She didn't have to stomp over people to get where she is now. And many people are engaged with that. But it was a fluke, as it so often is in the industry of influence.

#StopMakingStupidPeopleFamous

So, for all the people that would watch a show that featured Paige because they like her and her ethos, there are a similar number of people who hate her for being what she is. They don't feel that she has the expertise. Or she is too young, not enough life experience to offer such wisdom.

Hatred and fear are powerful emotions. For every influencer there is also a professional troll network. That is where people are now. They may not want to admit it but Lincoln/Lowell know it. They know that they can almost double their audience with Paige because viewers will tune in to witness her downfall.

It's easier to dislike her.

Lincoln/Lowell can exploit that.

They deal in misery.

But they need to strike now, while this feud with Ariel Dean is at tipping point. These shows can spend months in pre-production and planning, but Lincoln/Lowell are the best in the business. They need to get cameras in Paige's home this week because they know they can turn this around.

This is a surefire hit.

Or another unseen personal project.

^^^^^^^^^^

^^^^^^^^^^

ALYSSA

It starts tonight. At the party.

Sneaking up Rosie's front path and finding her door key beneath the mat was the first free bag of drugs the dealer gives you to get you hooked. It was a taster. A catalyst.

You hear about those serial killers who begin by burning ants with a magnifying glass aimed at the sun. Then they kill a cat. Eventually it's a person, a sex worker that they think nobody will miss. Then it's a couple making out in a car at some secluded spot near the woods. Then it's an entire college dorm room.

Rosie's path was the ant, tonight's party is the cat.

It's full steam ahead from here. And I'm taking Less along for the ride. He does so much for me, the least I can do is give him this.

Less arrives at my house on time, which is unusual. He has a bottle of champagne, as promised. I love him so much. It's not the price of the drink, it's the gesture, it's that his default is kindness and generosity.

'Oh, my God, your house always smells like the best restaurant in town. I've just eaten but my mouth is watering.'

'Hello to you, too.' I feel my expression brighten, and Less kisses me once on each cheek. It could look fake, but it's not. Ours is a deep understanding. We don't feel like outsiders when we are together.

'Shall we?' He holds out the bottle and I lead him into the house and through to the kitchen by his hand. He has that amazing mansion but it's like he somehow prefers it here.

I search through the kitchen cupboards, looking for something that resembles a champagne glass, but can't find anything. I take out two whisky tumblers and hold them up. I shrug.

Less looks over her shoulder into the cupboard and says, 'I usually like to drink my champagne out of a Snoopy mug but I guess you're not classy enough to have one of those around here.' He manages to kill the awkwardness with his quick observations and I love him even more for that.

We drink from the tumblers. I am already dressed to impress, so we sit with my grandmother and wait for our opportunity to leave.

'So I hear you're gay now,' Grandma says. I nearly spit out my drink.

'Well, I've always been gay, so I guess it's more that you've just heard now?'

'I thought you and Alyssa were courting.'

Less mouths the word 'courting' and shrugs it off. 'No. Nothing like that. We're just friends.'

There's a back-and-forth that follows where Less is very patient. The old lady's generation has a tougher time understanding this kind of thing. We forgive them.

The champagne runs out quickly and we are forced to look through the drinks cabinet for anything that will keep the buzz going. There's half a bottle of tequila and some unopened Blue Curacao. I place my discoveries on the kitchen counter, and Less decides on a cocktail we can make with the years of leftover dregs.

My mom returns home from work about five minutes early. It's clear that she has been on a long shift but, somehow, her scraggly hair makes her look even better and I'm thankful I don't have any straight male friends.

'*Hola*. Sorry I'm so late. Do you guys need a lift somewhere?'

Less and I greet her at the front door.

'No, Mom. Thanks. We have a car coming soon. Sit down and I'll heat your dinner through. Less will whip you up a cocktail in a mug.'

My mother looks confused but she goes along with the joke. Her own mother calls out to her from in front of the TV screen.

'You'll never guess what she did.'

'Mother, are you talking to me or the television?'

'She signed me up to be on one of my shows.'

'Alyssa, is she alright?'

'I put in an application for Grandma to go on *Jeopardy!*. I don't think I've ever seen her get a question wrong.'

My mother can't help but laugh at this. It tickles her. She can't stop. 'Oh, God. That is amazing. She will hate that.' She laughs, heartily. 'Well, I mean, she won't but she will pretend that she does.'

'She's invading my privacy,' Grandma calls from the living room.

'You see?' She tells us to ignore the old woman, and we all file into the kitchen where I warm through a bowl of the pork I prepared. It'll last another three days. Less finds some triple sec to go with the tequila and makes a margarita.

My mother takes a seat on a bar stool by the kitchen counter. She forks in the pork pibil and groans with delight. She washes it down with a gulp of the cocktail and nods her approval towards Less – she loves him, too. Then she asks, 'So, whose party are you going to?'

^ ^ ^ ^ ^ ^ ^ ^ ^ ^

^ ^ ^ ^ ^ ^ ^ ^ ^ ^

Davis Davis

102	**111k**	**335**
posts	followers	following

@davisdavis

This account is private

Follow this account to see their photos
and videos.

^ ^ ^ ^ ^ ^ ^ ^ ^ ^

^ ^ ^ ^ ^ ^ ^ ^ ^ ^

Davis Davis. That's whose party it is.

A&R guru for a couple of the big record labels over the years, he has discovered some incredible talent along with the most well-known but manufactured groups of the last twenty years. He broke away and set up his own label – Bedlam – eight years ago, and now he is a film producer, studio exec, philanthropist and is looking into purchasing a sports team. He has a finger in everything and, according to recent speculation, everyone.

Less's father has worked with Davis several times over the years. His company was responsible for the site that became Bedlam Studios. He also helped with retail space when Davis got into the restaurant game. He recently finished refurbishing and extending a place that was once the home of Alfred Hitchcock. Davis is selling his current house and tonight is the farewell party.

Less's father was invited but isn't going. That's how Less knows about it.

The place is obscene. Eight bedrooms. Five bathrooms. Pool. A hundred different corners for future pop stars to disappear with old music execs. There will be drinking and drugs and sex. At a party last summer, Davis Davis somehow got a white tiger and had it chained to the fountain in the garden.

His parties are the stuff of legend. He invites everyone, so Less and Alyssa have every chance of getting in. And that means anybody could be there. Actors, artists, tech billionaires, basketball players.

There's a Warhol in the entrance hallway that was given to Davis by the man himself. A signed Chicago Bulls vest is framed and hangs behind the desk in Davis's study. Jordan wore that shirt in his rookie season. But Davis Davis isn't flash. He's not showing off. If somebody took a liking to the Warhol painting and loved it as much as he did when he first saw it, he would give it to them. He's that kind of guy.

All the luck that helped him on the road to his success was matched by a tireless work ethic and refusal to quit. He has nice things because he can afford them and he has his parties because he works hard, still, and the rest of the time, he wants to live.

Davis Davis is fifty-eight. He's handsome and lean, with limbs like a basketball player. He had famously long hair in the eighties and held on to it for longer than he should before embracing baldness. He could retire now and choose to live every day to its fullest. There are hundreds of millions in his bank account. He could go to a Las Vegas roulette table, place half of his net worth on black, lose, and still live like a king for the next thirty years.

He's rich.

But he doesn't leave a key under the door mat because he doesn't even lock the door.

^^^^^^^^^

^^^^^^^^^

LESS

The cab pulls over.

'You sure you want to stop here?'

'That's fine. We can walk the last part.' I don't want to get too close to the house and draw attention to our arrival. There's a long, winding road that heads uphill. That's where we need to go.

Alyssa thanks the driver and gives him a five-star rating on the app. She booked the cab. She can't really afford things but she likes to make a gesture and not leave everything to me. It's her way of trying to make things equal. I like that she does things like that but I don't like the idea that it could leave her too out of pocket. I worry about her.

'Enjoy your night,' the driver says as I close the door. He swings the car around and heads back downhill.

It's dark. I point up at a terracotta-coloured mansion that is lit up against the dark sky and tell Alyssa that it's where we are going. Then I pull a joint from my inside jacket pocket and light it.

'I know how you get before we do anything like this. Let's make sure we go in there calm, huh?'

We start walking up the hill, passing the weed back and forth.

After a couple of hundred yards we spot a white electric Porsche. There's a line of expensive cars that lead all the way up to the Davis residence, undoubtedly the property of his guests, who will either be staying overnight or will drive them back home with a plethora of substances in their systems.

It's a Davis Davis party, you can do what and who you like. That's the rumour I've heard, anyway. He's pretty famous for that type of thing. More than for the music, to my generation, at least.

I'm wearing a purple hat with a long yellow feather attached to one side. I made it. I'm proud of it. But Alyssa doesn't think it's the best way to not attract attention.

^^^^^^^^^

^^^^^^^^^

ALYSSA

Less will be Less.

There's no sense in telling him that he can't do something, because that just makes him want to do it even more. He's sticking with the hat. He tells me that he's 'hiding in plain sight'.

There's noise coming from the house when we reach the top. Music is playing. It sounds live. Davis often likes to break new acts at these events, Less tells me. There are voices, too. So many voices. At a guess, there could be nearly two hundred people in the garden. There will be bar staff and waiting staff serving the guests, and Less is confident that this will be the easiest way in. They're being paid handsomely for their time but they'll take an extra tip and let you in through the back without hesitation. He's got the cash to flash.

But not tonight.

When we reach the stone driveway, I'm expecting some kind of security, but there's nothing. Everybody is inside or out the back. A Bentley pulls up and two women step out. We stop for a moment and watch them. I have no idea who they are. They can't be famous.

The women say something to each other, then they walk up to the front door and just let themselves in.

So that's what we do, too.

^^^^^^^^^

^^^^^^^^^

#AintNoPartyLikeADavisDavisParty #WhiteTigerOnCocaine #ElectrocuteTheBand

Of course, Edie Lincoln and Tammy Lowell are invited to the final party at the Davis Davis house. They're not Hollywood royalty but they are powerful and successful, but even more than that, they are fun. Tammy's deviated septum won't stop her taking a hit of whatever Davis has in bowls around the house. It's the reason she carries a silver straw in her handbag.

They exit the Bentley and tell the driver to wait in the driveway. They could be there an hour or six hours. He will wait.

The house is at the top of the hill. It would be an effort to break in. There are a hundred other houses around that have artwork and antique furniture and Persian rugs. It seems crazy to the producers that Davis leaves his house open but there always seems to be somebody there, even if he is not. Some band rehearsing or recording or partying. Davis is the Gatsby type, throwing these shindigs, waiting for somebody specific to turn up one day but nobody has any idea who that could be.

Tammy hopes it's her.

They say goodbye to the driver and see two people behind them. One in a purple hat. Looks like the fashionable type that would be invited to a Davis soiree. They push the front door open. It's heavy. Nine feet high. Oak. But it's like stepping back in time to the Jazz Age or the Golden Age of Hollywood. And they love it.

These are Edie and Tammy's people.

They pass fifteen guests who want to hug them or shake their hands before they reach the doors that lead to outside. Satmohan is already there. He is vaping and drinking a bottle of beer by the band. Edie and Tammy wave at him but don't want to get into anything. He's done well for them today, but they are there to make an appearance, drink a cocktail or two, do some blow and get the hell out of there.

Still, they need to find the host.

It shouldn't be too difficult. Davis is special. He's the kind of person who walks into a room and you know that he is there without even looking. Jack Nicholson or Frank Sinatra. It sounds like myth. Bluster. But it's true. There aren't many people like that. But Davis is definitely one of them.

There's a group over by the pool. They're laughing, and not the fake laugh you often hear at these industry events. If there's one thing the Lincoln/Lowell team know, it's when somebody is being fake. They head towards the joviality.

Davis spots them right away.

He excuses himself from the conversation and the crowd parts like he's Moses.

'TV bitches,' he says, walking towards them with his arms outstretched.

'Music-industry asshole,' Tammy smiles as Davis wraps his arms around both of them and kisses them on either cheek – Tammy first.

'I wasn't sure you'd show up.'

'Well, if we knew you were going to be here, we probably wouldn't have bothered.' Tammy winks. They have a silly shorthand repartee. It's the kind of relationship that looks like sexual tension that has never been acted on all these years. But it's not. They like each other. Genuinely. And they've had sex plenty.

'Let's get you two a drink.' He guides them over to a bar that has been set up outside. Large silver tubs filled with ice and bottles of champagne. One of the barmen asks how many glasses they would like. Davis tells him they will require two bottles and a couple of straws.

He laughs.

The barman doesn't know what to do.

'It's okay. Just three glasses. My friend Tammy here usually brings her own straw.'

Tammy blushes.

'Cheers,' says Edie, joining the conversation. She's third wheel once these two get going.

They drink.

'So, when are you ladies going to make something that matters again, huh?'

Davis has stopped joking now. He's deadly serious. Lincoln/Lowell Productions are a powerhouse duo, but they're stuck and he sees it.

Davis can spot talent. That's his superpower.

'We're developing new things all the time. We were doing it on the car ride over.' Edie is defensive.

'Nobody can deny how hard you two work, Edie. I'm surprised you're not checking your emails now. I just know how smart you both are, and I want you to leave the world with something more memorable than *The Poolboys of Tarzana* or whatever you have cooking up.'

'That's actually not a bad idea, Davis,' Tammy nudges.

'I'm serious. Edie, I know you've been thinking it. You're pioneers. You've got to shake things up.'

Davis walks the walk. His gift is unearthing future music stars, but he was also sick of the way artists were treated by the big labels. The contracts were ridiculously skewed in favour of making money for the execs and leaving little trickle-down for the talent. Sure, it was still a lot of money but it wasn't fair.

He changed that with Bedlam. He focussed on a new kind of artist, one with a story and something to say. One who could play the guitar or the piano, who wrote the songs that they wanted to sing. And he got them paid.

Edie and Tammy don't need the money. They need a legacy.

They talk things through for ten minutes or so. Davis isn't an ideas man, he doesn't have the answer, that's not his job. He's just there to grease the wheels.

Edie's brain is whirring. She wants to shake things up.

Tammy wants some coke. And maybe some Davis.

'Davis, I need you to do me a solid.'

'What do you need?'

Tammy reaches into her bag and pulls out the metal straw.

Davis laughs and suggests that they go somewhere a little more private.

'You'll be okay for ten minutes?' he asks Edie.

'I'm a big girl.'

'I've seen Satmohan around.' That's the last thing Davis says before Tammy grabs him by the hand and leads him back into the house and up the stairs.

Davis knows Satmohan because he knows everybody at that party. He makes a point of speaking with all of his guests. And that could be an issue for Alyssa and Less.

^ ^ ^ ^ ^ ^ ^ ^ ^ ^

^ ^ ^ ^ ^ ^ ^ ^ ^ ^

EP#3: Jerry Golding's Mind-Blowing Penthouse | *MTV Cribs* Collection
MTV
2.29M Subscribers 👍 1,333

Manhattan, New York
6,548 Sq ft.
3 Bedrooms
3.5 Baths

^ ^ ^ ^ ^ ^ ^ ^ ^ ^

^ ^ ^ ^ ^ ^ ^ ^ ^ ^

Jerry Golding has an apartment in New York on the Upper East Side that he doesn't even have a key for. He just goes into the lobby and a doorman lets him up in a lift that will open into the entrance of his home. It's this kind of lifestyle that leads to a person buying a Porsche and leaving it on the side of the road, unlocked, with keys predictably tucked behind the visor.

^^^^^^^^^^

^^^^^^^^^^

ALYSSA

Less and I split up at the party. I go to find us a drink while he heads upstairs to locate one of the five bathrooms.

I have to check myself repeatedly to make sure I'm not walking around with my mouth agape. I have to keep it breezy. Like I'm used to this kind of thing, rather than with a two-bedroom apartment that I share with my mother and grandmother, where sometimes the water is a little brown but you can still drink it.

The barman is polite and does his job, smiling and asking how many glasses I would like. I tell him I need two. To my left, a woman stands on her own with a drink, frantically scrolling through emails and messages on her phone.

'Enjoying the party?' I don't know why I enter into dialogue with this party guest. An actual guest who was invited. Fuck. I'm an idiot. I was just trying to appear natural.

We're going to get found out.

Shit. What am I doing?

^^^^^^^^^^

^^^^^^^^^^

Edie Lincoln knows when somebody is being fake.

'Do I know you?' Edie asks. She's not being rude, she is trying to force her brain to recollect the place that she has seen this young, attractive woman before. They have never met but Edie has seen her. She won't be able to remember where it was because she has seen a million faces on a million audition tapes. But this girl looks like a star.

Alyssa is willing the barman to just pour the stupid drink quicker but the bubbles aren't settling quick enough.

'I don't think we've met. I'm ... uh ... Alyssa. I'm friends with Alessandro.' She doesn't want to say 'Less' because nobody has that name and it's probably too memorable. Besides, there are twenty hunky Italian men within spitting distance. There's a good chance that one of them has a name like that.

Finally, the drinks arrive.

^^^^^^^^^

^^^^^^^^^

ALYSSA

I make sure I tell the woman my real name, just in case she is somebody I might need to know in the future. I could say something like, 'Oh, don't I remember you from the last Davis Davis party...?' Shit. This real-life networking is much harder than it is online. How am I supposed to talk to a real person?

What I want is to be remembered when the time comes but forgotten right now.

She doesn't let go, though. 'You could be on TV. You have a wonderful, offbeat quality.'

I don't know what she means by that. Is she saying I'm weird? Is she commenting on my ethnicity? 'That's very kind,' I say, and some of the tension goes away. It's enough for me to open up a little.

I talk about my various identities online and that I'm really just trying to discover my lane, and she tells me her name is Edie and that she is a producer. My eyes light up and I feel stupid again. That's when she lets me know something else. That she knows I'm not supposed to be at the house.

Ah, fuck. There goes that high. But she's not threatening to expose me, and we end up talking a little more before I excuse myself to find my friend.

'Anyway, enjoy the party.' I can't get out of there quick enough. This was my stupid idea and I blew it for both of us.

Inside, I'm looking for a purple hat with a god-damned yellow feather sewed to one side.

How hard can it be?

I have a glass of champagne in each hand and I'm trying to avoid the gaze of every model, director, actor and musician with influence in show business. All the people that could help me get to where I want to be.

Where the fuck are you, Less? I'm scared, now. I know where I belong and it's certainly not here. The only rich person I feel comfortable around is Less.

^ ^ ^ ^ ^ ^ ^ ^ ^

^ ^ ^ ^ ^ ^ ^ ^ ^ ^

LESS

I'm at the top of the stairs being quizzed by the owner of the house who has just blown a strawful of coke into the back end of a TV producer who can no longer take it up her nose. I know this because I walked into the one room of this huge house that I should not have walked into.

'Who are you?' Davis asks. He doesn't seem angry.

'My name is Less.'

'Hello, Les.' I don't correct him. 'But who *exactly* are you?'

Oh, hell. I don't think I should lie. I know who Davis Davis is. And he's not being aggressive or having me kicked out. Not yet, anyway. I don't want to pretend I'm a casting director or assistant editor or location scout. Davis Davis probably knows all of those people. So I tell the big-time music mogul that my father owns Donnaruma Construction and that he told me there was a party here tonight and that he couldn't make it.

'So you're representing your father? He's a good man, he's done a lot of good work for me.'

'I wish.' I almost laugh. 'He'd kill me if he knew I was here.'

Davis looks at the woman he is with. I heard him call her Tammy as he removed the metal straw from her ass. She's not really paying attention. 'Let's keep it between us, then, shall we? Grab a couple of drinks but then be on your way, okay?'

'Yes. That's very gracious of you. Thank you. I think we'll just go.'

'We?'

'My friend. Alyssa. She's downstairs. Probably freaking out. Even though we've crashed places before.'

Davis doesn't lose his cool. He says it's okay, he kind of admires the gumption – that's how you make it in this town. Apparently, that's often the time when opportunity strikes. Tammy even chimes in because she is interested in some of the other places Alyssa and I have crashed.

Davis is kind. He also tells me that my hat is *wonderful.* Tammy takes my details.

Downstairs, Alyssa looks anxious.

'Where the fuck have you been?'

'We're busted, Lyss. I'm sorry. Drink up, let's get the hell out of Dodge.'

'What do you mean we're busted?'

'We've been made by the host. The fucker knows every single person in here by name. I bumped into him upstairs with his girlfriend and he knew I didn't belong.'

'Then why aren't we running out that door right now?'

I was so honest with Davis that I earned myself a stay of execution, but, for some reason, I lie to Alyssa. I feel a need to protect her.

'I sweet-talked him a bit and he said that we could finish our drink before we left.'

She's suspicious. 'And how did you do that, exactly?'

'Look, just down the fucking champagne and let's get out of here.' I don't want to talk about it.

We both neck what we have and head for the door we pushed our way through about fifteen minutes ago. I open it. There are still people arriving. Alyssa spots a bottle of champagne on a console table in the entrance hall and swipes it.

It's not stealing. Davis said we could have another drink.

Outside, I feel despondent. 'That was a wash-out.' Those are supposed to be my kind of people but I still didn't quite fit in. Maybe I don't have a kind of people. Maybe I only have Alyssa.

'Not entirely.' Alyssa produces the bottle of Cristal. She pops the cork in the driveway and swigs straight from the bottle before handing it to me.

We begin the walk downhill, swapping the bottle every thirty seconds or so.

'What do we do now?' It's still early, and we've come all this way, I don't want to go home.

A car alarm sounds and it makes me jump.

'Calm down, Less. Nobody got shot.' She drinks and passes the bottle over again.

Twenty metres on, another car beeps. We run for a minute. Laughing and drinking.

'You're walking too close to the cars,' I tell her.

'Well how else am I going to lift the damn handles?'

'What? What are you talking about?'

That's when Alyssa reaches a silver Porsche owned by Jerry Golding. She pulls at the handle and the car opens.

'Fuck, Alyssa.'

'You still want to party? Get in.'

^^^^^^^^^^

^^^^^^^^^^

CONVERSATIONS WITH KILLERS – A LINCOLN/LOWELL PRODUCTION

EPISODE SIX: EDMUND J. HUBBARD – THE 'SWIPE RIGHT' KILLER

'Getting famous isn't that difficult. Sure, there are those people who learn from each failure, who never quit despite the challenges and rejections, who put in their ten thousand hours to master the skills that will project them from mediocrity into stratospheric stardom. A lifetime honing your craft. Painting, sport, filmmaking, music creation, everybody needs a little luck along the way, but the rewards will far outweigh the sacrifice.

'You could just kill someone.

'Maybe more than one.

'It doesn't require as much practice, does it?

'The problem with getting away with a crime is that there is this tremendous high. But it's fleeting. Returning to the scene of a crime can provide a similar sensation. You relive it. You feel it all over again, in a way. The moment is shorter, though. You know?

'So you try it again.

'But it's not the same.

'You need more.

'So you do it again but differently. Maybe you do something worse. Just to gain that euphoria once more. And you get somewhere close to that initial tingle you felt the first time you took something from a store or beat somebody up or murdered a person or stole a car.

'And then you want more.

'So you try again.

'But you need more to get anywhere near the way you want to feel. And with every extra minute of criminal activity, you get closer to being caught. And you don't get properly famous until you *are* caught. Which is maybe what I wanted all along.'

^^^^^^^^^

^^^^^^^^^

ALYSSA

Less and I drive around in that car for two hours. At one point, we pass the police. We hit the freeway and take it over a hundred miles per hour. We stop for snacks. We park up somewhere and lie on the front, looking up at the stars. We feel young and we feel invincible.

This is the gift that the poor girl can give the rich guy. We're not in a co-dependent relationship, though we both want the same thing – to belong. It's symbiotic. Because we both bring something different and each fulfils something in the other, making them fuller. That's real friendship. That's how strong our bond is. It's true.

We are *living* in that very moment. Uninhibited. No thought for consequence. We don't even have our phones out. There are no pictures of our crime. No video evidence of us tearing around the back streets.

The entire night is something of a blur and, though what we did was obviously wrong, it somehow felt pure. Because it gave us such joy. And it didn't cost a penny.

We dropped the car back somewhere near the spot that we took it from. We just pulled up along that same road, parked and walked off, leaving the keys inside. There were no scratches. No damage. The owner might notice that the fuel gauge will be slightly lower.

No harm done.

Less and I could wake up tomorrow and return to where we stole the car, but it won't have the impact we want.

We need something more, now.

Something bigger.

Something worse.

A new thrill.

^ ^ ^ ^ ^ ^ ^ ^ ^ ^

^ ^ ^ ^ ^ ^ ^ ^ ^ ^

LESS

Today's hangover feels more harsh than yesterday's. It's a bigger comedown. Speed is a filthy drug. Maybe crime hurts more because it is so pure.

It doesn't help that I'm also anxious that my father has somehow found out that I was at the Davis Davis party and I won't be able to explain my way out of that one. Davis seemed cool but you never know, my dad does a lot of work for him. I'd probably get a lighter reaction about stealing that Porsche than I would about possibly muddying the family name and business.

Oh, fuck. He's going to know. I don't want to spiral.

Davis seemed like a decent guy, though. He seemed to appreciate my honesty. Surely he has more important things to be discussing than a couple of chancers gatecrashing his party. There's no real story there. It's a detail at best.

That's what I tell myself so that I don't start hyperventilating.

I hear my father's voice and glance at my phone to check the time. He has usually left for work by now. He must be working at home today.

'I don't care. He's going in.'

I sit straight up when I hear those words. What is my father talking about? Go in? Where? The police station? Shit. I hold my breath so that I can hear.

I am worried. My father is a powerful man.

'I will drag him in there myself if I have to.'

Oh, God. They know. How do they know? Did Davis call and rat on us? God, you can't trust anyone. Someone is always taking a picture or a video, you can't get away with anything.

I slip into a pair of grey joggers and a white vest. I have no option but to come clean. I have to face the music.

When I get downstairs, both of my parents are in the kitchen. My father is drinking coffee and my mother is sipping a glass of fresh orange juice. (Though it could easily be a mimosa.) Her face is glowing and fully made-up. She looks too good for the shrivelled, mean addict I left in the hallway yesterday. I know that this is how my father likes her to look, even if she isn't going out. Which she never does anymore. I wonder whether she sets an alarm so that she can put her face on before her husband wakes up. When did things get so sad?

'Good morning, Alessandro.' My father also refuses to shorten my name. Proudly Italian. And stubborn. 'I was just talking to your mother about Davis Davis.' I wonder whether it might be better to just come clean before my father has some moment where he acts all superior and self-righteous. Maybe I should just own it.

Dad can act disappointed because he never came from money. I can hear it now. He never had all the advantages that I have. He is self-made. Blah blah. I would think that would make him more grateful, more accepting. But wealth did not give my father freedom, it turned him into an asshole.

I open my mouth to speak but nothing comes out.

My father continues. 'He had one of his parties last night. Turns out there was quite the furore later in the evening.'

Gulp. I could hear my father earlier. He didn't mention a party, he was talking about dragging someone somewhere. He was talking about dragging me to the police station. Why is he lying? He's trying to make one of his points. I just know it. I'm done for.

'What happened?' my mother asks, seemingly fascinated.

Maybe she is in on it, too. They're trying to torture me. It's working. They're doing a bit. Open fucking mic night at the shit parents comedy cellar. I'm paranoid, now. I feel like they both side-eye me, waiting for me to jump in with a confession. I keep my mouth shut.

'Well, it turns out that Davis had a live band there, as he usually does. Some up-and-coming rock group that he's been working with and will no doubt turn into megastars.' My mom nods along. 'Turns out the roadie – or whoever – set up the equipment but something wasn't earthed or there was a loose wire, but the frontman took one strum of his electric guitar and got hit with ten-thousand volts. Threw him across the stage. Had to call an ambulance.'

'My God, is he okay?'

Now, I'm confused. This appears to be a genuine conversation. Why are they not chastising me? What kind of sick mind games are they playing?

'He's fine. Shaken up. Burned his hand. There's always something at one of these parties. You got in late last night, Alessandro. What were you up to?'

Stay calm, Less. Stay calm.

'I was just with Alyssa. Hanging out. Nothing major.'

We went to the party you were just talking about and stole somebody's car to drive around all night.

'Not too tired for college, I hope.'

'No, I was thinking of going in early today, actually.'

There's a moment of silence, like two gunslingers sizing each other up.

My mother breaks the deadlock. 'There you go, no need to drag anybody anywhere.' My father gives her a look, but she's not stupid, it's a big house and the sound travels, especially when you're speaking in anger or frustration. She knows that I would have heard them talking in the kitchen.

She looks at me. There's something in her eyes. Like she is remembering how she treated me yesterday. I know that she doesn't want to be like that. She is struggling with life, herself. Things haven't quite turned out the way that she hoped. She feels trapped and stifled. I understand that. Yet she has everything she could want, so also feels guilty for feeling the way that she does. It's hard. I tell myself that I'm the only person she really loves, so naturally she takes it out on me.

I try to look unfazed. In fact, I may even smile slightly. I have always loved to get one over on my father.

But that's not why I'm smirking. My father was talking about dragging me in to college. I get a bad rap for missing classes, but it's a liberal arts degree that allows you to work in your own time. My father is a businessman. He wears a suit and tie to work. He has a schedule to keep. He doesn't understand. The world is different for creatives.

The point is, Davis Davis is clearly a top guy, and my father has no idea what happened last night. He's clueless.

I got away with it.

And, damn, it feels amazing.

^ ^ ^ ^ ^ ^ ^ ^ ^

^ ^ ^ ^ ^ ^ ^ ^ ^

ALYSSA

I have nobody to answer to this morning. When I get up, my mother has already left to start the next shift at work and my grandmother is in the living room with her nose a few inches from the television screen.

Another day in Paradise.

There's no comedown on this side of town. I am still buzzing. I'm a ball of energy. I may be the only person in my family to have gone to college but now I am also the only one who has ever driven a Porsche.

No wonder rich people are so smug.

This is what I want.

I've had a taste and now I want more. Not necessarily the opulence, but the freedom. It was exciting for Less but not in the same way as it was for me, because he's always had that independence.

Of course, I have seen what wealth looks like when I have been over to Less's house but it's not the same. Less's dad is working hard every day, and he will be able to retire at an age when he still has plenty of life left to live. But nobody really knows who he is. They've seen the Donnaruma logo on the side of building developments but they don't know or care who that is.

The world will not mourn when he eventually passes.

He has no effect on the people who have never even met him.

Because he's not famous.

I don't hate Less's father. I respect him and his work ethic and all that he has achieved. It's just not who I want to be. I want to be listened to. It's the millennial way. I just want to feel like I'm making a difference, having an impact, because we've all been brought up being told that's possible. I'm not even sure that I really understand what that means. It could just be buzzwords and marketing spin. Maybe we all think we're so self-aware but it's actually the opposite.

^^^^^^^^^^

^^^^^^^^^^

@Motiv8Me
'Not everything you say has to change the world, but you never know who really needed to hear the thing that you kept inside. Making an impact can be as simple as saying something real in a world filled with noise.'
♥ 15.7k

^^^^^^^^^^

^^^^^^^^^^

ALYSSA
I'm not afraid to work hard. I'm just trying to find my *thing*. At the moment, I have a handful of identities online that cover the influencer outlets. Fashion, food, fitness and lifestyle. I also have a book blog where I review upcoming titles. The one thing I don't have is any kind of musical ability.

But I know I want to say something worthwhile.

I just don't know what it is yet.

And this is where I differ from my best friend. He wants the same things, but he has a vision, he is devoted to fashion. And, like his father, he is happy to not be seen. He doesn't want to be in the spotlight. He's happy to be behind the scenes, creating. Less would hate to think that he is anything like his dad, though, I'm sure.

One thing I do know is that I want to go back to Rosie's. I want to wait for the influencer to leave for her daily run, then I want to casually walk up that garden path again, this time taking the key from under the mat to open the door, and then walk around her house, see how she lives. Feel it. Go through her cupboards, her fridge, her underwear drawer.

It starts with grand theft auto and moves to breaking and entering, it seems. Although we won't have to break anything.

Another thing I know is that when we are done with Rosie, I am going to want to go harder.

This feels like the beginning of another addiction.

I may not have a clear idea of what it is I want to say to the world, and I may not even have a clear idea of my own identity or who it is that I really want to be. Maybe it's my fate to fail. But I do know the way I want to live.

I want experience, and risk and reward, and maybe a little fame along the way wouldn't hurt. And I want to take my best friend with me on this ride. Because, even though he has everything and I have almost nothing, we are both disconnected from the world in some way. We are outsiders. We share that. And like so many of our generation, we're bored, and we feel a little lost.

^^^^^^^^^^

^^^^^^^^^^

HuffPost, July 23rd

What is an 'influencer accent'? Here's why all your favourite content creators sound the same...

^^^^^^^^^^

^^^^^^^^^^

Five things to consider before you leave your Uber driver a bad rating. The challenges they face every day that you were completely unaware of...

^^^^^^^^^^

^^^^^^^^^^

The three things you should ALWAYS lie about in a job interview. You're being too honest...

^^^^^^^^^^

^^^^^^^^^^

America's dumbest generation?

Or do millennials offer something that no other gen can...?

By Emily-Jayne Grafton

It's not their fault.

Every generation has its hardships. There are wars, racial injustices, health pandemics and terrorist attacks. Racing to the moon. Racing to build a bomb. Stock-market crashes and crippling recessions. The

Lost Generation will say they had it worst but so will Gen X, and it's the same for the Boomers.

But, without fail, they all look down on one generation.

The Millennials.

America's dumbest generation.

Intellectually anaemic.

The technology that is supposed to democratise them is ruining them. Social media teaches them to engage with one another. But it's all on the surface. There's no deeper understanding. Because they navigate this new world ephemerally, in short, sharp doses. Little truths that disappear as quickly as they formed and are impossible to stitch together into something whole.

There's online gaming and juvenile chat.

LOL this.

LMFAO that.

It's all about popular culture, so they skip more enriching activities like reading and philosophy and science and history. Instead of building their knowledge, they redistribute *bits* of knowledge they have picked up in passing but do not fully understand.

They may be a part of the generation with the highest number of mental-health issues, but they are also the most tech savvy.

And that makes them intellectually agile. They have the ability to jump quickly from one thing to another or perform tasks simultaneously. They may not be able to hold a conversation with their parents, but they can have thirty different conversations at once with people online. They have a better sense of community than the previous generation because they are part of a global society.

This makes them motivated by change rather than fearful of it.

They are less about thinking and considering and more about *doing*.

You want to work in fashion? Forget about college. Find an online tutorial that shows how to make a ruche on the garment you want to make, then post a picture on Instagram. Think you have a decent singing voice? Don't deliver your demo tape to every studio in town, upload a cover version of a popular song to your YouTube channel.

Feel like an outsider? Not part of the popular crowd? Tormented by the kids who are better-looking than you, wealthier than you, sportier than you? Just bored? Don't dwell on it. Don't get down. Find someone like you. It's easier than ever to do that. You only need one person. Somebody true. Somebody to trust. Suddenly you don't feel so outside.

Still bored?

Don't think, just do.

This millennial can-do attitude will feed into the next generation, who will be motivated to use that spirit and make a difference. They may not know how and they certainly won't know why, but they will try.

Why will they try? Why will they believe that they can achieve? It's very simple. The digital age could open up a world of history, art, literature, foreign affairs, but if you monitor the practices of their generation, you soon discover the thing that is most important to them.

Themselves.

^^^^^^^^^^

^^^^^^^^^^

LESS

My mum seems so unhappy. I think she feels trapped. It hurts me that she's like that. It's the reason I will always get her something to drink when she wants it, and it's the reason I would never say anything to her that would cause her further sadness, even when she is taking out her frustrations on me. I can empathise to a certain extent but at least I have Alyssa. And I'm so pleased that I do.

I'm lucky.

We have our own issues. We are just trying to navigate our world. If it wasn't so open and connected now, we would never have become friends – our lives are too different. That's the thing that is special about us, I think. In every other way, we are just like our millennial peers, we conform to that lifestyle. The difference with us is that our personal relationship with each other is profound. We are from different backgrounds, but we completely embrace that in one another.

^^^^^^^^^

^^^^^^^^^

ALYSSA

We are just trying to please ourselves. Entertain ourselves. Like anybody else.

In a world gone mad, we are making our own fun. The rich and the poor both struggle in their own unique ways. We are all just trying to get something done.

Just Do It, huh?

Get out the house. Maybe get into somebody else's house. Somebody famous or influential. We don't have to break in. We don't have to steal anything. Nobody will get hurt. It'll just be a bit of fun. It's wholesome, really.

Less and I are lucky.

Lucky that we have each other.

Lucky to be part of an ever-growing world that is at our fingertips.

Lucky not to have been caught.

Lucky nobody has been hurt.

But, I guess, at some point, luck has to run out.

^^^^^^^^^

^^^^^^^^^

#StrongWomen #FearlessFemales #FitAndFierce #BossBabeEnergy

The contract had already been signed by the time Paige's lawyer had a chance to read through it. He told her that it was brutal but honest. There was a good chance that she would not come out well, but it would certainly raise her profile even more, if that's what she wanted.

And the money was great.

She had emailed Satmohan that evening to say that she was ready to commit. And he had received the message while at the Davis Davis party. Then he went on to toast his success a little too hard. And now he has something demonic in his skull that aches so badly he doesn't even want his morning coffee. He needs water and to wear sunglasses inside and for people to talk in whispers for the next hour.

But he can't. Because he works in reality television and he is trying to walk off the effects of an epic party before arriving at Paige's home to get things rolling.

Satmohan is early. Paige answers the door after a short while. Moisture on her face and a perfect triangle of sweat on her grey vest that points down her cleavage. It's too perfect, Satmohan thinks. It looks sprayed on. Last time, he remembers how much her stomach was sweating, but it's dry this time.

Both days, she was wearing a full face of make-up.

'Sorry, I'm a little early, were you recording another workout?'

'No, no. Not today. Just doing something for myself. It's not always easy when you're training lots of people to find time to exercise for you. You know?'

'God, no. My genetics keep me slim. I haven't set foot in a gym since high school.'

Paige wants to tell him that skinny people can be fat on the inside, but she bites her tongue.

'Well, come in and I'll make you a coffee or a matcha or a chai tea or something. Is there a team coming today?'

'I wouldn't mind a chai, thanks. It's not a team, it's just one guy that we have used on numerous occasions. He's the best. He's going to install some cameras in the living space today. That's all. He'll want to have the entire area covered, but if you don't like where he puts them then we can work it out.'

'Okay.' She looks hesitant.

'But don't worry. It's very discreet. You won't even know they're there. We want you to forget about them, really, because that's when we get the real stuff.'

Paige is not sure how she feels about that. Every video she releases has been painstakingly lit and angled and rehearsed and edited so that it looks perfect.

She has to be perfect. That's how it works. And that's more exhausting than the exercise.

The cameras will pick up everything. The first day or so will be fine but, as Satmohan said, Paige will start to have moments where she forgets that there are cameras in that room and she will rub her nose or scratch herself or burp. Something that lets the viewers know that she is human. That she is normal and has flaws.

Maybe they will stop looking up to her.

Maybe they will like her more.

The deal is done. The ink is dry. The money transferred. And the cameras are about to be installed.

Satmohan navigates the installation. He introduces Paige to Rowan, who explains where he is going to put the cameras and how they will be mostly hidden, she won't even see red lights when it's dark because these cameras do not have them. There will be no coverage in any of the bathrooms or bedrooms. If they want footage in the bedroom, a crew will be present to set up the shots and instances. They can set anything up.

Paige nods along. She's nervous but excited. Success on a TV network opens so many more doors. She is already thinking about her own range of nutrition supplements and Paige Fitness Protein Powder. She will be an influencer and entrepreneur and a businesswoman.

She's on her way up.

That's the progression.

She only ever wanted to be one thing and it is none of the things that she is now.

'Rowan will probably come back once we've started filming to set something up outside in the garden, is that alright?'

'I just do what Tammy tells me to do.' He smiles. 'We'll give you your own camera for diary-room confessions, that sort of thing, but I'll go through that with you at a later date.'

It's true, Rowan is the best in the business but he is also unscrupulous. The cameras can be switched on remotely, so, at three o'clock, when Tammy calls Rowan and tells him to start recording a test run, all he has to do is flip a switch and invade Paige's privacy.

^^^^^^^^^

^^^^^^^^^

LESS

'Why are you calling me?' I ask.

'Because I don't want to write down what I'm going to say, you moody piece of shit.'

I laugh. Alyssa is so funny. She's straight to the point and she's honest.

'No sense in creating a trail or having proof.'

'It's not like we buried a body, Alyssa, we...' I look around to make sure nobody is listening, lurking outside the door, '...went for a drive.'

'It was pretty crazy, though, am I right?' Alyssa is relieved that I'm not freaking out about what we did. She thought I would be. Because, even though I like to think of myself as a natural rebel, I still like to make sure I toe the line on certain things.

'Yeah. It was wild. Fun, too.' I'm already at college. I'm in the studio with a ton of fabric. The phone is on speaker while I cut it to shape. Mine is the only station that is lit. Nobody else has arrived yet but some have left half-designs on their mannequins. The focus of this project is to make something with a strong silhouette, but it has to be editorial rather than veering into a costume. I'm in early to avoid the bitchy people from my course. The ones who never have anything positive to say to me, who insult with a smile, who praise with their backhands. The ones who take me right back to the way I used to feel at school. I haven't escaped that but at least I've managed to escape my home for the day.

'What are you doing? You sound distracted.'

'I'm in the studio, making a dress.'

'You're keen. I'm heading in now. But...'

She goes on to explain her plans for the day. She's staying at college until lunchtime but then she's leaving to go across town and hang out near Rosie's place again. She wants to get there a little bit before we did last time, just to be safe. The object of her mission is to scope out the influencer's place and make sure that this God-fearing jogger has some structure to her existence.

A lot of these influencers do have a timetable. They know they need to create content each day and they will focus on that to ensure that it goes out into the world at the optimum time. They're disciplined. They work for themselves, so they have to be. They make their own success.

Alyssa is fascinated; she always has been. She wants to witness how they live their lucky, luxury lives. She's seen how the other half live in my neck of the woods and she doesn't want that. And I get it, everyone seems so miserable and exhausted. But, these people, these influencers are her age. They are her peers. They're no more skilled than she is.

The plan is to wait and see whether Rosie Velazquez leaves around the same time for her daily jog. If she does, Alyssa wants to come back again tomorrow, with me, and get into Rosie's house to see what she is really about.

'You're fucking crazy,' I snort.

'Maybe. But you're still coming with me.'

^^^^^^^^^^

^^^^^^^^^^

@RosieVelazquez
'After a great night of sleep, nothing beats that morning matcha before my sun salutations.' #GoodMorning #Namaste #MatchaMatchaMatcha #VeganLife
♥ 2.2k

^^^^^^^^^^

^^^^^^^^^^

There is a routine.

But it's not that.

Sure, that is a part of it, but the picture of Rosie Velazquez, her face half covered by a giant mug of matcha tea, only her beautiful, big eyes peering over the top, did not happen as soon as she woke up. Nobody takes a picture of their face after they have risen from a perfect slumber.

These things take time.

Most days, Rosie wakes up and immediately checks her social-media messages from the night before. She is global, so she has hundreds of communications from the other side of the world. Emails next. There are multiple accounts. Personal. Business. The one from her website.

Stop.

She plays some game that will kick her brain into gear. It's not healthy to spend so much time scrolling, she tells herself. She checks her WhatsApp, in case somebody she knows in real life wants to talk.

Time to post a *Good Morning* picture. Something arty from her photos. A graffiti wall or broken bottle on the beach. Maybe that sticker she found on the Williamsburg Bridge that said, 'Trump has a tiny penis'.

If she's going to take a selfie like she's just woken up, she has to make sure she has already been up for an hour, she's hydrated and has perfect hair and make-up.

Then it's time to actually get up. Stretch. Do her breathing exercises. Eat something healthy. Take a shower. Plan her content for the day. Film something. Edit. Post. Catch up on the news. Death scroll. Coffee. Go for a jog before lunch.

Rosie often prays after her breathing. Some people like to sit in an ice bath. Rosie doesn't even like getting in a cool swimming pool. She hates gimmicks more. God isn't a gimmick. She takes Him very seriously. She loves Him. Without her faith, she would not have the strength for her activism. Without her activism, she is just another cute young woman with a quirky taste in clothing, hoping to forge her way into the fashion industry in some way.

Any way will do.

She needs the run to clear her head each day. To be with herself and her thoughts, without distraction.

Rosie is completely shut off from the world when she places her AirPods in and blasts some music or a podcast or an audiobook. So she knows that the Volkswagen camper van will still be across the road because it has been there since the day she moved in, but she is so absorbed in her nothingness that she fails to recognise the same woman as yesterday, standing next to the road sign for Rosie's street, puffing away on a nicotine vape flavoured like fruit.

It doesn't make an impending smoking-related death any cuter because you've made cancer taste like aloe vera.

But all the cool kids are doing it.

#LiveYourLife

#MemoriesOverMoney

Rosie jogs one way and Alyssa walks the other. She stands at the bottom of Rosie's front garden and looks up towards the house then at her watch. It's only six minutes earlier than the time Rosie went for a run yesterday. Perfect.

^^^^^^^^^^

^^^^^^^^^^

ALYSSA

So, it should be another hour before Rosie returns, that's how long it took before. It's tempting but I don't want to do this without Less. Besides, there is something to be said for delaying satisfaction. It's the longing that intensifies the pay-off.

One day left. I can do that. I don't have to have *everything* right now, no matter what Gen X thinks.

I take a quick picture of myself with the camper van in the background and text it to Less saying, *The van is still available, if you want it*, and I can't help but laugh to myself.

Then: back to college. Grab a sandwich on the way. Classes. Two buses home. Cook dinner for Grandma again. An hour of coursework. Grocery shopping. Four-hour shift at the bar. Home. Bath. Try to sleep through the excitement of my planned break-in. I have my own routine. It's not the one I want, it's not glamorous, but I don't complain.

I just want to see how Rosie lives. I don't want to hurt anyone. I'm not going to steal anything. I just want to see something new, experience the other side of the crossroads.

Is that too much to ask?

Damn. The next twenty-four hours are going to drag.

I suck in another lungful of my peach-flavoured death, sigh, and click back into the reality of my boring, regular life.

^^^^^^^^^^

^^^^^^^^^^

#OnSetLife #LightsCameraAction #TVMagic

There's a stack of papers on Edie's desk as high as her head. Every blog post @TheFitnessPaige ever posted back when she was *Paige Ponders*. Before she found her calling in health and wellbeing. Every printout is an invaluable insight into Paige's psychology. It's a window into her mind. It's a way to build up the perfect profile.

Edie Lincoln is old school. She likes things printed out. She wants the writing in ink rather than pixels. There are posts from a discontinued Myspace page when she was *Paige Plays*. It seems she has tried a bit of everything. Much like Alyssa, who once went gluten-free for six months even though she has no hint of an intolerance to wheat.

There are school records and reports. If Paige ever showed up in the local news for winning a beauty pageant or saving a cat from drowning or delivering home-cooked meals to the elderly, Edie has a copy. If Paige parked illegally or was found speeding and couldn't sweet-talk her way out of the fine, Edie knows about it.

She has to.

If you are going to be in a Lincoln/Lowell production, this is the level of research and due diligence that goes into your background – it's even more when it comes to her passion projects. That way, they know the best way to manipulate you. They know what incentives to offer to get you to play ball and they know what buttons to press in order to push your emotions in the directions that will ensure you are watched and ratings will increase.

Thought you made a subtle but devastating profile update to damn your ex and let the world know that you are over them? Thanks for that, they'll make sure you get a set-up segment in the show to bring back all those emotions you felt when you were together and then they'll break it off again. Watch the viewing figures spike.

Nothing is real in reality television but the emotional havoc.

Edie Lincoln really is the brains behind the team. Without Tammy Lowell, though, she may never have made it. If she had, she probably would have turned her hand to something like documentaries. She is where she is because Tammy possesses a ruthlessness that gets things done.

They wouldn't work as well separately.

Each has their own strengths.

This is one of Edie's. This pile of paperwork on her desk about the protagonist in their latest show starring @TheFitnessPaige.

There are three more piles of paper on Edie's desk and a monitor that shows every corner of Paige's living area. She has everything covered.

^^^^^^^^^

^^^^^^^^^

@TheFitnessPaige
'Even if you think you don't like eggplant, I guarantee you will love this. *Recipe in bio*.' #EatClean #RealFood #StrongWomen
♥ 9.9k

^^^^^^^^^

^^^^^^^^^

Once Satmohan and the guy who fitted the cameras, whose name Paige has already forgotten, leave, Paige makes herself some lunch. She has already planned the crockery that she will use and the gold Smonaco cutlery she was sent for free from La Redoute. She has also found a baked aubergine recipe with smoked tofu cream and chilli crumb.

It takes her thirty-five minutes to make. She knows that people don't want to spend that long making their lunches, but this post is not about the practicality, it's about the aesthetics. She wants the picture. She can add a link to the recipe and tag La Redoute on their product. And she gets a delicious lunch out of it.

Paige tucks her feet up on the sofa and eats from her lap with the sound of a playlist called *Aboriginal Dreamtime* playing in the background through a surround-sound system sent to her for nothing by Sonos. It seems to relax her.

She finishes her meal and places the plate on the cushion next to her before stretching out her legs and laying one hand on her stomach like she is absolutely fulfilled. Her phone buzzes. She takes a quick look at the screen then turns it upside down on the sofa. This is her lunch break. She wants to be free from distractions.

Just her, a full stomach and an indigenous Australian blowing into a tube of wood. She lies there, deadly still, only her chest moving up and down as she breathes. It's peaceful. There's something fascinating about nothingness.

In a world that is moving so fast, where it's a fight just to keep up, allowing herself to stop and breathe and let go for a moment is something of a luxury for Paige. It's a skill that people are having to, seemingly, relearn.

Like patience.

Everything is so instant. Television, music, food deliveries. People want everything, still, but they just want it now. This minute. This moment. So, when Paige lies down after eating her nutritious and colourful lunch and does nothing, it's captivating.

Edie and Tammy can't tear their eyes away from the screen.

Then Paige gets up. She takes her bowl and gold cutlery out into the kitchen, rinses them off under the tap and places them in the dishwasher. Edie and Tammy can't see this because there is no camera in the kitchen yet. So they also don't see Paige reaching up into a cabinet in the corner. She pushes three packets of protein powder aside, and behind is a jar.

She has to keep it up high. Out of reach. Otherwise she'd have a hand in it all the time.

Lincoln/Lowell Productions continues to watch an empty living room, not seeing @TheFitnessPaige balancing on a stool to reach her secret jar of goodies. They don't see her devour a chocolate brownie, a blondie and a bar of milk chocolate.

They don't see her wash it down with a bottle of Coke.

And there are no cameras or microphones set up in or near the bathroom, so the two TV producers do not see or hear Paige push her fingers down her throat and throw up the fizz and the sugar and the actual nutrition of the vegetables from her lunch.

They don't see her brush her teeth for three minutes.

They don't see her splash cold water on her face.

They don't see her look into the mirror and tell herself that she is disgusting. They have no idea how exhausted she feels, trying to project this wholesome, perfect existence. They just see her glide back into her living room with another cup of coffee and a book.

Edie and Tammy have millions in the bank but they never stop working. And they don't look anything like Paige. Maybe they are getting something wrong.

But it never takes long to capture something real.

They will continue to watch and record until Paige shows her true self and just what she is capable of doing.

^^^^^^^^^

^^^^^^^^^

ALYSSA

Nothing important happened today.

That's what I'm thinking as I pull my duvet over my shoulder.

It was a dud.

Sure, I got to see Rosie Velazquez running in Lycra, but, other than that minuscule moment, it has been an elongated taste of tedium. No parties or drugs or stolen cars. No cocktails or dancing. I didn't even get to see Less, today. Is this what my life would be without him? God, I daren't think about that. It's hard enough being on the outside, doing it alone would be intolerable.

I made black-bean tostadas and sat with my grandmother, knowing that each episode of *Jeopardy!* was bringing me twenty-five minutes closer to tomorrow.

Who is Rosie Velazquez?

What is Phrogging?

Mom was late home from work, as usual. Everything was usual. The endless loop of learning, consuming and defecating. Usual. Time slips by. Faster and faster. You find yourself saying things like, 'God, is it Wednesday again, already?' I don't want that. I don't want to be that person. I want more. I can't be specific about exactly what that is, but I know that today has not been how I want to live.

I understand that this is why my mother works as hard as she does. She wants to provide and she wants to make her daughter proud. I feel that way about her. I'm so proud of her. She is more of a role model than these influencers will ever be. I'm not stupid. I know my station. There are limitations for people like me. I know that, even though I am at college, I will probably end up like my mother. Working the same way when I get older. That's just how it is here.

We know our station.

But I'm allowed to dream.

Surely, I can, at least, have a taste of something that isn't expected, that isn't already laid out as my future.

The clock on my bedside table reads just after ten. I have gone to bed early in the hope that I will go to sleep and, somehow, that will trick my brain into thinking that tomorrow is a little closer.

I quickly look at my phone to see if Less has messaged, to see if he feels the same way about this laborious day of routine and stagnation. But there's nothing. Instead of setting my alarm and placing my phone, face down, on the bedside table, I decide to have a quick scroll. Perhaps the argument between @TheFitnessPaige and Little Miss Sperm Smoothie is heating up.

Nothing there, either.

Swipe up.

Sound on.

Some guy in a wig lip-syncs the wrong lyrics to songs.

Yawn.

A bearded, tattooed jock squares up with a smaller Polish man, who is with his young daughter in a McDonald's restaurant. He's telling him to get back to his own country. The kid looks scared. Mr Tattoo is deliberately trying to be intimidating. He pushes the smaller man. Then gets knocked out with one punch.

Skip to the end.

Four disturbing facts you didn't know: part eleven.

Don't care.

'Trying to scale your business?'

Drag your finger up the screen.

My eyes start to feel heavy. I set my alarm, just in case. When I look at the time, eighty minutes have passed since I picked my phone up. It feels like five. Scrolling my life away. Still no message from Less.

I take my vlogging camera and press the red button. I look directly into the camera to record my first diary entry.

'You see these things online. How to lose weight by drinking cider vinegar or free guides to building garden furniture from old pallets. Tips for better sex, or ways to earn ten grand a month by working from home for one hour a day. The people are beautiful. The clothes are stylish. The interiors are gorgeous. It's all the things we want but don't have, right?'

I hit a different button that uploads it straight to YouTube but it remains unlisted. For now, nobody can see it.

Now I have to sleep. I text Less, first, telling him to meet tomorrow at the same café we went to yesterday. We need to get there before lunch because we may need to hang out a bit and wait for Rosie to leave.

And when she does, we're going in.

^^^^^^^^^

^^^^^^^^^

#RunHappy #EveryMileMatters #BreatheRunRepeat

She always puts her bowl in the dishwasher when she finishes breakfast because she can't stand to have things out on the side in the kitchen. There's a place for everything. Storage solutions in every room. She just wants the place to look tidy.

Rosie has two new housemates. They are going to stay over this evening to try the place out for the first time, see what they think.

But Rosie has no idea.

And neither do they.

'Hello, beautiful man.' She speaks into her phone. 'I'm heading out now. You know ... I need to clear my head.' She nods at whatever the person at the other end of the line is saying. 'Yeah. Okay. Well, head over when you're done. I'm sure I can find some time to squeeze you in.' She smiles a coquettish little smile and hangs up.

AirPods in. Key beneath the mat. Turn right out the gate and past the woman sucking on a vape and her friend in the trucker's cap. Rosie is smiling because she knows she is about to set a personal best so that she can get home in time for her tattooed friend to arrive.

∧∧∧∧∧∧∧∧∧

∧∧∧∧∧∧∧∧∧

ALYSSA

I am playing it so cool until I see Rosie round a corner further up the road. Inside, though, I am ready to explode.

'Sure you want to go through with this, Lyss?'

'You're fucking funny. Come on. We're not doing anything wrong. We're just having a look around.' I think that sounds more true if I say it out loud. Like my morning affirmations.

He's trying not to look like an excited puppy. But I can tell. Less follows me. Like he did when we stole the car. Like he did when we arrived at the Davis Davis party. Like he always does. Like he always will.

I am so focussed. I'm not a felon, I'm just a normal person. Making fun for free. That's all. My mom is always telling me to get off my phone and do something that doesn't involve a screen.

I walk with purpose. Past a couple of Rosie's neighbours' houses, all set back from the road with long driveways. Less is not as cool. He's excited but he's also worried. He's on the lookout. It's not that he's scared of getting caught, rich people never are, he's scared of his father.

Less sees the camper van and watches for the curtains to twitch or a door to open or the old man to be out with a leaf blower or something.

He's sweating. But he wants to do this. I know he does.

'Wait up,' he says under his breath and picks up the pace, pushing through the front gate with me, I feel him next to me but my eyes are firmly fixed on the door mat.

I lift it and take the key.

Less wants to check on the neighbours one last time.

'Don't look back now, Less.' I can't even see him. 'It'll seem suspicious. Keep going.' I put the key in and turn it to the left. No troubles. I don't even have to wiggle it at all. It's smooth sailing.

This is it. The threshold moment. Less and I can decide not to do this. To go back to our lives. Our predictable lives where Less will continue to have his whims funded until they don't work out and he is forced to go into his father's business, to be hated by his peers because Daddy gave him a job.

And I will do well at college but still struggle because I will have to take care of my grandmother until she either dies or wins five episodes of *Jeopardy!*.

Less will be worried about what his parents will say if they find out.

I think of all the times that Christmas missed my family.

I step inside.

Of course.

We shut the door behind us. Everything will change. No going back now.

^^^^^^^^^^

^^^^^^^^^^

NOTE: DO NOT SIGN THIS UNTIL YOU HAVE READ IT COMPLETELY
<u>LINCOLN/LOWELL APPLICANT AGREEMENT WITH ARBITRATION PROVISIONS</u>
10. I understand that, in connection with the series, other parties (including, without limitation, other participants, Producer and network) may reveal and/or relate information about me of a personal, private, intimate, surprising, defamatory, disparaging, embarrassing or unfavourable nature. I understand that these actions may expose me to public ridicule, humiliation or condemnation.

Without limiting the generality of any releases set forth herein, I hereby expressly release, indemnify, discharge and hold harmless Producer, other participants, Network and other Released Parties for and from any and all claims and liability assessing a violation of my rights of privacy, intentional or negligent infliction of emotional distress, defamation, and/or damages in any way.

Print name ______________________________

Signature ______________________________

Address ______________________________

^^^^^^^^^

^^^^^^^^^

FIGHT #081 VIEWS: 283k COMMENTS: 4.4k LIKES: 267k

Jab, jab, cross, roll, cross.

Paige is working out to one of her own videos. She throws this combination for a minute, leading with her left hand. Then she switches to southpaw stance and repeats for a minute on the other side. For a further minute, she drops to the floor so that she is lying on her chest, then springs straight back up into a fighting stance.

And Edie watches.

There's a discipline there that is inspiring. Paige is dripping with sweat. It's real. She hasn't sprayed it on for effect. She hasn't poured water over her head and down her cleavage to ensure she gets the views. There's no lighting rig and the only cameras pointed at her are the ones she doesn't know are recording.

This is for her. This is Paige training herself, keeping herself fit and lean and flexible.

Hook, cross, push kick, superman.

She's intensifying the combination. The superman move comes after the push kick where she leans her weight over the foot that has just landed while simultaneously kicking the other foot back and punching forward with the same hand. It looks powerful.

Paige looks powerful.

Every time she performs the last movement, she grunts out the effort she is putting into it.

It seems the rumours are true and @TheFitnessPaige *is* a badass who can handle herself.

And this is exactly what Edie wanted to see.

If Paige is going to enter into this show after signing that flimsy contract that didn't really explain what the hell would be going on, she is going to need a degree of mental and physical toughness to handle the things that the Lincoln/Lowell partnership are going to throw the influencer's way.

Edie Lincoln is still in the information-gathering part of pre-production. Stacks of papers on her desk, three widescreen monitors in a horseshoe shape around the outside and Tammy Lowell in her ear.

'You think she's got what it takes?' Tammy asks.

'She looks strong.'

'But will she play ball? Can we set her up to get the sequences we need? Are we using her to pull in the ratings or are we just using her?'

'I mean, she signed the fucking contract.'

'They all sign. They're desperate. They want their time in the spotlight, they've got to risk it. You know that. I'm not teaching you to suck eggs. Are you going soft on me?'

Edie gives her partner an as-if eye roll. 'Oh, Jesus, you know me better than that. We've exploited plenty of these wannabes. And we'll do it again. Hell, it's not like we're going to kill somebody.'

^^^^^^^^^

^^^^^^^^^

ALYSSA

Click. Everything outside that door is now mine and Less's past. This is who we are now.

The hallway is bright white with a light olive-wood panelling around the bottom half of the walls. An iron-framed console table with oak top houses an old landline phone. Mid-century. Retro. There's no way it's functional but it looks the part. Above is a giant circular mirror, bouncing light from the kitchen, lounge and other rooms beyond.

That wall alone has been styled within an inch of its life. The lamp in the shape of a hare, hiding its identity behind the lampshade, would look garish in any other setting, but it lends the entrance an air of fun.

Of course, I've seen all of this before in pictures that Rosie has posted online but it looks even better in person. Everything has been thought about. Everything has a place and a purpose. My house is functional. Less's place is expensive. But Rosie has style.

'I think she has OCD or something, this place is spotless. Even the shoes are perfectly straight.' Less points to the right at an alcove designed to store shoes and coats but also have them on display for a pop of colour. It gives the illusion that this place is a home, to be lived in, rather than a showpiece or backdrop for the many lifestyle and design photos that Rosie takes.

'It's beautiful, Less. I thought you were into fashion.' My heart rate is spiking, I can feel it in my chest. Hell, my arms are shaking. 'Come on, this is the living room.'

A green antique French sideboard draws the eye. Distressed but striking. A one-of-a-kind piece. There's a natural linen armchair in one corner – curved mango-wood legs and brass riveting. It sits next to six piles of books just stacked against the wall like Rosie is oh-so-chilled about all the books she reads.

'The book stack. She's always reading something in this chair and adding books.'

Less moves over to take a closer look. He sits in the seat.

'What are you doing?'

'What do you mean, "what am I doing?", we are absorbing the energy, right?'

'Yeah, but she'll know if you move anything.'

'Well, let's see, shall we?' Less stands up and takes the cushion in his hands.

This is really where it starts.

'What are you…?'

'Can you please stop asking me what I'm doing? I'm taking this cushion and placing it back exactly where it was. Only, this time, the zip is not running along the bottom, it's up the left-hand side.' He places a hand over his mouth and makes a shocked face.

I don't know about this. What he is doing is worse than stealing something, somehow. I just wanted to have a look around, sit in a seat or lie on her bed or something. Knowing somebody has been in your house and taken something that belongs to you is scary, you don't feel secure, I get that. But Less is screwing with Rosie's mind. He's not doing it on purpose, he just thinks it's a bit of fun. He's embracing the project. He thinks it's harmless. Maybe it is. I don't know, I'm too busy sweating.

We believe that we have an hour to wander about. I admire the abstract wall art while Less makes his way into the kitchen.

'Wait for me,' I call after him.

We go through her fridge like it's an episode of *MTV Cribs*. Oat milk, tomatoes on the vine, gnocchi. There's half a bottle of white wine in the doorway with a Le Creuset bottle stopper to keep it fresh. Less takes a falafel from an open packet and puts it in his mouth. He's hungry because we arrived on the street before lunchtime.

I open all the cupboards and get jealous of everything. The frying pans, the ice-cream maker, the duck-egg-blue kitchen aid. Rosie has everything that I want and all she had to do was throw some paint over a few red-carpet events. Sure, she has a passion and a crusade but she's also a vandal. We might be in her house now but it's not like we broke in. We haven't wrecked anything. She is more of a criminal than we are.

Maybe we are all trying to justify our actions. We know it's wrong but at least we are out doing something. We're not just glued to a screen.

We head upstairs to look around the bathroom and bedroom and hallway library. There's a spare bedroom and a home office that looks as though it has been accessorised by Liberty London.

'What about up there?' Less points at the loft hatch. 'People keep all sorts of stuff in their attic. Stuff that's from their past lives.' He raises his eyebrows. 'I bet it's all boxed up and labelled beautifully.' It's like he's already forgotten what we're doing. He's just embracing the fun element.

I am torn. He's right. There could be stuff up there that gives a glimpse into her life before influencing. It might look just like my life. It might also be riding crops from her childhood pony and a selection of jodhpurs and horse-riding rosettes. Only one way to find out.

'Can you get the hatch down?'

'Yes. We have these on my side of town, too, you know?'

That's when I hear voices.

I run into Rosie's bedroom and look out the window.

Fuck.

I ran back onto the upstairs landing. Less is already halfway up the loft ladder.

'Go go go go go go go go go go.' I push him.

'What the…?'

'She's home … get the fuck up there and be quiet.'

^^^^^^^^^^

^^^^^^^^^^

#StrongerWithEveryStep #EndorphinRush #FindYourStride

It's not even been close to an hour.

Rosie opts for a sprint finish back down her road. She reaches the gate and hits stop on her watch then bends over and breathes heavily with her hands on her knees. The old man with the van sees and starts talking to her. It buys Alyssa and Less some valuable seconds.

^^^^^^^^^^

^^^^^^^^^^

ALYSSA

I pull the chain that retracts the ladder and shuts the hatch. Less and I sit on the wooden boards above and wait.

We're cooked.

This could be a very long night.

#TurnFromSin #GodsForgiveness #BreakTheChains

God, that guy can talk, Rosie thinks. She finally manages to peel herself away from Camper Van Man. He was being perfectly pleasant, talking about exercise and endorphins and how he still surfs even though it probably looks like he can't. She wanted to get away because she's expecting company.

He calls something after her as she walks towards her house, and Rosie throws out a hand gesture that she thinks is positive but also dismissive. She lifts the mat to retrieve her front-door key but it's not there.

She drops the mat and stands quickly. The old man has turned away and is walking back inside his home. She walks partway down her own path and looks down the road. Perhaps her friend arrived early and let himself in. But she can't see his car parked anywhere.

Rosie starts to worry. She has a large and loyal following for her activism, but it also makes her a fair share of enemies. She has had threats before. Not to kill her or anything that dramatic but certainly warnings to desist. A healthy dose of menace.

It frightens her.

But Rosie is tough. She has to be ready to fight the fights that she chooses. She goes back to her door and whips the mat up, the second key that she clearly forgot about flings itself down the step to her feet and she breathes a sigh of relief.

This job is making her paranoid.

Inside is quiet. She kicks her shoes off and lines them up with the others then throws her key onto the hallway console table. She's sweating and needs to get in the shower quickly, but she likes to take a coffee in with her, so flicks the kettle on and goes to the fridge for her oat milk.

Something isn't right.

Rosie looks over her shoulder. She feels like she is being watched. She takes the oat milk out of the door and spots the falafels on the middle shelf. She knows she had four left and now there are only three. The kettle clicks as it boils and makes her jump.

Things are slightly off.

She closes the fridge door and finishes making her coffee, wracking her brains about the falafel and when she may have eaten one last. She needs to get clean but her mind is racing. She tells herself that she's being stupid, too sensitive. So what if she doesn't remember grabbing a snack.

Still, Rosie takes the time to go into her living room, even though she is supposed to be in a rush. It's like she heard a noise. Except the house is deathly quiet.

It's so obvious, she spots it straight away. The cushion on her reading chair is not the way she left it. The zip always has to be hidden along the bottom. That's how she does it.

'Hello?' she says out loud but doesn't know why. As though somebody is going to pop out from behind a curtain and announce that they are pranking her. 'Adam, it's not funny to fuck with me like this.'

Adam is her tattooed friend. She thinks that maybe he has let himself in to surprise her. He knows where she leaves the key and she had told him that she was going out for a run.

Cautiously, she makes her way up the stairs. She checks the bedrooms and her office and, again, tells herself she's being paranoid, it's the social-media trolls in her head. Rosie breathes. She undresses and takes a scaldingly hot shower, but she still can't shake the feeling of unease and pokes her head out to check that the mirror doesn't steam up to reveal a message of some kind.

Too many horror movies.

She laughs to herself.

The doorbell rings and startles her. Rosie wraps a towel around her chest. It's just long enough to cover her modesty. She takes a quick swig of her coffee then opens the bathroom door, letting all the steam out.

At the top of the stairs she can see down through the window of the front door. Adam has arrived.

Rosie stops and tucks the top of the towel in further, so that it is secure. The loft hatch is directly above her head. She clasps her hands together and says, 'Dear God, please forgive me for what I am about to do and say.'

Amen.

^^^^^^^^^^

^^^^^^^^^^

ALYSSA

Oh. My. God.

It's so clear. We can hear everything from up here. Less and I are paralysed, not wanting to make even the smallest sound for fear of alerting world-famous fashion influencer and animal-rights activist Rosie Velazquez to our presence in her attic.

We don't want to get caught.

Ten minutes ago we were bored kids. Curious kids.

Now we are phroggers.

^ ^ ^ ^ ^ ^ ^ ^ ^ ^

^ ^ ^ ^ ^ ^ ^ ^ ^ ^

phrogging

[frog-ing]

Phrogging is the act of living in someone's home without their knowledge or permission.

^ ^ ^ ^ ^ ^ ^ ^ ^ ^

^ ^ ^ ^ ^ ^ ^ ^ ^ ^

ALYSSA

We hear her say a quick prayer to her God. I know how important Rosie's faith is to her but Less has no idea; he doesn't follow her. His idea of activism is liking a post about global warming or sharing an article about net zero. Less is more of a *slacktivist*. He'd rather plant a tree than go to a protest about cutting down forests.

Less shrugs his shoulders and screws up his face is if to say, *What is she praying for?* I respond with my side of the mime show and shrug my shoulders, too, in a how-am-I-supposed-to-know manner.

We listen.

The extractor fan has kicked in and sucks the condensation out of the bathroom, through a pipe in the attic, so their conversation is more muffled, but I can still make out what the pair below us are saying. The noise could disguise any movement we make but neither of us wants to take the chance.

'I wasn't expecting you this soon,' I hear Rosie say to whoever has rung her doorbell.

'I came as quickly as I could.' A man's voice.

'Well, I hope that's not a theme of the afternoon.'

Less and I look at one another, wide-eyed. I shake my head and mouth, 'No.'

The front door shuts and then there's a thud. I don't know what is going on but either Rosie has pushed the man against the door or he has done it to her. Rosie didn't have time to get dressed after her shower and now I'm starting to think that was never the plan.

Whoever this guy is that has arrived, Rosie already knows what she plans to do with him because she has apologised to her God in advance. It's all starting to make sense.

The falafel that Less stole seems to have made him even hungrier. His stomach rumbles. It sounds so loud in the loft, but there's no way they would have heard anything below. I want to hold my breath. Like that will somehow make me even quieter.

They're coming up the stairs, now. Slowly. They're kissing. I can hear.

Rosie Velazquez paints a picture of herself online as self-righteous with regard to the state of the planet and the way we are treating the world and the animals that try to live in it. When it comes to sex and relationships, you would think that she is waiting for the one that she will marry. That perhaps sex is simply for procreation rather than recreation, but the things that are coming out of her mouth tell a different story.

She is definitely not looking for this unknown man to make love to her. She uses the word 'fuck' and it makes me baulk. This is not the person I have been following online.

Is this the real influencer life? Take a picture of some tofu scramble, take a jog then screw the window cleaner. I spend a lot of time with my gay best friend – as a result, I haven't had anything between my legs, other than my own hand, for months. Less is pretty much the worst wingman ever.

We have to sit here and listen to the couple beneath us having sex. It's so noisy and Rosie is overly vocal. There's the sound of bodies slapping together and the bed scraping against the floor. Towards the end, the tapping of the headboard against the wall speeds up and Rosie lets out a moan to suggest that it all finished at the same time.

I'm not buying it for a second.

Overacting.

Pouting.

At one point, Rosie put on a childish porn voice that made everyone secretly living in the attic cringe.

There's a welcome silence as the couple bask in a glorious afterglow. At first, I don't realise that Less is waving to get my attention because I have my eyes closed and my head turned so that my ear is facing in the direction of the couple. I figure that shutting off my sight will somehow heighten my hearing. I saw a video online about a man who went blind and developed amazing senses of smell and taste. He's a top restaurant critic, now, with his own online review channel.

He was handed some lemons and he made a big old batch of virtual lemonade.

They're not saying anything downstairs, so I open my eyes for a second and find Less waving frantically in my direction.

'What?' I mouth.

'I need to go,' Less mouths back.

'They're still down there,' I point. 'We can't leave until they're gone.'

Less mimes by grabbing at his balls: 'No. I need to *go*.'

This is ridiculous. I look around the loft for some kind of container, just in case things get desperate. Then the amorous couple emerge from their fog of pleasure and start talking.

'I'm hungry now,' the male voice says.

'Did you eat one of my falafels?'

'No. That's a strange response.'

'Just that I was sure there were more in the fridge.'

I shoot Less a look that he feels. If he gets us caught...

I go back to listening with my eyes closed.

'You want to go out and get some food?' Rosie asks.

'No, no. You wait here. I'll whip us up something for now and maybe we can just spend the rest of the day in bed.'

Oh, great. I hear his footsteps move out of the bedroom and down the stairs. My heart sinks. Less is shaking his head as if saying, 'No more, please.' He squeezes between his legs and I gesture to him.

'You'll have to tie a knot in it.'

^^^^^^^^^

^^^^^^^^^^

LESS

Nothing brings a friendship closer than witnessing another person empty their bladder into an old camping canteen that has been left in the attic since the failed trip to Big Sur four years ago. Alyssa looked away while I did what I had to do but I know she could still hear what was going on. I couldn't do it quietly. Rosie and her fuck buddy were in the kitchen, so they were unaware, luckily.

'You might not want to hear this, but I saw a couple of sleeping bags in with all the camping stuff. We might need to keep warm later. I don't think they're going out.' Apparently, I can focus now that I have relieved myself. And we don't need to mime or use sign language because the couple are far enough away that we can whisper. It sounds like they are trying to christen every room of the house in an effort to satiate their libidos.

I can't even remember the last time I was kissed.

^^^^^^^^^^

^^^^^^^^^^

ALYSSA

After the high of getting into the house of one of my favourite influencers, I have crashed. The possibility of being caught was intoxicating at first, but I think that my body was so flooded with adrenaline there was only one way my mood could go. Now I feel hungry, and upset and tired. At least I'm not alone.

I text my mother to say that I am staying at Less's tonight, so that she doesn't worry. I've resigned to the fact that I won't be going home. That I will have to wait this out. As long as Rosie sticks to her daily routine, we can let ourselves out when she goes for her run tomorrow morning.

If she goes.

There's been a lot of sex today, though. I'd be surprised if Rosie could even walk by the morning. If that happens, I am going to need my own receptacle from the box of camping paraphernalia.

Luckily, Rosie's loft is as organised as the parts of her house that can be seen. Everything has been packed away in plastic storage boxes and labelled. Her winter wardrobe has even been vacuum-sealed, ready to be inflated when the colder months come around. This woman has everything under control.

Apart from the number of people who will be spending the night at her house.

There's a plastic box marked 'films'. There must be thousands of DVDs in there. They're not boxed. Each one has been unpacked and placed into a plastic sleeve so that it takes up a sixth of the space. She is the neatest hoarder on Earth.

'It's a shame she doesn't have a box labelled "steaks" because there's a gas cooker in with the sleeping bags,' Less quips.

'At least you've had a falafel.' I give him a side-eye.

'Look, we're going to be up here all night, let's just settle in.'

We lay the sleeping bags down on the floor and quietly climb inside. There's only Rosie left in the main part of the house now, so we have to be as quiet as possible again.

Rosie is coming upstairs. I can hear her footsteps.

She stops beneath the loft hatch.

My stupid mobile phone is in my pocket and vibrates with a notification against the floorboards above Rosie's head.

We hold our breath.

^^^^^^^^^

^^^^^^^^^

@RosieVelazquez
'Had the most relaxing day away from everything that has happened, recently. Reviving before fashion week.' #Friendship #TakeCareOfEachOther. #RenewedByFaith
♥ 2,134 ☐ 626

^^^^^^^^^

^^^^^^^^^

Usually, she would have posted five or six times throughout the day, that's her routine and it's important, but she has been otherwise engaged. She attaches a picture of her post-coital meal and a ginger tea she had later and a selfie of her and her man friend looking close but not necessarily like lovers.

It's not that she doesn't want the world to know that she has someone special in her life. It won't affect her following, people are generally supportive of that kind of thing. It's to protect her parents from the congregation at their church, but, mainly, it's to protect herself from her parents. The guy is covered in tattoos and people will draw the wrong conclusions from his appearance.

She types as she walks but stops when she reaches the top of her stairs to make sure there are no typos for the grammar nazis to follow up on.

She posts.

A second after, Rosie hears a noise above her head.

She freezes. And just like the two people she doesn't know are right above her, she holds her breath.

It sounded like it came from the attic. A couple of years back, she had a wasps' nest removed from up there. The things were buzzing around all night and keeping her awake. A local exterminator came and injected something into the hive. There was one more night of furious vibrations and he returned a couple of days later to remove the nest and clear up.

She wonders whether they have returned. She listens, carefully, reaching up towards the spot that she thinks she heard something, standing on her tiptoes. She thinks about that missing falafel and out-of-place sofa cushion. She loves her space, but Rosie doesn't want to live alone anymore because the noises at night scare her. It's the usual house noises, pipes and heating and settling but it's amplified when she is alone with only her imagination.

She reaches up.

Waiting for another sound.

Balancing on her tiptoes.

Her fingers are an inch from the button that will release the loft hatch.

She's close to the ceiling when she hears a gunshot.

It's not, of course. Not in this neighbourhood. But it sounds similar and it startles her back to the ground. She runs into her bedroom and looks out of the window. The old man across the street has tried to start up his old van and it must have backfired. There's a plume of black smoke coming from the exhaust pipe.

Rosie feels her heart beating so fast she can't even gulp. She watches the old man tinker about for a minute then give up, so she goes back out into the hall to listen again. There's nothing. She returns to the bedroom, drops to her knees and rests her elbows on the mattress.

And she prays, bookending her time with Adam in apologies and fear.

'Please forgive me, Lord.' She goes on to ask for absolution for taking His name in vain in the heights of ecstasy. For her lust and carnal actions outside of wedlock. And she begs for her parents to not feel any repercussions for her wrongdoing. She wants them protected.

'And I'm sorry for lying to all the people that trust me.' Rosie explains the etiquette of social-media practice to her God. She has to post something. She has to remain on brand and on message. She can't say that she's been on her back in every room of the house with a tattooed man between her legs for most of the day.

She says that she will make it up to Him.

That she's trying to save the world.

Then she puts her television on and gets into bed, turning it up loudly so that she can't hear any more scary noises in the house.

For Alyssa, listening intently from above, it would appear that without the crippling religious guilt, being an influencer is a life filled with health, pleasure and beautifully curated soft furnishings. What's not to like?

^ ^ ^ ^ ^ ^ ^ ^ ^ ^

^ ^ ^ ^ ^ ^ ^ ^ ^ ^

@FoodForThought
'Always Fighting'
♥ 4 ◻ 1,248

> **@GarfieldLeanne**
> 'Oh, my God. You're such a beg.' #unfollow
> ♥ 5k ◻ 345
>
> > **@SaraHornby35**
> > 'This is so cringe'
> > ♥ 1.1k ◻ 27

^^^^^^^^^^

^^^^^^^^^^

Left hook, right hook, knee.

Ariel Dean makes a video of herself beating the crap out of a punchbag. There hasn't been a response from @TheFitnessPaige like she expected so she has opted for a more subtle call-out of her new influencer enemy.

She writes something about letting the anger out. Hitting something hard. Releasing the poison. It's all a very obvious attempt at subtext, suggesting that she is feeling more energised over the last few days.

'It's not always what you put into your body but what you put into your mind.' ♥ **35k**

Pretentious twaddle.

Attention breeds false confidence.

The video is nothing like her others, where she has been documenting her hardships, her triumphs and her failures. It lacks heart. This is why Ariel is not in the same league as real influencers. She is reacting to how she feels, instinctively. These things take time. You have to bottle the emotion and portray it in a way that benefits you. She doesn't understand that, yet.

She came into this innocently, no matter what anybody suggests.

Her first response to the video is from a new follower that she picked up as a result of the feud. They suggest that Ariel should just kill herself.

Her die-hard fans know what she is doing and will forgive her this one indiscretion, but there is an onslaught of bad vibes. Ariel has never had this before. They're suggesting that she should put those boxing skills to the test and get in the ring with Paige.

This has happened before. Some YouTube prankster builds enough cash to release their own bottled water, which makes them a tonne more money, which inflates their ego even more, and pretty soon they're calling out an ex-professional boxer for a fight in the ring.

But Ariel isn't a real fighter. She made a stupid video and it backfired. Paige is highly trained. If ever they did meet, Paige would probably kill her.

^^^^^^^^^^

^^^^^^^^^^

LESS

I repeatedly shoot myself in the head with my gun fingers, like I'm Travis Bickle.

Is there anything worse than trying to decide what to wear in the morning?

Yes. Watching some fashion influencer walk you through her wardrobe and the possible combinations of outfit she is considering. But that is what Rosie Velazquez is doing now while Alyssa listens, completely engaged. It's obscene.

Every time Rosie calls a jacket 'cute' or a pair of socks 'cute' or the way a certain skirt and trainer combo is 'cute', I just want to cutely throw up in my mouth. But Alyssa is nodding along like she can see the outfits in question.

She's totally invested.

^^^^^^^^^^

^^^^^^^^^^

ALYSSA

If I was at home right now, I would be making my grandmother a cup of tea and telling her how to get to the quiz-show channel. Like I do every god-damned morning. My mother would either already be at the hospital, even though she just worked a night shift, or she'd be a zombie in the kitchen, fulfilling her role as the woman who has to take care of everybody even though the best way to take care of us is to take care of herself and get some sleep. I would love to be able to help more. A lot of the time, it seems like there is no way out. I'm stuck on my side of town. Not poor but just about getting by.

Meanwhile, this woman, who is only a few years older than me, has her own place, with jute rugs and Venetian floor mirrors and a dining table made from old scaffold planks. And she talks about why she can't wear a certain scarf with certain earrings and thousands of people tune in to listen to her.

It seems boring and puerile and vapid, and I want it. I don't even know why. Maybe it's because it seems easy and everything in my life has been so hard.

Then the front door closes and Less and I look at one another.

Less holds up a finger and whispers, 'Just wait. Make sure she's gone.'

Rosie has gone. She signed off her morning video saying that she was ready for her daily run, but it's best to be careful. We got through the night, we can wait a little longer.

Two minutes pass.

'Right. Let's get out of here. I don't know why you like that woman, Lyss.'

'She's inspiring. She influences people.' I tut. He doesn't get it.

'Influences me to want to set fire to her house.' He lowers the ladder carefully and quietly. I don't know why, Rosie is gone, she isn't going to hear us now. He's just being cautious.

'Don't worry about the sleeping bags,' Less instructs.

'What do you mean? We don't want her to find them.'

'It doesn't matter. She won't come up here for ages. Imagine Little Miss Tidy's face when she heads up for her box of Christmas decorations and it looks like two people have been sleeping in here.' He laughs.

'That's pretty fucking dark, even for you, Less.'

^^^^^^^^^^

^^^^^^^^^^

LESS

I bite my tongue. Alyssa was the one who got me into this. She's always encouraging me. I should feel liberated, the way a prisoner feels when he rubs his wrists after the cop takes off the handcuffs. But I don't. I'm annoyed that I had to spend an evening with that insufferable bore and her apparently insatiable sexual hunger. And that I left a flask of my own piss in her loft.

I put the ladder back up and close the hatch, noticing that there are two square indentations on the carpet where the bottom of the ladder was resting. I rub at them with my feet until they fluff up again. It's those stupid little details that will get us caught.

'I don't know how she missed those,' I say to myself.

'She was either looking lover boy in the eyes or staring at her phone screen. Whoever pays attention to the floor? Come on, let's get out of here before she gets back.'

'We've got time. I'm hungry.'

'We'll get something on the way. We can go to that café and debrief.' Alyssa tries to force a smile but she knows that I'm not biting. She doesn't want to get in trouble. These things don't end well for people like her.

'Yeah. We can do that after I eat something here.'

I make my way downstairs and Alyssa follows, trying to talk me out of it. I'm on a mission, though. I head straight into the kitchen, open the fridge and stuff the remaining falafels into my mouth. Then I take out the milk. Alyssa looks on, puzzled. I start opening cupboards until I find a bowl. I locate some cereal in another and a spoon in a drawer.

Alyssa watches intently as I lean against the worktop, feet crossed on the floor, shovelling Cheerios into my mouth, milk spilling on the tiles.

She says nothing. I'm trying to make a point and Alyssa doesn't want to give me the satisfaction of acknowledging it. But she can't help looking over my shoulder at the clock on the wall and I spot it, so I win.

'Okay. Let's get out of here.' I place the bowl on the kitchen table and start to walk out.

'Jesus, Less. The sleeping bags are one thing but she'd never leave a bowl out. Be more subtle.'

'More subtle than the box of piss I left upstairs.'

Alyssa rolls her eyes at this, she's not being as fun as usual. She washes out the bowl, dries it with a tea towel and places it back in the cupboard it came from. She wipes the milk off the floor, too.

'Okay, Lyss, you're right. You've made your point. Let's not be silly.' I haven't really thought about what is making me feel so disgruntled but it has something to do with Rosie's popularity, the popularity of anyone who refers to themselves as an *influencer.* School, college, work, it doesn't matter where I am, I've always hated popular people. Because popular people are mean.

Alyssa takes her own small win and moves towards the front door, looking out the window to make sure that nobody is there. She gestures for me to follow her closely like we're the front line of a S.W.A.T. team. I do as instructed but find time to place the spoon I held back from my friend on the worktop near the sink.

How's that for subtle?

There's nobody out on the street. These people don't want to live near other people. They don't want to associate with the riffraff. They want to keep themselves to themselves. That's what makes this so easy.

Still, there's a sense of euphoria that we got away with something again.

It's snowballing.

We are on a high all the way to the café, where we order everything we can. I'm buying, of course.

Part of the way through her French toast with butter and bacon and maple syrup, Alyssa's eyes widen like a Disney princess's.

'What? What have we done? What did you forget?' I'm worried.

Alyssa reaches down and fishes around in her pocket and then produces a key.

THE key.

The key to Rosie Velazquez's front door.

'But there were two, right? She probably won't even notice?'

'Less, we can't take that chance.'

I say nothing. I throw my black Amex card onto the table, grab the key from Alyssa's hand, and I run.

∧∧∧∧∧∧∧∧∧∧

∧∧∧∧∧∧∧∧∧∧

ALYSSA

Less takes off at full pace. I just watch him until he is out of sight. He doesn't slow down at all. He's crazy, but I have faith that he can do it. He can get the key back.

There are two sausages left on Less's plate that I drag on to my own with a fork. I find the idea of eating out to be something of an extravagance, so I can't waste food that has been bought. It wouldn't be right. I missed a meal last night and tell myself that none of these calories even count – I'm in deficit. By the time I start dipping the second sausage into maple syrup, Less is out of sight.

I ask for the bill. I rarely have to do this part, so I'm anxious when the waiter brings over the card machine to pay and I just hope that I can tap Less's credit card against it. If it doesn't work, I'll have to pay from my own account and it will wipe out my week.

It works, and I breathe a sigh of relief.

Seems I'm getting away with everything.

∧∧∧∧∧∧∧∧∧∧

∧∧∧∧∧∧∧∧∧∧

LESS

There is no way that I was going to be able to run all the way back to Rosie's house before she got home. I won't be able to replace the key that we took from beneath the mat. I won't be able to cover our tracks.

But I knew that.

When I grabbed the key out of Alyssa's hand, I knew that.

It was for effect, for the theatre.

I sit down on a wall and look at the key, twisting it between my thumb and forefinger. My breathing has already slowed considerably. I check my phone for the time. I'm going to wait here for another eight minutes, at least. That will give the illusion that I actually fought against the odds to get the key back to where it belongs. I set a countdown on my phone and kill some time by scrolling through videos. I haven't been able to charge it while in the attic overnight, but I also haven't been able to use it, so the battery is not as low as it could be.

There's enough time to watch somebody trying to cook thirty-five eggs in a cleaned-out paint tin that is hanging from a chain over a fire. Another video shows a couple pranking each other by dropping bags of flour over their partner's head in different rooms around the house. There are several videos of muscular men lifting weights and doing pull-ups on the beach; the algorithm is working. Dance troupes, lip-syncing, women fighting and pulling at each other's hair.

Scroll and scroll and scroll as intellect leaves my brain and disperses into the atmosphere.

Swipe and swipe until I don't even know what I'm looking at anymore but my finger still scrapes across the screen for the next mindless copycat showing me their latest IKEA hack.

I can't stand these influencers but I also can't stop watching them. I want to get off but I don't want to miss out. I know it's bad for me but I still do it. I'm not individual in that sense.

There's still some sort of spark in my brain that pulls me out of the death scroll, and I see that I have managed to waste eleven minutes of my time on Earth and that I can now, realistically, make my way back to Alyssa with the news that I ran as fast as I could; that I didn't check whether Rosie was back home, but I don't think that she was, and that I managed to get up the path and place the key back underneath the mat where we found it.

Alyssa hugs me gratefully at the news of my success and she gives me back my credit card.

'You're amazing, you know that?' she says to me.

'Oh, don't be silly. It was nothing.' I feel a little guilty. My right hand is in my pocket, fiddling with the key I had no intention of ever returning. My left hand waves the black plastic in the air as I suggest blowing off the afternoon and going for drinks.

I don't want to talk about Rosie Velazquez anymore. We had our fun together. It's done. 'We can celebrate our freedom while you plot our next adventure,' I say.

Tomorrow, I'm going to try something on my own.

^^^^^^^^^

^^^^^^^^^

#JoinTheMovement #EthicalLuxury #VFW25 #DoGoodLookGood

There's mail on the inside mat when Rosie gets back from her run. She's been waiting for it.

The envelope looks like it has been made from brown parcel paper but the invitation inside appears to have been handwritten by a master calligrapher on papyrus. It's supposed to have that recycled look.

It's Vegan Fashion Week. And Rosie is exactly the kind of person that the organisers want to see there. She's young and popular and stylish but she also stands for something. She believes in the ethics of fashion and design. She's an advocate for what these new-age, virtue-signalling, Green Party voters seemingly believe in.

So she won't have to pay to attend.

And she'll have a seat on the front row next to the catwalk so that she can be photographed just as much as the models.

Rosie reads through the invitation.

Make a positive impact without compromising on style.

That's what it says at the bottom.

Rosie reads it and sighs. She hates that kind of thing. It may as well say *Make a point without actually doing anything.* These people aren't getting their hands dirty. It's not front-line activism. It's a bunch of rich people who want to appear to be doing the right thing, caring about the right cause.

They don't really care about ethical style or sustainable, animal-friendly creations. They just want to be seen there. They want the chance to sit next to whichever pop star quit dairy this week or a film star who advocates meat-free Mondays.

The thing is, part of the festival is about fundraising for initiatives that support animal rights and, as the invitation says, *create a kinder world for all beings.*

Rosie reads that and looks around her entrance hall as though there are people there with her who share her despair. She hates Less-type people and he hates Rosie-type people. And the funny thing is that neither of them are the 'type' they are perceived to be.

There are going to be rappers in faux-fur jackets and stick-thin actresses in pretend-leather skirts that are really made out of mushroom protein or soya beans or something, and they'll be crying inside that it's not Dior.

Because they are not there to *help shape a more conscious future*; they just want to be seen.

And so does Rosie Velazquez.

She's earned it. She's still fresh from her fur-coat paint incident. She is real. She does care. She's not known for getting naked in films or painting with her own blood, she wants rights for every sentient being first, and her moment in the spotlight second.

But she does still want it. She never got into this to be an influencer, but that taste of fame gets to everyone. It becomes difficult to let it go.

Rosie walks into her lounge and takes a seat at her reading chair. She won't go into the kitchen and spot the rogue spoon on the counter until later, and she will assume it was Adam before he left, until she finds the food missing from her fridge. She'll ask Adam to stay over again because the whole situation is sitting uneasily with her, but she can't take any more sex because it feels like she has Tour de France level saddle soreness from yesterday.

She opens her phone screen with a look and searches her social media for any mention of Vegan Fashion Week. There are plenty of people with a blue tick next to their name that are posting about going along. They're excited, apparently.

Rosie has already confirmed that she will be attending, but looking at the number of stars who are also going, the chances of a front-row seat at the Stella McCartney show now seems unlikely.

She flicks through a hundred posts.

All of those superstars who are looking forward to seeing how they can help *change the world one dress at a time.*

All of them letting the world know that they care.

All of them telling Alyssa and Less the shows they are attending and exactly the times that they will not be inside their homes.

ΛΛΛΛΛΛΛΛΛ

ΛΛΛΛΛΛΛΛΛ

LESS

There's just a part of me that wants to fuck with Rosie Velazquez. It could be the bullied kid in me.

I'm not a vindictive guy. I could have easily gone that way based on the treatment I was subjected to at school and as a teenager, but I know how it feels to be targeted and shot at, and I wouldn't want to inflict that on anyone else.

Some of these influencers really get to me, though.

Hell, Rosie seems to mean well online. Sometimes her posts are a little preachy and others, they're sickly, but her heart is clearly in the right place. However, being locked in her attic while she got screwed in every corner of her country-chic show home was the last straw. I feel off balance.

Things aren't even.

Until now.

I watched Rosie leave and run into the distance. Then I let myself into her home. Again.

In the cloakroom area, I take the red raincoat on the left and swap it with the denim jacket on the right. I take the books from the shelf and place them in order of the colour of their spine rather than being alphabetised – I do the same with the stack on the floor. Then I push the sofa twelve inches to the right.

It's nothing. Just little things.

In the kitchen, I put the dishwasher on a cycle even though it was only half filled. I swap everything from the cereal cupboard with everything in the small crockery cupboard. It's all still stacked perfectly, it has just changed position.

I pour all the liquids from the fridge down the sink and place the empty containers back. It's crazy how all the ideas just come to me.

I make a cup of coffee and leave it on the table.

It's all more explicit than leaving my spoon by the sink. Rosie could have justified that, written it off. A moment of forgetfulness. Maybe it was her tattooed lover, he's probably not quite as tidy as she is.

But these changes are not as subtle.

She will know that somebody has been in her house while she was away.

Nothing is stolen, I'm not a criminal. There's no damage to the property – it doesn't even look like anyone has broken in but little things can set a person off kilter. There's a lack of harmony. Rosie will know something is off. There will be an energy. She'll find what it is. And explain it away. At first.

Then there will be something else.

And she will know it wasn't her.

And she will get frightened. Because she'll know a stranger has been in her home.

But I'm not really thinking of that at the moment. I'm just dicking around. Having some kind of fun. Doing something different. Just because I can.

Maybe I'm acting out.

I'm going to feel utterly shit about all this, afterwards. I'm lashing out at the wrong person.

^^^^^^^^^^

^^^^^^^^^^

#UninvitedGuest #HiddenInPlainSight #LivingInYourWalls #SomeoneIsThere

Rosie Velazquez does a double-take when she gets back from her run. She unties the long-sleeved shirt from around her waist and goes to put it on the arm of the sofa but the sofa isn't where it's supposed to be. It's moved. She almost laughs, it's so ridiculous.

Something in her mind tells her that the coats weren't hanging correctly in the hallway.

Then she sees the books and thinks – for a split second – 'They look nice like that.'

Then she freaks out.

She's scared.

Somebody has been in her house.

In a horror movie, she would then creep around her own home, discovering other misdemeanours, hoping nobody jumps out of a wardrobe. But Rosie just runs. She bolts back the way she came and when she gets to the bottom of her garden, she immediately calls Adam.

'Hey, you,' he says, sweetly.

'Have you been at my house?' she asks.

'What?'

'Have you been at my house today? While I was out for a run.'

'I've been at the gym for the last two hours.'

'Oh, God. Oh, God. Someone's been here. Shit, they could still be here.'

'Why the hell are you phoning *me*? Call the god-damned police, Rosie. I'm coming now.'

^^^^^^^^^^

^^^^^^^^^^

Jack Sandford
@TheJackSandford
'Rockin' and a rollin' and whatnot. New Album, BEDROOM CHAOS, August 25th.'
1 Following **81M** Followers

^^^^^^^^^^

^^^^^^^^^^

Jack Sandford is beautiful.

The lead singer of Troubadour, whose last five songs have hit the number-one spot almost instantly, he appeals to younger girls with his boyish good looks and a set of cheekbones that could cut granite, but he also has something of the rugged cowboy about him, which reaches out to an older demographic.

He has stubble that looks as though it is unkempt but has clearly been styled to look that way. His hair is long and sometimes hangs over his face while he plays the guitar but it's usually spilling out of the sides of some kind of hat.

Jack loves a Stetson, of course. But he has been seen in a flat cap, a baseball cap and a beanie during the colder months. He was pictured in the summer, coming out of a restaurant in a pair of long denim shorts with a T-shirt that showed the Ghostbusters logo, a flannel shirt tied around his waist, Jesus sandals and a trilby. On anyone else, it would have looked ridiculous, but on Jack Sandford, with his tattoo sleeve and his ultra-white teeth, it was a fashion statement.

Trilby sales went through the roof over that next week as men tried to copy and women tried to liven up their partners' wardrobes.

And he's not an asshole. There are no ex-girlfriends coming out with horror stories. No list of artist demands – he doesn't want body-temperature bottled water wherever he goes. He's not asking for a bowl of cocaine to be delivered to his hotel room. He doesn't have to dry his washed hands on Labrador puppies. In fact, he loves animals.

He's a vegan. And like so many vegans, he likes to talk about it. But unlike so many other celebrities, he has not jumped on this because it's a buzzword or hashtag. He doesn't care about trending.

He just cares.

Three minutes ago, Jack Sandford posted a picture of a pair of shoes resting on the bottom of his bed. Po-Zu shoes, of course. Creators of ethical and sustainable footwear. They think about their impact on the environment and they consider all workers along the supply chain. And now they have a poster boy for their products.

The image of the shoes was to push the brand, but he was also calling out to his legions of fans to help him decide what he should wear on his head when he goes to the opening of Vegan Fashion Week.

The post has already received over five hundred comments and more than fifteen thousand likes. One of those likes was Less.

For Less, it's more like love.

He adores Jack Sandford. Partly because of the cheekbones but mostly because of his no-nonsense, anything-goes fashion sensibilities and their mutual appreciation of millinery. On countless situations, Less has drifted off to the idea that Jack Sandford would wear one of his designs.

And now he has the opportunity.

Less has been following Jack for years. He feels as though he knows him. He was there when Jack cut his hair. When his dog died. When he toured Japan. When he lost a bracelet his mother had given him and somebody found it on the street. So, Less knows that Jack lives alone and that he never replaced the dog he lost and that he loves vegan sushi.

And he knows that Jack will almost definitely go for the trucker hat with those shoes in the picture and, most importantly, that he won't be at his house on opening night because he will be attending some catwalk show where every stitch of fabric has been sourced in the most ethical and humane way imaginable.

And, while Jack is there watching a parade of hemp skirts and jute bags, Less and Alyssa will be eating popcorn in Jack's living room with the giant screen blaring an episode of the latest Lincoln/Lowell production, *How Hot Is Your Gran?*

^^^^^^^^^^

^^^^^^^^^^

TMZ

HELTER SKELTER.

MANSON-STYLE HOME INVASION.

DO YOU KNOW WHO IS IN YOUR HOUSE?

^^^^^^^^^^

^^^^^^^^^^

They liken Alyssa and Less to members of the Manson Family.

Clickbaiting tabloids.

The police arrive at Rosie's home to find her standing in her front garden, afraid to go back inside. Adam is still a few minutes away.

'Ma'am, have you seen somebody inside?'

'No. I don't know. Somebody has been in there, I know that for sure. I don't think they're in there now but my boyfriend told me not to go back in. He's worried.'

'Okay. Well, we are here now. You're safe. We need to check inside. My partner is going to check the ground level first while you wait here with me.'

He asks whether there are any pets that he should know about, whether there is a basement or an attic room. The other police officer goes inside and clears each room, one by one, before confirming that the place is empty and they all go inside.

There is no sign of a break-in. No smashed windows. The doorframe is intact. The locking mechanism hasn't been scratched. There's also no sign of any of the rooms being ransacked. In fact, they look immaculate.

She is taken around the rooms to see if anything is missing.

'Whoever was here, they haven't stolen anything. I don't think that's what they came for. They want to fuck with me.' Then she has to explain who she is and what she does and how her activism can be divisive. How she does receive threats. 'This feels like some kind of mental torture. They rearranged my bookshelves. What the fuck is that all about?'

Adam arrives and knocks on the door. 'Rosie, it's me. It's Adam. Open up.' He keeps rapping against the window. A police officer appears from the direction of the lounge and opens the door.

The police have been questioning Rosie Velazquez about the apparent break-in. They want to take her seriously. She is a young woman who lives on her own. She's scared. It's not *nothing* but they are having difficulty in pinning down what is a crime and what could be forgetfulness.

But Adam confirms it. The sofa being out of position. The books.

The change-around in the kitchen. The officers record statements from both of them and garner a few leads on certain individuals that may have an issue with the way that Rosie conducts herself.

'Make sure you're locked up tonight. We'll look into some of the leads. Meanwhile, I'll make sure a car goes past here throughout the night just in case there is anybody lingering around.'

It makes Rosie feel better. Adam says he is going to stay with her overnight. She rubs his arm and gives him a smile. Then they lock up. Front door, back door and every window.

'Adam, the sofa is too heavy for me, can you pull it back so it's in the right place, please?'

Adam does as he is asked.

Rosie starts taking the books off the shelves. Then she says, 'No. Wait. I want to put something out there.'

'Rosie, come on, do you really think that's a good idea? We don't want to rile anybody up?'

'I need to show that they haven't got to me, that I'm not scared.'

'You're not scared?'

'I'm fucking terrified.'

'I don't know, babe. I don't feel like I can watch this, it's making me feel a bit weird.'

Rosie is understanding. Adam isn't quite at the same level as her when it comes to their influence. She is a full-time content creator. She asks him to go up and get her box of bags because there's one she can't find and will want to take with her to the fashion show. He obliges, of course. It gives him something to do. Anything to get out of that room. Rosie sets up her phone and hits record.

She tells her horde of followers that somebody broke into her house and moved her things around. She says that the police are now involved and that it is unacceptable to do this to somebody who is standing up for animal rights because she believes that all living, sentient beings should be afforded the same opportunity to not have their skin turned into a coat for some coke-snorting Amazonian model.

And while she films her outrage, Adam is performing his duty as the doting boyfriend of fashion influencer and activist Rosie Velazquez by unhooking the catch on the loft hatch and extending the ladder so that he can go up and find a box of vintage accessories that are saved for special occasions.

He doesn't get to the box because he sees the two sleeping bags and the piss-filled flask. Somebody has been staying up there. In the house. Probably while he was there. And it dawns on him that they would have been listening. He feels sick.

Adam doesn't want to disturb anything, so he goes back downstairs where Rosie has just finished her video and uploaded it to her social-media platforms.

'I think we need to get the police back. There's ... there's something up there that they need to see.'

The police return and are now more willing to understand what has happened. It's clear that two people have been staying there without anybody knowing. But, by this time, Rosie's post has taken hold and there are reporters outside wanting a statement or reaction. And TMZ irresponsibly run a story comparing Alyssa and Less's stupid prank to a cult family responsible for some of the most brutal murders in American folklore.

^^^^^^^^^

^^^^^^^^^

ALYSSA

'The fucking Mansons.' I call Less and I lose my shit.

'Come on, Lyss. You know those guys sensationalise everything. So I moved a couple of books. Big deal. I didn't stab some pregnant Hollywood actress.' He feels the need to stand his ground even though I know he regrets what he did.

'That's not the point and you know it.'

I don't really care that he pushed Rosie Velazquez's sofa to the side by twelve inches. I think it's kind of funny that he switched around the contents of her kitchen cupboards. I'm just pissed off that he went behind my back. That he lied to me about putting the key back. But, most of all, I'm annoyed that he did it without me. I'm in my dismal fucking life and he's out having fun for free.

I don't mention that part, though. I don't want to come across like some spoiled psychopath. I know that we could be doing something different with our time. We could join a club, or something.

But I like our club of two.

And we don't keep secrets. That's our thing.

'I don't even know why you did it,' I tell him. And the truth is, I bet Less doesn't even really know. Maybe it was a power trip for him. Maybe he was really annoyed with Rosie because we had to sleep in her loft and he had to piss in a tin. Or he likened her to those popular kids who bullied him at school. Maybe it was immaturity or that thing wealthy people have where they think they can do or say whatever they like and get away with it. Maybe he is annoyed at his dad.

Maybe all of those things.

Whatever it was, Less can't explain it to me. But he apologises. And he means it. And I know that.

'The fucking Mansons. I mean, come on, Less.'

We both laugh.

'Well, I guess it was kinda fun while it lasted,' I say. 'We got to go to a Davis Davis party, too.'

'What are you talking about?'

'What do you mean? We can't do it again with TMZ telling the world that we are serial killers, for Christ's sake.' I'm not rich. My family doesn't have a lawyer. I can't just walk around with reckless abandon.

'Alyssa, they don't know who we are. We didn't break in. We didn't wreck anything. We didn't steal anything.'

'You left your piss in the loft. Surely the police can identify you from that with DNA or something.'

'That's not how it works. I don't have a record. What are they comparing it against?'

There's a moment of silence on the phone while I consider this. He's talking like he's still on board with doing this.

Then Less hits me with his idea to go to Jack Sandford's house while he is at the Vegan Fashion Week opening. 'Just to check it out,' he says.

Without even skipping a beat, I tell my best friend in the entire world, 'I'll find out where he lives.'

^^^^^^^^^

^^^^^^^^^

ANFERNEE WASHINGTON
@RealAnfernee
'The guy from that movie. Oscar winner.'
44 Following **1.9M** Followers
'Almost every piece of plastic that ever existed, still exists. Sure, some is incinerated. There are certain types of plastic like polylactic acid that are designed to degrade quickly in sunlight or a composting environment, but if William Shakespeare had washed down his lunch with a bottle of Pepsi, that bottle would still be here now. Crazy.'
♥ 71k ☐ 2.2k

^^^^^^^^^

^^^^^^^^^

Plastic has got nothing on the internet.

Everything you think and then type and upload is out there for the world to see, forever.

Forever.

It's something we don't really think about. If you're a comedian who once made a joke about race or religion or gender, you'd better believe that it's coming back to bite you on the ass when you least want it. You are going to have to issue a full and public apology otherwise you're not going to get to host the Oscars.

For a joke you made.

A joke.

When your job is to make jokes.

Hell, you could be the president of the United States and, instead of focussing on the economy or policy or the opiate epidemic ravaging our country, you are on social media whining like a baby about 'fake news'. And that post you wrote a few years back about *all* Muslims having a propensity towards extremism is going to rear its ugly head when you praise Muhammad Ali as the greatest heavyweight boxer of all time – even though you deleted it. Because a thousand other people took a screenshot so that it would be remembered.

Forever.

Your kid filmed you while you were drunk and eating a hamburger off the floor? It's there forever.

The sex tape that you 'desperately' tried to get banned, even though you hoped it would spread to give you some much-needed relevance? It's been digitised and shared around the world. It will last longer than the plastic bag your grandmother got at the supermarket that has been sitting in landfill since the sixties.

^^^^^^^^^

^^^^^^^^^

ALYSSA

I do one quick search on the internet and find that the most famous musician on the planet has eight multi-million-dollar homes across the country. There's a West Village apartment in New York, a Tribeca penthouse, a neighbouring townhouse, an estate in Beverly Hills, another penthouse in Nashville. There are pictures of these places on the *Elle* Decor page. That didn't take me long to find, either.

Great. I know Jack Sandford will be in LA for the opening of Vegan Fashion Week, so he has to be staying at the estate in the Hills. The *Elle* website says that it was built in the 1930s and was once owned by a movie mogul from the old studio system.

I Google the mogul's name, plus the year the house was built, and the word 'home'. Another real-estate website is suggested that has fifteen different pictures of the house. It tells me how much was paid for it and that it was once owned by the movie studio exec, and that it is now in the ownership of Jack Sandford.

Further down the article, it tells me the name of the architect who is now restoring it to its former beauty. So, I find that architect online. Her website has a list of current commercial and residential projects. There's a 6,000ft complete interior renovation and remodel to former Georgian beauty. It tells me that the project is on Foothill Road, Beverly Hills.

Next, I type that in on my Maps app.

It's a long road but I notice that there's an historical landmark nearby. The former home of Milton Berle. I take a chance and type in 'former home' with the name of the movie mogul I looked up a few moments ago. Nothing comes up but a theatre nearby named after him – he was a big deal. It's okay. I'm not going to get it right first time, every time.

Back to the map.

Luckily, the first website has an aerial shot of the estate, so I know the scope and shape. It's a giant L with a pool and tennis court. I turn on satellite view so that I can see the actual houses along that road. Zoom out and scan along the road. Look for the L. Locate the green roof. Once I find it, I click on the roof. I'm presented with a Street View image of the house from the road. It matches up with the exterior shot from the initial article. I note the number of the place. Call Less back and tell him that I know exactly where Jack Sandford lives.

^^^^^^^^^^

^^^^^^^^^^

#StrengthInSisterhood #FierceAndFit #FearlesslyAuthentic
@TheFitnessPaige realises that she hasn't responded to Ariel Dean. Because she can, she hides behind her profile and performs something that has affectionally been coined as the *subtweet*. She responds directly and obviously about their apparent 'beef' without actually mentioning Ariel, but everybody knows exactly who she is talking about.

It's the classical cowardice that was once reserved for drivers with road rage who felt protected by the vehicle they were driving. Now people can bitch at or about anyone from the comfort of their own homes and, technically, it doesn't even need to be the real them that is doing the bitching.

Paige's video is blatant and immature.

Short but sweet.

Pithy yet degenerate.

She finishes her workout. A real workout. For her. Not for anybody else. She wanted to sweat. She wanted to move. She wanted to get something going in her body and her mind. She kicked and punched her way to an endorphin-filled high and then took to her social media to perform an abortion-skilled low.

'Just put all my martial arts training to use for a body-blitzing workout. I'd love to be able to replenish my energy with food but I'm not sure that's enough, so I've asked one of my male friends over and I'm going straight to the source.' Then she licks her lips and laughs.

The truth is, Paige doesn't have any male friends that she could call on even if she was offering a blow job. She puts so much into her own profile, into creating content and serving her audience that there is only really time for herself.

A million followers and nobody to be close to. She's so lost. This job has taken who she was.

Paige posts the stupid video. She doesn't really want an online feud but there is still something intoxicating about the notification of a new fan. And this will drum up a few more who are there for more than a chickpea-curry recipe and squat technique.

She sits on the sofa and scrolls through her contacts to see who she has to talk to, who she is close to. There are some friends. Acquaintances. Nobody she could get deep with.

It's depressing. She would get upset about it if she wasn't so tired.

It makes her want to eat junk. She's not allowed, though. She has to be aspirational. Her life is no longer her own. It belongs to everyone else. Paige thinks about calling her mother. She scrolls down to her contact details on the phone and feels so pathetic that she cries.

That's when her phone starts to ring.

It's Satmohan.

In an effort to compose herself, Paige sits up straight on the edge of the sofa and takes a deep breath. She wipes the corners of her eyes and answers the call.

'Hello?'

'Hi Paige, it's Satmohan. I hope I haven't caught you at a bad time...'

'No, no. It's fine. Just finished a workout.'

'Of course you have.' She thinks she can hear him smile. 'I just wanted to let you know that we want to run a test on the cameras to see if we can get them running remotely.'

'Um, yeah. Of course. Whatever you need.'

'Great. Thanks. We're going to turn them on now for a few seconds to make sure they are online. It's just so that we can download footage straight to our servers rather than bother you all the time by removing them and setting them up again,' he lies.

'Sure. That makes sense.'

'Thanks, Paige. One second.' Satmohan holds a hand over his phone for around twenty seconds then returns. 'Great. They're all working how they should. We just need to get one more above your front door and then install some very discreet microphones. Oh, and the diary-room cam. Are you around tomorrow?'

'Let me just check my diary.' She holds her hand over her own phone for a similar amount of time then tells Satmohan that she is out for lunch for a couple of hours but in for the morning if he can arrange for then.

'Perfect. I'll drop you an email once the engineer confirms a time slot.'

Paige goes to say goodbye but Satmohan has already hung up. He's watching her with Edie Lincoln. They saw her work out. They saw her make her post. They watched the post light up before they went back to her almost breaking down.

'Are you sure she's going to be strong enough for this?' Satmohan asks, concerned for the show rather than Paige's wellbeing. 'She could break.'

'She's going to be absolutely fine. Didn't you know ... Paige is *perfect*?'

^^^^^^^^^^

^^^^^^^^^^

@BlueJulie65
'That sounds so scary. Keep God in your heart.'
♥ 48 ☐ 12
@LAAlanG
'You threw a tin of paint over a stranger. Doesn't feel so good to be attacked, does it?'
♥ 11k ☐ 143
@Petey247653804
'Good to know how easy it is to get into your house.'
♥ 453 ☐ 71

^^^^^^^^^^

^^^^^^^^^^

The story catches hold of people's imaginations.

Because there was no real crime. Nobody had broken in. Nothing had been taken. Nobody was physically hurt.

Of course, there was an unlawful act: two people had clearly stayed at Rosie's place and fucked around with her stuff. But it's not like the house was set on fire or there were blood-spattered walls or a body was found stuffed into a flower bed.

Somehow, it's worse.

It's creepier.

It's all in the head of the viewer or the reader. They can create the story and the motive.

There's an outpouring of sympathy for Rosie, of course. Strangers telling her that this is an outrage, that people should be able to feel safe in their own homes. They are trying to empathise, though it's impossible to do so. How could they possibly understand? How many people has this happened to? How many don't even realise that it's happened? How many are wondering whether somebody is in their house right now?

She also receives her fair share of trolling. It's part of the job. You have to expect it. If you make the effort to climb up that social ladder, there are going to be plenty of people who want to rock you or knock you off completely.

Some seem to set up brand-new fake accounts whose sole purpose is to threaten and torment. No picture. No followers. Such effort to be needlessly mean.

Often, Rosie will post an outfit or design hack and she'll receive hundreds of comments and shares. She'll also get other influencers and celebrities to message her. This is an everyday occurrence, almost.

But nobody famous has commented on this. They can't understand it. Because Rosie is not famous enough. There's a hierarchy, a certain level of celebrity that feels like they are above such things.

They're too well known for somebody to break into *their* house.

They're too big to be worried.

But there's always somebody bigger.
Their arrogance is their weakness.
And it won't be long before they have to sit up and listen.
Everybody will.

^^^^^^^^^

^^^^^^^^^

#HelterSkelter #MansonFamily #AfterTheAttack #ActsOfHate

Adam checks the windows twice.

'I know I'm being crazy,' Rosie says.

'Babe, you're not. It's fucking weird and it's scary. I'll check these windows and doors as many times as you need.'

Rosie squeezes his arm. She feels protected. And he wants to protect her. He loves her. It's a real moment. When the events of the day have been so surreal, so alien, this is what Rosie needed most. Something genuine. An authentic relationship.

'Just check the back door. Double-lock the front. We'll take some ice-cream up to bed.'

She's almost obsessively tidy and organised. This is out of character.

'I'm sorry. What have you done with my girlfriend?'

'Oh, ha ha.' She slaps his arm playfully. 'I don't know, I just think I'll feel safer up there in bed. And I want to eat ice-cream. It's been a shitty couple of days.'

'Fresh out of the big house and now this. I hear ya.' He smiles at his own joke.

It's good that they can be like this.

Because Rosie can't stop thinking about what has happened. To her, it feels like the two people that were inside her house are still there. Watching from somewhere. Laughing. Tormenting. She wants to be in her room, with her man, with the lights on. It's stupid. She knows that. But the darkness will just put her into her own head, and that's where all the bad things happen.

This is the thing with terror. It lingers.

It remains.

It's like grief. It can hit a person from nowhere, for no real reason, because it's lurking beneath the surface.

It eats away at Rosie and makes her paranoid. And that's the intention. That is not what Alyssa and Less had in mind but they hadn't really thought about it enough. They only cared about what they wanted, how they were feeling, right there and then. In that moment. They, like most people, are the centre of their universe.

They've had their fun, and now Rosie's world is crumbling.

She eats almost the entire tub of ice-cream. Adam is on a strict diet, counting his macronutrients in order to maintain his shredded physique. That's his product, after all. He only has a few spoonfuls so that Rosie doesn't feel awful about devouring all of it.

He goes to the toilet and she worries about being on her own. He flushes and the sound of the pipes is louder than ever before. She notices every floorboard creak and every scratch in the walls. She imagines some noises, too.

Nobody is there but it feels like they are. She doesn't know whether that will ever go away.

'Just hold me,' she tells Adam when he gets back to bed. He obliges. But it's not enough. Rosie feels enveloped in his strong arms but he can't hug her mind.

'I've got you, babe,' he reassures her.

Rosie thinks about the sleeping bags.

Rosie rearranges her books in her head.

Rosie imagines loading the dishwasher.

'I know you do but, right now...' she reaches under the covers, moving her hand between Adam's legs, '...I need you to make me forget.'

^^^^^^^^^^

^^^^^^^^^^

#SunSalutations #BreatheAndShine #FlowWithGrace #StretchYourSpirit

Another lonely day.

Paige wakes up in her king-size bed for one. White sheet. White covers. Pale-grey walls with muted tones all around. Storage baskets and rope knot ornaments. It would be almost nautical if it had any personality. But it's like Paige herself, a blank canvas. Still trying to find out what it is.

She puts all the right nutrients into her body. All of her products, her face creams, her toners, her make-up, are organic and expensive and the best things that you can put on your skin. Because she knows that the things you put into your body come out through the skin and the things you put on your skin go into your body. She's pure.

And fit.

And healthy.

And miserable.

This is how her days begin. Nobody ever sees this because there is rarely anybody else in that room at the start of the day to witness the sadness of @TheFitnessPaige. And there were no cameras set up in the bedroom; it's one of the few truths told by the Lincoln/Lowell production team.

Paige sits up, grabs the laptop next to her bed and opens it. She needs to do her *good morning* post. Sometimes she'll add a picture of herself after 'just waking up' but she can't be bothered to cultivate that look right now, it takes too long.

She types something about yoga and chai tea and hashtags SunSalutations and a few other yogic buzzwords. Then she checks her emails. There is something from Satmohan saying that the engineer will be over at 10:30 and asks whether she would like him to be there, too, or whether she feels okay being alone.

Are you okay being alone?

She stares at those words for a while and ponders the question. Paige is so used to being by herself now, she hadn't even realised that was what her life had become. It's not even that she is craving a boyfriend or husband or BFF to gossip with over an Aperol Spritz, she just wants a connection that is true. She spends so much time portraying perfection, and being perfect isn't real.

After a while, Paige responds to Satmohan, telling him that she is perfectly fine to be alone, there is no need for him to be present while the microphones are set up. He seemed pleasant enough when he came over before but everything is fake in Hollywood, she wasn't buying his schtick and she certainly doesn't believe his concern.

There are still a couple of hours until the engineer arrives.

Paige is not going to do yoga like she said.

That was a lie, though she tends to think of it as social-media fiction.

And she's so sick of chai tea and matcha tea and turmeric tea. She'd be happier with a large black coffee and the newspaper. She's never even read the newspaper, she gets all her news from TMZ or the *HuffPost*. Maybe she needs to opt for the simpler life, for how people lived before technology advanced faster than anybody could keep up with.

When did it all change?

She never asked for this.

Could she just give it back?

With her phone above her face, Paige lies down and searches for a retreat where she can't be on her phone and the yoga isn't there to strengthen her core, it's to relax her. It's not for her to focus on her breathing, it's just a time to allow her to breathe. Maybe she could even read a book; she can't remember the last time she did that. She needs it. She feels like she's going to break.

Paige knows that she could message one of these places and say who she is and they would probably let her come for nothing and give her all of the best treatments. Massages, facials, mud baths. But they would be watching her all the time, making sure she was making the right expressions with her face to suggest that she would portray them favourably on her various platforms.

It's not what she wants. She wants to disappear.

Weirdly, she wants to be alone.

She's happy to book a place under her real name and pay for it and just be like everybody else at the spa.

Paige loses the next hour doom-scrolling through various versions of Paradise. It might be the best thing before this TV show starts filming, to get away for a few days. Or a week. To be in a different environment.

And if she announces to her followers that she is shutting down for the weekend, taking some time to recharge, Alyssa and Less will have their next victim.

^^^^^^^^^^

^^^^^^^^^^

@TheJackSandford *Image of a pyramid made from beer cans*
#VeganFashionWeek #PreDrinks @Heineken @ESPN
♥ 87k 🗨 765

^^^^^^^^^^

^^^^^^^^^^

Nobody wants to get to a party first, it looks desperate. Jack Sandford doesn't care about that because his party starts long before the opening of fashion week. Pre-drinks. It's all the rage with this generation. He has five of his friends over. Only one member of the band – the drummer – because the other two don't care about fashion and they really don't care about not eating animals or turning them into belts and shoes. The drummer doesn't care about any of that, either, but he does love a good showbiz party.

Downstairs at Jack's LA home is entirely open plan. The coffee table in the lounge area is as big as a bed. It's already covered in beer cans. There's a small, mirrored box filled with cocaine for anybody who wants it, but they're mostly smoking some weed and shooting some pool while a basketball game plays on the television.

One of the other three guys is Jack's best friend from school. They're still close. He does something boring with computers but helped Jack set up his home-recording studio because he's a bit of a tech whizz. The others are stragglers. Hangers-on, who seem to find their way to these bands and end up hanging around with them. They're the kind of people who make you feel important and disappear at the faintest sign of an issue. Jack doesn't care about them like he does his actual friend but he also enjoys the idea of having an entourage. So they all get something out of the relationship.

A couple of the entourage have taken some pictures of Jack playing pool and drinking. They know to not get any drug paraphernalia in the shots. Jack takes a photo of his own of a tower of beer cans on the coffee table.

He tags Heineken for the beers and ESPN for the sports on the TV in the background.

'Hey, Jack,' says Entourage Guy Number One. 'What time are we heading out? We hitting a bar or two first?'

'It doesn't start for another three hours. Play here for another hour, do some blow before we hit the strip. Grab some champagne and maybe talk to some girls before we head to the show. You three can keep the bar warm while we go watch the show.' He points at the drummer and his best friend, Ike.

'Sounds like a plan. Hey, Ike, you're up next once I've beaten this sack of shit.' Entourage Guy Number One laughs and the others join his laughter.

Ike gives him a thumbs-up, downs the rest of his drink, shakes an empty can as if saying, *I'll just grab myself some more beer* and he wanders back towards the lounge area.

'Fucking guys are parasites, am I right?' the drummer asks Ike.

'What?'

'This lot. I don't know where they came from. I don't know what they do. And I don't know why our man Jack keeps them hanging around, paying for their lifestyle. You know? He should be making music.'

There is a melancholy to his tone. He's an under-appreciated member of the band but he loves what he does and he doesn't want it to disappear because Jack is too nice to tell these wannabes to take a hike. He knows that Ike will understand.

Ike nods.

'He's always been like this. Confident and outgoing. Picking up the strays. He thinks he's looking after them.' Ike picks out another can of beer. 'You want one?'

'I think I'm gonna need it tonight. A fashion show isn't that rock 'n' roll, is it.' He laughs.

'I'll drink to that.'

They tap their cans together then each take a huge swig.

'Looks a bit conspiratorial over here.' Jack wraps his arms around his friends. 'You guys don't have to wait for me for the coke. But now I'm here...' He kneels on the floor next to the coffee table and opens up his mirrored box. He takes the small spoon hanging from his necklace, scoops a tiny amount of powder and sniffs it up his right nostril. 'It's important to stretch before you exercise, am I right?' He smiles, wide-eyed and youthful. Then he proceeds to divide a larger portion into three lines on the glass tabletop to share with his friends.

They willingly oblige.

'Right, Ike, you're up,' one of the entourage calls across the room.

'Okay, person who knows my name, you're going down.'

They play. Ike has more energy than skill. All six of them carry on in the same spirit for the next hour. It's fuelled by various substances, all paid for by Jack Sandford. And he's fine to do so. Because he has the money. It's not Davis Davis levels of money but it's a lot. It's global sensation, rock-star wealth. All his money came from music, but he has shrewdly invested over a hundred million in real estate.

Jack Sandford is not an idiot. He drinks, he screws around, he parties. But he doesn't get caught up with the tabloids. He doesn't read TMZ. He hates gossip.

But he is megastar rich.

So when that car arrives to pick them all up and take them across town to continue the party, they all leave and he doesn't even lock his door. Because someone might want to go home earlier than him and that way they can get in.

It's usually Ike.

He doesn't have the stamina. Having a kid took that away from him.

But he's up for it tonight. The cruising beforehand, the models wearing hessian dresses at the show, the after party. He's game. He's looking to get lucky. It's the other guys. The three stragglers. The begs. The fake entourage. The leeches. They don't have passes for the show. They could have bought them but they didn't.

They're not into it.

They would rather go back to Jack's place and wait. Shoot some pool, take his drugs, eat his food, watch the game on his giant screen.

It's always been the plan.

Leave the creatives at the artsy party.

Go back early to an empty, unlocked house.

No drama.

^^^^^^^^^^

^^^^^^^^^^

ALYSSA

Less and I are waiting in a bar near to Jack Sandford's house – getting in some of that Dutch courage – and refreshing Jack's social-media feed every few seconds, even though we have our notifications turned on.

'You know, Jack was a huge fan of Queen? Even as a kid. He had two cats. One was called Freddie and the other was called Brian May.'

I almost spit out my drink. 'What? He didn't just call the thing Brian?'

'No. He gave it a surname.'

'But the other one wasn't Freddie Mercury?'

'Nope. I guess everyone knows Freddie.'

'That is fucked up. It can't be true. How do you even know that?' Less is so funny, he's cracking me up.

^^^^^^^^^^

^^^^^^^^^^

LESS

I know everything about Jack Sandford. I've got a huge crush on the guy. I know where Jack went to school, what age he was when he first showed an aptitude for singing. Parents. Pets. Friends. I could have been a consultant on the Sandford biography. A human fact-checker. I know when Jack lost his virginity, and I don't mind saying that I feel weirdly jealous about it.

'This cocktail tastes like prison ass,' I share.

Alyssa seems particularly buoyant today. 'Yet, still, you've had two.' She laughs again. I think she's excited.

I'm hungry. I have the metabolism of a hummingbird. It keeps me slim. But I don't want to buy food in this dive bar. I want to eat something when we get to the Sandford mansion.

We wait.

'The food here is awful. And such small portions.' I wink, assuming Alyssa will get the reference. Even if she doesn't, she seems to be laughing at everything I say today.

Our phones buzz at the same time and it's like a Wild West quick-draw competition to see who can read it first.

Neither of us speaks.

^^^^^^^^^

^^^^^^^^^

@TheJackSandford
'There's definitely time for a few drinks at @TrulyLABar or @TheGraysonLA before hitting the red carpet of #VeganFashionShow am I right?'
♥ 19k 🗨 76

^^^^^^^^^

^^^^^^^^^

ALYSSA

Our lips move as we read.

'He's gone,' I say, first. 'Let's go.'

'Wait. I want to finish my drink.'

'You're kidding me.'

'We paid for these.'

'You paid for these.'

'Exactly. We have time. This is an all-night gig. Let's not rush, in case he goes back because he's forgotten something. He's quite forgetful, you know?'

'Oh, is he?' I fake roll my eyes and sip my drink through a straw.

'He is. And generous and charming and...'

'Get a room.'

'I wish.'

We knock back our drinks. It's the best way. Just get it over with. If the ice melts, it's worse. Feels like there's more to get through. Then we leave. It's a six-minute walk. A six-minute, nerve-shredding walk for Less, anxious but adrenaline-fuelled for me. I don't have the same emotional or sexual interest in Jack Sandford. I'm just here for the high. Maybe this is how Less felt at Rosie's place.

We're both trying not to get too excited, telling one another how we might not even be able to get in. The door could be locked with no key under the mat. All the windows closed. Cameras everywhere. Lasers. Guards.

It's quiet. The whole street is. Every house is different. Each one worth millions. They have to be. The place is ripe for the taking if you are of a criminal disposition. But that's what makes it so intimidating.

I feel like I stand out a little because my skin is not as white as Less's. And he walks like he belongs. Because he does. None of these houses are impressing him. They look like his house. Hell, a lot of these places have a separate garage that is bigger than the place I live.

^^^^^^^^^

^^^^^^^^^

LESS

There is a tall bush that hides the front of the house from the road. The driveway is empty because the cars are parked on a lower level. They're not supercars, Jack isn't into that kind of thing. He doesn't need a penis extension. He'd happily drop a small fortune on Jimmy Page's guitar but he prefers his vehicles to be practical.

'What is going on with these people? We just walked up the driveway. Why doesn't he have a gate?' Alyssa is incredulous.

'Lyss, nobody comes down this road that can't afford to live here. He's not worried.' This is my world. I understand it. I actually feel confident. So, just like we did at Davis Davis's house, I grip the handle on the front door and squeeze. I don't even take a breath.

Jack Sandford said that he put it out into the universe that he would become a rock star, he would be one of the greatest frontmen of all time. And the universe delivered.

Because he believed it.

He willed it to happen.

I remember reading that interview, so that's what I do. I will that door to be unlocked.

Click.

And we're in.

^^^^^^^^^^

^^^^^^^^^^

#Entourage #GroupieVibes #RollingWithTheStars #VIPByAssociation

There's no need to ask the universe for women, not with Jack around.

'He's a fucking magnet,' Entourage Guy Number Two smiles. 'He can't handle all of them, though.'

And the hangers-on will pick up the hangers-on.

Everything is free.

Some girl strokes Jack's arm in a bar and says that he is beautiful and he ignores it. Another mentions that he is talented and his ears prick up a little. It's not enough. If they can pick out a line in a song that resonated with them for some reason or a performance that moved them to tears then they're halfway to getting his attention.

He is charismatic as hell. He has to be, as the front man. It's not something that's quantifiable. It's more than just good looks. Good looks alone is not approachable, it can be intimidating. These women – and men – are drawn towards him. Some get enveloped, others are cast aside.

They feel shit.

Vulnerable.

And that's where the entourage comes in. The rescuers of the scorned. Vultures who feed on the dregs.

They're a couple of hours away from being left alone with these rejects. This part is fun, that part is boring. While Jack is around, even those left behind will make the effort. They will flirt with Entourage Guy Number Three and forget his name, because it's not important. They'll let Entourage Guy Number Two have a squeeze or a stroke because there's a chance to be in that world. If they can just cling on for a bit, they might be able to get closer to the prize.

As soon as Jack and Ike and the drummer go off to watch some size zero strut down a catwalk in shoes made from synthetic silken tofu rather than cruel leather, the groupies will deflate. They won't want to be out. They won't even want the opportunity to go back to Jack Sandford's house because it means they'll have to blow some nobody or they'll have to spend the night worried about something being put into their drinks.

They're women in a man's world, they've got enough to worry about already.

So, by the time the superstar and his band mate leave – with their actual friend – the entourage feel as crap as the discarded women. They just want to go home.

The difference is, they don't have to go to their home. They don't have to heat up some microwave meal in their one-bed palace. They don't have to kiss some sunset pig or wake up to a toothless wonder. They can go back to a multi-million-dollar mansion and play some more pool and drink some more beer and smoke some more weed.

That's their pay-off for being the lackey. They get a proper taste of this life but they have to swallow their pride. Suck it up. Get on with it. They're getting something for nothing. They feel like shit? Go get a job. Go work your arse off.

If only there was an easier way.

If only there was a chance to experience the lifestyle without feeling the degradation, to feel in control.

^^^^^^^^^^

^^^^^^^^^^

LESS

Alyssa and I have done a little coke. We've wandered around the house and taken a piss in two of the seven toilets in a rock star's home. I even went into the master bedroom to lay down the trucker's hat I made for Jack Sandford. It will be resting on his pillow when he finally comes home. My way of secretly saying that I love him. To thank him for letting us hang at his house. Eat his food. Sniff his bedding.

Now, we are sipping on champagne with our feet on the coffee table, watching the man whose house we are in walk down the red carpet. We are loving life and everything we are getting away with. And that's why we don't hear the front door open when three of Jack's entourage return for more free entertainment.

'Who the fuck are you?' Entourage Guy Number One steps ahead of the other two, puffing his chest and tilting his head to the side like he's going to pounce if we don't answer correctly.

Alyssa is scared. Of course. So am I. The three guys are huge. Not the lean, muscular type. They're like those guys who think that they can eat what they want because they lift weights at the gym. So there's muscle but it's covered in a decent layer of subcutaneous fat, and they have beer guts, too.

She's a statue.

^ ^ ^ ^ ^ ^ ^ ^ ^

^ ^ ^ ^ ^ ^ ^ ^ ^

ALYSSA

Oh, God. We're going to get caught. People are going to know that it was us in Rosie Velazquez's house. Shit. I'm panicking.

I'm going to jail.

I'm not like Less, I don't have my own lawyer.

My mother is going to kill me.

Fuck.

I gaze, wide-eyed at the men who have intruded on our intrusion.

'Who the fuck are we? Who the fuck are you?' Less bites back.

I did not see that coming. I don't know what game Less thinks he's playing but his scrawny ass is not going to do much damage to these three Neanderthals.

'We're friends with Jack,' one of the trio says from the back, like a henchman.

'Okay, well, I've never seen you around before. My uncle is Jack's best friend.' I don't know what Less is talking about. It feels like he is reaching. He got through the first question with confidence alone, but he's stretching a little on this one.

^^^^^^^^^^

^^^^^^^^^^

LESS

'You're Mike's nephew?' one of the goons asks, thinking he can catch me out.

I see right through this. I know what these guys are. They're in this for the same reason as Alyssa, the lifestyle, the perks, the experience, but they don't really *know* Jack Sandford. They're not fans of the work. I would never be able to bluff my way around true fans, but these guys won't know half of the things that I do.

'Uncle Ike,' I correct, without really sounding like I am correcting anything. 'I helped him fit the recording studio.' I remember reading about that, somewhere online. These thugs probably don't even know how to wire a plug, so I figure they won't quiz me on my knowledge of Protools or LogicPro.

'So, if I call Jack, he'll know you're here?'

'Uncle Ike said to come and have a few drinks and watch him feel uncomfortable on the red carpet, that we can hang out and wait for him to get back, if we wanted.' I take a swig from my beer, my hand so steady, I bet Alyssa can't believe how convincing I am. I see a little of her tension release. She's forgetting that she should feel worried and takes a sip from her own can.

That's my girl. Play along. We're such a good team.

The two people that the head goon could call are currently on the television, so I feel pretty safe that they're not going to pick up their phones while *Entertainment Tonight* shoves a microphone in their faces.

I'll bet that there are always people here. Different kinds of people, too. Young women, girls, models, sports stars. Obviously other people from the music industry, but not just artists, producers and A+R guys. Couples in their sixties. Families with kids at the summer barbecues. My story is not out of the realms of possibility. And it's not like we were stealing from the place, we were sitting comfortably, just watching the television.

Entourage Guy Number One decides that our story checks out. 'Well, we are gonna shoot some pool until your uncle gets back.' He takes off his jacket and hangs it up, then goes to the fridge for his own drink. The other two follow.

I grab Alyssa's hand so she knows I'm here for her. She smiles at the other guys, trying not to look nervous.

Out the side of her mouth she says, 'What the fuck are we going to do now?'

'Be cool. Let them get into their games, it'll be okay.' I reassure her, even though I'm winging it. 'Finish your drink, and then go to the bathroom.'

One of the mob calls over, 'We didn't catch your names.'

'I'm Tom and this is my friend Dana,' I answer.

'Dana. Hi.' Alyssa lifts her hand into a coquettish wave as she repeats her fake name. The group introduce themselves. I forget their names almost immediately, I bet Alyssa does, too.

Alyssa finishes her drink and stands up. She speaks to me loudly so that everybody can hear.

'I'm going to the bathroom, will you grab me another drink while I'm gone.' Her acting is awful.

'Sure. No worries. Same again?' I play along.

Alyssa nods and walks out. It means that I am left in the room on my own with the other *boys*. It gives me the same feeling I used to get at school walking into a class filled with jocks. That's what these guys are. The kinds of people who peaked in high school. Still, I play my role to perfection. I pour another glass of champagne for Alyssa and hunt for a can of beer for myself.

The gang says nothing.

In a way, I'm winning.

It feels odd.

I am looking at the TV but not really watching it, even though I love fashion and I love catwalks and I love Jack Sandford. I drink my beer. I didn't even really want another drink.

'I think your friend might have fallen in,' Goon three says as he hits a pool shot, and the other two laugh. 'Could be awkward when she comes back in and we all know that she has just taken a shit.'

Cue fits of hysteria, like Dave Chappelle has swung by to test out a new bit.

'I might just go and check on her, make sure she hasn't drowned.' I hate myself for making fun of Alyssa but it's just an act. I know a little something about that. That's how I sometimes managed to come home from school in one piece. It's about survival. I am not one of them.

I walk out of the room and into the entrance hall. Alyssa is waiting by the front door. She signals to me, pointing outside. I walk up to her.

'Let's get the fuck out of Dodge, Less.'

I say nothing. Just open the door and we run.

No looking back.

Running. Away from the house. Away from trouble. Away from capture. Adrenaline keeps our legs moving. The panic on our faces soon morphs into enjoyment. We smile and we sprint, eventually erupting in breathless laughter, hunched over with our hands on our knees, outside the damned bar we started in a few hours earlier.

'Hmmm. I wonder what the cocktails are like. Shall we?' I ask.

Alyssa grabs my arm and starts marching towards the awful bar that bookends our chapter of celebrity phrogging.

'Too scary, Less.'

'It was too big. Let's stick to the influencers.'

'Or maybe we just stop.'

But, like all good addicts, we agree to just one more.

^^^^^^^^^^

^^^^^^^^^^

The Late Night Show with Johnny Carmine – Opening Monologue:

'...You know, first these kids break into some influencer's house and move around her furniture, then they somehow get themselves into a rock star's mansion and clean out the contents of his fridge. I mean, why even wait for a reality show when you can just live that life, right now, am I right?...'

^^^^^^^^^^

^^^^^^^^^^

The difference can be seen in the news.

The next morning there's a sketch of Alyssa and Less on every showbiz website, online gossip column and daily chat show. It doesn't look exactly like them. And the 'journalists' are, of course, referring to them as Tom and Dana.

It turns out that the rock star came home with Ike and the drummer and a handful of models. They partied some more. The entourage was still there, melting vegan cheese on nachos, taking whatever they wanted. They were so enamoured by the dangerously malnourished women that it took over two hours of coke sniffing and dancing for one of them to mention to Ike that his nephew had been over that night.

'My nephew?'

'Yeah. Tom.'

'My three-year-old nephew, Tim?'

Less could tell you what colour Calvin Kleins Jack wore to last year's Video Music Awards but he wasn't as accurate with the information about his best friend Ike.

'Ah, fuck.' Entourage Guy Number Three knows he's messed up.

The police are called. They take statements. There are only cameras outside the house covering the driveway. The footage shows two people arriving. One male, one female. But their faces cannot be seen. He is wearing a baseball cap and she has her hood up with her long hair obscuring the sides of her face. Looks like they knew what they were doing.

Even though nothing can be seen, this twenty-second video circulates to all the major news channels and online social-media outlets.

The police bring a sketch artist to come up with something based on the testimony of the entourage. And then the media machine kicks in. They keep harping on about the Manson Family, suggesting that Sandford was lucky he didn't go home to a blood bath. They sensationalise it, of course.

They want readers.

Everybody craving likes and comments, from the blogger to the national news corporation. They rake up Sharon Tate and Rosemary LaBianca, reminding people how their murders changed the Hollywood landscape.

How people stopped feeling safe. How it altered the music scene in the LA canyons.

Nothing sells like sex but nothing controls as well as fear.

Alyssa and Less don't ever go over to that area of town. It's doubtful that they'll ever be spotted. The crappy cocktail bar was far enough from Jack's house not to be considered but also busy enough for nobody to really notice a couple who looked like they belonged there.

In the self-centred capital of the world, it's a wonder that everyone in the bar that night didn't think it was quiet and that they were alone.

The writers for the late-night shows are already constructing jokes about the situation.

^^^^^^^^^^

^^^^^^^^^^

SNL: 'WEEKEND UPDATE – TOM AND DANA'

TOM: Charles Manson didn't actually kill anybody himself, did he? He just convinced a bunch of people to do it for him.
DANA: Exactly. People have got him so wrong. If anything, he was one of the first influencers.
TOM: Hashtag grateful.
DANA: Hashtag blessed.

^^^^^^^^^^

^^^^^^^^^^

School kids are gossiping in the halls, thinking they know somebody who looks like one of the photofits. Security companies are targeting the more affluent areas with online marketing to exploit their worry that this is a crime epidemic. And in the image they use of Jack Sandford on almost every page, he is wearing the trucker's cap that Less left for him because he gets given so much stuff that he could easily afford to buy, he just assumed that it had been sent from some fashion label.

He posts about how his privacy has been violated while wearing a gift from the person who invaded his home.

And somewhere, hidden in the centre pages of the internet, there is mention of an ongoing feud between a couple of influencers.

Ariel Dean has hit back. A childish video with a stupid soundtrack. She has clearly decided to take the low ground. In a world where YouTubers are somehow getting into the boxing ring with professional athletes for exhibition fights, the last thing that needs to be added into the circus are a couple of health-and-fitness influencers settling their differences in the MMA ring. But that seems to be what Ariel is insinuating – without really following through.

But nobody really pays attention because a famous rock star, who has had a 'leaked' sex tape and text exchange and 'accidentally' put up images of himself in his underwear, had his privacy desecrated.

One person that does witness Ariel Dean's little stunt is @TheFitnessPaige.

And it breaks her.

^^^^^^^^^

^^^^^^^^^

@TheFitnessPaige
'TURN. IT. OFF.'
♥ 22k ☐ 2.1k
(Medium Close-up.)
'Listen. You can turn it off. Those things in life that are not a positive force. You can turn them off. If you are seeing pictures of somebody online and looking at them makes you feel worse about yourself, you can turn it off. Unfollow them. Mute them. Block them. Whatever you have to do to level yourself. If somebody engages with you just to dampen your spirit and ruin your moment, please, turn them off. We have one shot at this. One chance at life. It's not a rehearsal. It's not a warm-up. It's the main event. There's no time to be held back by those who can only feel good about themselves by making you feel worse about you...'

^^^^^^^^^^

^^^^^^^^^^

Paige would normally run through a speech several times before delivering it and putting it out into the world, but she wants this to come from the heart. Hell, she wants to be authentic.

That's what got her here, and that is what she has lost.

She explains that she started it. She entered herself into a heated discussion without having all of the information.

She says that she is a passionate person. That sometimes it comes out in the wrong way. That she should have been better at opening up the discussion.

Paige seems very careful to not say that she is sorry. Or that she herself is wrong. She still believes the things that she said but admits a better dialogue could have been started, had there been more listening.

She thinks that she was doing her job, tearing down the misinformation about nutrition or health fads. She's not in the wrong.

'As a result, I am going to turn things off. I've booked myself into a retreat next weekend to help cleanse my body and clear my mind. To regroup, in order to refocus. I'll still be here for the rest of the week and subscribers won't miss the *Live at Five* workouts. In fact, you won't miss anything but some posts over the weekend while I turn off the technology and get back together with myself.'

It starts to sound less authentic the more she stays off script.

She has to wrap it up.

'Thanks to my *fitfam* for all your support and kind words, I have no headspace for the trolls. Stick with me for the rest of the week and enjoy a short break from my ramblings over the weekend.' She smiles through the self-deprecation.

No edit.

Send.

She can't take it back now. It's out there forever.

Some of these other influencers love posting pictures of their food each day or reviewing books or testing strange products they find on Amazon, but for Paige it's a job. She sees it as work. It's not a jolly outing. Yes, it's her passion, but that saying about finding a job that you love and not working another day in your life, Paige thinks that's bullshit. She never stops.

She's always contactable.

So she is always on duty.

And just like anyone who has to work for a living, she needs a break. She needs a holiday.

Paige needs to turn it off.

^^^^^^^^^

^^^^^^^^^

ALYSSA

The person you are trying to call is not available. Please hang up the phone and try again.

I hate this.

Less and I keep calling each other at exactly the same time and receiving this message. And like good little millennials, we don't have the patience to just wait. So we keep hanging up, as instructed, then phoning the other person back, straight away.

We're excited, that's all. Thinking the same thing.

I skimmed over the headlines when I saw the sketches of 'Tom and Dana', but I had a similar reaction to that first time the press likened us to the Manson Family. The comparison makes me feel sick. We are nothing like them. But, then, maybe they didn't think what they were doing was wrong, either.

Please hang up the phone and try again.

Jesus Christ, this is frustrating.

This goes on for too long. It's farcical.

Eventually, I pause for a fraction of a second while listening to my grandmother answer one of her TV gameshow questions and my screen flashes with Less's name.

'Hey. I've been trying to get through to you. Who have you been on the phone to?' I ask.

'Nobody. I've been trying to call you, bitch.'

'Don't call me *bitch*, you don't get away with it just because you're camp.' I'm smiling at my own remark but the sentiment is kind of true.

'You've seen it, right?'

'Yeah. Wait, what? Are we talking about the same thing?'

'We must be.'

'It's everywhere.'

Many people are worried that their phones are listening to them or tracking them. You search for a new rug on a website and suddenly five different adverts pop up on your timeline. Maybe you don't even search for it. Maybe you talk about it and you think that the microphone on your phone has picked up what you were saying and then directed you towards those things in an effort to make you buy them but mainly to keep you on your device for longer.

Many people are worried and maybe they should be.

If you come from completely opposing standpoints to somebody on a political or ethical or religious enquiry, you will not be given the same top answers from a search engine. They will feed you articles that will help to perpetuate your self-view.

So, when I say 'it's everywhere', I am talking about the influencer wars. That centre-page story moved up the rankings for me because those are the types of people I admire and follow and quote – sometimes, out of context.

The disagreement between Paige and the semen swallower is the only thing on my mind. So it's the only thing I really see. It's the reason I called Less. And I assume that's what he is talking about, too.

'Want to say it at the same time?' I ask.

'What are we, girlfriends all of a sudden?'

'Don't be a prick and just do it.' This is all in jest. We both know it. People are easily outraged, they're sensitive. Not us.

I'm so confident that we're on the same wavelength. That we've both seen Paige's heartfelt plea for peace. I assume that he has seen that she is turning off her notifications while she has a little R&R, and the information he has also extrapolated is that Paige won't be in her house over the next weekend. And I *know* that Less wants to do it again.

'Ready?' I ask. 'After three. One ... two ... THREE. We are going to move into The Fitness Paige's house.' I'm so loud and excited that I almost don't hear what Less says.

His feed has not been the same as mine, this morning. Whatever he is thinking or typing or saying out loud, it means that his results are different. So, at the same time I speak about our next adventure, Less says, 'Jack Sandford is wearing my cap.'

^^^^^^^^^

^^^^^^^^^

#FifteenMinutesOfFame #BoredMillennials #Jeopardy

The week goes by like most any other. Days bleed into each other. Minutes are stretched out. They are forced back into their routines of school and work, longing for the blackout at the Fitness Paige mansion.

Things in the press die down quickly without any reports of further intrusions. Jack Sandford has returned to his home in Brooklyn for a while. They say that detectives are still looking into the trespassing but the cops don't have much to go on.

Alyssa's mother has worked four late shifts in a row and now has a couple of days off. Her grandmother continues her laborious road to death via the gameshow highway, though she has found a new lease of life in the mornings when the postman arrives, hoping that there might be a letter saying that she is going to be a contestant on her favourite show.

She's not like her granddaughter, she doesn't want her fifteen minutes, she's just in it for the cold, hard cash. And she's not afraid to admit that. Though she isn't going to admit her desperation for that letter.

^^^^^^^^^^

^^^^^^^^^^

ALYSSA

Oh. My. God. My week is dragging. I took Paige's advice about switching off the things that don't bring me joy, though, and deleted Ariel Dean from my 'following' list. Even though I have been travelling Ariel's journey with her for months. Even though I had the context of why she would try the semen-shot smoothie. Even though I had all the information. I delete someone from my life who I previously found inspiring. Because somebody with slightly more influence inadvertently told me to do so.

Because nobody wants to be the only kid at school not wearing Nike Air Force 1 shoes.

Nobody wants to order a decaf, extra-hot, dry cappuccino with two pumps of hazelnut syrup, chocolate sprinkles, double shot of coffee with skinny milk, because some part-time barista is going to spit in that.

We want to fit in.

We don't want to be individual.

It's not safe.

^^^^^^^^^^

^^^^^^^^^^

@DesignerLessD
'It's so awful that somebody would violate your personal space like that. But I love the trucker's hat you were wearing on the TMZ photo, where did you get it from?'
♥ 1

^^^^^^^^^^

^^^^^^^^^^

LESS

I have focussed my week on going to college, burying myself in my design work and trying to stir things up online.

I begin by publicly messaging Jack Sandford.

I don't post from an anonymous account, it is my personal profile. With my real name. I'm not stupid enough to have my picture on there. As much as the police sketches don't look like me or Alyssa, they have really nailed the shape of my chin; I don't want to be offering that direct comparison.

Sandford doesn't respond. My comment gets one like.

I start something of a campaign to get people talking about the hat that I made. I post pictures, trying to get my own followers to engage in the topic. A few people from my course comment. One is unfavourable and it upsets me – everyone has an opinion and nobody has any forethought. I hate these influencers but I also wish I had a little more sway to get the topic trending.

^^^^^^^^^^

^^^^^^^^^^

ALYSSA

I shuffle my way to the end of the week. I do the *Live at Five* workout with Paige, following along on my mobile phone in the kitchen while my grandmother watches television in the lounge and my mother collects Chinese takeout on her way back from the hospital now that she has bagged a few early shifts.

I have agreed with Less to go over to Paige's house tomorrow after dinner, just as it is starting to get dark. Less is convinced that we won't get in this time, that the last bit of bad publicity will see people battening down the hatches and setting up cameras and lasers and buying guard dogs.

But he's in. Of course he is. It's the last time. We could seek our thrills in Europe at the end of the semester or hitchhike to Vegas. We're young. Plenty of life ahead. Lots of time to make some mistakes and not pay too heavily for those choices.

Paige has posted that she will be away for the weekend on a retreat, so we will be able to stay there without worrying that someone is going to turn up while we're taking a bath or watching a movie. And it gives us plenty of time to figure out where we can continue to stay when she returns from her peaceful reset.

The fact that we were interrupted last time seems more of a personal hindrance than a deterrent from our new hobby. The closer we are to being caught, the greater the rush. Perhaps.

Maybe it's that we can't think of anything else to do.

Maybe it's that we think we'll never get caught.

Maybe we don't really care.

A millennial Bonnie and Clyde.

^^^^^^^^^^

^^^^^^^^^^

@TheFitnessPaige

'So pleased this package has arrived, can't wait to try out my new compression socks from @ripped_apparel'

♥ **100k** □ **743**

^^^^^^^^^^

^^^^^^^^^^

ALYSSA

It was so easy to find Paige's address.

Or maybe I'm just getting better at stalking.

Paige gets sent things all the time. And she always posts about it. Nutritionists send her advance copies of their books, hoping that she will read and comment favourably to her legion. She receives boxes of different protein powders and vitamins and supplements. She's lucky enough to receive beauty products and self-care items. Damn, I would love that.

Mostly, parcels arrive at her home containing fitness apparel. Trainers and leggings and vests. These companies want her to wear their clothing in her fitness videos and tag them in it, too.

It's not like being sponsored by Nike but it is a partnership.

If you start up your own compression-sock company from nothing and you are attached to a social-media post that gets a million views and a hundred thousand likes, it can change your fortune.

It doesn't always happen.

But it can.

Months ago, Paige posted a picture of a parcel that she had been waiting for. It had the company logo stamped on the front near to her address, which she covered up with her hand. The problem was the way that the package had been sent at the post office. There was a large sticker on the front with a gobbledygook QR code. Just a square filled with black-and-white shapes that mean nothing to the naked eye. But one of Paige's followers had commented on this picture saying that those shapes contain information and that she should probably take the image down.

Paige eventually saw the response and deleted the photo. She gifted the follower a free year of subscription to her workout app as a thank-you.

But I took a screenshot of that post. I don't really know why I did it at the time, but I did.

Nothing deleted from the internet is ever really gone.

A simple download of a QR reader app for $3.99 and I could extrapolate the information. A few numbers that didn't really mean anything and there wasn't a date or time stamp, but there was an address.

@TheFitnessPaige's address.

Online, for anyone to find out.

There must have been countless others who did exactly what I did. Some kind of stalker autopilot. People are snapping everything, videoing anything. There's no edit on the information we can ingest. But we've all taken a thousand pictures since then and have forgotten about the parcel photo. Some may not have even realised that they took it.

That's not me. I remember it, vividly.

So it's their own fault that they weren't as industrious as I've been, otherwise they could be on their way to move in with their idol right now like I am.

^^^^^^^^^

^^^^^^^^^

#DigitalDetox #UnplugToRecharge #LogOffAndLive #LessScrollMoreSoul

Paige turns it off.

Every social-media platform, every game, every shopping app. It's gone.

Do. Not. Disturb.

Nobody will be able to contact her or get hold of her for the next two days.

She's off the grid.

Relax.

Regroup.

Reset.

It's what she needs.

A couple of days away from creating content. She doesn't want to film herself cooking or working out or giving lifestyle advice. She just wants to be herself. She hardly ever gets to do that. She always has to be present, otherwise she will disappear, somebody else will take over.

Paige has never turned it all off before.

She could die tonight and nobody would even question it until Monday.

The cameras on the opposite wall zoom in on her from different angles.

She's being examined.

Always.

She has no idea that she is not really alone.

That the end is going to be filmed.

Paige goes into the kitchen and opens a bottle of wine. No workouts. No healthy eating. Not tonight. She pours a large glass of whatever white wine has been sitting in her fridge and she knocks it back like she's guest of honour at some college frat party. It's disgusting but she pours another large glass and takes the box of twelve glazed doughnuts with her to the couch. There's more calories in that box than she has had all week.

And she's going to eat them all.

Fuck it.

No throwing them up, either. She is going to drown herself in that perfect balance of fat and sugar before dropping into some kind of pastry coma.

Paige wants to be herself again. The way she was before all of this. When she was innocent and naive. She doesn't know how to get there other than punishing herself or just being the opposite of who she has become. Maybe she just needs a break. Maybe she needs to let go of the regiment and discipline.

Turn it off. For a night. For the weekend.

There's a screen that unfolds from the ceiling so that she can project onto it. The plan is to watch *The Notebook* because it always makes her cry. Paige wants her stomach to be bloated and her mascara to be running down her face.

She wants to feel fat.

She wants to look ugly.

She wants to just release everything that she has to be every day. Break the veneer of perfection and howl at the god-damned moon, for once.

It feels incredible to just let go.

Paige hasn't booked the spa. She doesn't want to be healthy. She's always healthy. She doesn't want to be mindful. She doesn't want to be caked in dirt to cleanse her skin. She's just eaten 2,340 calories of doughnuts and washed them down with a vinegary wine whilst trying to decide if she would rather spend a night with Ryan Gosling or Rachel McAdams. She wants to turn all the lights off in the house, go up to her en suite, run a bath and stew in her own filth for an hour.

So that's what she does.

^^^^^^^^^^

^^^^^^^^^^

ALYSSA

We can't get in the front door because it is locked. And there's no key underneath the mat, either.

Fuck. Maybe she's not that rich.

Maybe she's just normal.

It has been warm today and, when I look over the fence into Paige's garden, I can see that one of the back windows is ajar.

I thought Less was going to just give up, but the back door is open.

^^^^^^^^^^

^^^^^^^^^^

LESS

We creep around downstairs.

The screen in the lounge is even bigger than Jack Sandford's. The plan is to watch a movie and maybe order some pizza. I find a loaf of rustic bread in the kitchen on a chopping board. I check the date. It won't last until Paige is supposed to get back from her retreat, so I open it, take some cheese, pickle and pâté from the fridge and place them on the coffee table with a knife.

^^^^^^^^^^

^^^^^^^^^^

#SoakAndRecover #LiveLonger #HotToGo

Paige knows that there are many benefits to a piping-hot bath. It's great for relieving stress, obviously, but it's also helpful in relieving muscle tension and improving circulation. She works out a lot. Something is always aching.

She tells herself it aids her recovery but, in truth, she just likes the way it feels. There's pleasure in the pain.

Apparently, it also clears congestion and promotes better sleep, but a person should not endure the heat for more than twenty minutes.

Paige doesn't care about that. She's happy to spend an extra forty minutes in there. That's an hour to shrivel her fingers and disconnect from the world. Long enough for her visitors to really make themselves at home.

^^^^^^^^^^

^^^^^^^^^^

ALYSSA

Less looks so comfortable. I saw Paige's post about going on that retreat, I know she's not here this weekend. But I don't just sink into it like Less does. He went straight in and raided her cupboards and refrigerator, and now he's slouching on the sofa like he owns it.

Maybe it's a rich thing.

This life is so alien to me that I can't quite settle. It's high quality. It's luxurious, even. Everything I touch makes me feel a little nervous. And that's probably why I find phrogging so exciting.

But Less just seems relaxed, cutting his bread and eating his cheese, I wonder what's in it for him.

^^^^^^^^^^

^^^^^^^^^^

#SelfCareRitual #HolisticHealth #UnderwaterVibes

A company called Liquid Sound contacted Paige a year ago. They manufacture and install speakers that work underwater in pools and bathtubs. They offered her a free product if she endorsed it on her Instagram profile.

She took them up on their offer and held up her end of the bargain. They saw a spike in sales but have since gone under. But Paige believed in their product. She loves it still. It means that she can lie in the bath, her hair splayed out across the water, her ears beneath the surface, and she can't hear her two uninvited guests moving around downstairs.

And they are not disturbed by the soothing sound of Peruvian panpipes.

^^^^^^^^^^

^^^^^^^^^^

LESS

This place is nice enough, but it has no soul. I can see how enamoured Lyss is with the place, but it does belong to one of her influencer idols, so I think she has her rose-tinted glasses on.

'Lyss, come and sit down, for Christ's sake. You're making the place look untidy.'

She gives me a look and I pat the seat next to me. She sits down.

'It's weird, now that we're here, I don't really know what to do. It doesn't feel the same as Rosie's or even Jack's.'

'Look.' I hit a button on the remote and the screen lowers fully from the ceiling. 'Let's pick a movie, something with Ryan Reynolds is preferable. We can sit back, I'll order some pizzas, and then we can decide what the hell we are going to do for the weekend. Okay?'

She nods and starts flicking through the listing.

'I mean, we haven't even looked upstairs yet.'

^ ^ ^ ^ ^ ^ ^ ^ ^ ^

^ ^ ^ ^ ^ ^ ^ ^ ^ ^

As the screen descends, several of the cameras set up by Lincoln/Lowell Productions get covered up or obscured but enough have been positioned around the lounge of Paige's home that the sofa can still be seen from certain angles, as can the stairs that lead from the first floor directly into the main living area.

They recorded Alyssa and Less entering a home that is not theirs.

They recorded those young trespassers as they made themselves at home with food and drink and a movie.

And they will record what happens next.

^ ^ ^ ^ ^ ^ ^ ^ ^ ^

^ ^ ^ ^ ^ ^ ^ ^ ^ ^

#GoodbyeScrolling #NoFilterNoProblem #OfflineVibes
Paige has no idea.

She finishes her bath, gets dried and ties back her hair. No need to blow-dry and straighten it. She puts on some comfortable joggers that were sent to her for free and a loose-fitting T-shirt and heads downstairs.

She sees two people in her living room.

Her mind goes straight to the Tom and Dana story she saw on TMZ.

Paige is not somebody who scares easily but she has also had half a bottle of Sauvignon Blanc, so, instead of creeping back upstairs and calling the police, she confronts her intruders.

'What are you doing in my house?' She runs to the bottom of the stairs. 'Get the fuck out,' she screams at them and notices the back door is open.

^^^^^^^^^^

^^^^^^^^^^

ALYSSA

Less and I take a moment to register what the hell is going on.

Then the adrenaline hits.

My instinct tells me to freeze to the spot while Less's apparently tells him to pick up the knife.

'Less, what are you doing?'

'We've been made, Lyss.'

'Fuck, a knife, though? We're *not* the Mansons.' I plead with him, reminding him that we are not what the tabloids have said we are.

'Yeah, well, maybe we are.'

^^^^^^^^^^

^^^^^^^^^^

LESS

I'm not even thinking about myself. I want to protect Alyssa. I wave the knife in front of me and then lunge towards Paige.

Paige, the fitness guru and martial artist.

Paige, who refuses to be a victim.

@TheFitnessPaige, who gives a swift kick to the side of my knee, which buckles, giving her a split second to hit me again, this time in the face, before gripping my wrist and turning the knife around to plunge it straight into my chest.

^^^^^^^^^^

^^^^^^^^^^

ALYSSA

Now I feel the need for flight. But even with a gut full of doughnuts, Paige is a professional. It takes her no time to catch up with me. Paige grabs at my long hair and yanks me backwards. I cry out in pain before falling and cracking my head on the corner of the base of a marble statue.

^^^^^^^^^^

^^^^^^^^^^

#BlackBeltMindset #WarriorInTraining #StrongWomen

Alyssa twitches.

Once.

Twice.

Then stops moving.

Paige isn't even breathing that heavily. There's no way she was going to let intruders get away with coming into her house but, more importantly, she wasn't going to let it come out that she hadn't gone to her spa weekend.

Paige looks at the wreckage of her living area and then up at the screen. She walks over to her sofa, still warm from where her visitors had been lounging, she takes a piece of bread, spreads it thick with pâté and watches another film.

Now she is broken.

The cameras are still rolling.

PART TWO: GREEN LIGHT

----------STOP SCROLLING----------

[LIVESTREAM]
20:53

Edie and Tammy have never been so engrossed in a show before.

And nothing is even happening.

That's reality.

Paige hasn't moved. She is lying on the sofa and watching a movie. Occasionally she sits up to either dip her artisan bread into olive oil and balsamic vinegar or to scoop out some pâté.

She laughs at the jokes.

She baulks at the gratuity.

It's like she can't even see the two young bodies on her floor.

Paige has disassociated herself from her new reality.

'She's got to be in shock,' Edie says.

'Or she's a fucking psychopath.'

The producers look at each other. They've either made a huge mistake in casting Paige or it's another genius stroke from the golden pair. These high-achieving influencers do exhibit traits of narcissism.

There's rousing music and what sounds like Ryan Reynolds making a speech. Paige sits up in the centre of the sofa and gazes at her giant screen.

That's when she sees them.

First, it's Less, over to her right. Paige's eyes flit. Once. Twice. She pulls her feet up onto the sofa cushion in the way she always does when she's watching a scary movie.

The cameras that she can't see are pointing at her face.

She looks frightened.

Like she doesn't know what happened in that room. Or she's trying to remember how she got to this place. Then she jumps. Right as Ryan is receiving a standing ovation for his address. It's Alyssa. To the left. She doesn't look dead. She looks still, though. And there is blood on the floor beneath her hair.

Paige shakes her head to see if the memory of this female intruder's skull hitting the floor will somehow fall out and be forgotten. But it doesn't. Paige relives it. The sight. The sound of bone on marble. The crack.

The silence.

She doesn't know what to do.

Maybe if she sits still for long enough, it will all go away.

Tammy takes a handful of popcorn and hands it to the side for Edie to share. They wash it down with a glass of Riesling – Tammy's favourite. They watch and they wait. The inactivity is captivating.

'What is she thinking, Tammy?' Edie asks, not taking her gaze away from the monitors for a second.

'I'm telling you, this girl's a psycho. She's probably thinking about cutting up the bodies and burning them.'

'You're sick, you know that?'

'What's sick is that we don't have any cameras in the garden.'

They continue to watch their social experiment. They discuss the possibility of getting a camera down there discreetly. They talk about how the projector screen actually obscures two of the cameras that have been set up in Paige's lounge. They zoom in on the bodies that Paige is refusing to acknowledge.

And neither of them even thinks about calling the police.

– – – – – – – – – – –

21:42

'I should get this down. Even if it's just for me. So that I remember what happened, because it's all such a fucking blur right now.' Her voice cracks.

The film finishes and Paige is forced to confront the situation. But she's still unsure and her feet are still on the sofa because some childish memory is telling her that this stops monsters from pulling you under by your ankles.

Paige reaches for the camera that was provided by Lincoln/Lowell Productions to make the diary-room confessions. It was meant for her to record any thoughts she might have about health or exercise or fame or beauty, not the admission of manslaughter. But it's a good outlet because she is used to performing in front of a camera.

Her video will get two views.

Two 'likes'.

'These two people broke into my house.' She turns the camera to show Alyssa and Less lying on her living-room tiles. 'They didn't, actually, bust their way inside, they just walked in the back door and made themselves at home. Fuck, they were eating my food and watching a film on my screen, lying around like the place was theirs. What kind of…?'

The screen goes black for a moment as Paige places the camera on the sofa between her crossed legs and takes a few deep breaths.

There's no editing.

No perfect fifth take.

This is real.

'I don't know what to do. It's been a couple of hours and neither of them has moved. I'm scared. I put on a comedy movie in an effort to distract myself from what happened here. How crazy is that?' She laughs but it comes across as fake and forced and uncomfortable.

'Fuck. What the hell is happening to me?'

Paige holds her forehead in her left hand but the camera in her right stays fixed on her face. She may be distraught or in shock but she has spent so much of her life on camera, whether it was creating videos for herself or for her followers, it is second nature to her. She is framed perfectly.

A tableau of distress.

Capturing everything.

'*They* were in the wrong. I was defending myself and my property. I'm allowed to do that. Right? I didn't plan on killing them. I had no choice with the guy, and the girl was just … unfortunate. That was an accident. I could call the police and tell them that…'

But Paige can't alert the authorities because that would force her to have to come clean about her weekend. She was supposed to be turning everything off and relaxing at a spa somewhere. That's what she told everyone. That's what was going through her head when she saw Alyssa and Less. Not that she was protecting herself physically from potential criminals, but that she was protecting her reputation; without her followers, she loses everything.

So why would she go to the police and ruin things if that was what she was preserving in the first place?

'No ... no. I don't need to do that. Not yet. I'm supposed to be away for the weekend, so I have that long to decide. I'm not going to rush this. Think, Paige. Think.'

The credits come to an end on the film. It's quiet for a moment before going back to the home screen and letting out a loud burst of music.

Paige lets out a short scream.

Tammy laughs.

Edie drinks.

Alyssa bleeds.

Less is still.

There is plenty of the weekend left, but, now, it's time to freak out.

– – – – – – – – – – –

21:45

Ariel Dean finishes loading the dishwasher after her dinner, which didn't include even one fluid ounce of semen, and sifts through the bills and circulars that arrived in the post that morning to find a handwritten note. So old-fashioned.

Who does that anymore?

Why spend time scrawling with a pen when you can text or send somebody a direct message via social media? Everyone has an account, surely.

Everyone who's deeply unhappy.

Still, Ariel sees some novelty in receiving something so personal that isn't her annual pile of dispassionate birthday cards hoping she 'has a great day'.

The letter is from Paige.

Ariel can't believe it. Not only is there a written apology for calling her out about the morning smoothies, Paige is seemingly sorry for coming on so hard and doing it all so publicly, using her platform to incite vitriol towards Ariel.

It was wrong.

And that's not all.

She wants to meet.

Apparently, Paige didn't want to do this over the internet; it needs to be done right. The letter, scribbled by her own hand, is merely a token of her sincerity. She is inviting Ariel Dean over to her house. Tomorrow. So that she can apologise in person.

The old-fashioned way.

Face to face.

It seems that @TheFitnessPaige is on a quest for something genuine. A connection with real people. The letter gives Paige's address and asks that Ariel come over for a tea or coffee in the morning so they can talk.

Who knows, maybe we'll even end up being friends?

Paige's letter is signed off with a kiss and a smiley face drawn in a circle.

Ariel Dean is not that forgiving. She screws her face up at the possibility of them ever becoming friends. She doesn't want that. Ariel *is* real. She has been documenting her struggles and her condition in an effort to share her ordeal. If there is any benefit or motivation for others, that is a by-product of her own catharsis.

Sure, she got caught up in the furore of comments and likes and her following growing by thousands each day, but she doesn't need the negativity in her life. Ariel has decided not to be a part of the argument. She doesn't want to give any more energy to it, she doesn't want to fuel the fire or be complicit in what she now believes to be a publicity stunt on Paige's behalf.

But the idea of 'celebrity' is difficult to understand, it is even more difficult to avoid or discount. And Ariel is curious. What is Paige's house like? How does she really live? What is she really like when she's not on a screen with the perfect music and the perfect make-up and the perfect lighting?

There are no details of how Paige can be contacted to confirm or deny the apology, so Ariel decides that she will go to her house tomorrow morning and see what this is really about.

21:46

The screen retracts and *all* the cameras can see Paige.

She still won't leave the sofa.

Alyssa and Less still won't wake up.

She turns on the television and the sound lets Edie and Tammy know that the first show to come up is *So, You Want To Marry My Dad?* One of Lincoln/Lowell Productions' spin-off shows. Paige has watched it before. She remembers that parrot noise after the credits and it makes her think of the contract that she signed. She has money in her account already.

She might need it for legal expenses.

It's enough to pack up and leave, start somewhere new. Maybe she could put a few vitals in a bag, jump on a plane and go. Nobody is expecting her to be around for a couple of days. She could be long gone by the time somebody comes knocking and finds two dead bodies on the floor.

It's tempting. But the draw of her current lifestyle is too much. It becomes intoxicating. There's nobody around to keep her grounded, to advise her what's best.

The television catches her eye.

'Police are on the lookout for a couple, early to mid-twenties, going by the names Tom and Dana.' An image flashes on the screen. Some composite sketches, mostly outlines, no real detail, but the shapes of the faces and features are accurate to the description given. 'They have been letting themselves into people's houses and seemingly living there, undetected. Until they decide to move on, when they move things around in their victims' homes to torment them and let them know they were there.'

Paige focuses on 'Tom'. That sharp chin. She pauses the TV and finally gets off the couch. She steps towards the screen and really examines 'Tom's' features. Then she stands over Less's body and zooms her focus in on his face, too.

It's not perfect, but it's close.

She returns to the screen before repeating her scrutiny with Alyssa's lifeless body.

Her face is a little further from the drawing than Less's but they have captured the freckles on her cheeks.

It's her.

It's them.

It's definitely them.

'The pair are presumed to be unarmed but dangerous. Do not approach. This type of bravado indicates a spontaneity that could prove uncertain and threatening. If you have any information at all, please call the number at the bottom of the screen.'

Paige looks at the number. Maybe she would be considered a hero and her fans would forgive her minor donut indiscretion.

The newscaster reminds viewers to be on the lookout for anything suspicious and be vigilant with their home security.

'Los Angeles has not seen activity of this kind since the late sixties, when it culminated in the ill-fated incident at 10050 Cielo Drive.'

Paige, holding the remote control, drops both hands to her sides in disbelief.

'Oh, shit. I killed the Mansons.'

22:00

There's somebody at the door.

Tammy looks over her shoulder at the screen, which shows a man grinning and waving.

'Ah, shit. I forgot,' Tammy says.

'What?'

'I said Davis could come over for drinks and what not.' She didn't forget.

'What not?' Edie shakes her head in faux disapproval.

'Hey, a girl's gotta eat.'

'Look, there's nothing going on here, yet. I'll keep watching, you go and screw your fuck buddy, share some wine, then get rid of him.'

'Edie.'

'I love Davis, you know that, but we have a short window with this, and I want to stay on top of it. You go. Honestly, it'll be fine. Just get it in before the coke makes him go limp again, eh?' She smiles a knowing smile.

'You'd better not have any cameras upstairs, Edie.'

'Who would want to see that?'

Tammy hits the intercom button. 'Hey, Davis. I'm buzzing you in. I'll be over in a second.'

'I have a Lafitte Blanc that deserves to be quaffed immediately.'

'Wonderful.' Tammy releases the intercom button. 'Have fun with your Riesling.' She smiles and backs out of the door, seemingly unaffected by the double death she and her business partner witnessed only a couple of hours ago.

Edie is left with Paige, Alyssa and Less. Everything is being recorded directly to the cloud for editing. Though she finds the odd serenity of Paige's lounge fascinating, if this is never going to be seen by anybody else, Edie knows that something is going to have to happen. And that is what Lincoln/Lowell do best.

They manufacture reality.

They force situations.

They manipulate.

Edie puts in a call.

'...yeah ... as soon as possible ... no, no.' She watches as Tammy almost skips towards Davis. 'Maybe give it ten. Great. Thanks.'

She hangs up.

And she waits.

22:35

The doughnuts tasted better on the way down but, actually, it wasn't even really that bad when they came back up.

Paige forces herself to be sick. She doesn't know what else to do. Besides, she's good at it. The idea of having a break from the stresses of influencing hasn't really panned out, so she may as well get back to her regular routine. There are definitely still a few of those glazed beauties in her system that won't be coming back, though.

She realises that the lights are still off in her lounge. Only the blue from the TV illuminates the room.

It's almost as though she wants it to look like a horror movie. Maybe that makes it less real.

Just as Paige flips the light switch, her doorbell rings, making her jump and plunge the house back into darkness.

Her heart rate creeps up.

Why would somebody be ringing her bell when everyone knows she is supposed to be away?

What if it's the real Tom and Dana, she thinks, *trying to get in, and those two poor unfortunates were just in the wrong place at the wrong time?*

It rings again.

She looks at the bodies.

She looks back at the doors.

Back at the bodies.

It rings two more times.

It sounds so loud.

She has to answer it.

She thought she was starting to get a grip on things, now she is losing it again.

'Answer the god-damned door, Paige.' Edie speaks out loud to nobody. Tammy is upstairs with Davis, drinking and flirting.

Paige decides that she can't leave it. She paces towards the front door, looking back over her shoulder to see whether her two unwanted guests are visible. The back door is still open. She needs to get to the front door before this person starts looking for another way in.

God help me.

She doesn't even check through the peephole to see who it is.

As she opens the door, the person outside rings the bell again and Paige shouts, 'Jesus' in his face. 'You scared the life out of me.'

'I'm sorry, miss, I just...'

'You really want to deliver those pizzas, huh?'

She relaxes. She recognises the uniform. The guy is younger than she is. He has bad skin. Part of her wants to tell him to lay off the merchandise but this isn't the time.

'I get off after this delivery is all. Sorry if I seemed impatient.' He's young. He has a shitty job. Paige feels bad.

'No, no, no, no. That's fine. I understand.'

He unloads his bag. 'Two large, plus ice-cream, plus soda. That's $34.59.'

Those cretins got into my house and then ordered a pizza delivery. Paige is annoyed but also, strangely impressed. *How brazen? I guess they had to pay cash so there was no trail. Clever. They thought something through, at least.*

Paige acts as normal as she can. She's surprisingly good at faking it. It lends itself to her line of work.

'Okay, one sec, I'll just grab some cash.' She goes behind her wall into the kitchen. 'You said it was thirty-four...'

'Fifty-nine.' The pizza delivery guy is admiring the size of the front door. It makes for a grand entrance. He steps forward. Just one step, to get a better look inside. Human curiosity knows no bounds. He looks down towards the living area and Paige curses the architect who thought open-plan living was the answer.

Paige jumps out of the kitchen doorway, and it forces the delivery guy to jump backward. She doesn't want him to see anything. She doesn't want him pushing inside. Not that she's worried, she could handle him, she just doesn't want to get into anything.

'So, look. Here. I got fifty. Keep the change, okay?'

'Are you here on your own, miss?' He forgets to thank Paige for the tip. He's speaking slowly, like he's fishing for something, like he's suspicious.

'Look at the size of me, you think I'm eating two large pizzas and ice-cream by myself?' She forces a giggle.

'Huh. Yeah. I guess. That makes sense.' He's still trying to peer inside.

'Enjoy the end of your shift, eh?' Paige starts closing the door and he steps back outside. All the audio is picked up on the camera hidden above the door and there are a few angles to take the video from. Edie watches on several screens. She can edit in more tension. Add music.

Paige leans her back against the door, lets out a deep breath and slides down until she is sitting on the floor. The pizza smells great. She opens the top box and takes out a slice.

It's greasy.

It's fatty.

It's delicious.

Look at any image online of @TheFitnessPaige and you see her abs, the lines in her arms where she is so lean, you can almost taste the sinew in her shoulders. You look at the size of her and you'd think that there was no way she could eat two large pizzas and a tub of ice-cream to herself.

But, damn, she's going to give it a go.

This may not be the real Paige but at least it's different.

- - - - - - - - - - -

22:39

Davis doesn't have coke dick.

'I'm sorry, I didn't mean to finish inside you.'

'Oh, fuck, Davis, it'll be fine. My insides are such an inhospitable place, I probably killed all your best swimmers on contact.'

She laughs.

He laughs.

Their relationship is solid enough to joke in this vulnerable, post-coital position. Sadly, it's not strong enough to move to something more stable. There has been media speculation, of course, but many think Davis Davis is a playboy, that he can never settle. Some say that he needs to be seen with models, not some Botoxed TV exec who is similar in age. Some even suggest that he's firmly locked in a closet.

He's not what they say. Davis loves Tammy, he's just an idiot who doesn't want to ruin what they have by making it official. It's emotionally immature. Their bond could be even richer with some commitment.

They both want it.

Tammy would do it. Apart from the occasional fling with an intern looking to progress their career, she keeps herself for Davis and for her work.

'So, what are you working on?'

'Davis,' she strokes his cheek, 'don't think you can lower my defences in afterglow and get me to spill that information, you silly man.'

'Hey, it was worth a try.' He kisses her tenderly.

'All I can tell you is that it's going to be our most edgy project to date. We are filming now and Edie is editing things together. It's a personal one.'

Davis sits up in bed. He's excited. This is the kind of thing he has been pushing Lincoln/Lowell to do more and more. Projects that are just for them. None of this *Wives of Salt Lake City* crap that they keep peddling.

He reaches over to the bedside table. There's a little of the wine left and he fills the glass.

'We can share this but I just want to toast you, Tammy. Because I think that you are absolutely magnificent.' He drinks. She blushes. He hands her the glass.

Tammy wants to believe him, she truly does, but nothing in her life is real anymore.

23:08

Paige manages one large pizza and the entire tub of ice-cream. The second one goes into the fridge for later. Or the morning.

She leaves her kitchen feeling bloated and sluggish but still with the taste of cookies and cream in her mouth. It's almost enough to make a person forget they have two dead intruders in the lounge.

Paige has always been a go-getter. Focussed on what she wants. Hardworking. Forthright. Convicted. But right now she wants to throw up the half-pound of cheese and grease she consumed then curl up in bed and hope that this is all a rubbish nightmare, that she will come downstairs in the morning and they will be gone.

But she knows the truth. What she has to do is get rid of the evidence. She has to make sure nobody finds these people, because surely somebody is going to come looking for them at some point. There's no reason that they would suspect Paige's involvement, unless these idiots were stupid enough to post about their crimes on the internet.

It wouldn't make them the dumbest criminals of all time if they did.

Paige is devastated. She has to switch things back on. She couldn't even go for half a day without the internet.

What have we become?

She Googles herself, which is not as fun as it might sound.

'@TheFitnessPaige house'.

She figures that they may have posted something to say that she was being targeted. Thoughtlessly putting something out there to say that they had selected her as their next target, the way that idiot did who killed those cats online.

What she finds is much worse.

Pictures of her actual house.

The front gate. The door. A view from above that looks as though it was captured with a drone. There are even a couple of images of Paige inside doing yoga, from a magazine article she did a couple of years back.

Anybody could find it.

Two people did. But there's nothing that Paige can unearth, with her limited search skills, to suggest that they were reckless enough to document their prank.

There's nothing there, Paige. Turn it back off.

Paige convinces herself to go dark. There seems to be nothing about the incident online. She needs to take herself off the grid. Off the map. She slides all of her settings back to *off*. She needs to not be at one with her technology like she usually is, where every thought, meal and workout is distributed to her adoring legion.

She can do it.

She can focus on what's important and not what content can be created. This would not even be a consideration in a rational person's mind.

Paige places her mobile phone in her pocket and walks to the centre of the lounge. She tries to take in Alyssa and Less at the same time. Alyssa is by no means overweight but she has curves in places that Paige could only wish for. And Less, even though he is a man, is so slight in stature. She can't get rid of them both at the same time, there's too much risk, so she chooses the one that will take the least effort, especially after the day she has just had.

She can deal with one of them tonight and one of them in the morning. Or maybe tomorrow night when it is dark again.

She opts for Less this evening.

But, before she drags him outside by his wrists, Paige goes back to her diary-room camera so that she can capture her true emotions before possibly dismembering somebody for the first time.

23:13

The best thing Paige can do is keep her phone off. She's seen enough movies and listened to enough true-crime podcasts where people have searched 'how to dispose of a dead body'. It's the kind of thing that not only leaves a trail, it leaves the perpetrator looking ridiculous in court.

The last thing she needs is some intelligence agency becoming interested in her search history or the things she has been buying from Amazon. There are terrorist threats every day and presidential assassination attempts and Russian cyber-hacking to consider, so the NSA probably isn't concerned that some *bookfluencer* is buying their books cheaper online rather than supporting their local independent bookshop, as they claim. Or that some left-wing politico has been bidding for Nazi memorabilia. Or that @TheFitnessPaige bought pruning shears, a hacksaw, black bin liners, duct tape and a shovel at ten-thirty in the evening.

'We are approaching a time for action. I'm sorry to sound so clinical but I'm finding I can handle this situation better if I keep myself removed from it, emotionally.' She looks over at Alyssa. 'Though that isn't always easy.' She's mumbling as though she is creating content. Habit perhaps. Delusion, more likely. Her voice cracks on the last word and she inhales sharply as though she is about to cry.

She doesn't. She's @TheFitnessPaige. She's strong.

It comes across on camera like Paige is resilient, dealing with an unprecedented situation the best way that she can. But there is a correlation between successful people – entrepreneurs, CEOs, heads of state – and psychopathy.

Not in the sense that one becomes a serial killer, rather in the way that they can switch off. They can compartmentalise. They can look as though they are going to cry at the dead girl on the living-room floor but they are just forcing a reaction that is deemed the societal norm.

'I'm going to move *him* first. It's getting late. I just ate a pizza and now I feel super sluggish. That's the problem when you put crap food inside your body. Food is supposed to give you energy, not zap it completely after some fleeting moment of pleasure.'

Paige can't help it.

It's ingrained in her now to lecture on the subjects that she has become known for. Health. Fitness. Nutritional wellbeing. It's also ingrained in her to document the moments of her life on video. It's automatic. She may not be Googling body-disposal techniques but she is keeping a record of the things that she could just be thinking. It's an indication of how detached she is from her situation. The video could be edited to make Paige look however Lincoln/Lowell want her to look.

Maybe Paige just needs somebody to talk to. 'I don't have the energy for what I have to do. Fuck. I'm either going to have to dig a large hole in the garden or I'm going to have to dig a smaller hole but chop him up into smaller pieces.' Paige baulks a little and tastes the pizza in her mouth again.

She moves the position of the camera so that it is closer to her face, but also higher, to give her the best angle.

Everything has been switched off but Paige.

'I don't know how anybody could ever murder somebody intentionally, to premeditate such a crime. That part must be hard enough. It's afterwards that the real work begins. I can't even think about that, right now. It's just too much. I can't. I just can't.'

The camera lowers and turns to black, like Paige is too upset to continue. But Edie is watching her on one of the other cameras and thinks she sees Paige nodding. Like she is counting with each nod of the head, giving herself enough time to emotionally recover.

Or perhaps she wants it to look that way on the diary-room footage. It's a deliberate pause.

'I'm going to drag him out into the garden and leave him in the shed at the bottom for now. He's very skinny. It wasn't difficult for me to turn things around when he tried to attack me with a knife.

I'm sure I'll be able to get him out of the house. This has taken everything out of me. I don't think I have the energy for anything else right now.'

She does have enough energy to call the police and explain what happened, though.

She just doesn't want to.

There's a pause, a moment of reflection perhaps. She's in and out. She's not a psychopath, she's just broken. Paige lowers the camera again. It stays in her hand, resting on the sofa. 'Fuck. I'm getting this all wrong. I'm getting everything wrong.'

She leaves the camera rolling. It doesn't take any video footage of what she does next but it does capture the audio of her struggles. Paige leaves the camera running until the battery is drained.

None of that matters because there are six other cameras pointing at her. Recording her every movement. Uploading to the cloud. Where it will exist forever.

23:15

'What did I miss?' Tammy bounds back into the editing suite. Glowing.

'Jesus, woman, you couldn't have showered? You smell like sex.'

'Well, I should damn well hope so. I thought I'd had enough wine to cover it up.'

She smiles a filthy little grin, but she looks so happy. Davis gives her that. He won't commit to it, but when they are together, there's nothing else.

'So, what *did* I miss?'

'Not much. She ate an entire pizza and actually managed to keep it in her system this time.'

'I don't understand why you'd need to throw up your food if you work out as much as she does and you look like that.' Tammy is naive, as many people are about fitness and nutrition now that everyone with an eating disorder and matching spandex is an expert.

There's too much information and it's all conflicting.

Too much choice of food.

Too little self-control.

Edie nods along as she takes another handful of popcorn and pours more wine. 'Maybe *we* should order some pizza. Could be a long night.'

Tammy says she has an app on her phone and can order right away. She's built up an appetite.

'She wants to get the bodies out of the house.'

'What?'

'That's what she says. She's going to move the boy first because he's the lightest.'

'Edie, you were right. I was sure she was going to break down and piss her pants. But this one is really stepping up to the plate. We could have something golden here. I can't wait to show Davis.'

'You've shown him plenty already.' Edie laughs.

They sit right next to one another, staring at the same screen. Edie, short mousy-brown hair and brown eyes. Tammy, long fake-blonde hair and eyes as blue as a robin's egg. They are so dissimilar in appearance, each could be the photo negative of the other. But, in front of those screens, watching some lucky internet sensation sweating and moaning as she tries to pull a deadweight wannabe haberdasher across her living-room floor, the two women couldn't be any more alike in their demeanour and glee at the fitfluencer's strife.

They look the same.

They have been working together so long that they are completely comfortable with one another. It's like a marriage. In fact, Tammy is just as close to being married to Edie as she is to Davis.

These women are ambitious and creative and wealthy beyond their means. If that is the measure of success, then they are done. What is left?

These things often go one of three ways:

Philanthropy: they've earned containerfuls of cash. More than they could ever spend, so they either give it away to charities or they get involved in a cause that is, apparently, close to their hearts and they feel gratified by doing something good, something worthwhile.

Something for somebody other than themselves.

Art: commercial success is one thing, and it can provide stability and a bucket less worry, but it doesn't feed their souls. There's no critical acclaim. They want to make something in black and white. Or French. For a smaller, more discerning audience. Because Joe Public is an idiot, and if that's who is watching their show or reading their book or listening to their music, then they are probably an idiot, too.

Power: they want to do what they want to do, make the things that they want to make. They want their own record label or movie studio. That way they can make their commercial crap AND their artsy garbage that nobody will watch. Hell, they'll even throw a couple of million at some blind kids or treatable cancer.

This thing with @TheFitnessPaige, this is Lincoln/Lowell's art. It's their *Citizen Kane* moment. They are orchestrating everything. They are writing, filming, directing and editing. They know how small the final audience will be but they don't care about that. It's not about the money. They're not worried about the box office take on opening weekend.

The thing is, when you can have anything you want, you start to want the things you can't have or shouldn't touch. Billionaires are having private parties with tinpot presidents and corrupt princes and underaged girls because they know it's wrong. Music moguls are shipping in vats of baby oil and drugging their guests. So why wouldn't a couple of TV assholes make a snuff movie to watch with their friends? As long as they don't get found out.

They drink wine and look the same and watch the screen as Paige tries to pull Less by placing her hands underneath his armpits, but the movement is too slow and jolting. She grips Less by the wrists and tries things that way, and it works a little better.

Edie and Tammy can't help but see the absurdity of the situation. They laugh at it. Paige pulling Less along by his hands and then letting go so that his head hits the hard floor. It's like a scene from a Marx Brothers movie.

A farce.

Paige gets into a rhythm eventually and disappears off the screen with the boy she stabbed, the front of his shirt soaked in blood. The producers don't see her for another eight minutes because there was no time to rig up a camera out the back, in the yard.

But Paige has already confessed that she is leaving Less's body in a building, outside, overnight, until she can get her head clear about what she should be doing in order to get away with this.

Paige re-enters her house through the door she left open earlier. The one her accidental victims used for easy entry. And she knows what she wants.

She wants her life back. The one she had before this evening. The one she was so ungrateful for, that she needed to escape for the weekend.

And she needs to sleep.

Her body is working hard to digest that pizza, and she just wants to lie down, shut her eyes and not think about what she's done.

But on her way back in, walking past Alyssa, she notices a bag lying next to the body. She doesn't know why she didn't see it before. Once she had accepted that both intruders had been neutralised, she didn't want to pay too much attention to them. A bag has been lying there all this time.

There is so much that you can miss in a stressful situation, when you are adrenalised or shocked.

She desperately wants to go to sleep but there could be something in the bag that identifies the people she has killed.

There's a purse with a driving licence, which displays Alyssa's name and address.

'Alyssa,' Paige says out loud. 'So pretty.'

Then she does the one thing she needs to do in order to learn a little more about Alyssa. She looks her up on social media.

Alyssa is prolific. Several accounts. Followers in the thousands on each of them but nothing that will get her noticed. One account is dedicated to food and cooking and baking. The pictures are well thought out and vibrant. The recipes are accessible.

Paige finds a video on another account where Alyssa is moving clothes along the rail in her wardrobe, trying to decide what to wear. She is talking towards the camera as though she has a captivated audience. It makes Paige cringe.

Swipe up.

Paige can see that Alyssa is desperate to become some kind of influencer but hasn't really settled on her product or brand or unique selling point. It's clear she doesn't have a vision, she just wants to be famous, be seen.

There's nothing personal there, though. It's all a front. A persona. An avatar. It doesn't garner much sympathy. Paige doesn't feel that the world of social-media influencing lacks something without this Alyssa girl. There has to be a profile somewhere of the real Alyssa. Maybe there is an account that shows her breaking into another house, maybe bragging about it.

Where is she from? Why did she come here? Was she following the boy? Did he lead her astray? Anything.

Search. Scroll. Tap.

Paige accidentally double-taps a picture of Alyssa, and the corpse beeps.

'Shit.' Paige double-taps again to take off her like. She doesn't want Alyssa's friends in 'the real world' seeing that. Hopefully she deleted it quick enough.

The vibration and noise from the phone in Alyssa's pocket jolt Paige out of her focus. She turns off her phone screen and goes back to the bag.

Inside is a small, black neoprene case that holds a video camera. It's the same brand as the one that is running low on battery on the sofa. It may even be the same model. Some big-time gaming influencer probably recommended it after receiving a couple of free ones in the post.

Paige is intrigued.

She taps the power button. The blue light flashes three times before the screen on the back lights up and shows her the part of the house the lens is pointing at. She presses the play button to switch from camera mode to video mode.

Twelve images of the dead woman on her floor pop up on the screen. Each one is a different video. If Paige wants to learn about who Alyssa is, or was, and just how she ended up at her house, she now has everything she needs.

23:20

It's strange to hear Alyssa's voice. Until now, Paige only ever heard her question Less about having a knife. The knife that Paige turned against him.

Paige was expecting more content like the videos of Alyssa she had found online. Maybe some raw footage of her baking something that was then condensed into something more palatable: a bite-sized recipe, edited to music with Alyssa perfectly made up and styled. Or another of her fashion guides or outfit selections.

It's none of that.

But it is raw.

There was a trend a few years back where young girls would video themselves crying. They would talk about how a boy had treated them or a friend had let them down or a parent hadn't understood them. They would be in their bedrooms or locked inside a closet for privacy, and they would unload their apparent troubles in front of the camera and then cry, their eyes packed heavily with mascara so that it could run and help create more drama.

It's difficult to know where it started. A cry for help or a cry for attention. It doesn't really matter. The girls (and boys) who then followed suit didn't ask that question. They just saw that somebody had done it. Then eighty people had done it. Then four thousand. And they wanted to be a part of it.

To stay on trend.

To be relevant.

Perpetuating the myth of reality.

There's a video like that on the camera that Paige found in Alyssa's bag. But Alyssa is in her early twenties. It's clear from her public content that she wants to be noticed, but this is private. This isn't for the world. This must be for herself.

Paige watches this video first.

Four times in a row.

It does seem real.

Alyssa is upset with herself because she got mad at Less for messing with Rosie's house. It's clear that she wasn't entirely mad. She was jealous. Jealous that she hadn't had the opportunity to go back to one of her favourite influencer's houses so that they could mess with her stuff together.

The video does not endear Alyssa to Paige in the slightest. She seems spoiled and desperate. Paige could probably empathise with Alyssa a little if she had the capability to feel such an emotion.

But the tears seem real, not just for the camera. Not just to add poignancy. Alyssa goes on to say that she feels guilty for dragging Less into this, that it was all her idea and he tends to follow her because he's so lovely and lively. 'He's like an excited puppy. He just wants somebody to play with him and have fun and rub his belly from time to time.'

The dead girl on the floor does not garner much sympathy for herself, but Paige does think about the boy in the shed at the bottom of her garden.

She killed a puppy.

Fuck.

He didn't seem at all confident while holding that knife, she sees that now, waving it about in front of himself, aimlessly. He was trying to protect his friend. Like a puppy barking at somebody threatening its master. It all makes sense.

Paige watches the same video over and over, and Edie and Tammy watch Paige.

Fascinated by nothingness.

– – – – – – – – – – –

23:29

'Maybe she's going to cry now,' Tammy says.

'I wouldn't bet on it. I don't think she has it in her. Those eyes don't even water when she makes herself sick after a meal.' Edie is cold.

Tammy is drunk.

Paige looks tired.

'Why do you think she keeps watching the same clip over and over again?' Tammy asks, taking another sip from her glass, washing her liver to oblivion.

'She stupid?'

Tammy doesn't respond to her partner's cutting remark.

'I'm sure we'll find out, Tam. Maybe she's still in shock. Maybe she's hoping it tells her something.'

'You know what I think?'

'What do you think?'

'Look at the way she punishes her body on a daily basis. All that training. Lifting weights and jumping around and kicking and punching stuff. And then she's eating more food than she needs and she has to keep throwing it back up. It must take its toll, but she continues to do it to herself, day in, day out. I think she's watching that video over and over again because she doesn't like it. Because she feels guilty. Because it makes her feel bad. And maybe she can only feel good when she feels bad. Or maybe she can only *feel* when she feels bad.'

Tammy seems triumphant at her pop-psychological breakdown.

Edie doesn't buy it.

'That's very observant, Tam, and I might think that you're on to something if it wasn't for one small thing: this woman can't feel any of those things because she's a fucking psychopath.'

Edie looks over at the clock on the wall then back at the screen. It's getting late. They have what they need for a captivating opening sequence.

Paige keeps the camera in her hand. She goes over to her back door – off camera – and checks that it is locked. She does the same with the front door. Then she walks back up the stairs towards her bedroom.

Edie and Tammy wait for another half an hour. When Paige doesn't return, they go to bed themselves, leaving the cameras rolling.

– – – – – – – – – –

23:58

There are no cameras in the bedroom.

Paige is exhausted.

But she's not going to sleep.

Another video shows Alyssa in her bedroom again:

'Ho. Lee. Shit. We just spent the night with Rosie Velazquez. Well, not with her but at her place. We didn't have to break in – there was a key underneath the mat. How stupid do you have to be? We looked around. Less ate some of her food and then we hid in the loft overnight. The worst part was listening to her having sex most of the time with that Adam guy she pretends is just her friend. Like we're all that stupid.'

Paige doesn't finish the video. She hits the back arrow. There are maybe another ten.

Is that how many times they've done this?

She watches the first ten or fifteen seconds of each one. Alyssa doesn't mention Less in all of them. There's one where they both stole a car and drove around all night but they gave it back. Apparently, they went to Jack Sandford's house, too.

Something clicks in her brain about Tom and Dana.

There are six videos where Alyssa doesn't mention Less at all. She says that she has been in somebody's home. Some of the names don't mean anything to Paige but there are a couple of influencers that she has rubbed shoulders with. One of them has a small vegan donut place that has become something of an LA hotspot for people who want to be seen.

Alyssa is definitely more into this than Less, Paige thinks.

The videos make it seem like Less has no idea that Alyssa is making a video diary about this stuff. He's complicit in the act but not in documenting the crimes.

The poor idiot.

He probably thinks that they are close. Best friends. That they tell each other everything. All the while she is going behind his back, then getting upset when he does it to her.

The more Paige sees of Alyssa, the more she feels sorry for her. She wants the fame. She wants what Paige and Rosie have but she has no idea what it does to you when you get it. Even if Paige could explain how lonely it is having so many followers, Alyssa would still have craved it.

The difference is that Rosie and Paige both have a passion for something and the notoriety is secondary. Alyssa wanted the fame to find herself, Paige knows that it's the reason she is lost.

Paige turns off the camera screen. She can't take any more of this. It's a god-damned farce. There's a dead woman in her lounge. How is this real?

The camera looks almost identical to the one that she was given by the production company to upload her diary room files. There's a button that you can press and it uploads anything that you have recorded to YouTube. In Paige's case, it was explained to her that it was already set up so her diary entries would go to the Lincoln/Lowell account but would be unlisted. Meaning that they could not be accessed by the public unless the link was given. And that could only be done by Edie or Tammy.

But they didn't want it shared.

Paige, for whatever reason, thinks that it might work to her advantage if these videos could be seen by *real* people in the *real* world. Maybe, if this whole thing ever makes it to court, it will help her defence if it is shown that Alyssa has prior form, that she has a history of invading people's privacy.

The clips certainly do not show Alyssa in her best light.

She hits the upload button and waits.

It feels like a minute passes, but it's only ten seconds. Paige hears the noises that houses make when you are alone in the dark. She convinces herself that someone is in the garden and that another person is moving around downstairs.

Then the camera beeps.

Not connected to a wifi network. Please check settings.

'Oh, for God's sake.'

Paige finds her phone and scrolls through her photos. She took a picture of the wifi code on the back of her router a while back. She doesn't want to go downstairs again tonight.

She eventually finds the image she is looking for, locates the settings option on the camera and gets the equipment onto her home network.

She presses the button again.

This time, Paige doesn't have to wait long.

File has already been uploaded.

She tries the most recent video.

File has already been uploaded.

'Fuck.' It's frustrating. Paige doesn't know where the file has been uploaded to.

She knows that her videos get saved as 'unlisted' to the Lincoln/Lowell channel. She assumes that Alyssa is keeping hers online somewhere, to be seen, to show off. To get her fifteen minutes of fame, even if that is for committing an offence.

Paige could post the videos from Alyssa's camera. Share them on her platform. Maybe somebody online would put together the obvious link between Alyssa and this Tom and Dana ghost duo that the media have created and run with. Maybe then she will be able to get ahead of this thing.

The information could be out there. And information shared is out there forever. Whether it's right or wrong.

00:05

Alyssa's mother texts her. She had a little time off before the weekend but has managed to pick up an extra shift, and now wants to know whether her daughter would like to go shopping or to the cinema. Just to spend some time together. There are three generations of women in that house, so most of the time together is very functional. It's cooking dinner and fixing drinks and washing the dishes.

They don't have much time, or money, for fun. For downtime. They focus on their food. Spending time together for dinner when they can, but other than that, Alyssa is studying or breaking into people's homes, her mother works shifts at the hospital, so every week is different timings, and her grandmother sits eight inches from a TV screen that broadcasts quiz shows 24/7.

Alyssa's mother can't really afford to go shopping for clothes but also doesn't see the sense in working all of these late nights or early mornings to not use some of the disposable income for fun and frivolity.

There has to be some kind of balance.

And she doesn't want her daughter to feel like she is missing out. Especially when her best friend comes from a wealthy family.

Above all, *she* doesn't want to miss out on time with her daughter. She has accepted that, from the age of twelve or thirteen, Alyssa didn't need her as much as she once did – she was always naturally independent and had been forced to fend for herself from a young age while her mother worked, getting herself up and dressed and fed. But all kids get to an age when their friends become the most important thing in their lives and their teachers become the smartest adults they know. And the parents are just the annoying people with stupid rules.

She just wants some time with her daughter.

One on one.

To talk about anything and everything. To have a coffee or a glass of wine. They have always been close, they have always got on, but it would be good for them to have some time together away from the one-woman general-knowledge machine.

To be themselves.

To be real.

Alyssa's mother sees these millennial/Generation Z types, running around not knowing what the fuck to do with their lives. Vaping and filming every private moment and just hoping to be seen and liked. They say they want to make an impact. Like it's their duty. But they don't realise what that means. And they don't know how they should do it. Wandering through life, oblivious about what it means to be living.

They don't know who they are.

They don't know what they want.

And Alyssa's mother knows exactly what her heart desires. And it's simple. And it's a little selfish but with the best intentions. She wants some time with her daughter. With the person she loves the most. Because, to her, time is wealth, not money.

What she doesn't know is that, sometimes, the things we want, we want too late.

00:10

Don't even ask.

A three-word social-media post.

It's clickbait. Everybody knows it is. People are reading and getting annoyed by it because it's so blatant. A friend – not a real friend, a social-media friend – has had a bad day and they write these three words on a post and hit send.

They want somebody to ask.

Nobody wants to ask. They really don't. It's just begging for attention.

You okay, hun?

It's a relief. Somebody else has asked. A bullet has been dodged. Just wait for the response, read, fulfil any voyeuristic urges and life can continue.

I'll message you.

Damn. That doesn't help. Then somebody else remarks with something that indicates that they already know the full story, and it eats away at those in the dark because human curiosity is a cancer.

#FOMO.

#MakingMemories.

It's stupid to get involved in the affairs of others. And nobody *really* cares because this pretend friend is always putting up cryptic things like this or wishing their dead grandparent a happy birthday or saying something to the person who cut them up in their car while on the school run, even though that person will never read the message. So it's best to resist and not to get into it.

It would be playing into their hands. It's exactly what they want.

But it eats away. That spirit of inquiry. And, while it is annoying, people still want to know.

So they ask. Even though they don't really want to.

This is how it works. It keeps even the most sane and rounded person on the edge of madness or self-loathing.

Ariel Dean was never like that. She belonged to a very exclusive group of the few who are honest online. Who hoped that what they are writing and sharing would somehow benefit another person. It would make a small difference.

At least, that's what she was like before her following grew overnight. Now she has to be interesting and relevant all the time.

She wants to keep some things back, but the bug takes hold quickly. It changes people. Fame changes people. An audience changes people. Ariel doesn't want to talk about her apparent feud with @TheFitnessPaige anymore. She certainly doesn't want to publicise that they are going to talk face-to-face tomorrow. She doesn't want to tell anybody about the letter she received. Ariel just wants to be brave and confront Paige on her own. Hopefully resolve things. And never mention it again.

Still, there are people listening now, so she posts 'Important meeting tomorrow. Scared, obviously, but hopeful.'

#DontEvenAsk.

- - - - - - - - - - -

03:33

It's quiet. It's dark. It's so late that tonight is already yesterday. And nothing moves but the trees in the wind and the nocturnal wildlife.

And Less.

Paige is sleeping soundly. No nightmares. No flashbacks. No guilt. She is wrapped in her quilt. Warm and comfortable. Protected. There's a cold pizza in the fridge for tomorrow and the other is slowly working its way to her thighs, which is where the weight always seems to go first for her. It's nothing that anybody can control.

Genetics and luck.

The cameras in the lounge are on standby mode in the evenings. They only turn on when there is movement. So, if Paige goes sleepwalking or can't resist refrigerated margarita in the middle of the night, three of the cameras will whir back to life to capture the moment in fuzzy green night-vision footage. But there's no sense in leaving them running all night and taking up valuable space on the servers.

None of the cameras will come on until morning.

There's nothing moving in that house until Sunday dawns.

Less lies on the floor of the shed. Paige dragged him through the doorway, scratching his back against the wood, hitting his head against an upright, eventually dropping him on his side with his head resting on a bag of sand that was left over from the path she'd had laid.

Paige threw a picnic blanket over Less's body that is keeping him warm. She took the shovel and rested it against the outside of the shed, then padlocked the place shut.

He's locked in.

The moon shines in through the small window. It's directly above Paige's house, looking down on the pathetic scene below. Less, staring up, hoping to witness a shooting star that he can wish on. Maybe he could ask to turn back time, to be more prepared when Paige came down the stairs. Or maybe he could wish that the whole thing stopped after the Jack Sandford close call. Or that they never stole that car or went to the Davis Davis party, at all.

Because that's where all of this started.

That's how this came about.

That is why both he and Alyssa are here.

That stupid fucking party.

Rich people are assholes.

Less looks at the sky through that shed window. The door remains locked. The ground remains cold. The front of his T-shirt remains crimson red.

And no shooting star appears.

– – – – – – – – – – –

SUNDAY

SCROLLUP

^^^^^^^^^^

^^^^^^^^^^

@RosieVelazquez
'#ItsSunday. God's day.'
♥ **321**

^^^^^^^^^^

^^^^^^^^^^

It's the only day of the week that Rosie Velazquez doesn't go running. Because she walks to church, upholding her online bio description that she is a servant of the big, bearded man upstairs. Monday to Saturday, she nourishes her body and her mind, but today, Rosie focusses on her soul.

She's still not right after the incident and posts regularly about Tom and Dana, and how we need to be vigilant and alert in order to stop them from terrorising anybody else.

She's also looking to move because she just doesn't feel safe in her own home anymore. Even though it's unlikely for the perpetrator to return in these sorts of crimes, it has made Rosie increasingly paranoid and anxious about every creak and movement of her once-perfect house.

^^^^^^^^^^

^^^^^^^^^^

@TheJackSandford
'#ItsSunday. Hangover day.'
♥ **46k**

^^^^^^^^^^

^^^^^^^^^^

One of many for Jack Sandford, who gets invited to parties all the time. Who can work whatever day and whatever time he wishes. He can go through the night, laying down tracks at the studio for a new album, or he can stay up until morning doing coke and screwing whichever groupie is ready to spread her legs that day.

But Sunday morning is a different level of hangover because it follows Saturday night, and on a Saturday night Jack Sandford *only* parties. No work, unless he is playing a gig, in which case the night is even bigger. He will eat out with somebody, drink and then hit the clubs. It doesn't have to be exclusive, it doesn't have to be a VIP area, cordoned off with velvet ropes. It can be some backroom dive or late-night Japanese karaoke booth. Jack Sandford has one thing on his mind and that is getting fucked up.

He's not waking early on a Sunday for church.

When you're a rock god, you don't need to look up to anybody.

Jack Sandford has not been affected in the same way as Rosie Velazquez. He isn't sitting around in one of his mansions, worrying about somebody getting in who shouldn't be there. Because there are always people at his house that shouldn't be there.

For Jack, it's a funny story about how his knuckle-dragging entourage had no idea that they were hanging out with the New Manson Family, trying to get them to play pool and mix cocktails. Sharing hummus and pretzels.

He doesn't see it as something malicious. Just a couple of kids trying to get their kicks in a way that isn't through their phone screens.

Life goes on for Jack Sandford.

And it is a glorious life, lived fast and full.

^^^^^^^^^^

^^^^^^^^^^

PAIGE

It's Sunday.

Sweat day.

I post all of my own workouts throughout the week and I perform my livestreams and online classes for all of my followers, but Sundays are for me; I don't even jump in on the #ItsSunday trend.

It's difficult to find the time to work out for myself when I spend most of my life training others and getting them into shape. But you have to make that time. And I always do that on a Sunday.

I found a couple online who run their own fitness business. They're both vegan and probably ten years older than I am but I love the way they work out. It's full-on, balls-to-the-wall, digging as deep as you can go and pushing until you want to throw up.

It's that kind of workout.

And I absolutely love it.

I love it so much that I keep it to myself. I could probably help to grow their business exponentially with the flick of a switch. A quick mention or some kind of endorsement online and a good percentage of my followers would add them into their monthly fitness budget, even if it was just for a Sunday workout to be more like me.

But I don't.

I see how many followers they have and I know that they probably struggle a little and rejoice at every extra person they get, but I don't help them. Even though I boost a mediocre leggings brand by tagging them in a video or I bump profits for a protein bar that tastes the same as all the others – they send me boxes for free – I don't do it for my favourite workout of the week.

That may seem horrible. But it's mine, and I don't have anything that's just for me anymore.

It feels personal.

And I don't share personal stuff.

And I won't miss my Sunday workout just because I killed two people the night before.

None of this feels real. None of this feels like anything. I'm numb. A zombie. It's like I'm not even really here. So I need this. I need something that I know is real. I need something that can remind me how to feel.

^^^^^^^^^^

^^^^^^^^^^

It's Sunday.

Shocked day.

Edie and Tammy look like shit. And they feel even worse. Everything they planned is coming together but they still eat like children and drink like fish and stay up like a couple of rock stars. They don't go to church for fear of bursting into a ball of flames when they walk through the doors.

They sit there, mouths open, unable to tear themselves away from the screen that shows Paige squatting and jumping and sweating while doing a live online workout with Alyssa's body lying next to her on the floor. They can only see part of Alyssa at the bottom of one of the screens, but she is still there.

'See? This girl is cuckoo,' Edie says, with a knowing raise of the eyebrow.

'Yup. But she is solid TV gold.'

^^^^^^^^^^

^^^^^^^^^^

Davis Davis
108 **111k** **335**
posts followers following
@davisdavis

This account is private
Follow this account to see their photos and videos.

ʌʌʌʌʌʌʌʌʌʌ

ʌʌʌʌʌʌʌʌʌʌ

There are bathrooms in the new house that Davis hasn't even used yet.

It's that huge.

But it still didn't have everything that he needed when he bought it. He hasn't unpacked all of his furniture and memorabilia yet. Luckily, the new place has an attic that feels like a football field with rafters. His platinum records are already on the wall, as is his Andy Warhol painting, and his framed Michael Jordan vest is hanging behind the desk in his new study.

Upstairs, out of sight, is a French Kingwood Escritoire writing desk in mahogany with marble top that deserves to be seen every day. But it is tucked away behind a framed cinema poster of Rita Hayworth in *Gilda*. There are rows of items like this. Treasures that should not be hidden from the world. That may never be seen again.

Davis Davis bought the house almost a year ago. It was almost perfect. Acres of land for his legendary parties, extra rooms for all of his guests and the bands that visit and play and audition for him. There's even a recording studio out the back that would make Brian Wilson blush.

But it didn't have a screening room.

Somewhere to watch early releases of nominated movies, for his consideration. Somewhere to gather and cheer through game seven of the NBA finals or the Super Bowl or any major sporting event. But it's also where he gets to see the Lincoln/Lowell passion projects. The programmes they want to make but the industry is too scared or too cautious or too risk-averse about, even with their track record of success.

There are no phones allowed in there. They *are* allowed but they won't work. No reception. No wifi. No disturbances. It has to be a complete surrender to the art.

Wall-to-wall screen. The highest definition. He spent a quarter of a million to get the same speaker system that George Lucas uses. Many cinemas opt for Dolby Atmos because it is more immersive, but THX sound is cleaner and comes out closer to the way the artist intended.

Davis Davis is a sound geek. He knows his stuff after a lifetime in the music industry, but he invested in this because he wants to watch the Lincoln/Lowell production in the way they want it to be seen and heard.

As artists.

He did it for Tammy.

He built it all for Tammy.

Davis believes in her. He wants her to move away from trash TV and make art, something that she can be proud of. Something that means that Tammy is taken seriously as a producer, a creator.

Maybe then, *he* could take her more seriously. He could take their relationship more seriously, and people out there would judge in a way that would mean Davis would not have to explain himself. He wouldn't have to justify his reasons for being with her. Nobody ever asks him about the models he is seen with.

He is rich enough and powerful enough to not have to care about this kind of thing, but he wants it to work with Tammy so much that it has to be perfect from the off. Davis doesn't want any complications.

In his caution, all he is doing is wasting time when he could be with the woman he adores. Instead, their relationship remains like the French bureau in his attic room.

Unseen.

Unappreciated.

And if Davis is not careful, if he waits too long and does not do the right thing, he will see it all go up in flames.

^^^^^^^^^

^^^^^^^^^

#CleanEating #HealthyLiving #EatTheRainbow
There are days when Ariel Dean finds it difficult to get out of bed. If she doesn't give her body the correct nutrients, she's screwed. She wakes up and flatlines for the morning.

There has been such a tremendous amount of trial and error to get her to a place where she knows the foods that her system will absorb adequately and keep her going, so that she can live a relatively normal life.

For a while, doughnuts seemed to help until she realised that the crash was harder. The comedown from that perfect mix of sugar and fat is worse for Ariel than speed is for Less.

She is in tune with her body now though. But there are still days when she struggles. When she wants to pull the covers over her face and try again tomorrow.

Today is not one of those days.

^^^^^^^^^^

^^^^^^^^^^

@FoodForThought
'#ItsSunday.'
♥ 47

^^^^^^^^^^

^^^^^^^^^^

Closure day.

Ariel is going to respond to Paige's letter of apology and visit her at her home. This could have been done over the phone or a Zoom call or with a post on one of her social-media platforms, but Paige seemingly wants Ariel to visit her at her house.

There's an address but no phone number. It wouldn't be difficult for Ariel to message, but she got so annoyed with the last childish response that she unfollowed her former inspiration and blocked her.

So she has no idea that Paige is currently offline and is supposed to be away on some kind of recovery retreat.

Ariel Dean doesn't have the time or energy to deal with these kinds of high-maintenance, high-functioning narcissists. But she is so intrigued about what Paige could possibly want to say to her that wasn't already covered in the letter, she has to go.

Human intrigue is worse than the curiosity that killed the cat.

She could have knocked back a six-pack of Dunkin' Doughnuts with a gallon of full-fat Pepsi last night and she still would have leapt out of bed this morning like she'd rolled onto a Lego brick.

Her male friend is no longer coming over with his yoghurt pot of semen. As much as the entire situation could have been handled more sensitively, what Paige said was right. Ariel had been duped. She has worked hard to get herself healthy but she is still looking for that magic pill to make everything okay, to make it a little easier.

It's all anybody wants.

A tablet that you can take that will melt fat from your body so you don't have to go to the gym six times a week or only eat lettuce and ice cubes for dinner. They want the potion that will lead them to their one true love. Or they want the job working from home for six hours a week that pays five times as much as their full-time office job.

Or a pump that makes their dick twice as big.

Or the Nigerian king who really needs to transfer thirty million into your bank account before he flies over to meet you.

Now, all Ariel wants is to see why @TheFitnessPaige wants to see her, why the letter wasn't enough. Because it was more than enough for Ariel.

She finishes her breakfast smoothie bowl. Another ridiculous invention. Frozen banana and mixed berries blended with a non-dairy milk. But she doesn't drink it. No. That would make too much sense. She pours it into a bowl then chops more fruit to go on top and sprinkles it with chia seeds and coconut. Maybe some granola.

And she eats it with a spoon. Sure, she could have blended the initial ingredients and then stirred in some extra fruit and seeds or oats but that isn't as Instagrammable.

#CleanEating.

#Food4Thought.

#PointlessGimmick.

It may have a placebo effect on Ariel Dean but that doesn't matter, surely, if it *is* having an effect. If she thinks it's working. What harm does that cause anybody else?

She finishes eating her liquid. Out of a bowl. With a spoon. Then makes herself a coffee to go. She is only allowed either four instant coffees each day or two 'good' coffees. By that, she means either from her machine or from a coffee shop. She says it affects her cortisol levels.

They can't be too high.

Or too low.

Too high and you risk weight gain, acne or female facial hair. Too low and you risk continual tiredness, nausea and muscle weakness. So now that the fitness industry has cottoned on to something that nobody really considered before, it's another way for people to aspire to perfection.

Just the right amount of cortisol.

Of course, cortisol is released when people are stressed, and nothing stresses a person out like aiming to get things perfect.

Ariel has a handle on this now, like she does with most things. She has learned through failure. And today will be no different.

She leaves her house and gets into her modest but practical Ford. She'd love a hybrid or an electric car but the initial outlay is too much right now. She doesn't want any recognition for her environmental concern, she just wants to do her bit, she wants to live her life. She wants to be kind to herself, other people and the planet.

She even plans to be kind to the person who rubbished her to a million people on the internet.

Ariel puts the address into her Maps app. It's thirty-five minutes across town. She's never been there before. It'll be interesting to see the neighbourhood, she thinks.

She is a laid-back and thoughtful individual but she is a little nervous about this meeting.

And she should be.

Paige has no idea Ariel is coming.

^^^^^^^^^

^^^^^^^^^

#RedCarpetReady #AndTheOscarGoesTo

'Wow. Thank you. That's a wonderful reception. Thank you.' Satmohan holds up a can of spray deodorant as he looks in the bathroom mirror. 'Of course, I would like to thank the Academy for this great honour. When my parents migrated from Jalandhar, it was because my father wanted more opportunities than the sporting-goods industry. He wanted his children to have more possibilities than he ever had.'

Satmohan opens his mouth and licks at something he thinks he sees in his teeth.

'It's sanctimonious, Sat. Nobody cares about the American Dream anymore.'

He sprays under his armpits and pulls a T-shirt over his head.

Every year he watches the Oscars and it leaves him feeling buoyant and energised for success in his chosen industry. When his parents came across the ocean, they had certainly set their sights on something more stable and worthwhile. A doctor, preferably. A lawyer, at a push. But Sat had gone his own way.

And he wants to do it again.

He feels like he has paid his dues, getting Edie's caramel macchiato, fetching Tammy's laundry. They've certainly imparted some of their wisdom and experience in his direction and have given him more and more responsibility every time he proves himself.

And he's grateful for all the parties and events he has been able to attend and the people he has had the chance to meet. He's seen some things at those parties, too. Women (and men) being drugged and taken off to rooms for god knows what to happen to them. He has woken up in his bed and can't remember a thing that happened the night before. But he knows he didn't have a good time.

Nobody wants to say anything though, because they are scared that they will never become relevant or they won't remain that way. Yet, still, Satmohan is somehow grateful for the experience and the opportunity.

The first series he worked on, *Never Met, Now We're Married*, he was credited as a runner. On the next he was cited as being Edie's personal assistant. He didn't like that. Now he gets production assistant before his name. It's gradual but it's in the right direction.

He is so Westernised, though, that he wants it all now. Before he has had a chance to work for it. To fail. To learn. These influencers become successful overnight, why can't he?

Satmohan wants to make documentaries. They are real. Reality television is not real. He wants to get out, move on. But nobody leaves Lincoln/Lowell Productions without Edie and Tammy hearing about it first. There's no way he could get time off in the week to meet up with someone in the industry before somebody else called Edie to let her know.

But it's Sunday, and the bosses are knee-deep in one of their vanity projects that will never see the light of day. It's Satmohan's chance. He approached Martin Quartermain about being a part of one of his projects in the future. They have been talking online. Satmohan is lined up to be a part of a documentary feature film about the People of Choice cult. At the moment, he is down to be a researcher.

He sees it as another step towards the speech he has been practising in the mirror.

But the director wants to meet for coffee to finalise a few things.

Satmohan picks up the deodorant again. 'My thanks should also go out to the two people who took that first chance on me: Edie

Lincoln and Tammy Lowell. They taught me so much about the industry – its people and talent and how to succeed. They showed me how to make a TV show and, more importantly, how *not* to make a TV show.'

This is where he seems ungrateful, a clever little shit.

He's decided that he's bigger than his position at Lincoln/Lowell. In his head, he has moved on to greener pastures, already.

What he should have learned from those two stalwarts of the industry, as morally bankrupt as they are, is that you don't celebrate anything until the ink is dry.

^^^^^^^^^

^^^^^^^^^

PAIGE

It seems like everybody's life is moving forward but the two people that broke into my home, whose lives have seemingly stopped.

Everywhere else, it's just another Sunday.

I am dripping with sweat after my online workout.

'Take some time if you need to stretch a little more. Refuel your body with good food. Eat colourful stuff.' They say almost the same thing after every workout. Their marketing could do with some work, but they do have a brand and they do have these repeated sayings that clients and viewers would remember.

They are amazing but I just don't want them to hit. I know it will change them, like it changed me. They think they want what I've got but they have no idea. They're perfect the way they are, and I don't want to lose that. I don't want them to lose that.

I feel myself smile as I log off. Then I take a mouthful of water as I walk to the kitchen to completely ignore the advice of my trainer by eating a slice of fridge pizza. I manage it in three bites and wash it down with more water.

Usually, on all the other Sundays when I have not suddenly

become a murderer, I would make myself a protein shake with many of the same ingredients that Ariel Dean would use in one of her smoothie bowls, and I'd take it into the shower with me.

There's no point in having a shower now because I'm only going to get sweaty again by digging holes in my yard, big enough for an adult to lie in and decompose.

God, what have I become? The idea should haunt me, but I think I lost who I was some time ago. I don't know if I can ever get her back. Physically, I'm in great shape, but I'm mentally unhealthy. All the videos say that we should talk about these things, but what if we have nobody to talk to?

Alyssa's camera is still in my bedroom, but I made sure to plug in mine, which is identical, before the workout started. It has enough battery for me to make a diary entry.

'Last night was a total fuck-up. It was instinct more than anything else and I've always followed my instincts. Today, I am torn. There is still a part of me that thinks I should call the police but there is a larger part that says it was a mistake. And people get away with mistakes all the time.'

I have a plan and I go on to explain it.

My home is designed in a way that the back of the house is balanced over the rear patio. There are no uprights. No pillars or steel beams. It's a cantilevered structure that keeps the patio slabs dry but it all pushes out over some of the grass.

That is where I am going to dig.

The neighbours would be able to see me from the rear of their properties if I took a shovel to the bottom of the yard. The area closer to the house seems more private. Of course, this will be the day that the people next door will suddenly try to have a conversation with me, I bet. That's just how it goes.

The weather is mild outside and brightening up. That's LA. There's not much chance of me hitting soft, wet earth. If this was a movie, there'd be an image of me digging in the rain, hair wet and hanging over my face, grey skies, red eyes from the tears. But it's not like that here. The sky is blue. There are no clouds. The ground is dry. I could take a selfie, digging in the sunshine, sweat glistening on my toned arms and it would look almost happy. Maybe even sexy and energetic.

Sinister, if you're in the know.

Which only I am.

I'm on my own. Like always.

I'm still ignoring Alyssa. I walk to the bottom of my yard, to where I left the spade out last night. The door to the shed is padlocked. There's no reason, other than paranoia, that I would look in through the side window, but I can't help it. I can just about see the blanket that I draped over the guy, to keep him concealed.

He'll be first.

I've seen enough TV and movies to know that the creators cut corners with even the shallowest of graves. These things take a long time. I'm not looking to put him six feet under, but I need him to be completely covered and ensure that the smell of his rotting body doesn't seep out into the atmosphere immediately behind my home.

I don't even flinch at this thought. What the hell is wrong with me?

As I pick up the shovel, my neighbour appears at their back window. All of the houses are different along this street, so I don't know if that is his bedroom or not, but he is looking directly at me.

At first, he just stares, and I think, 'Oh, God, I bet I don't look like I'm here to do some yard work, I look like I'm ready to bury a body.'

So I wave. I try to look friendly. Breezy.

And, straight away, I feel stupid and awkward. Why am I entering into a dialogue with this person? We have lived next door to one another for over a year and hardly acknowledged that the other person exists unless we are caught out the front at the wrong moment and have to give a furtive glance.

He doesn't wave back.

He's suspicious. I know it.

But then he does. He gives an awkward smile, too. He's not

wearing a top so I can see his body. He looks healthy. He must work out. Judging from the size of his place, he can probably afford to shop at Wholefoods, too, so he definitely eats the right things.

But now we're stuck. Where do we go from here? I have very few flowers and plants in my yard because I'm not interested in that sort of thing and they would just die and look ghastly. I mow the lawn and that's about it. So why would I need to dig anything up? Shit. I don't even remember ever buying a shovel, it must have been left in the shed by the previous owner.

I do grow my own tomatoes because they are easy. Anyone could do it. But there are three pots lined up against the wall, I wouldn't need a giant spade for that.

If I was sweating during my Sunday-morning workout, it doesn't compare to now, in this agonising moment of nothingness where I look as guilty as hell about something.

I think about giving him a thumbs-up, and my cheeks start to blush at the stupidity of it. At least I can feel that, I guess.

Oh, God. Do something, Paige.

I can see the bottom of Alyssa's feet through the lounge window and instinctively turn towards the shed. I can't think about that, right now.

Then my neighbour opens his window.

'Nice day for it.'

For what? What does he know?

'I mean, I don't know what *it* is, but it is a nice day,' he adds, and smiles. It's disarming.

'Digging around the garden,' I say back. It's not really a response to his statement. It's not even a full statement in return. Or a question. It's just some words, thrown into the world.

He nods.

Another pregnant pause.

'Hey,' he finally breaks the silence, 'I hope you don't mind me asking but you're The Fitness Paige, am I right?'

'That's right. Um, Paige is just fine.' I don't know whether to ask his name. He could be somebody famous but I don't feel like I have seen him before. He's probably some tech guru.

'I subscribe to your app and do the workouts.'

'You can tell.'

#Cringe.

#KillMeNow.

He can see that I'm struggling with this interaction, surely. Great behind the screen but awkward in real life. Please just go back in. Don't prolong the agony.

'I'm Nolan. I know we've been neighbours for a while, I just ... People don't talk much in real life anymore, huh? It's all done online. I guess I'm just as bad. Anyway, I'll let you get on with your ... digging. I guess I'll see you tomorrow for the fight workout, but you won't see me.'

I lift the shovel, half like I need to get on but half in recognition of his efforts.

He shuts the window.

I lower my head and walk to the top of my yard where I mark out a four by one foot rectangle with the spade by pushing it an inch or so into the lawn. The body doesn't have to be lying straight. The hole just has to be deep enough for it to be tipped in.

I jut my head out from beneath the roof and look up cautiously at the window. He's not there. And even if he was, he wouldn't be able to see what I am doing.

I'm safe. Alone again.

I start by removing the top couple of inches of lawn, trying to keep it as intact as possible so that it can be laid back in place once the hole is refilled.

Then I dig. Shovelling the dirt into a pile on the paving slabs. I don't even think about the fact that it won't all go back in once the body is taking up space in the cavity. That's for future Paige to worry about.

Those movies are fucking lying. It takes me forty minutes to clear a foot of earth. If I'd killed a couple of rabbits, I'd be done. But there's a young man in my shed. He has a slight frame, sure, but I still have work to do. It's taking longer than I ever thought or hoped. Maybe checking that I'm not being watched every few minutes is adding to the time. Maybe I'm tired and under-fuelled after my workout.

I need more fridge pizza.

I jab the spade into the ground and go back inside. I pick up the camera from the sofa because I feel like I should document this journey. It's become second nature to do this.

Another bite from another slice and I melt into myself.

Why does everything that is so bad feel so good?

I have tomato sauce on my cheek where I tried to cram in as much as possible, I can feel it. My hands are dirty from the mud in the yard. I am caked in sweat. No way am I fit for a picture, but I don't mind making the video diary. Because this is supposed to be reality. A documentary of sorts. To show the real me, not the perfect version of me.

The camera goes on.

I swallow and think about my opening line.

I hit record.

The doorbell rings.

^^^^^^^^^

^^^^^^^^^

#Starstruck #UnrealMoment #HeroInRealLife

Deep breath in. Count to three. Exhale.

Count to three again.

Repeat.

Shift your weight from side to side.

Breathe again.

Ariel is freaking out. She is nervous. There is no gate to the front drive of Paige's home, but it feels rude to just park next to her house. There was no time on the letter, it just asked for Ariel to come over and talk.

She drove around for twenty minutes trying to find somewhere to leave her car. Every house bigger than the last. More intimidating. Ariel doesn't belong here. From what she has seen of @TheFitnessPaige, she wouldn't think that Paige belonged here either.

Ariel is polite. She is thoughtful. She didn't want to leave her car on the side of the road. Her shitty Ford, lowering the value of the properties on that street. After feeling out of place and stupid for going on what seems like a wild-goose chase, Ariel parked outside Paige's house.

And now she is on the doorstep, counting her breaths and shuffling her feet. Terrified of what lies behind the door. Like she is confronting her childhood bully.

In. One, two, three.

Exhale.

She presses the doorbell.

Her heart rate increases. Maybe Paige isn't even home and this is all for nothing.

But Ariel hears a crash.

^^^^^^^^^^

^^^^^^^^^^

[LIVESTREAM]

Paige is inside, dropping the camera on the floor. She won't be filming her diary entry now.

She needs to clean her face.

She needs to obscure the dead body in the lounge, just as she did when the pizza was delivered.

And Edie and Tammy need to watch it all unfold.

^^^^^^^^^^

^^^^^^^^^^

@TheJackSandford
'Starting to feel more human after breakfast and a little hair of the dog. Forgot to mention my new trucker's cap. I love it. I don't remember buying it and, I'm sorry, I can't remember who sent it to me. But I am grateful.'
♥ 19k ☐ 245

^^^^^^^^^^

^^^^^^^^^^

[LIVESTREAM]

'Shh. Shh. Shh.' Tammy taps Edie on the arm to quiet down, even though she is not talking. 'I want to hear how she reacts.' She points at Alyssa's feet in the bottom left corner of one of the screens. 'She has to be in view, right?'

They could have called the police. But the viewing is too interesting. The evidence is there, it has all been recorded. They could lie and say that Paige knew the cameras were on but just forgot, then it wouldn't look as though they were illegally surveilling her. (They have money and lawyers who can make things go away, anyway.)

Edie and Tammy have never had a single intention to alert the authorities.

And they never will.

What they did do, however, is send a letter to Ariel Dean, via Satmohan, apologising on Paige's behalf and inviting her over. Because this is what reality television is all about. It's not about filming what is real, it is about staging something that looks real, it's about manufacturing and controlling the situation.

If you are making a show about rich kids from Chelsea, you set the filming in a VIP area at a club or the designer section of a department store or an exclusive eatery. Because you want them to look spoiled and out of touch.

If you are producing some kind of matchmaking programme, where couples are placed together by experts and are made to live together, you set them tasks to discuss what they don't like about the other person. You dress it up as 'talking things out' or 'confronting problems' but it's because the audience requires conflict if they are going to remain tuned in. Nobody wants to see a happy couple for too long. There's only so much time you can watch a car pootle around picturesque country roads before you want to see it crash and burn.

And, if you are filming a renowned fitness and nutrition influencer – somebody who is self-aware and in tune with themselves and their surroundings, and they get their ten thousands steps in each day without even leaving the house, and they eat all the fruit and vegetables that are recommended by the World Health Organisation, and they never get sick, and they are beautiful and toned, and eloquent when they speak – you want to disrupt their life. You want to throw a spanner into the works.

You want them off kilter.

Knocked from their perch.

So you send a letter to somebody with whom they have recently had an online spat. You invite them over to create a confrontation.

If there has been no spat, it's very easy to create one of those, too.

And, if that influencer happens to have murdered a couple of people the night before, this will only add to the paranoia and tension.

Lincoln/Lowell Productions are so pleased with themselves.

It's fun to play God.

^^^^^^^^^

^^^^^^^^^

PAIGE

The camera isn't broken.

I pick it up off the floor and test it. Any hope I might have had of ignoring the doorbell has evaporated after making such a noise. The screen lights up and I place it on the chopping board next to the sink. I wipe around my mouth with the back of my hand and run my fingers through my hair. This is not how I want to open the door. To anyone.

It's probably just another product that some start-up is hoping I will endorse.

I'm not even supposed to be here today.

I was very clear about that.

Why can't people just leave me alone?

^^^^^^^^^^

^^^^^^^^^^

#NeverMeetYourHeroes #FifteenMinutesOfFame

It has been a moment since the crashing sound, Ariel has waited patiently, performing her breathing exercises. Maybe it's not the right time.

This is a stupid idea she tells herself.

Just as she turns away, the door opens.

^^^^^^^^^^

^^^^^^^^^^

PAIGE

'Can I help you?' I ask, only opening the door a crack.

'Paige?' the woman asks. Like I should know who she is. Maybe I look so disgusting that she doesn't think it's me. I probably don't look a lot like the woman on The Fitness Paige social-media platforms. I'm not as perfect-looking. Not lit from above. I want to cower behind the door even more.

'Yes, and you are…?' It takes me a split second to register the woman in front of my eyes. Not because she doesn't look like her online profile – she looks exactly the same. In fact, she's hardly wearing any make-up and she is positively glowing. It's just that she is the last person I ever expected to see on my doorstep. Especially this weekend when *everyone* knows that I am supposed to be away. '…Ariel Dean. Ariel Dean is on my doorstep.'

It's an odd way to express myself, I realise. Like I am talking to somebody who is not there.

I guess we are a generation of performers.

#HeyGuys.

#DontForgetToLikeAndSubscribe.

How do people not know that I am not supposed to be at my house this weekend? The two people who broke in clearly saw my video. How did Ariel Dean miss it? Maybe she tried to message me. I wouldn't know. I've turned everything off. Nobody is supposed to be watching me.

God, if I had just told the truth and gone away, I could be sipping sangria in a rooftop bar, right now. The two dead people would be alive, watching my big screen and ordering more pizza, not actually causing anybody any harm.

'I'm not away this weekend,' I say, awkwardly.

'Yeah. I can see that.' Ariel looks at me like I'm on something. Like I'm acting weird.

'I mean, I'm here. And you're here.' It's still odd. Shock, plus paranoia. A cocktail for mistakes.

'Look, this really doesn't have to be that awkward. You apologised in your letter, and I accept that, you really don't have to do it in person as well.'

I know nothing about this letter, but I play along.

'No no no no no, it's fine. Sorry. You just caught me off guard. I've got this new camera and I dropped it on the floor and I thought I'd broken it. Why don't you come in? Have a cup of tea, or something. We can talk.'

^^^^^^^^^^

^^^^^^^^^^

[LIVESTREAM]

It's another turning point. Edie and Tammy can hear what is being said and can see Ariel through the camera embedded in the porch ceiling. Paige has to obscure the view of Alyssa somehow or act in a way that will keep Ariel quiet.

Maybe Paige is trying to double-bluff, inviting her unwanted guest inside and knowing that she will probably refuse.

The producers hold their breath.

They dare not blink.

'Well, if you're sure?'

If Lincoln/Lowell are looking for the moment to set up their new TV show, this confrontation would be a great place to start, whether this show is for the world to see or not.

^^^^^^^^^^

^^^^^^^^^^

PAIGE

I step back, open the door wide and stand in the gap between the edge of the door and the wall that leads to the kitchen. I couldn't say for sure that I am blocking the angle of sight towards Alyssa, but I feel fairly confident. I hold out a hand and guide Ariel into my kitchen, closing the front door behind her.

God, I hope I don't have to kill her, too.

Why am I even thinking about that?

Ariel follows the cues and enters the kitchen. Phew. It's small but it's functional, and stylish. She probably recognises the quartz worktops from some of my recipe videos. There's no getting away from the pizza box across the other side. I spot her trying not to look at it.

'That's a nice camera,' she says, diverting her gaze.

I pick it up. 'I know. Apart from the huge dent I just put in one corner. It was given to me by a film company. They're interested in making a documentary or something.'

'Wow. That sounds amazing.'

'I'm not sure, I have to be honest. I kind of said yes but maybe I shouldn't have.'

'Well, you already do so much.'

She seems so genuine. So nice. I wonder if I was nice before all of this happened to me. I can't remember, anymore.

'I was going to have a coffee because I've been working out. You want one?'

'Do you have matcha?'

I want to tell Ariel that it's the weekend, that nobody is here. That we don't have to talk while sipping on wheatgrass and eating kale sandwiches made with gluten-free bread. But, instead, I say, 'I never run out of matcha. Or kombucha.'

A fake smile.

Posing for pictures that aren't being taken.

We are both in the kitchen. Alyssa is in the lounge. The guy is in the shed. Nolan's next door. There are twenty cameras dotted around the house that aren't switched on yet, luckily. I look over at the dented camera and imagine striking Ariel across the back of the head with it, knocking her to the tiled floor and repeatedly bringing the thing down into her face until she stops moving.

Who have I become?

When did this modicum of fame and influence become so all-consuming that I could premeditate a murder? The first two were passion kills. Heat of the moment. Self-defence.

Self-preservation.

But there's no way I could really follow through with something I imagined or planned. I know that much.

Maybe, sometimes, you have to completely lose yourself in order to find out who you really are. That could be the tagline for my show.

I hit a button on the machine and it starts to drip fresh espresso roast into a mug. I take the matcha powder from the cupboard and spoon it into another cup for my latest uninvited guest.

Ariel is looking around the kitchen, she glances out into the hall and moves towards the doorway. I don't want her to look out there otherwise I'm going to have to act, I am going to have to shut that beautiful face up.

'Hey,' I say, suddenly, and Ariel turns back to give me attention. 'You know, I'm sorry about how things went down. I'm in a weird place at the moment, wondering if this is really what I want to be doing with my life.'

^^^^^^^^^^

^^^^^^^^^^

[LIVESTREAM]

Edie hears this and imagines another reality star breakdown. Always so good to watch. Great for ratings.

She can smell another Lincoln/Lowell hit.

This could be their masterpiece.

^^^^^^^^^^

^^^^^^^^^^

Ariel is gracious and poised in her own quiet way. Paige continues to talk while filling the matcha cup with boiling water straight from the tap. It can also produce ice-cold water immediately. Ariel marvels at such an invention, like boiling a kettle is such an inconvenience.

They talk things through. Paige goes along with this mysterious letter story – that she does not believe – and she tries to be as accommodating as possible. She tries to come across as humble. Then she says, 'Will you post on your socials that we met?'

'No. I don't need to do that.'

'You don't want to say that we buried the hatchet?' Paige imagines burying a hatchet into Ariel's spine as she tries to leave.

'I'm okay knowing that we've put this whole issue to rest. I don't think it's anyone else's business.'

Ariel is not cut out for this world.

^^^^^^^^^^

^^^^^^^^^^

[LIVESTREAM]

It won't take too much editing to make Paige come off as some spoiled content creator who thinks she is above other people. She will not emerge from this exchange in a favourable manner to anyone who watches it.

Edie loves it. It's exactly what she hoped it would be. (Even without any hair-pulling.)

'I guess you got a ton of new followers out of it, at least.'

Ariel is slightly disgusted at the comment. 'That's not the reason I was sharing my story. Not everyone bleeds for publicity. I just hoped that it might help somebody who was experiencing a similar hardship.'

This is gold, Edie thinks. Ariel Dean is purity personified.

'But now you have the opportunity to maybe help more people.' Paige is trying to claw back some dignity.

'Sure. It starts with one, though. And I hope that our little incident and resolution means that one more person doesn't have to suffer an onslaught like that.'

The producers can't help but howl with laughter at this. She's got

Paige, there. Nothing to come back with. They're not going to become gal pals after this, of course, but the animosity is gone – on Ariel's side, at least.

^^^^^^^^^^

^^^^^^^^^^

PAIGE

'Well, thanks for coming over.' I pour the remainder of my coffee into the sink but keep hold of the handle. It may seem like an abrupt and possibly aggressive gesture. I don't care. I've had enough. I've got more important things to be doing. I've switched off my socials, now I'm switching off this encounter.

Ariel is only halfway through her matcha, but she gets the hint that she is being asked to leave. She's naive, but she's not stupid.

I imagine cracking Ariel across the back of the head with my *I Heart Yoga* mug as she walks out of the kitchen. And, as I daydream about my third kill, Ariel Dean is heading towards the door. She exits the kitchen and looks down the hallway into the lounge area as she leaves.

Straight past the sofa and the coffee table. In the direction of Alyssa. Ariel moves quickly to the door and opens it herself before I have even clicked back into reality.

I clock this sudden change in behaviour, though. And I speed over to the door, looking towards the body as I do, to see whether Ariel might have noticed Alyssa's feet. Again, I'm confident that she didn't but she does seem to be trying to exit as quickly as possible.

By the time I get to the door, Ariel is already out onto the driveway and is walking towards her car.

'I'm glad we did this,' I call after her.

Ariel lifts a hand and waves. She turns back to see that I am standing in my doorway and throws a false smile back at me. I can't work out what just happened. If I run at Ariel now, I won't make it before she gets into her car and drives off.

Maybe I should have hit her while I had the chance.

I slam the door shut.

'Fucking bitch.' I walk back into the lounge, mumbling about what a cow Ariel Dean is. I scratch an itch between my legs and mumble again. I'm just annoyed because I try so hard to be perfect and it seems as though Ariel Dean doesn't have to try at all.

I'm aware that these are the kinds of things I might do when I forget that I am being filmed. When I'm off guard. It's more real. Even the voice that I use on my diary-room videos is different.

Because I know the camera is there.

I am being watched.

I'm performing.

Now, I am not.

Now, I can show my ugliness. I can let my freak flag fly.

I need to get digging again. If Ariel saw anything, it is probably only a matter of time before the police come knocking.

I need to get these bodies in the ground.

^^^^^^^^^

^^^^^^^^^

#CarpeDiem #MakeItCount #CreateYourChance #NowOrNever

But first, coffee.

That's what it says in every Alfred Coffee shop. In Palisades Village, it's a white neon sign over the soft-drinks refrigerator. Out on Ventura Boulevard, giant yellow letters hang from the ceiling but, on Melrose Place, one wall covered in black wooden cladding has the three words painted in white, above the opening that leads downstairs. And that's where Satmohan's Sunday meeting is.

He wants to turn off his phone so that he can't be contacted. Edie and Tammy are busy on their secret project, so he knows that they probably won't try to get hold of him today. He hates that he is always contactable and that they have requests at all hours of the day. He knows how unhealthy it is to have no downtime from work, to have no work/life balance. He knows that he struggles with a lack of sleep and that working like this will end up killing him, somehow, through stress. But there is also a part of him that doesn't want to let them down.

And he knows how unhealthy that is, too.

So he leaves his phone on.

He needs it, anyway, in order to listen to music as he walks down Melrose, pretending not to be window shopping for celebrities.

Satmohan wants to make sure that he is there on time. He wants to be early but not appear too desperate. He doesn't need this job, they need him. That's what he wants to project. He loves a chai tea latte but orders an Americano because he thinks it will help him to fit that scene.

Nobody is real in this town.

In the end, the producer he is supposed to be meeting turns up thirty-five minutes after the time that they agreed, because that's the industry. Execs are rude. They've always just been in another meeting that overran. Maybe they're on a power trip. Or they want to fuck you or get fucked by you in order to give you the career boost you are looking for.

He doesn't even apologise when he finally arrives. He just says that the traffic was a nightmare and asks Satmohan if he wants a drink. Satmohan orders another black coffee and the producer says, 'Well, I'm going to have the chai tea because it is fucking beautiful.'

This is Satmohan's big chance, so he lets this guy walk all over him in much the same way that he lets Edie and Tammy.

'You look on edge. You're worried about those two ball-breakers, right?'

Satmohan doesn't want to badmouth them, whether they are here or not. Whether they exploit his position. He doesn't want to get into a slagging match. He's been taught to be ruthless but also to understand who he's dealing with.

'Don't get me wrong, Satmohan, they are great at what they do, it's just that what they are doing is outdated. They're dinosaurs. It's a slippery slope down but those women are savvy enough to get out before the descent, you know?'

He's looking for some kind of confirmation from Satmohan but he won't give one. Instead, he sips at his coffee and stares, waiting for more words. People love to talk. Satmohan knows to listen.

Eventually, he has to break the silence. 'I've learned a lot from them about the way things are run in this town. Even the bad experiences are good ones.' Satmohan's mobile phone doesn't ring, but it vibrates on the table. It's face down but he knows it's probably Tammy. Edie is the real boss, everybody knows that. She's the ruthless one. She would never call.

The producer that Satmohan has been dying to meet up with to finalise his position tilts his head to the side. It looks like pity but it's not. He's disappointed in Satmohan. He's allowing himself to be walked over. Working on a Sunday. Always contactable.

Satmohan is sick of Edie and Tammy. And he can see himself getting sick of this guy pretty soon. But he won't miss the opportunity. He's a climber. He's playing the game.

But he's also terrified.

Scared that this could be a test.

It sounds paranoid but Satmohan is smart, he sees what goes on, he knows how Lincoln/Lowell operate. They are clever and they have more power than people realise. They have so many projects in development or production or being tied up. And they have a host of characters on hand when they need them. Desperate actors who will play a role because they are being paid some actual money but they won't be appearing on television or film.

This guy could be a plant.

It sounds ridiculous but Edie would do it, Satmohan knows that. She would call on somebody to play the part of a producer, maybe get him to call a meeting at the Coffee Commissary by Siren Studio for added authenticity, then entrap Satmohan.

This scenario is running through his head every time he hears a slur against Tammy that he agrees with but is too scared to say anything. He knows not to trust anyone. Maybe that is a positive lesson that the Lincoln/Lowell partnership has taught him. He should be grateful but, instead, he's impatient.

They have done some awful things, all in the name of creating reality television gold. They manufacture the truth so well that they even believe it themselves. Satmohan has watched them get excited over a stunt they have pulled because the characters have reacted in the way that they wanted.

And that is the way that they see people. As characters. Not as individuals. They are pawns that can be moved around to do whatever is bid. They are there to be toyed with, to create entertainment rather than observe reality.

Satmohan looked up this producer. (Maybe he is paranoid. Maybe he's just a little jaded.) Dan Kapinos. He's real. He has credits. He's worked with some talent. But he is a producer, so his face isn't over every magazine or blog article. He's on the red carpets but he's not getting interviewed or asked who he is wearing that day. It took a little digging, but Satmohan found his image and it looks exactly like the man across from him, right now.

He still doesn't trust it.

Lincoln/Lowell are everywhere. And they will ruin him if he stays too long.

Success at a cost.

So he plays the diplomat. He doesn't say a bad word about his current employers. Anything that has gone wrong or has not worked out has been something to learn, rather than a failing. He spins things, just as he has been taught to.

Kapinos gets into more detail about the feature documentary, detail that Lincoln/Lowell would put into any of their characters, their sleeper agents.

Satmohan has to get out. He's anxious all the time and that is not who he is. It's like they have created a new Satmohan. Another character that they can use to do their bidding.

'I'd like you to come across for this project. We don't start filming for a month, so you have time to tie up anything you're doing with L and L. It's going to be a good six months. Are you sure you're okay with that? There will be some travel.'

Satmohan is fine with travel. In fact, he wants it. He wants to get away from the bright lights for a while.

Kapinos shakes Satmohan's hand and leaves, saying that he'll be in touch. Satmohan waits around before ordering a chai tea to go. He's full of joy and a sense of possibility.

Finally, he checks his phone. There is a missed call from Tammy. Normally, he would call her back. In fact, normally, he would never have missed it, but today is different. Satmohan is feeling brave. So, if she wants to get hold of him on a Sunday, this glorious Sunday, she will just have to call him back.

ΛΛΛΛΛΛΛΛΛ

ΛΛΛΛΛΛΛΛΛ

PAIGE

I can see no joy or possibility.

I'm still shut off from the real world. Partly by choice and partly through necessity.

This is my world now. One where I kill people, apparently, and bury them in my back yard. I didn't really understand or appreciate the things that I had before all of this happened to me.

I was so privileged. Lucky. Now I'm fucked.

And the doorbell rings again.

I've never been so god-damned popular. What the hell is going on?

I have been digging and checking that I'm not being watched. Digging. And checking. Physically, I can handle it all. But mentally, I'm starting to struggle. I feel like I'm imagining things: Alyssa moving, the coffee table moving, the walls moving.

And now I am being interrupted again.

I've never had so many visitors.

I have to take a breath by the door, and I use the back of my hand to wipe the sweat from my forehead, leaving a dirty smear behind.

A handsome, light-haired, well-built man is standing in front of me. His eyes are almost turquoise. His teeth are white and straight like a movie star's. He's the kind of guy that I would normally find attractive but my heart sinks when I notice his perfectly starched and ironed police uniform.

Shit. That bitch, Ariel Dean. She saw Alyssa in the lounge.

This is the end.

It was never going to turn out well.

'Good day, ma'am,' he says politely, a hint of southern drawl. 'We have had reports of strange goings-on in this area. Unknown vehicles, people walking where they don't usually walk, that kind of thing.'

'Okay.' I'm waiting for the punchline. *Oh, and the dead body in your living room.* Something like that. *You mind if I take a look around your yard?* I don't know where he is going with his line of enquiry.

'Obviously, we are being a little more vigilant knowing that these Tom and Dana characters are roaming around, doing whatever they want to do. You've heard about them?'

'Yeah. I saw that on the news. Kinda creepy.' I'm trying to sound as natural as possible but I'm no actress.

'Quite right. You can't be too careful. Have you seen anything out of the ordinary today?'

'To be honest, I can't say that I have, but I haven't really been out. I had a friend over earlier for coffee...' I let that linger in the air to see whether he responds or not. He doesn't seem to, so I conclude that he is not here at the behest of Ariel Dean. But then I worry that one of my neighbours saw 'Tom and Dana' creeping around last night.

'And that's it? No noises in the garden? No security lights coming on in the night? Nothing like that?'

'No. Nothing like that, at all. I mean, I have been out in the yard.'

I feel the need to explain away my dirty hands and face. 'But the only weird thing was that my neighbour spoke to me for the first time since I moved into this place.' I try to laugh but it comes out awkwardly.

I'm not good at this. How is that possible? I spend most of my time faking it through the day.

'It was reported that somebody was driving around the neighbourhood for twenty minutes in a red saloon. Do you know anybody with a red saloon?'

'Yes. My friend who came over. She's not from over here, she didn't know where to park. She's a nervous kind of character,' I lie. 'It was probably her, Officer, really nothing to worry about.' I start to close the door but the cop starts talking again.

'Ah, I'm sure you're right. It's nothing. People round here are just a bit paranoid with everything that is going on.'

'Really? I thought it was all over. A couple of freak instances. Kids being kids, or whatever.'

'Maybe you're right but it's best to be safe.'

I just want to get rid of him. This is too close for comfort. It doesn't seem right that the police would knock on my door at the report of something suspicious. Some poor, young stud in uniform has been demoted to door duty.

'I'm going to patrol the area for the rest of the day. And I'll drive by a few times throughout the night, so, if anybody is watching, they'll know that there is a police presence.'

'That's very kind of you, Officer. I'm sure that's all that is needed. I feel safer already.' I smile, poke my chest out a little, and I try to shut the door again.

'You don't want me to check things out inside? For peace of mind.' He takes a step forward as if he's going to come in and, instinctively, I ready myself.

He steps back.

'You seem nervous,' he says, almost accusatorially.

'I don't like the idea of a man stepping foot inside my house without an invitation.'

I remember seeing a video online about how women living with domestic abuse can subtly signal to a police officer at the door by running a finger down their face, or across their heart, or along their neck. I can't quite recall the exact details, but I know that I certainly gave no indication to the man on my doorstep that I was in trouble, either verbally or with a swipe of the hand.

I've split my feet. I'm in a fight stance.

I am not letting any more strangers into my home.

^^^^^^^^^^

^^^^^^^^^^

[LIVESTREAM]

There's a short moment of awkwardness. Edie and Tammy are listening in. Recording everything. They can read the officer's name on his shirt. Malone.

'I apologise, miss…'

'Paige.'

'I apologise, Miss Paige, I didn't mean anything by that.'

'It's okay. Thanks for stopping by but, as I said, everything is fine here. Nothing out of the ordinary.'

'Just to be safe, my superiors have asked that I knock again later. I just want to give you advanced warning.'

'I guess I'll see you again tonight.' And she closes the door, breathes, slides her back down until she is sitting on the floor. And she cries.

^^^^^^^^^^

^^^^^^^^^^

#FailForward #LessonsLearned #GrowthFromFailure

Satmohan's euphoria is short-lived. His phone rings. It's Edie this time.

'Where are you?' This is how she greets him.

'I'm sorry?'

'Where the hell are you?'

'I'm out. What's wrong? You need something?' There's a part of Satmohan that thinks they might be cloning his phone or somehow they've turned on the location services so they can see if he's in some dive bar when he says he's at the gurdwara. They could be tracking him. Then the rational part of his brain tells him he's not that important.

'Tammy called you and you didn't pick up.' She's looking for an explanation or some kind of apology for not being at her beck and call. Satmohan would usually grovel, but not today. He's out. Or, at least, he's getting out. So he doesn't play her game.

'Is there something I can do for you, Edie?'

'We're filming.'

'On a Sunday?'

'Yeah. The Fitness Paige thing. We didn't expect it to kick off so soon or with such style, and we don't have the place covered.'

'There are eight or nine cameras in the house and one at the front door.'

'Exactly. It's not enough.'

'We can't get one in her room, Edie.' Satmohan looks across the road and takes a swig of his chai tea. It's even better than he expected.

'Jesus, man, I'm not a sicko. I'm not some kind of pervert, I don't want to watch her in bed. We need eyes on the yard. Nothing permanent, just some footage of what it's like out there. She's been outside for most of the day and we are missing it.'

Satmohan knows that this is unethical. Paige could be sunbathing topless or she could be painting her fence. It doesn't matter, they'd need her permission for that. He also knows that ethical considerations are a grey area in the world of reality TV. Sure, she doesn't know she's being filmed in her house but at least she knows the cameras are there. Somehow, that feels different. Not as underhand.

But he can't go against Edie Lincoln. Not now. It would be career suicide, even if he has another job lined up. He has to play it smart. No contract has been signed yet.

'When do you need these shots?'

'Four hours ago. We don't have time to play nice and get her to sign off on it. We can do that retroactively. Just get recording.'

'I doubt I'll be able to hook anything over her back fence.'

'I don't care how you get it or how much it costs us, I want some footage of her back yard, and if she's in that footage it's even better. And I want it in the next hour.'

'Fuck. Okay. I know where she lives. I won't even need to get close. I can fly the drone cam overhead. She'll spot it if it's too low, but we'll have the footage. The camera is good enough to stay at a distance and you can zoom in on the edit.' He's ashamed of himself. He used it before to catch a glimpse of a Davis Davis party from above, sweeping across the crowds of guests.

'There you go. That college education is something that Tammy and I don't have. That's why we have you, Satmohan. You're one of us. Part of the team. We don't work without you. Upload to the shared drive once you have something.'

She hangs up.

Satmohan doesn't have time to lament his decisions. He can't dawdle. He can't second guess. But all that stuff about being a team and only working together has his mind racing.

Oh, God. She knows.

^^^^^^^^^^

^^^^^^^^^^

PAIGE

Two more pieces of fridge pizza.

I'm so disgusting.

Food should be a joyous thing. Something of a celebration. Lincoln/Lowell made a show where chefs from countries all over the world competed against one another to see who made the best food. It was called, *If You Can't Stand the Heat.* There were so many stories of how these cooks watched their grandmother baking or slaving over a giant paella or rolling their own tortellini but, for me, food is a source of guilt and punishment and agonising discomfort.

I know that I am only hurting myself to eat in this way, but I also think that I deserve to feel like this.

Like, I really do believe that.

I haven't had much today other than pizza and coffee. I know that with my exercise class and the digging, I am almost certainly working at a calorie deficit, but that doesn't help me at all. It doesn't make me feel any better. Because nothing really does anymore.

Food feels like poison.

That's why I have to throw it up, sometimes.

I take the throw from the sofa and drape it over Alyssa's body. I want to keep it covered up because that police officer said he was coming back, and it definitely looked as though he wanted to come inside. He made me feel uncomfortable.

So is the sight of Alyssa's face. I can't remember whether her eyes were open or closed. When things first happened, I seem to remember them staying open. But yesterday they looked closed.

Or maybe it was the other way around.

I meant to look up whether dead people can do this but I forgot, with all my visitors. But if Alyssa is covered by a blanket, it's okay to forget. It's like she's not there.

I am tired from the digging and now I'm losing the light. But that is kind of what I've been waiting for. I can't drag Less from the shed up to the house until it's dark. I also have to remember to turn off the motion sensor on the garden floodlight before I go out to collect the body because it'll alert Nolan next door, who now wants to be besties, it seems.

Everything is done. The hole is ready. The top layer of turf has been preserved. There's a body safely locked in my shed. I am covered in mud and sweat and tears and tomato sauce. I need to shower and wait until it's safe. It seems pointless to get clean, knowing that the hole will have to be refilled, but I have to find a way to pass the time that won't drive me insane.

I take a moment at the back door to admire my handiwork. A perfect rectangle. I look up at the sky and see something. I don't know what it is and the light is still strong at this angle. There's a buzzing, though. Bees did swarm a tree nearby last year but that was so much louder.

I cup my left hand over my eyes and squint to try to make out what it is.

^^^^^^^^^^

^^^^^^^^^^

#ChaseOpportunity #BoldMovesOnly

Satmohan has a perfect ten seconds of Paige squinting and looking to the sky, standing next to a large hole in the ground. He also has more natural footage of Paige walking out her back door and staring at the empty grave. He knows that's the part Edie will want to use.

It has to look as real as possible.

Maybe it's because he knows he is going to leave that he feels a little more reckless, but Satmohan decides to drop the drone fifteen feet lower, so that Paige doesn't have to squint. She will know what she is looking at. And maybe it will make her question what she sees. Maybe she will wonder about the cameras in her house.

Maybe it will ruin Edie's and Tammy's special show.

Maybe they'll have him whacked.

It's only for a second. But long enough to capture a decent still of

Paige's confused expression before the drone flies off. She doesn't know it is a camera. She thinks it's probably kids nearby with a toy. She thinks that just because she has turned off her social media, nobody is watching her.

For all the paranoia she feels after what she has done, the one thing she should worry about, that could trigger a realisation, is given minimal consideration.

^^^^^^^^^^

^^^^^^^^^^

PAIGE

Rich kids and their toys.

I casually stroll back toward my house, taking one last look to the sky, then to the house next door to see whether Nolan is catching another glimpse.

He's not.

I shut the door and lock it.

I don't like it. It feels like somebody is watching me. Somebody knows. I'm overly suspicious, but maybe I have to be. For a while, at least.

'What the fuck was that?' I speak out loud because I'm scared, the way that people often do when they go to bed in the dark. The sound of their own voice is comforting. Try to tell themselves and anybody that might be listening that they are not afraid. That everything is normal.

I look at my sofa and it seems as though it is further to the left. It can't be. And was the body facing that way before? I can smell something burning and think that I might be having a stroke. Then I remember hearing that people taste lemons before they have a stroke.

I'm so confused.

It could be something else.

They smell sulphur, maybe.

Where is the camera?

What is happening?

I have to get rid of them, I think to myself. *Tonight*.

To myself, I say, 'I need to get the hell out of here.'

Then I run upstairs.

^^^^^^^^^^

^^^^^^^^^^

[LIVESTREAM]

Tammy looks at Edie and says, 'She's going to run.'

Edie doesn't seem as bothered.

'There's nobody in her life, Tam. That's why I chose her. She's got nowhere else to go.'

^^^^^^^^^^

^^^^^^^^^^

CNN AFTERNOON EDITION with VICTORIA BANNERMAN

'Paranoia is an increasingly prevalent emotion in a society where we are constantly putting ourselves out there to be watched and judged and ridiculed and attacked, as well as congratulated and applauded and supported.

'There may be an increasing feeling that everyone is out to get you in some way, to tear you down from whatever pedestal you have been placed on.

'Of course, there is a genetic component to this, as with so many mental-health issues, but it can also be triggered by chemical imbalances in the brain, or when a person is thrust into a difficult or stressful event.

'Los Angeles is feeling the stress, right now. There is a creeping sense of disquiet in the canyon area after the recent spate of break-ins. Residents are increasingly cautious but also overly suspicious in their own homes. If they misplace a magazine, they think they are being toyed with, they check the cellar room and the attic. If the cleaner polishes a surface and moves a candlestick out of position, it's suddenly easier to assume that a person is living in the pool house without you realising. Let's go over to Gina Ashby to discuss the recent craze among young people ... of phrogging...'

^^^^^^^^^^

^^^^^^^^^^

PAIGE

I try to tell myself that I'm just being paranoid, I'm crazy, in shock. But something isn't right in this house. I may have incapacitated my intruders, the same duo who have been terrorising the area, but something is definitely *off*.

I'm sure that Alyssa's eyes were open for half a day and now they are closed.

Fuck, I need to get this done. I'm losing it. I may have turned everything off for the weekend but I don't know whether that was the real world or this one is.

I feel like I can say with almost absolute certainty that the position of my sofa is different. It's exactly what Rosie Velazquez said about her own furniture in that news article I read.

I'm scared to look at my bookshelves.

It's paranoia when you think that people are out to harm you in some way. But sometimes they are. Sometimes, somebody is fucking with you and you have no idea who it is or why it is happening.

Two days. I wanted two days where nobody was looking at me. I switched it off. But they're still watching. Oh, God, they're still watching.

I don't feel like I am being irrationally anxious, I know that there could be outside influences at play here. That somebody wants to take me down. It could be any of the other *fitfluencers*. It could be Ariel Dean. It could be my neighbour, Nolan. It could be all of them. I don't know who it is but I know it is happening. My mental strength has taken a dent. A mania is taking over.

Because it is true.

I know it.

But, then, that is exactly what a clinically paranoid person would think.

^^^^^^^^^

^^^^^^^^^

[LIVESTREAM]

The officer is back on Paige's doorstep.

Tammy pours Edie another glass of wine as they watch the camera. Paige ran upstairs forty-five minutes ago and has yet to emerge. Tammy was worried that she had gone up there and done something stupid in her room, taken a mouthful of painkillers or something. But Edie has backed Paige all the way.

'She'll come down when she hears the doorbell. I guarantee. When you have nobody else, there's no choice but to make yourself the most important person in your life. She won't throw that away,' Edie says, like some pop-psychological Western guru.

It's annoying to Tammy how right Edie has been about this woman the entire time. She half hopes that she has topped herself just to prove her friend wrong for once. The police could eventually find all three bodies and wonder what the hell had happened. And the only people that would know the truth would be Lincoln/Lowell.

Paige emerges. Making her way down the stairs when she hears the doorbell ring again. She's wearing nothing but a towel around her chest. It's short but it covers her modesty. Her hair is still wet.

'It's a sexy look,' Tammy comments.

'I'll be sure to let Davis know about how your tastes have changed.'

Tammy rolls her eyes and it makes her yawn. She thinks Edie might be jealous, but she's not.

Paige takes a look at the dead girl in her lounge, and Edie and Tammy look back at their very alive protagonist. The sofa seems to be back in place. Alyssa definitely hasn't moved. It must have been the drone playing havoc with her mind. That's what she tells herself.

She looks through the peephole and sees who it is.

'Officer Mahone,' she says as she opens the door, deliberately getting his name wrong.

'It's Malone, ma'am, and I'm sorry to disturb you but your neighbour called in saying that he thinks somebody was looking in through his bedroom window.'

'And he thinks it was me?' She almost laughs.

'No, no. A drone.'

'A drone?'

'Yeah. One of those remote-controlled flying things with a camera on the front. He says he saw one outside his window, thought it might be filming him.'

'Well, the guy has a great body. It wasn't my flying thing, though, Officer.'

'I wasn't suggesting that. We think that these people use them to case houses, waiting to see when nobody is home so that they can sneak in.'

'I'm always home.'

'And you didn't see it? Or hear it? Those things aren't always quiet.' He looks her up and down, there's too much leg on show.

Paige clocks it, though, and pulls the towel around her, protectively. 'Are you knocking on everybody's door, or just the ones who have recently finished in the shower?' She lifts an eyebrow.

'I was just next door, actually,' he lies.

'Well, I didn't hear or see anything, so thank you for your time, and I'm sure I'll see you again before the night is through, and I'll hopefully have more clothes on.'

She shuts the door.

Tammy sees the police officer's face on the front-door cam. He gives a wry smile, breaking character for a second, he clearly noticed the way she looked in that towel, with her wet hair, and he liked it.

^^^^^^^^^^

^^^^^^^^^^

PAIGE

I race back up the stairs. I don't even want to look in my living room in case the coffee table is facing the wrong way or the console table has moved to the other wall.

I need this whole thing to be over.

In my room, there's a suitcase on the bed, half packed with some essentials. Underwear, jeans, vests, face products. I drop the towel and slip into a pair of black joggers with matching black hoodie. It's my attempt at being stealthy.

After the lies about going to a spa this weekend, I think I might just head to the airport and hop on a flight to wherever. I have the money. I have my phone. I can work anywhere. My avid following won't care, as long as I keep posting content.

I look in the mirror.

Who the hell am I?

Now is not the time. I can figure this out later.

It's time to dump some bodies in a hole.

^^^^^^^^^^

^^^^^^^^^^

[LIVESTREAM]

Edie is on her own again. Davis swung by twenty minutes ago because his throat is dry and his dick is dry, so he brought a bottle of wine and requires Tammy to open her legs. Edie knows that they love each other but it doesn't always look like love to her.

She looks through the drone footage while waiting for Paige to reappear. It's magnificent. There are definitely some reaction shots that can be spliced in, but that long shot of Paige in the yard next to the hole in the ground is like something out of a John Huston Western. Satmohan outdid himself, this time.

Edie can't hear the bed squeaking or the headboard crashing furiously against the wall, but she knows what is going on. Edie has nobody. Not even someone to pop by for a glass of wine and a quick screw over the dining-room table. Maybe that's why she knows how Paige will react.

Edie has her work.

It's her baby and her lover and her outlet.

Of course, she has Tammy, but they're so close it's almost like being alone; they come as one. But Edie does know what it is like to feel alone, to experience pure loneliness. Just like Paige. So she should empathise with her situation. Unfortunately, after a lifetime in an industry where only the greatest of actors can tap into that emotion, Edie has been left with an almost psychopathic level of apathy.

She's not a naturally mean person. She is driven and focussed and somewhat obsessed with leaving a legacy, but she just doesn't care about Paige's problems, her mental health or her struggles. It's more interesting to witness strife and hardship.

It's better television.

And that's all that matters.

Tammy re-enters the editing suite.

'Holy shit, that was quick. Is this why they call Davis *The Panda*?'

'The panda?'

'Yeah. He eats, shoots and leaves.' Edie laughs.

'Ha. There wasn't any time for eating.' Tammy laughs, too. She's unapologetic about her actions. She sits back down and places the bottle of wine on the table.

They talk as they wait, and they drink. And they reminisce over some of the shows they have made in the past, where they started and that first tiny flat.

'This is probably going to be one of our best examinations of human nature and nobody will get to see it.' Tammy does this. She tries to provoke her friend from time to time. They are very similar in so many ways but Tammy wants more than the shows. She wants love and family meals at Christmas. Edie seemingly only cares about her work.

'They'll find it when I die, I'm sure. I have a shelf filled with our best work.'

'Well, if you could let me die first, that would be great because I won't have to deal with the fallout from that.'

They clink glasses.

'This will be our best yet, Tam. Don't worry about who does and doesn't get to see it. Just know that we made it.'

It is true, they both made it. Like they both always do. But Tammy's eye is off the ball with Davis sniffing around and her uterus seemingly aching for something more. So she is involved, but it's not equal.

No partnership is equal.

One person is always smarter than the other or hotter or more needy, depressed, ambitious. Nothing is fifty-fifty. You play to your strengths and you compromise where needed and you do what you have to do to make the collaboration work. It's like any relationship.

Even the best ones have their secrets.

And if there is one person in the industry who can keep something quiet, who doesn't need the adulation of others to feel success, who would even go behind her lifelong colleague's back to make a TV show the absolute best it can be, it's Edie Lincoln.

She's one step ahead of everybody.

She knows that Tammy is imagining a simpler life with Davis.

She knows that Satmohan plans to leave.

And she knows that the next time Paige comes down those stairs, the show is really going to kick off. Paige has to finish what she started.

It's time.

^^^^^^^^^

^^^^^^^^^

PAIGE

I feel safe in the kitchen.

It's a mess, so things could be moved around and I would have no idea, which means that it is not as scary as the lounge. Plus, there are still a few slices of pizza left.

I turn the dented diary camera on myself, because I can't live without a screen of some kind, it seems.

'I'm losing it. This house is no longer a home. It's a fucking crime scene. For a crime that I committed. I have nobody to call. Isn't everybody supposed to have one friend who would take a bullet for them. Who would lie down in traffic for them? There's supposed to be a friend that I could say "I need your help to get rid of a body" to, and they wouldn't ask any questions. That's a thing. I know it. And I know I don't have one.'

I stare into the lens for twenty seconds or so, trying not to cry at this pathetic realisation. Breathing my way through the terror.

'I'm alone. So I have to do this alone. I have to bury a god-damned body on my own. No questions.'

I press the button to stop the recording. I don't hit the upload button. I don't need this information out there. I don't even know why I'm recording it. Catharsis perhaps. It's just an outlet. I save it for myself. Because there is nobody left to talk to. Or maybe it is simply because I am young and my entire life has been spent in front of a camera.

That's who I am, now.

The world owns me.

Whether it was my parents taking a hundred photos of me each day as a toddler or creating my own online content. Or all of the dances and push-ups and parties that I documented along the way to where I am now.

Whatever it is, I think it helps.

Because it's what I know. It's all I know.

I eat a slice of fridge pizza and steel myself for what I have been putting off.

^^^^^^^^^

^^^^^^^^^

[LIVESTREAM]

Edie and Tammy watch as Paige powers into the living room from the kitchen. She doesn't look up. She is determined. She doesn't want to take in any of her surroundings. She just wants to get down to that shed.

Paige has to stop at the kitchen table because her keys are there. She picks them up and walks past the blanket-covered Alyssa without even considering her. It's Less that she wants.

She unlocks the doors and steps into the garden. The floodlight comes on and illuminates the entire area.

^^^^^^^^^

^^^^^^^^^

PAIGE

'Fuck.' I forgot to turn off the god-damned sensor.

I go back inside and disarm the trigger. I have to wait another two minutes for the light to turn back off naturally. I wait another three minutes after that, my head in my hands on the sofa, not looking at anything. Tapping my foot in frustration and impatience. I had already built myself up, now I have to do it all over again.

^^^^^^^^^^

^^^^^^^^^^

[LIVESTREAM]

'This part isn't the best TV to watch,' Tammy says, captivated without knowing why.

'Don't you worry, she's on the edge.'

Tammy trusts her partner. She's been right all the way.

^^^^^^^^^^

^^^^^^^^^^

PAIGE

The three minutes pass and I go for it again. This time, the garden remains in darkness. I don't even look back to see if Nolan is at his window. I don't have time for that. I don't have the headspace. I prepare the correct key for the padlock as I move.

I don't look into the window on the side of the shed.

I am focussed. I am efficient.

I unlock the door, open it and step inside. I breathe deeply. Safe. For now. I can see the blanket that I placed over his body.

Then I look at the open shed window.

Then back at the blanket.

I hadn't noticed at first. But it's so obvious.

He is gone.

I panic. I look back at the window and see blood on the edge.

'No.' My eyes are wide. Unblinking.

I go back to the spot that I know I left him. He was dead, I'm sure of it. The blanket is still there. I lift it, slowly. I don't know what I'm expecting to find. He's gone. But he has left his T-shirt behind. I remember the front being covered in blood. But it has been left draped over a bag of soil with only the back showing.

There's blood but it's deliberate.

It looks like writing. It looks like he has written something on there.

I only pull the blanket back enough to see the bottom of the T-shirt but it is all I need.

I read.

Five words.

Cameras on.

They are watching.

^^^^^^^^^^

^^^^^^^^^^

[LIVESTREAM]

Edie Lincoln and Tammy Lowell sit, staring at a still image of @TheFitnessPaige's living room.

Maybe the sofa is slightly more to the left.

They wait.

Then the sound of sliding doors.

Paige appears. She's not frantic but she's not calm. She is looking for something on the coffee table. She pushes a magazine to the floor and a book of black-and-white pictures of New York that she has never read but saw something similar on an interior-design show. It looks good when visitors come by. Paige doesn't have many guests.

She turns around with the television remote control in her hand. The producers watch. It's almost as though she is looking directly at them. That hasn't happened before. It's creepy. They have spent the last two days in some voyeuristic haze, but when the tables are turned, they feel uncomfortable being viewed.

But Paige is not looking into the cameras. It's hard because she knows they are there now and that they are filming her. But she tries to act the same.

The problem is, there is a huge difference between acting natural and being natural. Even though Lincoln/Lowell are famous for their reality shows, it's always obvious when a situation has been forced. When something has been set up to occur in a certain place in a certain time for a certain reason to ascertain certain information or reactions. It's interesting TV but it's the least real part of it.

Something is slightly off with Paige, and Edie senses it.

Then she's flicking through the news channels.

Swipe. Scroll. Tap.

'Come on. Where are you?'

She stops on a story about Tom and Dana that suggests they have gone quiet after the police net started closing in on them. Some police captain is taking the credit.

'Oh, please,' Paige says out loud.

Another channel has some local college basketball results. Another says that the Dow Jones is down.

'There's nothing.' Paige looks agitated.

Tammy gives Edie a look. 'She's gonna break.'

They watch as Paige presses the button to move on, eventually going past the news channels into soap-opera territory.

'Nothing. Nothing. Nothing.' She turns the television off and throws the remote across the room.

'He can't just fucking disappear.' She runs to the kitchen.

There's one last slice of pizza in the refrigerator, but she doesn't touch it. Instead, she goes straight to the diary cam. Edie has been disappointed that Paige hasn't hit the upload button yet. They are capturing distant sound but she keeps recording in her bedroom or the kitchen, so they may have to be creative, maybe get an actress in to voice the lines.

This time is different.

Paige is more manic. More animated.

She hits record and holds the camera up in front of her, walking back into the living area.

^^^^^^^^^^

^^^^^^^^^^

DIARY ENTRY 004 'UNLISTED' VIEWS: 1
COMMENTS: 0 LIKES: 0

'So, it seems that pushing a knife through somebody's chest doesn't always fucking kill them. In fact, they can last for a day then climb out of a god-damned window and disappear into the night without a trace. I've checked the news and there's nothing. I've stayed offline because that's what I said I was doing. That's what I wanted for my own mental health. Ha! A fat lot of good that has done me.'

(Paige realises that she's shouting and forces herself to breathe more calmly.)

'If he makes it to a hospital, I'm done. Maybe I'll get lucky, and he'll collapse somewhere. Fall off a bridge or into a ditch.'

^^^^^^^^^^

^^^^^^^^^^

[LIVESTREAM]

'She's not right, Edie.'

'You sense it, too?'

'Sense it? She's being pretty damned obvious about the state of her mind.'

'I mean, she doesn't seem different to you?'

'Yes. Of course. That's what I'm saying. She's lost the plot.'

'Not that. I mean her voice. The way she moves. It's not that it's not her, it's obviously her, it's just ... I don't know, maybe it's the wine, it just feels more open. More ... to the camera, maybe.'

'Her already crazy situation just got heightened. It's the adrenaline. She's back in that fight-or-flight mode. And she wants to fight. She is charged. That's what it is.'

'Maybe you're right,' Edie concedes.

Talking to the camera, Paige says, 'I've got a fresh grave and a less-than-fresh body that will fit into it. I have to get it down now because that Officer Malone seems to turn up at the exact moment I need him least.'

Paige stops the video.

Edie is shouting at her screen for Paige to hit the upload button. This is the footage she wants. A slow descent into the heart of darkness. A beautiful, athletic and smart young woman with so much of her life ahead of her, throwing it all away over something a judge would probably see as either self-defence or an accident or both.

She doesn't upload her video.

'Damn it!' Edie slams her hand on the desk in exasperation.

Paige drops the camera on the sofa and walks over to the crumpled human beneath another of her favourite blankets. Alyssa is still there. She hasn't got away like Less.

She would never have left *him*.

Paige grabs Alyssa by the ankles and starts pulling her towards the door. She was right from the beginning, Alyssa does weigh more than Less. The adrenaline helps. But it's not easy.

She pulls her out of shot, but Edie and Tammy can still hear her struggling. Paige drags her to the doorway, hitting her head on the framework as she jolts the body out into the garden. She drops her on the patio and shuts the back door. If Officer Malone comes back knocking, Paige doesn't want to hear it. She doesn't want to be a part of it. She can ignore him. This is more important.

Edie and Tammy would give anything for that drone right now but it's too late. Maybe Satmohan can fly it over again tomorrow and show that the garden is back intact.

For now, all they can do is wait.

^^^^^^^^^

^^^^^^^^^

Alyssa's mother is starting to worry. She never goes this long without hearing from her daughter. And Alyssa knows that she has to be at home to help her grandmother. The old lady is more than happy to sit with a cup of tea and a blanket over her legs as she watches her shows. But, if she takes a tumble on the way to the toilet or there are pains in her chest or she gets confused and forgets where she is, it's not right that she is alone.

Alyssa's mother is annoyed with her daughter about that. But she's also worried. There's a feeling. Maybe mother's intuition, but something isn't right. Alyssa could move across the country without saying a word, if she desired. She's old enough to do what she wants. Technically, she can stay out as long as she wants. She's an adult. There's no sense in reporting it to anyone because it'll be laughed at.

Woman in twenties doesn't text mother back straight away.

So Alyssa's mother is stuck. And she has to work a long shift at the hospital. She already worked the Saturday night shift because she was offered the overtime, and she doesn't like to say no in case it never gets offered to her again. It was supposed to be her day off. The emergency room is a circus of overdoses, stomach pumping, car crashes and broken limbs. And Saturday night is the worst. Asshole drunk drivers a plenty. And the damn drugs are ravaging the suburbs.

The world is going to shit. And that's why Alyssa's mother is worried. She knows that her daughter goes to some parties and clubs that she would not be able to attend if she were not friends with Less. The wealthy have access to everything. Including the best private healthcare. She's not seeing too many of the richer classes on a Saturday night because they're in their mansions sipping Châteauneuf du Pape, discussing didacticism while listening to Stravinsky. Or they're accidentally killing a stripper at the country club and getting their lawyers to make the right calls.

Alyssa's mother is left to deal with the students and the minorities. A fourteen-year-old took a ricocheted bullet to the arm at a convenience store drive-by. Some gang dispute, no doubt. He wouldn't give details. There was no lasting physical damage, but he shouldn't be going through something like that at such a tender age. At any age.

Sunday night is a little quieter; this is her scheduled shift. The mornings are busy with sporting injuries. The elderly are waiting for the Monday-morning rush. It gives Alyssa's mother a little time to worry some more. She doesn't have Less's parents' details, otherwise she would check in with them.

She met Less's mother once when she picked Alyssa up from their incredible home. His mother said she had had a little too much to drink after lunch, but Alyssa's mother has seen a lot at the hospital and she can spot the difference between too many mojitos and opiate use.

If she worked in a hospital across town, she would see that people crash Bentleys as well as Fords. That rich bones splinter just like poor ones. And, on a quiet Sunday night, a kid in his twenties could turn up with an apparent stab wound and receive the best care in the land.

And maybe he would have some idea where she could find her daughter.

^^^^^^^^^^

^^^^^^^^^^

LESS

I know exactly where Alyssa is. I know the address. I know what state she is in. I know how long she has been there.

I know everything.

The cameras don't lie. But people can.

I am out of that house, and that's what matters, right now. I'm out. But I'm not going to the hospital. I'm not going to the closest hospital or the rougher hospital, where Alyssa's mother works, or the clean, everyone-gets-a-private-room hospital that my father pays a premium for.

I'm going home.

And I'm leaving my best friend behind.

All that BFF talk. All that brother from another mother, sister from a different mister banter. Alyssa and I are supposed to be inseparable. We're supposed to tell each other everything, be each other's confidantes. We are from different sides of the tracks but we are two sides of the same coin.

And I left her there.

Would Lennon have left McCartney?

Would Bonnie have left Clyde?

Would Pippen have left Jordan?

I walk through the night, shirtless, down back roads, in the shadows of hedges and houses. It's possible that I could get picked up by the police, but there are plenty of odd people to see if you walk down Skid Row or you're out on Robertson, by the American Apparel, and see that leather-skinned, uber-tanned homeless guy, who skates around in spandex shorts and rollerblades. Who is really going to care about some skinny wannabe hat-maker with no shirt on?

I'm not even covered in blood because it's all on the T-shirt I left behind with the message for Paige.

I left behind a message, and my best friend in the world.

It's all I could do. That's what I tell myself.

In those rare situations where a person is faced with a difficult, life-threatening problem, adrenaline kicks in and forces the individual to either run away or stand their ground. I froze. And then I chose to play dead. And I kept it up until it was time to escape.

I'm not hurt enough to go to the hospital. I'll go tomorrow. I'll find Alyssa's mom, and I will explain everything.

At least, then, she will know she won't have to worry anymore.

My parents won't be worried. I've stayed out plenty of times. I've even come home without a shirt on before. My mother is probably dropping into some gin-drenched, opiate-infused coma while my father works late and fucks his secretary like the walking cliché he is.

I plod my way up the drive, undetected. I walk up to my front door. I don't need a key, I just let myself in. All is as expected. I down a pint of water, take some rolls from the breadbasket and a tub of hummus from the fridge and I gorge.

I go upstairs.

I shower.

I dry.

I slip into some loungers and a T-shirt and shut my bedroom blind.

And, as I settle into the warmth of my bed with my thirteen-tog duvet, the person I love most in the world is probably being dragged outside towards a hole in the ground that was originally meant for me.

^^^^^^^^^

^^^^^^^^^

[LIVESTREAM]

They try not to breathe too heavily because there is a slight sound of scraping as the shovel scoops up the dirt that Paige previously piled on her patio stones. Edie thinks that they can use it over a black screen. Maybe some text to say what is happening. Add in a little of that *Texas Chainsaw Massacre* industrial noise.

Make it more sinister.

They know what is happening. They saw Alyssa get pulled out of shot and into the garden. They know there is a hole. They could have called the police at the beginning, but they didn't. They could still call them now, but they won't. They have a show about an ordinary person thrust into extraordinary circumstances and how she dealt with the complications that were placed in front of her.

How she remained strong and resilient.

Before eventually descending into paranoia and fleeting psychosis.

And only the people involved will ever see it.

But it will get made. Edie and Tammy will know how good it is. They'll forget about the collateral damage, the lives ruined, because they got more than they were expecting. They can pick another influencer to follow, to make the show that regular people will watch. They could throw a stone in The Valley and hit eight influencers who are trying to break through to the next level so they can move closer to the Hills.

'We could end it there,' Tammy says. Exhausted. Drunk. Missing Davis.

'Let's just see what she does next. It's nice to be surprised.'

They hear the patio doors sliding open again. Paige walks into shot, dirty, hair in disarray. She goes into the kitchen and takes out her last slice of fridge pizza. The tap starts running. Paige emerges back into the lounge with a wet sponge and some kitchen roll, the pizza hanging from her mouth. She hums a tune that neither Edie nor Tammy have heard before. Then she gets on her knees and scrubs at the blood on the floor where Alyssa was lying.

It's not that interesting to watch. Both producers are on their phones writing text messages while Paige dries the floor with paper towels.

^^^^^^^^^

^^^^^^^^^

PAIGE

I go back to the kitchen. I throw out the wet paper towels and hurl the sponge into the sink. I head back to the fridge and take out the half-bottle of white wine and pour myself a large glass before returning to the sofa and the diary cam.

'I'm done,' I say into the camera lens. 'This was supposed to be a relaxing weekend, and it has turned into one of the worst times of my life. I feel used. I don't know. I just ... I feel like I've been used, somehow. I don't know what's going to happen now. Maybe the next time Officer Malone comes back, he'll slap some handcuffs on me.'

The bell.

'Right on cue.' I roll my eyes, stand up and move to the door.

Deep breath. Hold. One, two, three. Release.

'Officer Malone, what is it now? Are there urban foxes roaming the street with flick knives? Fireworks? A light is on in my attic?'

'No, Miss Paige. Nothing like that. I'm here to see you.'

What does he know?

'What? You want to cuff me and take me downtown?'

He screws up his face. 'No. Of course not. What? No. Nothing like that. Just that ... I've knocked on a lot of houses today and yours has stuck with me. Maybe it's my police gut, but I was worried about you.' He leans in and speaks quietly. 'Maybe you're in trouble but you can't say it out loud.' He moves back and talks at a normal level, like he wants the person that's possibly inside to hear him. 'Maybe I should just come in and take a look around, anyway.'

'By all means. Be my guest.' I open the door and take a step back into the hallway. 'That isn't what you were wearing earlier,' I say. It's not a question.

'We're supposed to wear a body cam, but it's not to every situation, and I tend to put mine on at night when we run into the more unsavoury characters, you know?'

'Like me?' I flutter my eyelashes a little in flirtation.

'You'd be surprised what goes on behind the closed doors of the wealthy, ma'am.'

I shut the door behind Officer Malone and hold out a hand for him to lead the way. He walks to the living area, taking in the finer details of his surroundings, making sure he turns his body so that it can be caught on the camera stuck to his chest.

It's so obvious.

He walks over to the back windows and looks out into the yard. He slips where I have recently cleaned the floor. I tell him I spilled some wine.

The light doesn't switch on automatically because I have disarmed the sensor. Nothing looks out of place. The yard doesn't have a lot of plants, it's mostly grass and, from his angle, Malone will not be able to tell that a hole has been dug because the grass is flat and I fit the rectangle I cut out back into its place.

'You know your shed window is wide open?'

'Sorry?'

'Your shed at the bottom of the garden. The window has been left open.'

'Oh, God, I don't even really use it. How often does it rain here? I'm really not that bothered.' I think about the blood that has been left in the shed. And the T-shirt with the message. I forgot about that. I haven't cleaned that up, yet.

That's how people get caught. They plan for everything, but one stupid oversight costs them dearly.

'I'm not worried about the rain. Hell, it'll be fire season soon enough. I was thinking more about squirrels and pests like that.'

'Sure. I'll go and shut it.'

Malone moves away from the back doors. He asks if I would mind him looking around upstairs. Says he just wants to make sure I am safe. I let him wander around. There's nothing to see now.

^^^^^^^^^^

^^^^^^^^^^

[LIVESTREAM]

Edie can't believe how confident Paige is now that she has buried Alyssa and cleaned up the blood. Maybe she thinks she has nothing to lose.

'Going somewhere?' Malone shouts from her room.

'I'm sorry?'

'You seem to be packing a suitcase. So ... are you going somewhere?'

Malone stands at the top of the stairs and Paige is at the bottom.

'No, no. More like *was going* somewhere. I was packed to go to a spa retreat this weekend but something came up. It's not a half-packed suitcase, it's half *unpacked*.'

He seems to buy it and starts walking downstairs.

'Your place looks good. Keep the windows and doors locked, we don't want anybody sneaking in and moving your books around or whatever these freaks are doing.'

She escorts him towards the door.

'You know, Officer, I'm just not too worried about it. I haven't seen anything for a week. I think they've had their fun and moved on.'

'Well, I sure hope you're right. Enjoy the rest of your evening. Maybe you'll get to the spa next weekend.'

'Loooong week ahead, but I sure hope so.'

He tips his hat and leaves.

Paige goes straight back to the sofa, puts her feet up and drinks a mouthful of wine. She hits record one last time. 'That was close. I'm sure Malone will be back when they find the one that got away and I won't have any way out. Maybe I'll just drink wine and eat pizza until then. There's no use running. Looks like there won't be a show about me now, huh?' She finishes the glass. 'Could have been fun, too. So ... uh ... I guess this is me, Paige, signing off, even though I never really got to sign in.'

She stops the video.

Fiddles with the camera.

Presses the upload button.

Edie was right. Paige has nothing to lose. It's like she went through with all of that and now she is giving up.

^^^^^^^^^^

^^^^^^^^^^

Crazy Facts @CrazyFactsOrg
'Ten of the craziest social-media influencer downfalls.
A thread.
Number seven will shock you.'
♥ 4.3k ◻ 61

^^^^^^^^^^

^^^^^^^^^^

[LIVESTREAM]

Lincoln/Lowell Productions have everything they need for a one-hour special. If the police don't come around in the next week to arrest Paige, Edie can edit the footage together and leave the end dangling, forcing the audience to crave more.

A two-part mini-series.

Throw in some talking heads, interviews with family and friends and former work colleagues. Bulk it out a bit. Delay the gratification. Make it a six-part limited series.

Edie isn't thinking about any of that, though. She has days of footage to condense, but she can break it up with the drone shots and the diary-cam videos that have uploaded to the privacy of the Lincoln/Lowell YouTube channel.

Tammy is worried that Paige might not make it to the end of the week. She watches the fitness and health guru chug a bottle of white wine. Now she is opening a bottle of red to go with her bread and cheese. It wouldn't be too difficult to wash down a bottle of pills and make all of this go away.

Edie is not worried. She tells Tammy that she's going to go to bed, get some sleep. But Tammy can't. She needs to wait until Paige goes upstairs or she passes out on her sofa.

Maybe it's her need to be a mother.

Maybe Hollywood hasn't totally destroyed her.

Maybe it's just that she can feel empathy and Edie cannot.

Tammy watches Paige do nothing, and, for her, this is the most captivating footage. Because it is real. Nothing has been heightened. There is no outside interference. No drones or pizza deliveries, it's just a woman, on her own, having a lonely drink and feeling lost. Paige is on the verge of something. Either a breakdown or a breakthrough. But this tipping point, this is the real examination of the human condition.

Tammy watches until Paige's body gives in, then she gives in herself.

Almost everybody is asleep. Paige, Edie, Tammy, Less, Malone, Satmohan, Davis.

Alyssa's mother is not. She doesn't finish until six. She will be worrying about her daughter until then, hoping that she's safely in her bed when she gets back from work.

It's late and tomorrow is the start of a new week. Paige will have thousands of notifications to deal with. Edie will be buried in the editing process. Davis and Tammy will be engaged in something more romantic than the eight-minute knee-trembler they had today. Satmohan will be running his last errands for Lincoln/Lowell and updating his resumé.

And Less will have to lie to his parents.

He will tell them that he had a weekend-long rager. He'll make up the name of a friend he doesn't have and say that they partied hard for two days straight. He'll lie some more and say that he's going to work hard to finish his college project this week. He won't mention the money he made from a TV show that will never be seen, or that he intends to use the money to start his own fashion line without their input and judgement. And control. And disapproval.

Less will lie his way through the morning. He will lie through breakfast to his father. He will lie to his mother when she walks in on him getting dressed and sees what she thinks is a huge bruise on his chest.

He will say that he probably fell.

He will say that he didn't even notice it.

That she needs to get out of his room.

And then he will leave the house, unlocked, of course, with all the lies out of his system, so that he can get across town and tell Alyssa's mother the truth.

Tomorrow, she will find out where her daughter is.

By Friday, this entire ordeal will be over.

MONDAY

SWIPE RIGHT IF INTERESTED - - - - - - - - - - >>>>>>>>

LESS

'What is it?' my mother asks. 'Anything interesting?' She knows it was hand-delivered.

I run a thumb along the inside of the flap and open the envelope. I read.

You are cordially invited to a private screening of THE WEEKEND RETREAT.

The invitation says that it will be held on Friday afternoon. It gives an address and I know that whatever house is there will make my own look like a garden shed. The soiree is happening in the afternoon. It is signed at the bottom, *Davis Davis.*

It's exclusive. I'm supposed to burn after reading but I don't. I don't have to do anything they say. I won't remember the address from one view but I've also never been great at following the rules. So I fold it in half and place it in my pant pocket.

'Nothing interesting. A party invitation for this weekend. I don't think I'll go. I probably need a break from all that.' The lies are coming more easily to me. Maybe I've changed. Maybe I'm worse than I was before.

^^^^^^^^^^

^^^^^^^^^^

PAIGE

I have nobody to lie to because I'm still by myself. How depressing. When I open my envelope, I have to act surprised. Like I have no idea who Davis Davis is or what a film called *The Weekend Retreat* could be about. I get asked to attend events and wear specific clothing or accessories all the time, so it isn't out of the ordinary to be invited to a premiere.

I take the invitation into the kitchen because I worry that I am still being watched. I stick the envelope to the fridge with a magnet I bought on Brooklyn Bridge while walking across it. I hope the two producers assume that I am saving the date because it could be something important to me, but I have no intention of attending. I have been exploited enough.

In fact, I leave the envelope on the fridge, walk myself upstairs to the bathroom, where I know there are no cameras, and I light a corner of the invitation and watch it burn in the sink.

They can all burn.

^^^^^^^^^

^^^^^^^^^

#ThereAintNoPartyLikeADavisDavisParty
Satmohan will attend because he loves Davis but also as a farewell to his mentors.

Davis even sent an invitation out to Officer Malone.

The only person involved who didn't get one is Alyssa.

There is no way to RSVP, so Davis Davis has no idea who will come. It may be nobody. It may be everybody. He doesn't care. He only wants to see Tammy, and watch what she and Edie have come up with this time.

^^^^^^^^^

^^^^^^^^^

LESS
This is not going to be easy.

What the hell am I going to say?

I'm going to have to tell her everything. From the beginning. I'll have to say that we went to the Davis Davis party. That we stole a car while we were there. That all the crap on the news about Tom and Dana, well, me and Alyssa are Tom and Dana.

Fuck.

Maybe I could just say that. Then I don't have to explain how we stalked Rosie Velazquez or spent the night at the home of a rock legend.

There will be no need to go through the details of how amazing Alyssa is at finding out where famous people lived. It really is a gift.

Just say, 'We are Tom and Dana' and all of that gets explained away.

But there is nothing in the news about Paige's home. Nobody knows about the knife and hair-pulling and the shed and the fitness goddess throwing a box of Krispy Kremes into her mouth. I'm going to have to talk about that.

I'm going to have to say that we both got hurt and that I played dead. And that Alyssa was considerably better at doing that than I was.

And I won't need to say it because it will be frighteningly obvious but I will have to tell Alyssa's mother that I left her daughter there.

And that she is in a better place.

That's it.

I think I have a plan.

I make my way across town after breakfast, pretending that I am going to college, getting all the lies out to my own mother before I have to tell the complete truth to Alyssa's.

I'm scared. My chest hurts. Part of me wonders whether Alyssa's mother could help me because she is a nurse. She may not want to once I begin my story.

I take a couple of deep breaths and ring the bell. I can't just let myself in around here, not in this neighbourhood. Alyssa doesn't live in a mansion. Her family is not wealthy. There's nothing of value to insure inside their home. So, of course, there are three locks on the front door.

I wait.

One lock.

Two locks.

Three.

Then Alyssa's mom's beautiful smile.
She looks relieved.
It won't last.

^^^^^^^^^^

^^^^^^^^^^

PART THREE: **SHOWTIME**

^^^^^^^^^**KEEP SCROLLING**^^^^^^^^^

FRIDAY

'THE WEEKEND RETREAT'
@LincolnLowell 👍 4 👎 |
7 Views

^^^^^^^^^^

^^^^^^^^^^

Davis Davis has a personal chef, who prepares all his meals.

But not today.

Not for the world premiere. He can't have any of his staff around.

His new place is palatial, of course, but it has character. In comparison to many other parts of the world, the United States is still young. They don't have 500-year-old churches and county halls. They tear their history down. Most European capital cities have multi-storey car parks that are older than American monuments.

But Davis's new place looks like a Tudor mansion. The craftsmanship is evident in the wooden roof beams and trusses. Part of the house is thatched. So the noises are different from his city crash pads and more modern real estate.

He poaches three eggs and listens to music. His realtor assured him that the roof is like a magnet for martin nests but it's nothing to worry about. All very natural. Hardly an infestation.

He places the poached eggs on some rye toast and cracks black pepper over the top, then sprinkles with rock salt. And he scrolls through his emails.

His assistant has been trying to get some pest control in to look around the thatching and get rid of any nests. Davis just wants his new place to be perfect.

He pops a yolk with his fork and emails his assistant that he doesn't want to be disturbed today and to just get the pest guy to come along in the morning. But not too early because he always sleeps well on Premiere Night.

It's an intimate affair. There are so few people involved in the production. Davis has a screening room in the basement. It's soundproofed and the speakers are so loud, any rats or starlings or possums that want to crawl through the walls and ceilings will probably vibrate to death.

Edie and Tammy are coming over after lunch. Satmohan will, obviously, attend, as well as a few of the actors that were involved. The room can fit twenty Senso Modular Reclining Cinema Sofas, and there's a fully stocked bar and popcorn machine.

Davis is lucky enough to be sent early screenings of films and TV shows, and he'll often fill the space with friends and industry professionals. But Premiere Night is different. There's a circle of trust.

This is for the shows that Lincoln/Lowell do not plaster with their logo. There's no memorable catchphrase after the credits. They haven't made this for the world.

They've made it for themselves.

And Davis loves what they come up with.

He can't wait.

Nobody is allowed to discuss what they see here tonight.

Nobody ever will.

^^^^^^^^^^

^^^^^^^^^^

WHEN YOU'RE NOT HOME...

THEY BECOME THE OWNERS

- - - - - - - - - - - -

Call 1-800-THE-PEST

RATS|WASPS|POSSUMS|COCKROACHES

When you need the best, call THE PEST

Skip Ad in 5...

^^^^^^^^^^

^^^^^^^^^^

#OpeningNight #BigScreenMagic #RedCarpetEvent

It's exactly 3:30 when Satmohan arrives. He's always on time for a Davis Davis party. Nobody else is sad or desperate enough to arrive on time because they want to project an image of coolness, like they don't have to be there even though they absolutely do.

Satmohan is always grateful for the one-on-one time with the famed record-label owner. Satmohan doesn't want to work in the music industry, but business is business. He's learning from the best.

'Satmohan, my boy. As keen as ever.' Davis smiles. He's not making fun of Satmohan, he's not like that. He likes the kid. 'Now, I'm on bar duty today, so I'm not sure about your fancy cocktails.'

Satmohan sees glasses fizzing on a tray in the entrance.

'Anything with bubbles will work, sir.'

'Davis. Please. Sir is my father's name.' He places a hand on Satmohan's back and ushers him inside. 'Take a glass, take two, if you like. The rest will be along shortly, I'm sure. Edie and Tammy will be last, of course.' He fake laughs.

'Of course. Build the suspense.' Satmohan takes a sip of champagne. His hand is shaking.

'Have you seen any footage?' Davis asks.

'No way. They keep these projects very close to their chests. You know, I don't even think they tell each other everything.'

Davis laughs haughtily. 'You know, that wouldn't surprise me one bit. Couple of sneaky bitches. You have to love them.'

Satmohan nods, though he doesn't quite agree. The producers he works for are prolific and inventive and encouraging, but it's not always easy to even like them. They do some deplorable things, and they are not interested in the welfare of the on-screen 'talent' in the slightest.

'Are you okay to wait up here, Sat? I need to go down to the screening room and sort a couple of things before the rest arrive. Just hang here or in the kitchen and let anyone in if they're as punctual as you. Okay?'

'Of course. Of course. Do what you have to do. There may not be any champagne left if you take too long, though.' He is desperately trying to sound casual and like he belongs in this situation. He's nervous because Edie and Tammy have been so understanding about him leaving.

Satmohan downs one of his glasses when Davis leaves and takes another from the tray before wandering around the new house. He has been to three Davis Davis parties so far. All at the old place. He was there when the guitarist got electrocuted and the one where the tiger was chained up – he swears the thing was coked-up at one point.

Satmohan has seen some things.

At the other party, a prominent leading actor was present. His wife was not. The actor was spotted out of his mind with worry because his special friend could not be found. Twenty minutes of searching and the A-list actor was reunited with the young Thai male and they excused themselves to one of Davis's bedrooms for the next hour.

Everybody at the party was forced to sign a non-disclosure agreement.

World Premiere Night has no such agreement. Not in writing, anyway. There can be no trail.

The dining room has a table large enough for twenty. Davis lives on his own but he is almost never alone. The furniture matches the house. It's all clearly antique, from the patinated mirror to the pair of nineteenth-century Howard Ivor armchairs beneath the bay window. It's opulent but it's tasteful.

Satmohan goes out the front of the house to see if anyone else is arriving. There's no life in sight. Not even a gardener. It's the quietest movie premiere of all time.

He goes back to the kitchen, places his empty glass on the tray and picks up another. This is a celebration, after all.

Davis returns from downstairs.

He looks at the tray. 'Someone's thirsty today.'

Satmohan is embarrassed, he doesn't want to look like he is taking advantage of the hospitality.

'I'm so sorry, I don't know what came over me. Excitement, I guess.'

'My boy, I have an entire room dedicated to wine and whisky, there's more than enough to go around.' He takes a glass for himself. 'It's all set up down there. I think I'll join you now.' Davis has always come across as nice, like a stand-up guy. But Satmohan forgets that Davis is ambitious. That he is powerful. That he always wants more. And that he wants the things that he can't have, that nobody else can have either.

'I actually thought you'd finished and gone upstairs, I thought I heard you up there.'

'Stupid birds, I'm afraid. Lodged in the roof. I need to get rid of the thatching but it just makes the place from the outside, don't you think?'

Davis leads Satmohan into the kitchen and tells him it's the quietest room in the house. They talk a little bit about music. Davis finds out what Satmohan is listening to at the moment and Satmohan tries to give some different answers to the ones he gave at Davis's last party.

He wants to appear more interesting than he is. Davis Davis has a million stories from his illustrious life. He's halfway through one of them when Edie walks into the kitchen, a glass of champagne in one hand and a briefcase in the other.

She let herself in.

Like she always does at Davis's house.

Like anybody could.

'Edie, my dear.' Davis stops the story and greets her with a kiss to each cheek. 'Tammy not with you?'

She tries to hide her disappointment even though she knows those two are much closer to one another.

'We have to travel separately on days like today; if we both got hit by the same truck, there would be no screening.' She taps the briefcase and winks.

'How very diligent of you.'

Then, 'Started the flirting without me, huh?'

It's Tammy. Loud. Brash. Overly confident. A glass of champagne in her hand. She greets everybody with a customary double-kiss. Edie first, as she is closest, then Satmohan, then Davis, who gets an extra playful kiss on the lips. 'Thanks for hosting our little soiree, Davis.'

'My absolute pleasure. So how many more are we waiting on?'

Tammy looks up to her right and counts in her head, then she looks at Edie.

'Four,' Edie confirms.

There have been another four invites sent out.

Two actors, Gabriel and Michael. They won't pass up the opportunity to spend time at the Davis Davis mansion.

And two victims. Less and Paige.

One of them isn't coming.

^^^^^^^^^^

^^^^^^^^^^

LESS

Looks like I'm the last to arrive; I don't want to hang out with these people, these vultures, these puppet masters. I just want to witness their film, their personal project that took so much effort and required MI5 levels of subterfuge to carry off.

I want to know what I have been paid so handsomely to never discuss with anyone.

Ever.

I let myself in. The door is always open at Davis Davis's house. There is still champagne in the entrance hall, too. I knock one back for added courage. I place the empty glass down and take a deep breath. The thatched roof rustles above me. I breathe again, I'm weirdly aware of it. I drink another glass in its entirety. Then I take two more glasses and head downstairs.

I know where I am going. There are voices.

'Ah, Less,' Tammy says as I enter the screening room. 'Just in time. I see you found the drinks. Come on in and take a seat.'

I don't know everybody in that room. I have never met Edie or the two actors in the corner or the camp Asian guy. It feels like a lot of nobodies for such an intricate operation.

Maybe that's how it works. Nobodies can be destroyed and discarded.

^^^^^^^^^^

^^^^^^^^^^

#AcceptanceSpeech #PlayTheMusic #AndTheAwardGoesTo

'Thank you all for coming today to another private screening.' Edie takes centre stage. 'As you know, these are our real passion projects. We produce shows all the time for many different networks and streaming services, but these are just for us. And this was a real experiment in psychology. We wanted to look at the price of fame in influence and entitlement, and how somebody in that position would act if thrust into extraordinary circumstances.'

Tammy joins in. 'Yes, and, unfortunately, the subject of the show chose not to be here with us today, it seems, but that will not take away from the enjoyment. Edie had the final cut, so I'll also be seeing a lot of this for the first time.' The friends smile at one another.

Edie jumps back in. 'We would like to thank Davis for hosting the event, today. Thanks, too, to Gabriel and Michael, who did a sterling job acting in the show.' One played the pizza delivery guy, the other was Police Officer Malone. 'Satmohan, as always, we couldn't function without you.' He grins at this, it's the validation he needs, and it seems genuine. He still plans to leave. 'And, of course, Less, who played such a pivotal role in pushing Paige into action. Thank you all for your efforts.'

^^^^^^^^^^

^^^^^^^^^^

LESS

There's no mention of Alyssa and that upsets me. I drink down my third glass of champagne in as many minutes. It's crazy to me that she wasn't even acknowledged. Everything she went through. The accident. There's nothing. They are going to have to show it on the screen, surely.

And why did they expect Paige to show up? She's back on her social platforms and continuing like nothing happened, like she actually went on that spa break.

Jack Sandford has released a new song and Rosie Velazquez has moved home because her old place was creeping her out. Everybody out there is acting like this is totally normal.

And everyone in the room is now expected to do the same thing: watch the horror and commit it to memory. Because it will never be seen by anyone again. And we can't talk about it. This footage will become the stuff of myth. An urban legend that circulates Hollywood auditions and script readings. Rumours of a snuff movie. Conspiracies about producers' power.

'So, without further ado, please, relax, drink, and enjoy *The Weekend Retreat*.'

Everyone claps but me.

The lights dim. The screen lights up.

A Lincoln/Lowell Production.

Then the title.

And straight into some footage of Paige kicking and punching and sweating in her living room a few days before she thought she had stabbed and killed me.

I can't watch. It's making me cringe at the thought of what is to come.

I finish my last glass of alcohol. I stand up. 'Sorry, too much. This stuff goes right through me. I'm just going to go to the bathroom.' I speak quietly so not to disturb too much but it's loud enough for them to hear. They're too engrossed to even wave me off.

They don't care about me.

They don't care about anybody.

Davis locked the door from the inside so that nobody could get in. He wants the moment preserved, clearly. The guy leaves the front door of his house wide open with a Warhol original in the hallway but locks up his screening room for a not-for-profit, homemade documentary he will never even own.

I let myself out, putting the key in my pocket before I leave; I don't want to get locked in the hallway.

I walk upstairs to the entrance. There are thirteen bathrooms in this huge building. I walk straight past the first one and go into the kitchen. I look through the refrigerator, take a few grapes and a bottle of white wine then head upstairs.

I have no idea how much the wine would have cost, but I swig straight from the bottle. I look around at a few of the bedrooms, whistling loudly as I do so. Then I find a bathroom. I can't hold it much longer.

It probably looks like I'm going off the rails a little since the incident of *The Weekend Retreat*, drinking straight from the bottle in my left hand while holding my dick in my right and emptying my bladder.

#MenCanMultitask

I flush, swig, and I only lay the bottle down to wash my hands.

There's a noise outside the door.

I take a deep breath – maybe it's a sigh – and I unlock it.

Then I open the door.

It's a ghost.

^^^^^^^^^

^^^^^^^^^

ALYSSA

Three days.

And not a starling in sight.

I have been living in a mansion for almost half the week. I'm well stocked up on food. Besides, this is no ordinary attic, where people box up all the belongings they should have thrown out years ago. There are lights and plug sockets, so I can keep my phone charged. There's regency furniture that deserves to be seen and fifty framed one-sheet cinema posters of some of the greatest movies of all time. If this is the kind of stuff that is locked away, never to be enjoyed, nobody was ever going to find me up here.

I've actually been very comfortable. There are chairs to sit on and it's not cold at all. The house is so huge that I've been able to get down and use one of the many bathrooms without ever being seen, so there's been no need to find a bowl or some old camping equipment when I need to take a piss.

It's not like Rosie's place. You don't have to pop the loft hatch and extend a ladder. There are stairs and a door. Nobody comes up. There's never been a noise near the stairs. It's the easiest phrogging I've ever done.

Screw the influencers, the über-rich is where it's at.

I know it's safe to exit when I hear the whistling.

I would recognise Less anywhere.

We have been inseparable for years now. Peas in a pod.

A brother from another mother.

A sister from a different mister.

Bonnie and Clyde. But better. Because they got shot.

Less and I may not have shared a womb, but we are just as close as any twins out there.

^^^^^^^^^^

^^^^^^^^^^

#SorryNotSorry #ZeroRegrets #IDGAF

In the screening room, they whisper about what a shame it was that Alyssa's life was cut so short but, at the same time, they revel in the forced drama of the show. It's sick. The rich feel untouchable.

If they don't talk about it, then it didn't happen.

^^^^^^^^^^

^^^^^^^^^^

ALYSSA

I get up. There's no need to tidy away my wrappers and empty packets. I pick up a bottle of Macallan whisky that I spotted on the first day. It's in a lacquered-wood presentation box. The bottle says it has been aged seventy-two years. I don't know a lot about whisky, but I know that means it's probably expensive. I Googled it. The bottle is actually a Lalique decanter. The entire package cost Davis a hundred and thirty grand. Ouch.

I know the staff are off today, so there is no need to sneak anywhere. I am three floors higher than the screening room. So I take my whisky bottle, without the box, open the attic door and walk straight down the stairs, leaving it open.

I don't fucking care anymore.

I swing the hundred-grand whisky as I walk, like a child with a teddy bear. Down the stairs. Across the corridor. Towards the whistling.

The toilet flushes.

The tap pours.

The door unlocks. Opens.

And I am reunited with the friend who left me in that house with a woman who thought she had killed me.

^^^^^^^^^

^^^^^^^^^

LESS

'Jesus Christ.' I step back, putting a hand to my chest.

'Not quite. Take another guess.' She stares at me. Those big brown eyes.

We look at each other for a moment. Then I say, 'Bitch, get over here.'

She smiles at me. Her best friend. Then walks over and wraps her arms around me like she hasn't seen me for years. I love her. She has been in Davis's house for three days. That's the longest we have been apart, since we've known one another.

We're better together.

'Are you ready to do this?' Alyssa asks.

I put a hand in my pocket and pull out the key. 'I mean, it's the least we could do, right?'

^^^^^^^^^

^^^^^^^^^

#JustForTheFunOfIt
#TheStrangestDamnedGangYouEverHeardOf

Edie and Tammy think they are so clever. Making their personal projects. Creating their art. Playing God.

Edie, with her four piles of paperwork, one for each of *her* characters in the show.

An extensive background check was done on Paige, a lot of which involved Satmohan stalking her online and in person. She had to know that Paige was psychologically sound to handle what was thrown at her but also the best way to manipulate her paranoia and sense of self-interest. And she thinks that last part is so easy with this generation because they're all only interested in themselves.

The two actors, Gabriel and Michael, had to be desperate for roles and unscrupulous in character to enter into such a situation and not want the plaudits after. There would be no credit on IMDb for their first feature-film role. Essentially, they did it for the money. And they will keep quiet because of the money. It will keep them comfortable enough to continue on their chosen career path without having to wait tables at a TGI Fridays.

The fourth was Alyssa. Taken from the hundreds of audition tapes. She was attractive and entrepreneurial, but the key was that she clearly knew exactly what she wanted. She wanted some time in the spotlight and she wanted to support her family. She was friends with someone who came from wealthy stock, and she had difficulty feeling like she belonged. And, damn, she wanted to know how the other half lived.

She was desperate, as so many are, but she was desperate and poor.

Edie couldn't believe it when she walked into Davis's party at the old house. That's when she knew she had the final piece to her puzzle. Alyssa was the last part to *The Weekend Retreat.* Give her a camera to record her life, document her journey. Promise her some money if she just keeps it all quiet.

Of course, Tammy is just as smart. Or so she thinks. It doesn't matter how close two people are in Hollywood, there is always going to be a battle of egos.

They're not Butch and Sundance.

And they're certainly not Bonnie and Clyde.

These kids sending in their audition tapes are clamouring for glamour and fame and everything that goes along with it, but every actor, director and producer is suffering from a version of imposter syndrome. All of them are constantly having to prove themselves.

They're insecure.

When Tammy was coked out of her mind at Davis's, she met the kid in the purple hat who had snuck into the party. And she admired the balls on him. Davis clearly did, too, because he would have had the boy ousted, immediately, otherwise.

She asked him if he wanted to be on TV. He said no. He wanted to be in fashion. Hell, he was already in fashion, but he wanted to be bigger.

She asked him if a TV slot might help boost his profile.

He said he didn't want to do it that way.

Integrity isn't something that is admired in this town.

So she asked him if an influx of cash would help him start his own line.

He said yes.

She could give him money to be on a show that nobody would ever see or talk about, and he would still get paid. All he had to do was take a fall and play dead. The only catch was that he would never be able to discuss it with anyone.

Again, he said yes. It worked for Less. He didn't want to tell anyone, anyway. He would have his own money. Real independence. Making it on his own like his father had. His dad would be proud of him for once. And nobody would ever know how it started.

It was clever. They were clever. That Lincoln/Lowell partnership was going to produce another show for themselves and their rich friends. Something edgy, something unpredictable, but nonetheless, something that they could control.

And they are so used to getting their way. They know that everybody signs the contract. They know that they can send around a fake policeman to up the tension or drop off a pizza to stop their victim from alerting the real police.

It's all under control.

Everybody signs.

Nobody talks.

But Alyssa and Less are not everybody. They're not one of the hundred percent. There's a bond there that cannot be broken. There is no way they would ever betray one another.

Sure, no relationship is 50/50. Alyssa is hotter than Less. He is richer than her. They are both ambitious but she is more ruthless. But they are equal. They feel the same about one another. And, when they are told that they cannot tell a soul about something, they don't think that includes each other.

They have no secrets.

Edie and Tammy thought they were the strongest duo.

Another rich-person mistake, thinking they can dominate everyone beneath them.

Another Gen-X screw-up, thinking they are smarter than everyone younger than them.

^^^^^^^^^

^^^^^^^^^^

#MovieMagic #LightsCameraAction #CinematicVibes

Davis Davis is transfixed. He's at the part where Alyssa gets grabbed by the hair and smashes her head into the floor.

There's blood.

That was real.

She twitches.

That part wasn't real.

Then she stops moving. He has watched some fucked-up videos in the Lincoln/Lowell personal collection, but nobody ever died.

He should be shocked. Outraged that they let this happen. He's not like these women. His fortune was earned honourably, through grit and a talent for spotting *other* people's talent. Davis is a good guy. But, when you can have everything you want, there's no value in anything. Only the one-offs.

'Where the hell is this going?' he says out loud to anyone who will listen.

Edie and Tammy are smug. Heartless.

Paige was panicking, she was never going to check their pulses. As long as they didn't move, she would assume they were dead.

When she finally came out of the shock, maybe after a night of sleep, she would have the mind to consider her options.

Moving the bodies.

Disposing of the bodies.

Making a run for it. (That would ruin the show.)

'But he's not dead, he's...' Davis looks around the room for Less.

'Gone to the bathroom. You see how much he drank when he got here?' Satmohan is so aware, he thinks. It's more that he's judgemental.

'No. He's not dead. The knife for the bread was a plant. We gave him that,' Edie explains. Proud. They have access to the wardrobes and effects departments of every studio. Fake bottles, blood packs, retractable knives, stunt guns, blanks, you name it.

'Hollywood magic.' Davis nods.

He should know better. In this town, you shouldn't believe anything.

'What about the girl?'

'Very unfortunate. An accident.'

This was not the plan. There were back-ups and contingencies and fifteen different scenarios, but it hinged around the planned incident with Less. At first, some playfulness with the phrogging. Moving things around in the house, getting Paige more paranoid about the Tom and Dana figures in the news. Alyssa wasn't supposed to get hurt.

'She's...?'

'Just watch, Davis,' Tammy jumps in. 'You don't want to miss anything.'

He's excited. Like this has all been created for him. He could buy anything that he wants but this is one of a kind. Like Tammy. That's what the super-rich want. The object that exists only for them.

Everyone turns back to the screen. They've forgotten that Less is not there. Everyone but Satmohan. But he doesn't want to ask questions. He doesn't want to disturb the show. He also doesn't want to leave.

#FOMO.

It's an exclusive club, though only God knows why anybody would want to become a member.

Gabriel enjoys his pizza-guy appearance and Michael is more self-critical about his portrayal of a police officer. He feels he could have played it with more menace or been more creepy. He didn't fully commit to either. They take drinks from the bar and continue to be interested. Something eats at them, knowing Alyssa is being seen as collateral damage, but their bank accounts have never been so healthy.

Michael has an audition for a commercial in three days.

Gabriel has been offered a part as a prince at Disneyland. He doesn't need to take that now, but who says no to Disney?

^^^^^^^^^^

^^^^^^^^^^

ESCAPE TO YOUR #HAPPYPLACE

WALT DISNEY World®

1-407-WDW-SAVE

Skip >|

^^^^^^^^^^

^^^^^^^^^^

#LessonLearned #BurnMeOnce #DonePlayingNice

It's getting close to the part where Paige shows her physical strength and drags Less out to her yard. She knows that she can't keep the bodies there, but she doesn't know what to do, so she leaves him outside.

Everybody knows that he gets away because he was planted there. Because he is at the Davis residence, right now. But there were never cameras in the yard. Less could move freely. Less could escape. He could make it look like he left his dead best friend behind because he wanted the money to begin his own fashion label. He could use the remains of that blood pack and write a message on the T-shirt he would leave behind.

Cameras on.

They are watching.

And, above that, when Paige moved the blanket.

She's not dead.

Bring her out.

Paige didn't mean to do what she did. She's not a monster. Less knew that she would trust him, that she would try to save herself, because that's all she had been doing since she found them.

She did the same thing with Alyssa. Dragged her out. Spoke to her. Realised what the hell was going on and then recorded those diary-room entries. Those TV-worthy stories of dismembering. Those award-worthy performances where she cried and howled at a God she didn't even believe in.

Manipulating the manipulators.

It's all make-believe.

That's show business.

^^^^^^^^^^

^^^^^^^^^^

LESS

There's still time left in the show, I'm sure. I didn't leave that long ago. The speakers are loud in there. No way they can hear Alyssa and me outside the door. They don't realise that we have used the key I took to lock them in. It'll be too late once Alyssa has poured the hundred-grand lighter fuel over that door and carpet and set it alight.

We watch it ignite and spread like liquid light, dancing down the hallway and up the walls. It's strange how loud it gets. Once it obscures the door to the screening room, Alyssa and I turn to leave.

Up the stairs.

Back to the entrance.

One more champagne.

Our work here is done.

Everything in this wonderful and impeccably refurbished house will burn. The signed photographs and baseballs. The gold and platinum discs that line the walls. The antique furniture and rugs. The wine collection. All gone.

^^^^^^^^^

^^^^^^^^^

ALYSSA

'Follow me,' I instruct Less. I take the original Warhol off the wall and tap it with my hand as if to say, *I think I probably deserve this*.

Less agrees and, like always, he does as I ask.

We walk outside, turn left and go around to the back of the building. There are two wooden cellar doors that open to reveal a flight of stairs that lead down to the back of the screening room. I assume that fire regulations mean that there has to be an adequate escape route for a moment like this.

The thing is, I came down in the night and took the key from the inside of that door.

I'm not a fire marshal. I don't want them to have an adequate escape route.

'Shouldn't we be getting out of here?' Less asks. 'What do we need from down here?'

'You'll see. Just wait.'

I open my rucksack, which was filled with snacks three days ago. I take out the expensive vlogging camera supplied to me, kindly, by

Lincoln/Lowell Productions. The same model they gave to Paige for her video-diary confessions.

'What's that for?'

'I'm making a documentary.'

'Lyss, I don't know if that's a good idea.'

'It'll only be a minute.'

^^^^^^^^^

^^^^^^^^^

#InCaseOfEmergency #HelpIsOnTheWay

Inside the screening room, the film goes off. Wires are melting in the wall. Switches are being tripped. Davis goes over to the locked door and tries to open it but burns his palm slightly on the handle.

'Oh, shit.'

'What's wrong?' asks Tammy.

'Okay. Don't panic but I think the place is on fire and this door is locked.'

'Why is it locked?' Satmohan chimes in.

'That's not important. What is important is that we get out. The fire exit is over behind that panel. Don't worry. Come with me.'

Davis keeps his cool and moves the panel aside to reveal a door that takes them down a corridor that will lead them out to the garden and safety. He thinks about his thatched roof and how easily that will ignite.

When they get there, the door is also locked from the other side and, through the small pane of glass, Davis sees the kids from the video.

Alyssa and Less.

There's no mistaking them.

Alyssa is holding Davis's Warhol painting in one hand and a camera in the other at her waist. She is filming his reaction. Then Edie's reaction as she pushes her way to the front to see what is going on and why they are not walking through that door to safety.

She screams something at Alyssa, who responds by placing a hand to her ear and shaking her head like she can't quite hear.

Edie and Tammy scream obscenities in Alyssa's direction, conveniently forgetting what they had done to her, how insignificant her life had been in their struggle towards creating something artistic. Because you're supposed to be able to do what you want with the poor and the desperate, the rich and powerful are supposed to be untouchable; they have their own set of rules.

Satmohan is crying.

'You stupid fucking bitches. You just think you can ruin people's lives and get away with it forever?'

'Now is not the time to grow a pair of balls or a conscience, Sat. They signed. They knew there was a chance it would ruin them,' Edie reminds him, as cold as ever.

'But not kill them.'

'Stop it.' Gabriel is animated. 'It's not in here yet, call the police. Call the fire service. We have time.'

He's right. They do have time. What they don't have is reception. When Davis had the screening room built, he made sure that it was a black spot. He wanted focus in there, not people checking their phones or taking calls or swiping through current trends. The internet does reach that far – just – but that doesn't matter because Alyssa switched that off before she lit the fire.

^^^^^^^^^

^^^^^^^^^

ALYSSA

I wave those assholes goodbye, and Less and I go back up the stairs, shutting the hatch behind us. I don't even turn back for one last look. I place the camera in my bag and the Warhol under my arm. It's the first thing I've stolen and kept.

'Let's go home, Less.'

'We're just going to leave them? There's six people in there, Lyss.'

'One less than Charles Manson.'

^^^^^^^^^^

^^^^^^^^^^

#Fin #Ende #Koniec #结束 #Конец #終わり

Inside, Edie has left the fire-escape corridor and is back in the screening room with her laptop. It's not the big screen but she does have a copy of the video on her hard drive. She fixes herself a stiff drink, fires it up and drags it to the point where they left off.

'Davis,' she calls. 'There's about twenty minutes left, want to see how it ends?'

He knows how it ends. In their death, burning and screaming for help.

But what else is he going to do?

Satmohan is incredulous. 'The fire will come through those walls at some point, and you want to watch TV and stroke your egos one last time?'

'Sit the fuck down, you big baby,' says Edie. 'I don't want to die but I'm going to. I've had a great life and I've done a lot. It could've been worse. What have you done, eh? Apart from sit around and piss and moan. Maybe you need to go in a corner and stroke your own ego one last time before you burn to a crisp.'

A bitch to the end.

Finally, Edie does something that is actually real.

^^^^^^^^^^

^^^^^^^^^^

#TooBlessedToBeStressed #LivingMyBestLife #SpiritualGlowUp #GratitudeAttitude

Paige looks at her watch. Edie and Tammy will be trapped by now.

They made her think that she had killed two people. Just so they could watch how she would react. Just to examine her behaviour, like she was some kind of lab rat.

They poked and prodded her and pushed her around in whatever direction they wanted. Each ring of the doorbell brought with it tension that the truth would be uncovered. Some of them perfectly timed to prevent her from giving up, others to push her into action.

And she was ready. She had motivated herself to bury Less.

And then he wasn't there.

Part of her feels stupid. She can't even remember what it felt like to hold a knife as it went into somebody's flesh. But, then, she doesn't remember because it never happened. And she just assumed they were dead. She didn't check their pulses. Who would? If they hadn't moved for hours, you'd guess that they weren't breathing.

As soon as she thought they were dead, her focus shifted on to what to do next. Something just switched in her brain. Self-preservation is a powerful motivator.

If she had started to look at them more closely, Officer Malone would have called around to misdirect her. Or Ariel Dean would tap at the door to talk about apologies and the benefit of removing dairy from her diet. All orchestrated by Lincoln/Lowell Productions, but really, it was Edie.

Paige tried to block it out. Covering Alyssa in a blanket and dragging Less down to the shed until she was ready to do the unthinkable. The unreal situation had pushed her into unreal territory.

She had to save herself.

Paige had to psych herself up to throw a young man into a hole and cover him in the earth she had spent most of the morning digging up.

She pushed herself into the zone, with Edie and Tammy viewing her every thought process, drinking their wine and eating their popcorn like they were at the cinema watching the latest romcom.

And then Less wasn't there.

He wasn't fucking there.

And Edie and Tammy knew he wouldn't be there. They knew because they had orchestrated it. They wanted to break Paige. They found a young, healthy, vivacious and optimistic woman online, seemingly conquering her own corner of the world and they wanted to tear her down.

Just because they could.

All Paige wanted was to help build people up.

Edie and Tammy.

They came as a pair.

Inseparable.

Powerful.

But not as inseparable as Alyssa and Less.

He was gone. Through the shed window. Easy to do when you haven't really been stabbed. But Alyssa wasn't, either. She was still on the living-room floor. And now Paige knew that she wasn't dead. She just had to pull her out of shot. Out of the eye-line of those two old, manipulative crows, trying to ruin her life. Just as they had said they would in the contract that Paige signed so easily.

#TheyAllSign.

#TheyAllGetRuined.

Alyssa hugged Paige as soon as she was out of shot. She had been lying almost in the same position for over a day. Thinking about the money and what Edie had told her. Playing her part. If she becomes Paige's friend then she has to be her best friend. If she gets her head smashed into the floor, then she stays on that floor. See how it plays out.

Keep it real.

Even though none of it is real.

Apart from Paige's reaction, which is all they really wanted. Those puppet masters. Those heartless black alchemists. Those Botoxed bitches.

Alyssa told Paige everything. She and Less were not supposed to tell each other how they had been recruited. But that's not how they work. Screw the contract. Friendship first. They would never go behind each other's backs like Edie and Tammy.

And that's why they have money in their banks and an original Warhol painting on their lap.

And Paige will never be the same. She stopped being real when she started to become famous. But now everything seems even more fake. She doesn't know who she is or who she wants to be, anymore. Her followers haven't noticed yet. But they will. People can smell inauthenticity.

Paige doesn't know the entire revenge plan. She doesn't need to. She doesn't want to. Alyssa and Less will take care of it. Paige just had to force herself to continue as normal. She played out the week, pretending that she still had no idea that the cameras were on her. Edie had an eye on the edit, Tammy had two eyes on Davis.

They had other things going on, so didn't check to see whether Paige was still being genuine. She can understand the oversight better than most.

Lyss and Less have confirmed that it ends today.

Paige can stop pretending.

All the cameras are still there, including the diary cam.

^^^^^^^^^

^^^^^^^^^

DIARY ENTRY 007 'UNLISTED' VIEWS: 0 COMMENTS: 0 LIKES: 0

'I can't believe it's been a week since everything happened. A week since you came into my life and tried to fuck it up. Since you thought that somebody who spends most of their time on camera would not know that they were being filmed. Since you assumed, as you probably always do, that you were the smartest person in the room.

The smartest people in the room. Well, you weren't. Alyssa and Less played dead for a day. And they played you like a fiddle. It's pretty much the stupidest thing you can do, and they still outwitted you. You're out of touch. You're irrelevant.'

^^^^^^^^^

^^^^^^^^^

Paige holds on to the diary cam as she walks around her room picking out the cameras from their hidden locations and pulling the wires. She needs to demonstrate that she is not the idiot.

That she is in control.

She doesn't have to tell Edie and Tammy the truth, she owes them nothing. Paige just wants to hammer home her point.

She bites back at Lincoln/Lowell. She tells them that they didn't have to do what they did. That if they had played it properly, if ethics and morals played any part in what they were trying to make, then they could have just told her what was going on.

Like Alyssa and Less had.

'Alyssa and Less, who are free. And, now, so am I. You're the ones who are trapped. And I hope you burn in hell.'

That last part is what Alyssa told Paige to say.

And now Paige has pressed stop and she is uploading her video. And maybe it feels cathartic or like she has some closure, but she hits the upload button and sends that message straight to the Lincoln/Lowell cloud. She hopes that Edie will see it and feel awful.

But the only way Edie Lincoln will feel choked is if that room fills with smoke. She watches the end of the movie as the room becomes hazy. Satmohan continues to cry. The insignificant bit-part actors are banging against the back door, screaming into nothingness. And Tammy and Davis are soaking up whatever time they have left with each other.

Edie knows that she has lost, she doesn't need to see a video of

Paige telling her that. She assumes that her other passion projects will be found if she dies in this room and whatever legacy she was going to leave will be tarnished after her death.

There's nothing she can do. She's as helpless as the people she has ruined over the years. Part of her is just pleased that she won't be around to experience her own downfall.

Being rich and powerful doesn't mean you're not a coward.

And she may not be able to see Paige's final video right now but it is saved to Edie's private, unlisted account. It's out there. It exists. Like every piece of plastic or anything that has ever been on the internet.

Paige doesn't care about that because, right now, she is free.

^^^^^^^^^^

^^^^^^^^^^

ALYSSA

Less and I are off the hook. We sit on that grass verge for a short while, watching a beautiful mansion burn.

It didn't take the fire service long at all to show up. I called them before we even started the fire. If I'd given them *my* address, I bet they'd have taken their sweet time, but a rich music producer gets special treatment, I guess. I don't even know if they were in that room long enough to get scared.

That would be a shame.

We wait at the top of the hill, looking down until all six people are free. I left the key in the outside lock of the back door. The first fireman on the scene would have been able to just open the door and let them out.

The two actors come running out first. The Indian-looking guy is next. He's a little slower. Coughing. Looks dramatic. Then Edie. Then Tammy. They each get an emergency blanket to wrap around their shoulders.

It's another couple of minutes before Davis Davis emerges. He gets put into the back of an ambulance and taken away with Tammy at his side. I don't know what took him so long to get out. Maybe he was trying to save some of his belongings. Or destroy them.

They're huddled together talking to paramedics. The police are arriving now, too. Edie has her back turned to them. She's looking up the hill at us. I drink some disgusting, overpriced whisky and stare right back.

We weren't going to let them die. Despite what the vultures at TMZ think, Less and I are not the new Manson Family. We just wanted this moment. Where Edie Lincoln and her asshole friends would look up at this hill and know that a couple of kids got the better of them.

We just wanted to take away their power.

Less stands up and holds out his hand. 'Come on, you. It's time we got out of here. Let's go home, eh?'

I get to my feet, the Warhol tucked beneath my arm. 'Sounds like a plan. Whose home are we going to next?'

'Oh, Lyss. I think we might need a new hobby. Maybe ethical hacking or something.'

He holds my hand, and we walk away.

'Yeah, or a pirate radio station. Or urban exploration.'

'I'm not getting involved in any more of your crazy ideas,' Less laughs.

But he's only laughing because he knows that he will. We are best friends. Besides, he always says yes to me.

^^^^^^^^^

^^^^^^^^^

DEADLINE, August 8th

ENTERTAINMENT

Legendary music producer Davis Davis in hospital after fire at home.

Rock, pop and rap stars, alike, are sending out their thoughts and prayers for music scout, producer and label owner, Davis Davis, who was caught in a house fire yesterday afternoon at his recently purchased mansion in the Hills.

Police are investigating the incident, but early information suggests the cause may have been faulty wiring in the owner's viewing suite. Five others were also trapped but escaped without injury, including long-time on-again/off-again partner, TV producer Tammy Lowell.

Davis is responsible for discovering and nurturing some of the biggest and most influential musical artists of the last forty years. Below are some of the good wishes that have poured in on social media:

^^^^^^^^^^

^^^^^^^^^^

^^^^^^^^^^

^^^^^^^^^^

@TheFitnessPaige 'Thank you so much for all the messages of support. Don't worry, I will be back, and the app is still running with plenty of workouts to keep you busy while I recover. My weekend retreat was glorious, but I plan to take some time to do something different. I haven't lost my passion for fitness and I will continue to help as many of you as I can. Thanks again for your understanding.' #SelfCare #RestIsProductive
♥ 278k ◻ 4.9k

^^^^^^^^^^

^^^^^^^^^^

PAIGE
Edie was wrong about me.

I did break.

I managed to hang on for another week, pretending that I didn't know the cameras were still on me. It was exhausting. And then I lasted another three days until the story broke about the fire.

I didn't know that Alyssa and Less were going to take things that far but I can't say that I was upset. I have no idea who Davis Davis is. I'm surprised that Edie and Tammy have lasted so long without somebody putting out a hit on them, to be honest. I didn't bat an eyelid when a picture of Satmohan's young, still-have-the-rest-of-my-life-ahead-of-me face was plastered across the news. I never liked that snake.

Seeing the actors who played the police officer and the pizza delivery guy brought that night back. Because they had been there with me. They shared the experience, even if theirs was not real.

That night.

That stupid, fucking night.

Everything comes back to it, and I was scared that it would end up defining me. So I took to my pages and told them that I needed to take a break. A real break. That I was burnt out and needed to rediscover myself and what was important to me.

#YouAreEnough.

#Healing.

#SelfTalk.

This time, I wasn't lying. I thought the TV show would be a way to show my true self. To demonstrate my work ethic, my business acumen and my self-discipline. Maybe I needed it so that I could discover something about myself. That was all taken away from me.

Maybe I just need something new. A new business venture. A new partner. A new hobby. I don't know. But I do know I'm not going to find out by doing what I had been doing every single day, never having time for me. For regular Paige. Never meeting anybody new in real life. Staying in that house all the time where *it* had happened.

So I've taken some time for Paige. And, largely, my followers have been supportive, sending me messages of positivity, telling me I should take time to process. Talking to me like they know who I am, like they're my real friends.

I want to try to find myself or at least find something to fill the part that has been missing since the ordeal that I will never talk to anybody about.

And now, I am lying in a hot bubble bath, in absolute silence, on a Thursday afternoon, after trying pottery and three tango lessons and hooking up with a stranger on a dating app – swipe right for disappointment. And I have read two books and tried smoking weed. All fun.

Fun is fleeting. It's just moments. Fragments. Hardly a change in lifestyle.

But this, right here, right now, lying in the bath in the middle of the day, it is both relaxing and exciting.

Because the owner could be home any minute.

ACKNOWLEDGEMENTS

This is my tenth book with Orenda. They are all very different and I am proud of each of them for varying reasons.

It takes a lot of people to turn my ideas into novels that can be found in bookshops, but it all begins with Karen, who plucked me from a very dark pit a decade ago. When several publishers wanted *Good Samaritans* but were not brave enough to pull the trigger, she showed belief and vision for the project. Without that support, I would never have been able to express myself through my writing in the way that I have.

I've been allowed to write crime, thriller, horror, speculative fiction and now, something that will appeal to a younger audience, too, I think. I've written as evil itself. I've written chapters where every sentence is a question. I've written as a psychopathic woman, a cult leader and an angel. It hasn't always worked but that is the risk you take when you have artistic freedom. And, in an industry that is increasingly risk averse, I appreciate the space I've been given to develop my voice, and that only comes from having Karen in my corner.

I should thank West, with whom I have developed an editing partnership that just works. The last one was a little sticky, but we were right back on track with this book. Speedy and painless. Just the way we like it. Thanks to Cole, Anne and Amanda, who ensure that as many people as possible see the book in all its beauty and that it lands in the hands of all the right people. And to Mark for another wonderful cover. I asked for pink...

My agent, David, who says I am his most *interesting* author, and I have decided to take that as a compliment. Writers need a champion at every step of the way. David encourages me to write the things that I want and then he makes them sound better than they are to the people that matter.

Tom, Sarah and Steve, my writer friends, who support and despair of me in equal measure. It's been a long time, but I think I'm starting to figure this thing out.

I wouldn't be able to continue doing this without my hardcore readers, who stick with me even when I try something that is too weird or goes too far. There are not a million of you (yet) but, damn, you are loyal to this literary cult and I'm very grateful to have you along for the ride.

And to the real-life people who keep me going. There are five teenagers in this house, and I have enjoyed looking into your world for this book. It's scarier out there for you than it was for me but, on the plus side, I've finally written a book that you can read. Sadly, getting a teenager to read a book is not as easy as it sounds...

Finally, Kel, who inspires me each day with the way she works. Who takes the piss out of me when I'm being too clever. Who tells me to go outside and get some sun on my forehead. It's not easy living with any kind of artist; as a writer, I ask lots of questions of the world, I try to have hope, and I strive to *see*, but it is comforting to know that there is one person for whom I feel totally seen.